"Abramowitz to away team, priority one."

"I have good news and bad news."

Stevens, Hawkins, and Gomez swapped dismayed reactions.

"The camp's public-address hardware is a closed system. I wasn't able to access it."

"What's the good news?" Gomez said.

"I'm using an alternative method to trigger your snowfall."

Stevens suppressed a stab of panic. "*What* method?"

"I found a derelict Tenebian satellite that was scheduled for atmospheric reentry and changed its descent profile."

The trio's looks of dismay turned to terror.

"You're crashing a satellite into the mountain?" Hawkins said. "Isn't that a little . . ." His voice pitched with disbelief. "*. . . imprecise?!*"

"We'll know in about thirty-five seconds. I suggest you take cover." Stevens was about to say something about the importance of leaving engineering to engineers when a fiery streak slashed low across the sky overhead. *Oh, no,* he thought, then he sprinted to catch up to Hawkins, who was already running between the tents, shouting to wake up the other male prisoners. Gomez ran through the women's yard, shouting for the women to retreat to the far side of their camp.

A crimson flash on the mountainside above the camp lit up the night sky. One second later, a cataclysmic boom shattered the night. X'Maris and Venekans alike awoke in terror. A surreal, deathly silence washed over the camp . . .

STAR TREK®
CORPS OF ENGINEERS

GRAND DESIGNS

Dave Galanter, Allyn Gibson, Kevin Killiany,
Paul Kupperberg, David Mack, and
Dayton Ward & Kevin Dilmore

Based upon *Star Trek®* and
Star Trek: The Next Generation®
created by Gene Roddenberry
and *Star Trek: Deep Space Nine®*
created by Rick Berman & Michael Piller

POCKET BOOKS
New York London Toronto Sydney Kharzh'ulla

POCKET BOOKS, a division of Simon & Schuster, Inc.
1230 Avenue of the Americas, New York, NY 10020

This book is a work of fiction. Names, characters, places and incidents are products of the authors' imaginations or are used fictitiously. Any resemblance to actual events or locales or persons, living or dead, is entirely coincidental.

This Pocket Books trade paperback edition July 2007

POCKET and colophon are registered trademarks of Simon & Schuster, Inc.

Manufactured in the United States of America

These titles were previously published individually in eBook format by Pocket Books.

10 9 8 7 6 5 4 3 2 1

ISBN-13: 978-1-4165-4489-0

ISBN-10: 1-4165-4489-5

CONTENTS

RING AROUND THE SKY

Allyn Gibson

Dedicated to the memory of my grandfather,
Donald Gardner. He never read science fiction, but he
would have wanted to read *Ring Around the Sky*

Engineering is the art of modeling materials we do not wholly understand, into shapes we cannot precisely analyze so as to withstand forces we cannot properly assess, in such a way that the public has no reason to suspect the extent of our ignorance.

—Dr. A. R. Dykes, 2003

CHAPTER 1

As Tev woke from his nap, he smiled and felt completely refreshed. The past few weeks had been trying, and to be able to sit, lean back, and relax for hours on end put him quickly to sleep. He snorted, clearing his nose, and stretched his facial muscles to loosen them. He took a deep breath and exhaled slowly. This had been a very good nap.

He turned to the Kharzh'ullan seated next to him. "How long until we reach the base station?" he asked.

The Kharzh'ullan checked his wrist chrono and frowned. "I never was good at math. Should be soon. Half an hour, perhaps."

"Good," said Tev as he leaned back into his seat and closed his eyes. He had traveled from Kharzh'ulla to the Ring and back many times in his life, and he had always enjoyed the passenger cars. They were oriented differently than subway trams he had used in and around San Francisco when he had been at Starfleet Academy—the subway trams had seating on a single, long level, but the Kharzh'ullan passenger shuttles had seating on five levels, with chairs arranged in a circle around the central ladder that ran from level to level, and the conductor's station at the base of the passenger car. Like the trams, the Kharzh'ullan shuttles traveled through tunnels, but where the San Francisco trams traveled beneath the city, the Kharzh'ullan shuttles moved through the space elevators between the planet's surface and the Ring.

The passenger beside him shook Tev's shoulder. Tev sat up, turned his head, and half-opened his eyes. "If you wouldn't mind my asking . . . ?" Tev's neighbor said.

Tev shrugged.

"You're an off-worlder," said the neighbor. "Have you been to Kharzh'ulla before?"

Tev smiled. "Many times." He leaned back in his seat, his eyes focused on some distant point beyond the central ladder. "I used to live on Kharzh'ulla. In Prelv, actually."

A skeptical look crossed the Kharzh'ullan's face. "Been away long?"

"Years."

"Why did you leave?"

Tev sighed. "Starfleet." It wasn't the complete answer, but it would suffice for a stranger.

His companion nodded. "What brought you back?"

"Business," said Tev after a lengthy pause, his voice low. He closed his eyes. His companion seemed to take the hint, and said nothing more.

Tev had spent too long in space. He could feel the shuttle's movement through the elevator just as he could feel a starship's, down the superconducting magnets that ran thirty thousand kilometers from surface to terminus at the Ring.

Tev's eyes shot open. Something felt wrong. Very wrong.

"*Aeh-hvahtin,*" said Tev.

"What are you talking about?" said his companion.

"We should be decelerating, but we're not." He did a quick mental calculation—the passenger shuttle should have been decelerating rapidly from its speed of five thousand kilometers per hour. If the passenger car didn't begin braking soon it wouldn't have the time or space to slow to a stop when the car reached the elevator's base.

Tev unfastened his shoulder harness and began to rise from his seat. A hand on his shoulder stopped him. "What do you think you're doing?" his companion asked.

"There's some sort of problem, probably with the passenger car's brakes. I'm a Starfleet engineer. The conductors need my assistance."

The other passenger unclasped his hand from Tev's shoulder. Tev nodded in wordless thanks and lunged for the ladder.

The climb down the ladder felt endless. Time seemed to slow for him. What should have taken at most a minute, from the fourth passenger level to the conductor's booth, seemed to take hours. Tev heard the voices of the other passengers, their fright and anger as they too realized that the passenger car was in grave danger, that their lives might soon end. He paid them little attention; he was an engineer with a job to perform, and he would save them.

The conductor's cabin was dark, with computer monitors ringing the compartment. Some consoles flashed red, others were dark. A Kharzh'ullan stood over one of the consoles, his hands frantically working the controls.

"What's happening?" Tev raised his voice over the din of the cabin's alarms.

The Kharzh'ullan turned, startled. "Who are you?"

"Lieutenant Commander Mor glasch Tev, Starfleet Corps of Engineers." Tev steadied himself against the base of the ladder as the passenger car rocked.

The conductor nodded, his eyes dark. "The brakes appear to have failed." He paused. "We're in free fall."

"What of the emergency brakes?" Tev asked, referring to the friction brakes that explosively deployed against the interior of the elevator shaft.

The conductor shook his head.

"There must be something we can do," said Tev.

"Your ship," said the conductor. "Can they beam us away?"

Now Tev shook his head. The superconductive sheathing of the elevator shaft made transporter locks on objects within the shaft difficult, and with the passenger car increasing its speed with every passing moment, such a lock would have been impossible.

Tev staggered against the g-forces toward one of the computer readouts. The electromagnets that slowed the passenger car showed a reversed polarity—instead of breaking the car against the shaft's sheathing they were accelerating. "I think," said Tev, "if we restart the computer system, we might be able to restore the electromagnetic polarity." He reached over to the next console and began a shutdown sequence. The console went dark.

The cabin rocked again as the passenger car bounced off guide rails. Tev fell to the floor. He felt a stabbing pain in the right side of his chest. One of his ribs might have cracked. He tried to push himself up, but his right arm felt weak. He looked across the dim cabin and saw the conductor leaning heavily on one of the consoles.

"Can you restart that console?" Tev's voice was muffled as he felt his mouth fill with blood. The broken rib must have punctured one of his lungs.

"I don't know how," a voice said.

"What?" said Tev, uncomprehending. The conductor had been male, yet this was a female's voice he had just heard.

"Tev? Tev, I don't want to die," said the conductor, and she turned.

Tev's eyes widened as they lost their focus. Tev couldn't believe what he was seeing.

"Mother?" he said as he reached out across the cabin with his left hand. His mother had slumped to the cabin floor and rested her back against the base of one of the control consoles.

"Tev?" she said again. "We're not going to stop, are we?"

Tev's mind felt dizzy and disoriented. "We will," he said, his voice hollow and weak.

Everything stopped as the passenger car plowed into the base of the elevator shaft at seven thousand kilometers an hour.

Tev sat up, his eyes open wide. "*Fvirhiehs*!"

The covers of his bunk were drenched with sweat. He felt his heart hammering in his chest. Closing his eyes, he took a deep breath.

He had had the nightmare again.

"Computer," he said as he rubbed his eyes, "how long since I doused the lights?"

"Thirty-four minutes."

Tev frowned. He sighed and lay back on his bunk.

He first had the nightmare five years before, while he served aboard the *Madison.* It resurfaced from time to time, especially when he was under great stress, but he hadn't had the nightmare for over a year, and he thought himself past it. But this mission, to return to Kharzh'ulla, to return to that very place where his mother died, Tev had been expecting the nightmare.

What he hadn't expected was for it to be quite so vivid.

Lying on his bunk, Tev stared at the ceiling. He had thought he might be able to squeeze in an hour-long nap after his bridge shift before presenting the Kharzh'ullan mission briefing. Re-experiencing the nightmare, though, removed that option. He needed to put his mind on other things, alleviate the emotional pressure.

He turned his head and looked at the clock on his desk. The mess hall would be empty this time of morning. He could prepare the briefing there in relative peace.

Sonya Gomez stopped by the mess hall to get herself some tea, and found Tev sitting alone at one of the corner tables. Something that looked like a plate of twigs sat untouched on a plate next to him as he riffled through several padds at once.

"Mind if I join you?" she asked.

He looked up from the padds and flared his nostrils. Placing all but one of the padds on the table, he said, "I am endeavoring to complete my mission briefing, Commander. Is there something you want?"

Gomez sat down across from him. "How's the briefing coming along?"

Tev snorted. "It will be ready in time for this afternoon's meeting."

She reached across the table and began to pick up one of his padds until he snatched it away from her. "I just wanted to take a look at your progress," she said as she pulled her hand back.

"My presentation," Tev said, his voice heavy, "will be ready."

"Is there a problem, Tev?"

Tev fell quiet and said nothing. Gomez sighed. It always seemed to be one step forward and two steps back with her second officer. Every time she thought he was making progress in integrating himself with the rest of the crew, his behavior would remind her that he was still the insufferably arrogant twit who had reported to the *da Vinci* at McKinley Station weeks ago.

"Commander," said Gomez, "we can stare at each other across the table all day if that's how you want to play it. If there's a problem, I'd prefer to know about it now, when we can do something about it, rather than later, when the mission's on the line."

Tev took a deep breath and scrunched his snout. "I request that I be taken off this mission," he said at last.

"Why?" Gomez asked as she shifted in her seat.

Tev looked at her quietly from behind impassive, bleary eyes. Finally he spoke, with a depth of emotion that Gomez had never heard from the Tellarite before. "Had Starfleet given me any choice in the matter, I would have chosen not to be here, Commander." Gomez began to cut him off, but he held up a hand. "*Yes,* I was raised on Kharzh'ulla. But I left there many years ago, and I would prefer not to return. My life there—" He paused, then continued: "—ended badly."

Gomez shook her head. "You'll have to do better than

that, Commander." She paused. "Whatever your misgivings about returning home, whatever happened in the past, the fact remains that I need you and the team needs you. Captain Scott pushed for the *da Vinci* to be assigned this mission on the strength of your experience, and you would be doing the team a disservice if you sat out this mission."

Beneath his beard, Tev's face flushed red and his nostrils flared in anger. "Kharzh'ulla IV is not my home, Commander. I am from Tellar. I merely lived on Kharzh'ulla."

"There's no one aboard who knows more about Kharzh'ulla IV than you do," said Gomez, hoping to appeal to his overweening pride. She stood, planted her hands firmly on the table, and her stare bored into Tev's eyes. "I won't take you off this mission, Commander, not now. If you want to put in a request to the captain, I won't stand in your way, but I will go on record as believing you are putting your personal history ahead of the mission. Understood?"

Tev nodded slowly, his eyes and expression unreadable.

Gomez stood up from the table. "Good. You'll have the briefing ready?"

Tev nodded again. "As I said I would."

"Then I won't keep you from your work, Commander."

As she left the mess hall she heard Tev munching on his twigs and humming softly to himself. She shook her head. This mission promised to be simple, but Tev's attitude made her question just how simple it would be.

CHAPTER 2

Captain David Gold drummed his fingers on the conference room table. He never liked to be kept waiting, and certainly not for a routine mission briefing.

"Where is he, Gomez?" he asked, looking pointedly at his first officer seated next to him.

Gomez frowned. "I don't know, sir. He was preparing for the briefing earlier this morning, and he assured me he would be ready. Should I page him?"

"Your call."

Gomez tapped her combadge. "Gomez to—"

The doors opened, and Tev bounded into the conference room, several padds clutched in his arms.

"You're late, Tev," said Gold.

"My apologies, Captain. Commander," he said with a quick nod of his head in Gomez's direction. "Preparing one of the simulations took longer than I had anticipated."

"Let's get the briefing started," said Gomez. "The floor is yours, Tev."

Tev took a deep breath and looked at the team seated around the conference room table. He touched the table's computer interface, and the viewscreen image changed from the Federation emblem to an image of a Class-M planet, mottled blue and orange. "This is Kharzh'ulla IV, a Tellarite colony on the fringe of Federation space," Tev said. The image zoomed in, and the planet grew larger. Continents took on distinctive features. An archipelago near the planetary equator came into focus. Solid structures rose from the planet's surface like spokes on a bicycle wheel arrayed around the equator and reaching far into orbit. A solid ring encircled the planet, connecting the terminus points of each of the shafts rising from the surface. The viewing angle shifted suddenly from the equatorial approach and the profile view of the structure to a more polar view and a straight-on view of the planet and the artificial ring surrounding it.

"Wow," said Fabian Stevens, the *da Vinci*'s tactical systems specialist. "I'd heard stories, but never thought I'd see it."

Tev ignored him. "The structure you see is called simply 'the Ring.' It has no other name, and perhaps no other name would suffice. Until the discovery of the Dyson Sphere by the *Enterprise*-D eight years ago, the Ring was the largest and most complex artificial structure known in the Alpha Quadrant." The camera closed in on one of the shafts. "These shafts are a functioning space elevator system, capable of delivering any payload—people, merchandise, raw materials—to and from orbit without resorting to transporters or shuttles. Cargo can be off-loaded at the port terminus atop each elevator, and then delivered to the base a few hours later." The image panned across the shaft, zoomed out, and began moving toward the Ring at the terminus. "The Ring itself is inhabitable, essentially a space station one hundred and sixty thousand kilometers long, five hundred wide, fifty deep. In terms of living space, the Ring's interior can support comfortably the population of this entire sector." The view panned past the terminus, curved over the edge of the Ring, and zoomed in toward the outer edge, revealing massive docking bays. "The Kharzh'ullan Ring was utilized extensively during the Dominion War, both as a staging area for fleet deployments and as a drydock facility for damaged starships. The fleet yards here, if developed to their full capacity, would be capable of supporting tens of thousands of starships."

Tev paused and regarded his audience. He then touched the computer console.

The image on the viewscreen changed dramatically. What had been a vibrant, functioning structure on the viewscreen—brightly lit and with starships in the drydocks under repair—was replaced by nothingness. The camera panned to one side and something metallic, frayed and twisted, came into view. As the camera moved onward, the image came into focus as the wreckage of what had once been the Ring. The camera pulled back, and perspective revealed itself. A section of the Ring simply was gone, destroyed.

Someone let out a gasp.

"What happened?" asked Dr. Lense.

Tev sighed deeply. "The Jem'Hadar." The viewscreen image changed again, and the Ring returned intact to the viewscreen. "One month before the cessation of hostilities, the Dominion attacked the fleet yards. The attack force was small"—three Jem'Hadar warships appeared on the screen—"but Kharzh'ulla's defenses were negligible, and what few ships were able to leave the drydock facilities to engage the Jem'Hadar attempted to defend the planet." On-screen, starships that had been decommissioned decades before tangled with the Jem'Hadar cruisers, destroying one, disabling another. "With the battle turning against them, the commander of the undamaged Jem'Hadar vessel made an attack run on the Ring itself, rather than engage the defense fleet." The image changed quickly, following the Jem'Hadar ship as it skirted the edge of the Ring. "The Jem'Hadar ship took several phaser blasts and photon torpedo hits. The ship lost control and crashed into the Ring's edge." The Jem'Hadar ship collided with the Ring, and the screen flashed white for several seconds. When the image cleared, a debris field radiated outward from where the Ring had once been.

The viewscreen image altered again, with the image of the shattered Ring changing to a high-angled schematic of Kharzh'ulla IV and its elevator and Ring system. Tev took one last look at the viewscreen, turned, and came to the end of the conference room table. "Not only did the Jem'Hadar destroy a large section of the Ring's structure, they also struck at one of the elevators, cutting deep gashes into the shell of the elevator shaft closest to the section destroyed by the Jem'Hadar ship."

"How big a hole in the Ring did the Jem'Hadar make?" asked Stevens. "The damage you showed looked rather extensive."

Tev grunted. "And rather complete. The kinetic energy from the impact, combined with the matter annihilation from the collapse of the ship's antimatter containment fields, was sufficient to destroy the Ring's structure over a four-hundred kilometer section."

"Then what are the Kharzh'ullans expecting us to *do?*"

Before Tev could answer Stevens's question, Gomez said, "The Kharzh'ullan government approached the Federation Council asking for assistance in rebuilding and repairing the Ring. The Council passed the request along to Starfleet, and they assigned the *da Vinci* to make a survey of the damage done to the Ring and the elevator, evaluate any repairs the Kharzh'ullans might have made, and then provide whatever assistance we can."

Stevens looked to Gomez. "The last time I checked we didn't have the personnel or the hardware aboard to essentially build a space habitat four hundred kilometers long." He paused. "No offense meant, Commander, and I know we'd do fine work on a job like this, but this doesn't sound at all like our sort of mission."

Gomez nodded. "I would agree with you, Fabian, *if* that's what the Kharzh'ullans wanted from us. There are any number of private contractors and engineering firms that would line up for work on this scale, if only for the notoriety of being the ones that repaired the Ring. I have no doubt that once we've made our report, Interworld or another of the habitat builders will descend on the Kharzh'ullan system looking for the work." She stood, crossed to the viewscreen, and tapped the computer terminal. The image zoomed to focus on one of the elevator shafts. While most of the shaft showed as blue against a black background of deep space, a portion showed as red. Gomez pointed this out. "As Commander Tev mentioned, one of the elevator shafts took phaser damage during the Jem'Hadar attack. The Kharzh'ullans haven't repaired the damage, either because they don't know how or they don't have the resources. If the elevator shaft isn't repaired, then there's the chance the elevator might collapse onto the planet's surface."

"What would that do to the Ring?" asked Lense.

Wordlessly, Tev called up another simulation on the viewscreen. The elevator shaft toppled, and as it fell, it pulled the Ring attached to its terminus down with it. Halfway to the surface the Ring structure snapped, but the elevator to the west had already begun to fall. Like dominoes, the elevators fell to the ground, and large sections of the Ring tumbled out of orbit and crashed into the surface. When the collapse was finished, the time-index counter read twelve hours. No elevator stood standing, and the planet's equatorial region showed the ravage of the impacts from orbit.

"We think," said Gomez, "that if one elevator fell, the entire system would as well. Each part supports the others. Much, if not all, of the debris would impact with the surface. It would be like asteroid strikes all the way around Kharzh'ulla's equator."

Tev continued: "Sixty percent of the planet's population resides within five hundred kilometers of the equator. Another fifteen percent lives in coastal areas near the base of the ocean-based elevators. These areas would be ravaged by the falling debris, either from direct strikes or from tsunamis caused by the fall of the elevator into the ocean." He paused for dramatic impact. "Kharzh'ullan civilization would not survive."

"What about evacuation?" asked Lense. "If we can't repair the elevator, then there's always the chance that it would fall."

"It's an option," said Gold. "If we have to take it, Federation relief agencies will step in and handle the matter. But that's the final option, not the first."

Carol Abramowitz, the *da Vinci*'s cultural specialist, cleared her throat. "Tev, you said Kharzh'ulla is a Tellarite colony. I wouldn't think a colony would be capable of building a space elevator, let alone fifteen *and* an inhabitable ring around the planet."

Gomez smiled. "The Kharzh'ullans didn't build the elevators and the Ring. They found it."

"*Found* it?" said Bart Faulwell, the ship's linguist. "Useful artifacts like that aren't usually left around for anyone to find." He looked to Tev. "Where did the Ring come from?"

Tev placed both hands on the table and leaned forward slightly. "Two and a half centuries ago a Tellarite ship surveyed the Kharzh'ulla star system and located several planets, with the fourth planet apparently inhabited, as the Ring was detectable by telescopic observation even from far outside the system. As the survey ship drew closer to the fourth planet, however, they detected no life save for some lower animals and vegetation. When they made planetfall they found the Ring and elevators intact, but no intelligent life, and as the planet seemed in all respects to be capable of supporting a civilization, a colony ship was dispatched from Tellar. Several years after the colony's founding the mechanism for working the elevators was discovered, and a few years after that archeological expeditions placed the age of the elevators and Ring at nearly fifty thousand years."

"Who built it?" Faulwell asked.

"For a long time they were called the Tomeq."

"The Tellarite word for 'unknown,'" said Faulwell.

"Correct, Bartholomew," Tev said. He touched the computer terminal, and the viewscreen image changed from the schematic view to the image of an old *Consti-*

tution-class starship. Gomez read the sensor tag at the bottom of the image—NCC-1701, *U.S.S. Enterprise*—and concluded it was at least a century old. "Analysis of the wreckage of this starship, the *Rath,* led xenoarcheologists to conclude that the original inhabitants of Kharzh'ulla IV and the builders of the elevators and the Ring were"—he turned to the screen, toggled the image it displayed, and waited for the crew's reaction—"the Furies."

On the viewscreen a pale yellow humanoid appeared. He had red eyes with slits for irises, and instead of eyebrows red horns protruded outward and upward from his skull. This was one of the races known collectively as the Furies, inhabitants of the Alpha Quadrant some five millennia before, then cast across space and banished to the Delta Quadrant. They had attempted to invade the Alpha Quadrant and take their homeworlds by force at least three times in the past century, each time stopped by only the slimmest of margins.

"You mean, Kharzh'ulla IV is the Fury homeworld?" said Abramowitz.

Tev flared his nostrils slightly. "Analysis of the native lifeforms on Kharzh'ulla IV shows few genetic links between them and the Fury corpses retrieved by the *Enterprise*-D at Brundage Point eight years ago. The evidence is inconclusive that the Furies evolved on Kharzh'ulla IV. It may have been one of their colony worlds."

"Why build the Ring, though?" asked Faulwell. "The cost in resources would have been immense. Plus, there are easier and quicker ways to get into space. It seems like too much effort for too little benefit."

"We know from Captain Kirk's encounter with the Furies a hundred years ago that they didn't have transporter technology," said Gomez. She pulled up a galactic map on the viewscreen. Kharzh'ulla IV was indicated by an over-sized red dot. "This is Kharzh'ulla IV's present location. Run its location backward through time"—the location of Kharzh'ulla IV moved, as did the positions of many other stars—"and fifty thousand years ago Kharzh'ulla IV was here." She zoomed the image to focus on a single sector of space. "The heart of the Culostan Expanse. A region of space twenty thousand light-years wide in which spatial density is such that transporters do not function and warp travel is limited. If the Furies had the knowledge of transporter technology, even the theory, within the Culostan Expanse that knowledge would have been useless. It could be that they built the Ring because they needed it to expand outward into space."

"Another possibility to consider is this," said Tev. "The docking facilities of the Ring are capable of supporting tens of thousands of starships. In the Furies' war against the Unclean thousands of years ago, they would have needed extensive ship facilities to build and support their fleet. They might have built the Ring for the sole purpose of building the ships they needed to prosecute the war."

"Which doesn't make Commander Gomez's theory wrong," said Faulwell, "or your own theory negate hers. It could have been a bit of both."

"Or one facilitated the other," said Tev. "Or neither may be correct." He shrugged. "We haven't the evidence to make a definitive conclusion."

Faulwell stroked his chin, as if lost in thought. "Commander," he said, "how long did it take the Tellarite colonists to work out how to use the elevator system?"

"Twenty years, if memory serves," said Tev.

"You mean that this structure the Furies built fifty thousand years ago works without regular and ongoing maintenance?"

Tev nodded. "Essentially, yes."

"One thing about Fury engineering," said Gomez, "is that they build using 'brute force' principles. One hundred years ago the *Rath* wasn't shielded; it had thick plate armor, instead."

"Correct, Commander," said Tev. "The elegance of the Kharzh'ullan solution to building a space elevator is that the structure is self-supporting and requires no outside assistance for its own maintenance. The Ring and the elevators were built to stand the test of time. Except for a single incident a few decades ago, the safety record of the elevators has been impeccable."

"What happened?" asked Abramowitz.

"A passenger carrier coming from orbit down the elevator crashed into the base when the braking magnets failed to engage," said Tev softly.

"Survivors?"

Tev shook his head wearily and looked downward. "None. Estimates placed the speed of impact at nearly two thousand kilometers per hour. Many of the bodies recovered were never positively identified."

Abramowitz nodded when it became clear that Tev had nothing more to say on the matter.

"This mission sounds too simple, Commander," said Stevens. "A vacation compared to some of our other missions."

Gomez smiled. "We can't go black-hole-diving on *every* mission, Fabian." She paused. "The Kharzh'ullans want to use the S.C.E. as consultants on the rebuilding, to give them advice and point them in the right direction. If they have matters in hand, I can't imagine this mission requiring any more than myself, Commander Tev, and Pattie for materials analysis."

Around the conference table heads nodded.

Tev looked to Captain Gold. "Sir, what is our ETA to Kharzh'ulla IV?"

"About sixteen hours," said Gold.

Gomez nodded. "Tev and I will meet with the planetary leaders, and then we'll proceed from there as events develop." She took a look at each of the faces around the conference room table. "Any further questions?"

Other than a few head shakes, there was no response.

Gomez smiled. "Very well, then. Dismissed."

CHAPTER 3

Sonya Gomez caught her breath as the transporter effect dissolved around her, surprised at how light she felt. "Gravity, Tev?" she asked.

"Eighty-two percent of Earth normal, sixty-seven percent of Tellar's gravity."

Gomez nodded. The air seemed thinner, too. She knew Kharzh'ulla was a small world by Class-M standards and not especially massive, poor as its crust was in the heavier metals, but there was a world of difference between knowing that intellectually from reports and experiencing directly the effect of the planet's lesser gravity upon her body.

She glanced around the entrance hall to the presidential palace. "I'd have thought there would be someone waiting for us," she said, seeing that she and Tev were alone in the massive hall.

"Patience, Commander," said Tev with a flare of his

nostrils. Gomez smiled. Tev got annoyed at the slightest provocation, and there were times when she couldn't resist baiting him.

The ceiling vaulted far above Gomez and Tev. White marble columns rose to support the roof, and a fresco depicting the Tellarite planetfall two hundred years before adorned the ceiling. Ringing the hall stood statues of important Kharzh'ullans, perhaps past presidents and other notable leaders. But to Gomez's eye every statue looked wrong, almost as if they were carved out of proportion.

She turned, startled by both the sound of footfalls on the marble stairs at the end of the hall and the snort of derision Tev made. She looked to Tev, and saw him scowl for the briefest of moments, then turn his attention away from the stairs and back to her. Descending the stairs was the oddest Tellarite she had ever seen—lanky, but not thin; stretched out, but full on his frame. She thought Tev short even by Tellarite standards, but by this newcomer's measure Tev was a veritable dwarf. Evolution adapted organisms for their environments, and at two hundred years Kharzh'ulla was old for a colony world. Each successive generation born on Kharzh'ulla would no doubt be taller than the generation that preceded it as bodies designed for a much higher gravity could grow taller than the Tellarite norm in a vastly different environment.

Gomez and Tev crossed the hall to meet him at the base of the stairs. "You must be Commander Gomez," he said. His voice was pitched higher than Tev's, an alto tenor to Tev's bass, and his enunciation was drawn out, his *s*'s sibilant, his pronunciation precise in the manner of a speaker whose native language wasn't Federation Standard.

"I am," she said, and she held out her right hand in greeting.

The Kharzh'ullan took her hand and clasped it with both paws, then brought his forehead down to touch the joined hands. The traditional Kharzh'ullan greeting, she remembered from Abramowitz's cultural briefing.

He straightened, and his hands fell away. "I am Eevraith, the minister of transportation. We've been expecting you."

Gomez smiled. "We're glad to help."

Eevraith bowed slightly. "Thank you. We haven't the resources or the technological expertise for such a massive undertaking, and any assistance your crew can provide in repairing the Ring and the damaged elevator will be greatly appreciated."

"After our last few missions, Minister, this one should be a walk in the park."

"I have no doubt, Commander." He turned and gestured up the stairs. "Come. The first minister awaits."

Gomez nodded, and she and Tev followed Eevraith up the staircase. But upon reflection two things bothered her—Tev had been unnaturally silent during the greetings, and Eevraith hadn't looked in Tev's direction even once, even though he had been standing just off to her side the entire time.

By any standards, First Minister Grevesh was *old*. Tellarite fur colored from brown to yellow, with Tev tending toward the ruddy and Eevraith toward the blond, but Grevesh's fur was uniformly near-white, and his face was nearly hairless and deeply lined with wrinkles. He sat in an antigrav wheelchair, and Gomez decided by the lengths of his arms and legs that if he stood he would be no taller than she was and certainly nowhere near Eevraith's height, yet still taller than Tev.

"First Minister," said Eevraith as they entered his office, "I would like to present to you Commander Gomez of the Starfleet Corps of Engineers, here to look into our . . . problem." He gestured toward Gomez. She bowed slightly, and wondered why Tev hadn't been introduced as well.

"Follow me, Commander," said Grevesh. He turned his chair toward the French doors at the far end of his office, and began moving in that direction. Gomez, Eevraith, and Tev followed "Eevraith, the doors, please."

"Of course, First Minister." He pushed forward, and threw open the wide doors. Grevesh motored out onto the balcony, and Tev and Gomez stepped out into the sunlight.

The city of Prelv stretched out before them.

Much of the city was modern. Off to the south a complex of modern skyscrapers, thirty and forty stories tall, shiny and gleaming in the mid-morning sun, rose in a cluster perhaps a few blocks wide. Past those skyscrapers and to the east Gomez could see the ocean beyond—Prelv was a coastal city and a major port, with cargo ships running routes from the city to the elevator launches to put cargo into orbit and bring the cargo of the galaxy to Kharzh'ulla. Closer to the palace, the buildings were older and reflected a different design philosophy. Where the skyscrapers were undistinguished and the sort seen on dozens of planets, the older buildings were short and squat, built of piled mud or brick with tiled roofs, in a style that Gomez would have labeled Mediterranean on Earth. The area around the palace, she realized, was the old town, dating back to the very founding of the Kharzh'ullan colony, with much of the area turned to the workings of the planetary government, while the more distant area represented the modern economy and the trade interests that relied upon the Ring to drive the engines of Kharzh'ulla's industry.

But what dominated the view from the balcony was not Prelv.

From east to west a thin line, shining bright in the sunlight, cut across the sky. Gomez looked up. Her gaze caught the Ring in the southeast, and she followed it upward through the blue sky and the wafting clouds. Here and there she saw thin, bright lines intersecting the Ring—the elevators—and she followed one or two down to the horizon or until the clouds obscured them. She continued westward along the Ring, and to the southwest, not far below the Ring's maximum elevation in the sky and one of the elevator junctions, the Ring's reflected splendor was broken. She hadn't known the position of the destroyed segment of the Ring, but the thought that the first minister of the planet could come on his balcony and see it every day saddened her deeply, and she turned from the sky and looked to Grevesh who, as she had been, was looking up into Kharzh'ulla's morning sky.

Grevesh turned to her and smiled. "An impressive sight, is it not, Commander?"

Gomez nodded. "Yes, First Minister, it is."

He moved his chair to her side, and he took her right hand in his hands. "The Ring matters to my people. It stands as a symbol of everything that we are." He looked up into her eyes. "Please, we need your help, your expertise." Grevesh then looked past her to

Eevraith and nodded in his direction. "When he was but a student at the university, my minister of transportation wrote the definitive work on the Ring, how to build it and how to work it, but repairing it is a different and difficult problem."

Gomez turned and looked at Tev. He wore a neutral expression on his face, and she thought his eyes especially sad and pained. She gave him a reassuring nod, turned back to Grevesh, and said, "We'll do what we can, First Minister."

"I knew you would."

Eevraith seated himself on a nearby couch on the balcony, and he gestured at the couch opposite. "Please, Commander, be seated," he said.

As Gomez moved to sit, Grevesh asked, "Who would this be? We haven't been introduced, Eevraith." He stared directly at Tev, whether out of shock or confusion Gomez could not decide.

"First Minister," began Eevraith, "this is no one—"

"Nonsense," said Grevesh just as Gomez was about to object to Eevraith's assertion that Tev was "no one."

Tev stepped forward quickly, knelt at the arm of Grevesh's chair, took Grevesh's right hand in his, and touched them to his forehead. "It has been far too long, sir," he said as he stood. "You were a friend of my father's. I am Mor glasch Tev, second officer of the *U.S.S. da Vinci.* I knew your granddaughter, Biyert, quite well, and my family and hers spent summers together at your vacation home."

"Tev," whispered Grevesh, recognition dawning on his face. "Your father—"

Tev nodded. "When you were the chancellor of the Kharzh'ullan University, my father was the chair of the political science department, and he served as your campaign chair during your first campaign for the Kharzh'ullan Assembly."

Grevesh smiled widely, his teeth yellow with age. "Yes, I remember! Oh, so long ago."

"Thirty-seven years ago, sir," said Tev. "Twenty-five Earth years," he amended, no doubt for Gomez's benefit.

"How is your father?"

"He passed away, six years ago."

Grevesh's blurry red eyes narrowed, and Gomez thought she could see tears welling in them. "I should very much have liked to talk with him again. He had a fine political mind, and I valued his counsel highly." He looked about his office, nodding slowly, then settled his gaze once again on Tev. "And your mother?" Tev did not answer. "Ah, I remember now. The accident . . ."

Tev nodded slowly. "Yes, sir. The accident with the passenger transport."

Gomez blinked rapidly. Suddenly the unelaborated mention during the mission briefing of a passenger transport accident in one of the Ring's elevators made sense. Tev's mother must have been a passenger aboard the shuttle that plunged into the elevator base.

"Tev," said Eevraith as he rose from his sofa, "these reminiscences are all well and good, but haven't we more pressing concerns?"

Tev turned and faced Eevraith. "I would think, Eevraith, that if matters were more pressing, your government would have approached the Federation Council long before they did. What was it, two months ago, that you asked for help? The war ended almost a year ago. If that time wasn't pressing, five minutes of reminiscence is hardly more so."

Eevraith glared at Tev. "You were never so leisurely, Tev."

Tev's nostrils flared. "You were never so lacking in basic decorum, Eevraith. What was my father's favorite dictum? 'A polite politician is an oxymoron.'"

Eevraith's face flushed red beneath his pelt.

"Gentlemen," Gomez said as she stood and moved to break them apart, "our time *is* pressing." Eevraith shook his head, muttered a curse beneath his breath, and sat back down on his couch. Tev simply glared at him. Gomez looked hard at Tev and put her hand on his left shoulder. "Tev?" His gaze turned from Eevraith and he locked eyes with Gomez. She saw something in those blurry eyes, something distant and haunted. These two, Tev and Eevraith, knew one another, Gomez realized, and more than just as colleagues and fellow engineers. What was their past relationship? Childhood friends? Fellow students? Something else entirely? Would the history between them impede the mission? Whatever their story, it obviously had a bad ending.

Grevesh looked to Tev and smiled, as if oblivious to everything else that had just transpired. "That dictum of your father's—he said I was the exception that proved its inherent truth. He wondered if that might have been why I proved so popular with the people, that I was polite and solicitous of them." The first minister inhaled deeply and sighed slowly.

"I would rather not discuss the past," said Eevraith. "We have far more pressing concerns, such as the damaged space elevator."

Grevesh nodded slowly. "I agree, Minister Eevraith." He turned to Gomez. "Did you know that Eevraith is the galaxy's greatest authority on the elevator?"

"So you've implied before."

Eevraith nodded, but his eyes remained fixed on Tev, and there was no mirth in them. "The first minister overstates my reputation. A study I did on the elevators from an engineering standpoint won me a doctorate. The first minister thought it an important enough work to bring me into his government as a transportation expert, and years later to appoint me transportation minister."

"What's your evaluation of the damage to the Ring and the elevator shaft, Minister?" asked Gomez.

Eevraith breathed deeply and relaxed into the couch. "The damage to the Ring does not concern me nearly half as much as the damage to the elevator. Rebuilding the Ring would be no different, except in matters of scale and curvature, to building a space station four hundred kilometers long." He paused. "The elevator concerns me far more."

"How so?" asked Gomez.

"The structural integrity of the elevator was severely compromised by the damage inflicted by the Jem'Hadar. Had the Ring above it remained intact, the elevator's structure would have been supported from both ends, by the base and by the Ring, against gravity's pull. But as the very segment of the Ring that supports the elevator from above was compromised by the impact of the Jem'Hadar ship, the elevator structure is not receiving the support from above that it requires, and both the elevator shaft itself and the Ring structure west of its terminus are beginning to show strain from the stress and buckling."

Grevesh shook his head. "Forgive an old fool, Eevraith, but this makes no sense to me. How does the Ring hold up the elevators?"

"Counterweight, First Minister," said Tev before Eevraith could answer. "The centrifugal force on the Ring from Kharzh'ulla's spin throws the Ring outward from the planet, but because it's anchored to Kharzh'ulla by the elevators, the same centrifugal force pulls the elevator shafts taut."

"Should the destruction of the Ring section not concern us equally to that of the elevator damage?"

"It would," said Eevraith, this time cutting Tev off, "but the Ring's geosynchronous altitude serves to keep the Ring in place. The centrifugal force counterbalances gravity's pull. A lower or a higher altitude for the Ring would be a concern for us. The builders put in place a system so finely balanced that it keeps itself intact."

"Until something happens to upset that balance," said Gomez.

Eevraith shook his head. "The elevators and Ring are quite resilient. Even the accident with the passenger transport two decades ago posed no threat to the stability of the system."

"Only now there is a threat," said Tev.

Eevraith scowled. "Would you not consider the possibility of the system falling onto the planet a *threat,* Tev? Or have you grown too indifferent to the plight of our people . . . ?"

"I think that if the elevator truly posed the threat you claim, Minister, you would have asked for Federation assistance a year ago."

"There was never a need to ask for assistance. Not when we were able to deal with the problem ourselves. We were able to shore up the elevator shaft, but when we discovered several months ago buckling and stress fractures in the Ring to the west of the damaged elevator, the problem had become larger than our ability to contain it."

"'Shore up,'" repeated Gomez. "How? Did you patch the phaser scoring?"

"Have you seen the damage?" asked Eevraith.

Gomez shook her head. "Not up-close, no. From the *da Vinci,* yes."

"The phaser damage is not insignificant, and certainly more than mere 'scoring.'" He looked to Grevesh, who nodded slowly, his eyes closed. "The Jem'Hadar phasers cut a gash into the elevator shell nearly forty kilometers long. Sensor analysis of the battle shows it was probably not deliberate, merely a shot gone awry. Regardless, the damage was done, and we installed starship-rated structural integrity field generators along that section of the elevator shaft, until we were ready for a permanent repair."

"What sort of repair do you have in mind?" asked Tev.

Eevraith's eyes narrowed on Tev, and then he quickly looked away to Gomez. "We have manufactured a new shell to bridge the gap. Our hope"—he looked to Grevesh—"is that your team will be able to install the new elevator shell."

"What about the superconducting magnets within the shell? Will the transport pods be able to travel up and down within the shaft?" asked Tev.

"Replacements for those have been fashioned as well." He looked hard at Tev. "You of all people should know, Tev, how the elevator housing is put together. The new shell we've built will suffice for all of Kharzh'ulla's needs."

"Minister," said Gomez as a thought occurred to her. "You said the westward Ring segment *and* the elevator were buckling under the strain of the damage, yet you also said you were supporting the damaged elevator by using structural-integrity fields. How can you have buckling if you also made the elevator artificially rigid?"

Grevesh was silent, his eyes still closed. Eevraith sat back on his couch and said nothing.

Tev turned and looked at Gomez. "The structural integrity fields. The elevator shafts require a certain amount of movement and oscillation, but by making the damaged elevator shaft artificially rigid in the middle—"

"—the elevator shaft couldn't oscillate as it should have," Gomez finished. "The oscillation wave would reach the structural integrity field and die."

Eevraith nodded. "By artificially supporting the elevator, we actually increased the stress on the shaft and the adjoining Ring segment."

Gomez said, "I'll want to examine the new elevator housing you've constructed, and I'll want to examine the damage to the elevator shaft personally." She looked to Tev. "You'll be with me, Commander." She turned to Eevraith. "You, too, if you're interested."

Grevesh opened his eyes, blinked a few times, and fixed on Tev. "You can repair the elevator?"

"We'll try, First Minister," said Gomez. She rose from her couch, and Tev followed suit.

He smiled. "Good. Very good."

"You should know, sir," said Tev, "that the damage may be more extensive than even we can repair."

Eevraith stood quickly. "Tev!" he cried. "The fact remains that the replacement shell need only be installed for the elevator to be repaired."

"The fact remains, *Minister,* that Commander Gomez and I know nothing of the sort." Tev turned from Eevraith to Grevesh. "If we cannot repair the elevator shaft, the likelihood is that Kharzh'ulla will have to be evacuated."

A look of cold fury crossed Grevesh's face, and the white skin flushed dark red. "I once thought you worthy of being a Kharzh'ullan, Tev, but I can see now that you are only a Tellarite. Your father would be most disappointed in you." He turned his chair and retired to his office, leaving Gomez and Tev alone on the balcony with Eevraith.

Gomez looked to Tev. "You have a way with tact, Commander."

He shrugged. "It needed to be said." He looked to Eevraith, and his eyes narrowed. "I imagine, Minister, that you have been keeping the truth from him."

Eevraith crossed the space between Tev and himself. "Evacuating the planet is not the truth, Tev, but merely a possibility." He spoke his words with precision and barely veiled anger.

"You hadn't told him," Gomez said. "You hadn't told him that the damage might be so extensive that even we might not be able to repair it."

Eevraith nodded slowly. "You've seen him. He's barely conscious of where he is. That was the fifth time in a month I've had to explain centrifugal force to him. Telling him that the Ring poses a danger to the entire planet is more than he can deal with."

"And what will you do, Eevraith, if you must abandon Kharzh'ulla?" asked Tev. "Return to Tellar? Where will your political career be then?"

Eevraith reached out, grabbed Tev's uniform collar, and pulled his face into Tev's. "I would be very careful, Tev."

Tev shoved Eevraith away. "Is that a threat, Eevraith? You're the one putting personal politics before public safety." He nodded toward the city beyond the balcony. "Those lives are on your head, not mine."

"Gentlemen!" said Gomez as she came in between them.

Eevraith stamped the balcony tile with his foot. Tev

turned and looked at him. "You left, Tev. In the end, you *left*. Tell me truly that you know better than I what is best for these people."

Tev narrowed his eyes, shook his head, and wandered to the balcony's railing, leaning on it to look out over the city.

Gomez planted her hands on her hips. She looked at Tev, frowned, then turned her attention to Eevraith. "Will you join us, Minister, in surveying the elevator damage and the replacement housing?"

Eevraith nodded slowly. "Of course. I presume you will want to see the housing first."

Gomez shook her head. "I'd rather examine the elevator shaft and see firsthand what needs to be done before passing judgment on the housing." She raised her hand, cutting off Eevraith's coming objection. "I'm sure what you've assembled is fine, but I want to see what will work without any preconceived notions of what *you* think will work."

"Very well," said Eevraith. "If there is anything else?"

Gomez sighed. "Tev?" she called.

Tev turned. "I have nothing more."

Gomez nodded. "Then I think we have everything we need at this point, Minister Eevraith. How would 1600 hours strike you?"

"That should be fine." Eevraith paused. "Should I have someone escort you to the entrance?"

"I think Commander Tev and I can beam out from here."

Eevraith nodded. "Sixteen hundred hours, then." He turned and walked crisply back into Grevesh's office.

Gomez came up to Tev's side. She nodded in the direction of the departed Eevraith. "An old friend, Commander?" she asked with a flash of humor.

"Friend?" Tev snorted derisively.

Gomez rolled her eyes. She tapped her combadge. "*Da Vinci,* two to beam aboard."

Gomez's last sight of Prelv was of the Ring glittering in the daytime sky. As the transporter beam took them, she wondered who would suffer more this mission—the people of Kharzh'ulla if they had to abandon their world, or Tev.

CHAPTER 4

Gomez reached up, took the environmental suit helmet in her hands, and gave it a sharp turn counterclockwise. She heard the hiss of atmosphere as the pressure seal broke, and she lifted the helmet off her head. She closed her eyes and took a deep breath through her nostrils. She smiled. Every planet had a distinctive smell, and Kharzh'ulla IV was no different. The air was tangy and sharp, but not unpleasant—a welcome change from the processed smell of the *da Vinci,* or the earthy or industrialized smell of far too many worlds she'd visited in her career.

"Commander," she heard. She turned to Pattie, standing beside her, and the only one not wearing an environmental suit. The Nasat was pointing up with three of her limbs.

Gomez, Tev, Pattie, and Eevraith had beamed from their inspection of the elevator shaft damage to the manufacturing plant at the base of the elevator that was constructing the new hull to replace the phaser-damaged areas.

The elevator rose upward from an artificial island raised in the middle of Kharzh'ulla's ocean. Gomez followed Pattie's gesture to view the structure, and she found her mind temporarily unable to comprehend the size of the thing. In orbit as they floated in environmental suits scanning the damage with their tricorders, the elevator lacked scale. She knew instinctively that in orbit the elevator shaft was forty or fifty kilometers in diameter, and she had seen and worked with starships or space stations of that size many times in the past. Even though it dominated her experience, she could conceive of it as an object. But here at the base, the elevator was two hundred fifty kilometers around, and even at a kilometer's distance she lacked the perspective to see it as anything more than a wall that stretched from horizon to horizon. It had curvature, but she couldn't see it. It had shape, but it was formless to her. It rose before her, and as she craned her neck upward it filled the sky. The Ring was overhead, but she couldn't see it. Someone envisioned this, someone *built* this. She felt small, she felt insignificant, she felt . . .

She felt a hand on her shoulder. "Sonya," said Tev in an uncharacteristically soft voice. "Turn around. Please."

Her eyes blinked a few times rapidly, and she turned at the sound of Tev's voice. "What . . . ?"

"The sight of the elevator from the base can be . . . overwhelming, if you don't know what to expect."

"But . . ." she began.

Tev nodded. "You knew, up here," and he tapped his head. "But knowing doesn't mean understanding."

"Is everything all right?" asked Eevraith as he hurried to their side.

Gomez nodded. "I'm fine, Minister. Just a touch of agoraphobia."

Eevraith looked from Gomez to Tev, uncomprehending. Tev merely shrugged in response.

Two Kharzh'ullans approached the group. Both were tall, nearly three meters in height, and wore red coveralls and yellow helmets. Seeing Eevraith, the Kharzh'ullan in front smiled.

"Commander Gomez," said Eevraith, "may I present the restoration project leader, Gringa."

Gomez held out her hand, and Gringa took her hand in his and touched them to his forehead. "A pleasure," he said as he rose.

"Commander Gomez and her team have come to assist in our repairs of the elevator," said Eevraith. "They wished to inspect the new elevator shell."

Gringa nodded. He turned to Gomez. "I believe you'll find our work satisfactory."

"Let's take a look," said Gomez.

Gringa led them down a metal staircase, across an open field, and into a large warehouse. Inside the entrance, Gomez, Tev, and Eevraith placed their environmental helmets in a storage locker. Gringa in turn handed all four of them hardhats to wear. "For your protection," he said.

Pattie refused hers, using her top left limb to point to her head. "This is harder than the helmet—besides, it won't fit."

Looking down at the helmet in his hand, Gringa saw that the helmet was too small to fit over the Nasat's exoskeleton. He shrugged and replaced it on the shelf.

They stepped from the entrance alcove into the warehouse. The interior was cavernous. Kharzh'ullans operated machinery and metal presses, and a forklift passed them as it drove down an aisle. "This is where we're fashioning the replacement shell," said Gringa. "These workers are taking processed ore and molding it into panels." He pointed to an area far to the left. "Over there, we take the panels and bolt them together into a 'sandwich'—the outer casing, a reinforced skeleton, an electromagnetic sheath, and then the inner shell."

Gomez looked up as she heard something above her. A large panel, three meters square, passed overhead on the end of a crane arm. Gringa noticed her attention. "Those panels will form the inner shell."

"The outer tiles are the same size?" Pattie asked.

"No," said Eevraith. "They're much smaller, half a meter across."

"Why the difference in size?" asked Gomez.

"Different materials and repairability," said Gringa. "On the inside of the elevator shaft we use a frictionless ceramic tile to facilitate the transports up and down the elevator, while on the outside of the shaft we use a shielded metal panel to withstand and reflect the solar radiation to protect the delicate electromagnetic sheath within. More importantly, the smaller panels on the outside will enable us to access the interior of the elevator shell should we need to effect repairs in the future."

He then led them further into the warehouse. They stepped through an open doorway, and in the room stood hundreds of the replacement panels on their ends, which showed the different construction materials—black on the metal side, beige on the ceramic side. As they walked down the central aisle, one or two might stop and examine a panel before continuing on.

"How will these be installed, Supervisor?" said Tev.

Gringa stopped, turned, and looked down on Tev. He took a deep breath, and Gomez thought he might have even frowned. "We will bolt them onto the elevator shaft, beginning from the edges of the phaser gashes and then working inward."

Tev flared his nostrils in annoyance. "The phaser gashes are not even. I presume that special panels are built to match exactly with the damage done."

Eevraith nodded. "We will cut out more of the elevator shaft, if the special panels do not work."

"Could we examine one of the custom panels?" asked Tev.

Neither Gringa nor Eevraith answered.

"They don't exist," said Gomez.

"Not yet, no," said Eevraith quietly, confirming Gomez's sudden suspicion.

"How do you know these will work?" said Gomez, gesturing at the panels around them.

"They will," said Eevraith. "While the Furies left no instructions on how to work the elevators or how to repair them, they left us the elevators to study and reverse engineer. That is what we have done—studied the work they left us and replicated it. We know what the Furies did. We know how they did it. Rebuilding the elevator shaft poses no great difficulties if we follow their example."

Gomez looked to Tev. His expression seemed neutral to her, but when he caught her gaze he nodded sharply.

They inspected the panels for an hour, with Pattie and Tev taking extensive tricorder readings for analysis aboard the *da Vinci* to compare them to the earlier scans of the elevator shaft. Gomez performed a quick tally of the number of panels in the warehouse, and to her it seemed as though there weren't enough. The phaser gashes were kilometers long in some cases and many meters wide, yet the panels here might have been enough to stretch only half a kilometer if set end on end. *What were the Kharzh'ullans hoping for?* she wondered.

Gomez stepped outside onto a grassy field, and she was glad enough to be outside the warehouse.

"Have you seen Commander Tev?" said Pattie.

Gomez looked about. While she saw a number of Kharzh'ullans—Eevraith and Gringa were standing with a group near the facility's exit—she couldn't see Tev. Where had he gone?

Gomez frowned. "Pattie, take a look inside. He might be with some of the engineers or inspecting the new elevator shell." She looked back to Eevraith. "I'll look around out here."

Pattie nodded and went back into the warehouse.

Gomez went over to Eevraith. Seeing her approach, Eevraith said, "What's your analysis, Commander?"

She shook her head. "I don't know yet. Give us some time, and we'll let you know."

Eevraith grimaced. Gomez knew he was impatient. Every day the elevator went unrepaired it posed a threat to Kharzh'ulla.

"Have you seen Tev?" she asked.

Gringa shook his head. "Not for some time," he said. "I believe he left the warehouse before Eevraith and I did."

Gomez scowled. She tapped her combadge. "Gomez to Tev." No response. She repeated the hail, but still nothing.

"Would the elevator be blocking communicator signals?" she asked.

Eevraith shook his head. "Follow me."

He led her around the warehouse and past the observation platform where they had beamed down to. Gomez knew they were walking toward the elevator's base, and she forced herself not to look at it, lest its size overwhelm her. They climbed a short hill, and Eevraith stopped at the top. He pointed. "You'll find Tev there."

Gomez looked down the hill. Sure enough, she saw Tev. "What . . . ?" she asked. "What's going on? What's down there?"

Eevraith shook his head. "My apologies. I must return to Prelv."

He turned and began walking back to the warehouse.

"Minister!" Gomez called.

He stopped and turned.

She closed the distance between them. "I don't understand. Why is Tev down there?"

"That is Tev's tale to tell. Not mine."

"There's history between you."

Eevraith said nothing.

"If that poses a risk to this mission . . ."

Eevraith held up his hand. "Tev will do as he will. Whatever the differences between us, he will never endanger your mission." He turned and continued back toward the warehouse.

"No, he won't, Minister," Gomez called after him, "but what of you?"

Eevraith continued walking as though he hadn't heard her.

Shaking her head, Gomez proceeded down the hill. She looked at Tev. He stood near what she took to be a monument of some sort. Might this have been the elevator that had suffered the transport accident?

If Tev heard her approach, he gave no notice.

"Tev?" she said.

He turned. "Commander Gomez," he said, his voice flat and low.

"You didn't answer my hail."

He said nothing.

Gomez frowned. She looked past Tev to the monument. It was a simple granite obelisk. Curvy writing that she recognized from the *da Vinci*'s past missions to Tellar and Maeglin as the Tellarite script ran down the obelisk's face.

"What does this memorialize?" she asked.

Tev's nostrils flared. He looked back to the monument. "The victims of the transport accident."

Her guess had been correct. "Your mother."

"She was returning from family business on Tellar. She had been away for six months."

"How old were you?"

"Twelve."

Gomez nodded. She placed her hand on his shoulder and squeezed lightly. "I'm sorry, Tev."

"My father . . ." he began, but his voice choked. He closed his eyes and took deep breaths to center himself. "Nothing was left in the wreckage. No bodies. The force of the impact, the speed of the transport, it left nothing to be identified. My father . . . hoped she hadn't been aboard, that she missed the transport when it left the orbital terminus. Until he died, he hoped she would come through the door to our home." He shook his head. "She never did."

Gomez understood. The monument was all Tev had to remember his mother by.

"Come on, Tev, let's get back to Pattie," she said. She turned and started back up the hill. She stopped, turned, and saw that Tev had not moved. "Tev?"

He turned, and his eyes were damp and blurry. "I blamed myself."

"You couldn't have done anything if you had been here."

Tev shook his head. "I had a dream." He took a deep breath. "I was serving aboard the *Madison.* We were ordered to Brundage Point, to stop the Fury invasion."

Gomez nodded. The Furies had attempted their third invasion of the Alpha Quadrant a few years before, and Starfleet sent three ships—the *Enterprise,* the *Madison,* and the *Idaho*—to counter the invasion. She had transferred off the *Enterprise* to the *Oberth* by that point, but she remembered the late Kieran Duffy telling her about that invasion attempt, which had come very close to succeeding.

"They used a fear weapon," Tev said, his voice still and quiet. "It made nightmares real."

"Your mother's death."

Tev nodded, biting his lower lip. "I hadn't thought of her death for a very long time. When the Furies used their weapon, I was there aboard the passenger car. I saw my mother." He closed his eyes tight. "I saw her. She begged me to help her. She didn't want to die. No one did. I couldn't do anything."

"The accident wasn't your fault, Tev."

He nodded. "I knew that then. I know that now." He paused. "Knowing that doesn't keep me from feeling, though."

Gomez sighed. She walked up to him, put her hands on his shoulders, and looked straight into his eyes. "Tev, we can't change the past, neither of us. If we could, we would. Kieran, your mother . . ." Her voice trailed off. "We can't make yesterday, but we can make tomorrow. I have to believe that to keep going forward."

"I know, Commander," said Tev softly. "I know."

She dropped her hands from Tev's shoulders. "Let's get back to Pattie and the *da Vinci.* I want her analysis of the Kharzh'ullan repairs." Tev scowled. Gomez found this unsettling. "Something bothering you, Commander?"

"I have my doubts about the Kharzh'ullan solution," said Tev as he walked up the hill back toward the warehouse.

Despite her asking him to elaborate, Tev said nothing more on the subject until they beamed back to the ship.

CHAPTER 5

"Computer, pull up file Eevraith-Ring-One," Gomez said with a sigh as she collapsed backward onto her bunk. If Eevraith's was the definitive study of the construction of the Ring and the elevators, she decided that comparing the study's analysis of the elevator's composition, particularly its structure and flexibility, to the newly fashioned shell would be of immense aid in the repair job.

"Acknowledged."

Gomez rubbed her eyes, as much out of exhaustion as out of habit. The morning's visit to the palace had begun a promising day, but the next six hours of survey and analysis of the damaged elevator shaft and the Kharzh'ullan replacement hull took its physical and mental toll. "Begin playback, from subsection 14, paragraph 4."

"Playback in Tellarite or Federation Standard?"

"Standard," she said, momentarily confused.

"Acknowledged."

Gomez closed her eyes as the computer's recitation began. *"The structural demands placed upon the shafts lessen exponentially as the elevator shaft approaches terminus—"*

"Computer," she said, interrupting the playback, her curiosity piqued. "What was the language of the original text?"

"Tellarite," the computer replied.

It made sense. The study had been written by a Tellarite—Eevraith—for a Tellarite audience—his university professors—and the speech had the telltale sign of a speaker of Federation Standard who used it as a second or third language—too mannered, the syllables drawn out and the stresses misplaced. Kharzh'ulla IV, like so many non-human worlds, spoke Standard only when necessary, and oftentimes the universal translator worked just as well in everyday conversation between native and non-native Standard speakers.

"Computer," she said, "resume playback from beginning of sentence."

"The structural demands placed upon the shafts lessen exponentially as the elevator shaft approaches terminus, hence the narrowing of the shafts as they progress from surface to geosynchronous orbit. Theoretical models formulated of space elevators prior to the discovery of the Kharzh'ullan system relied upon ungrounded skyhooks that reached into the upper atmosphere, space tethers, or extensive cabling systems to counteract the gravitational effects a structure the size of an elevator would experience. The Kharzh'ullan elevator shafts by contrast support their own weight over their thirty-thousand kilometer length in two ways.

First, the Ring structure itself acts as a counterweight to the elevator shaft, thus anchoring the weight in orbit and providing an upward 'pull' that prevents the structure from collapsing due to gravity. Second, the base itself distributes the weight of the shaft by spreading the gravitational pull across a base two hundred fifty kilometers in diameter. The elegance of the Kharzh'ullan solution is that the structure is self-supporting and requires no outside assistance for its own maintenance."

Gomez sat up in the dark with a start. "Computer, halt playback. Repeat last sentence."

"The elegance of the Kharzh'ullan solution is that the structure is self-supporting and requires no outside assistance for its own maintenance."

Hadn't Tev said exactly that the day before during the mission briefing? Would Tev knowingly quote Eevraith, if their relationship was as damaged as she thought it was?

Gomez glanced at the wall chronometer, an idea half-formed in her mind. "Locate Bart Faulwell." Very likely he was off duty—the current mission afforded him nothing to do—but she wanted to be certain. But the time—would he be awake?

"Dr. Faulwell is in his quarters."

"Computer, download Eevraith-Ring-One to my padd." The padd bleeped as Gomez grabbed her uniform jacket, threw it on hastily, and headed out, padd in hand. At the late hour—0130 hours, in the middle of gamma shift—she met no one in the corridors.

She stopped at the door to Faulwell's cabin, tapped the chime, and waited. Seconds later the door parted.

"Commander," Bart said as he rose from his desk. "Please come in."

Gomez stepped into the cabin and waved him down. "I hope I'm not interrupting anything." She glanced about. "Where's Fabian?"

Faulwell shrugged as he sat back down at his desk. "The surface, I think. The captain approved a sightseeing trip to see the Ring from the planet."

Gomez nodded. "You didn't go, obviously."

Faulwell shrugged in his seat. "I wanted to catch up on some reading. I've gotten behind."

Gomez smiled. "I know the feeling. Anything good?"

Faulwell handed her an old book, hardcover, its spine bent and tattered. "A gift from Anthony."

She gently opened the cover and read the title page. "*The True History of Planets,* by Reginald Tyler." She looked back at Bart. "Never heard of it."

"Few have. At the time it was one of the great works of heroic fantasy in twentieth-century Terran literature, standing alongside *Lord of the Rings, Gormenghast, The Swords of Lankhmar,* even *Thieves' World.*" He sighed. "Unfortunately, heroic fantasy has never been my particular choice for recreational reading."

"Then why—"

"—did Anthony give me this? Because of the dogs, I'm sure."

"Dogs?"

"Poodles, actually. With opposable thumbs."

Gomez shot him a quizzical look.

"Seriously, it's a heroic fantasy with super-intelligent poodles as the heroes, caught up in a revolution against the vaguely medieval tyrant that rules their world."

Gomez shook her head and handed the book back to Bart. "Doesn't sound all that serious to me at all. Why dogs?"

"Growing up, my grandparents raised purebred

dogs." Faulwell shrugged. "I suppose Anthony thought I would have a particular affinity for the book because of my childhood. It makes a certain perverse sense—I spent a lot of time around dogs, so I would have some emotional connection to them."

"Not a dog person, eh?"

"When I was completing my postgraduate work I had three cats. It may have been an uneasy relationship for the four of us, but we each respected the others' space. Dogs, though, are like children, needy and loud. Cats are a bit more self-reliant than that." Faulwell laughed. "I *hated* dogs. Raised around them for so long, I grew tired of them, the way children grow tired of peanut butter and jelly sandwiches because their parents make them all the time. When we had that big gathering at the captain's house a few weeks ago, I was so grateful that he had that dog of his tied up, you couldn't believe it."

Gomez shook her head. "I never knew."

"That my parents raised dogs?"

"No," said Gomez with a smile, "that children *ever* liked peanut butter and jelly."

Faulwell laughed. He set the book down on his desk and leaned back in his chair. "I don't imagine you dropped by my cabin to talk about childhood."

Gomez's smile upturned at the corner, and she nodded slowly. "I have a little project for you, Bart."

Faulwell gave a noncommittal shrug. "Public or private?"

"Private."

"What do you have in mind, Commander?"

She handed him her padd. "How good are you at analyzing writing styles?"

"I'm a linguist, not a literary scholar."

Gomez smiled. "You're the one reading twentieth-century fantasy fiction."

Faulwell shrugged. "Just because I work with words on a daily basis doesn't mean I have any special facility with style analysis."

"I can think of no one better equipped for this little project than you."

Faulwell looked at the proffered padd and reached out gingerly. He looked directly into Gomez's eyes, and in that moment took the padd from Gomez's hand. "You don't believe Eevraith glasch Tremen," he said, reading the author's name off the padd, "wrote this text?"

Gomez shook her head. "I have my doubts."

Faulwell called up the document and looked at the first page. "Original text in Tellarite." He looked back up at Gomez. "This will definitely stretch some mental muscles." He paused. "Sounds like a challenge. It might take weeks."

Gomez nodded.

"What do you want to know?"

Gomez took a deep breath and exhaled slowly. "I want to know who the author is." She paused. "The *real* author."

CHAPTER 6

Gold stood at the ready room window as he listened to Vivaldi's *Four Seasons,* and looked out over the *da Vinci*'s saucer at the Ring and Kharzh'ulla beneath it. From the ship's position in orbit the damaged Ring segment could not be seen, but behind the ship Gold could see an elevator thousands of kilometers distant move out of the terminator and into the dawn. Few sights he had seen in his Starfleet career could inspire such awe at the power of technology to add to the beauty of nature. The Dyson Sphere Montgomery Scott and the *Enterprise*-D had discovered represented the ultimate in stellar engineering. The Kharzh'ullan Ring was so much smaller than that, but no less impressive. Planets always held a fascination, each unique in its coloring, its features, and space stations reflected the sensibilities of their designers. Here, however, was a synthesis of both the natural and the artificial—functional, yet inspiring.

He heard distantly over the strains of violins the sound of the door chime. He sighed, asked the computer to mute Vivaldi, and took a seat behind his desk.

Gomez and Tev entered the ready room, and they took their seats opposite the desk.

Gold leaned back in his chair. "Anything to drink?"

Both Gomez and Tev shook their heads.

"How did the surveys go?" Gold asked.

"Exhausting," said Gomez.

"Long," said Tev.

Gold nodded. "Care to elaborate?"

Gomez looked to Tev. He nodded, and an unspoken communication passed between them.

"The Kharzh'ullan plan won't work," she said.

Gold folded his hands together and lazily tapped the tip of his nose. "Why?"

Gomez bobbed her head from side to side in thought, then scrunched the side of her mouth. "The Kharzh'ullans' makeshift solution—using the structural integrity fields—actually damaged the elevator shaft more than the Jem'Hadar attack did. Pattie found stress fractures all along the shaft. The SIFs held the structure too rigid, and it wasn't designed to take that kind of stress."

"They had the right idea," said Tev. "The system's design was rather ingenious—the Ring holds the elevators up, but that centrifugal force would have pulled the elevator apart eventually. The structural integrity fields were meant to hold the elevator together. Ironically, they hastened the Ring's collapse."

"How long until the system fails?" asked Gold.

Gomez shrugged. "We can have an answer for you in a few days. If I had to take a guess, we have some time, perhaps even a few years." She took out her padd and passed it across the desk to Gold. "Pattie's preliminary report hasn't been able to pinpoint an exact time."

"There may not *be* an exact time," added Tev. "There are too many factors in play."

"What about the Kharzh'ullans? I thought they were building a new elevator casing."

Tev nodded. "They are. Unfortunately, fixing the hole the Jem'Hadar made in the elevator shaft would be the beginning of the cure, not the end, as the stress fractures themselves also need to be repaired."

"What about welding the fractures back together? I thought the Kharzh'ullans were building a new skin for the elevator shaft."

Gomez shook her head. "It wouldn't be as strong if those areas were simply torn out and replaced."

"To keep the structure stable while replacing the stressed areas, we would need to use structural integrity fields to hold the elevator in place," said Tev. "More importantly, what the Kharzh'ullans are building will not be as strong or as stable as the original shell."

"Which would exacerbate the problem," Gold said.

Gomez nodded. "The Furies built the elevator shells of solid diamond."

"Diamond?" repeated Gold.

"Diamond has one of the highest natural tensile strengths," said Tev.

"I thought tungsten was harder," said Gold.

"It is," said Gomez. "But diamond is easier to find. Or fashion, if the Furies used molecular engineering."

Gold drummed his fingers on his desk. "Tev brought up how the Ring holds itself up. If the Ring were repaired first, wouldn't that be enough to hold the elevator in place?"

Gomez scratched at her nose in thought as she considered the idea. "We'd have to run a simulation, but I don't think that would work. There are two problems I see. First, the Kharzh'ullans aren't even ready to rebuild the Ring; they focused on building the new casing to repair the elevator as that was the more obvious threat. Second, while the Ring itself orbits at a geosynchronous altitude and has an angular momentum to remain in place at that altitude, the elevators move at a greater angular speed than they should at all altitudes because they're held in place by the anchoring effects of the base and the Ring. The damaged elevator, because of the stress fractures, would fly apart and rain debris down onto the planet."

Gold took a deep breath and exhaled slowly. "It sounds to me that you're both saying this is a problem we simply cannot repair. If Captain Scott wants recommendations, what do you suggest?"

Gomez looked to Tev and frowned. "If we can't repair the elevator, I don't see that we have any choice but evacuation. The Ring will fall to the surface, and that will render Kharzh'ulla uninhabitable for generations."

"I don't like that option, Gomez."

Gomez shook her head. "I don't either, sir. But looking at what we're facing, I don't see any other option." She looked to Tev. He sat impassively, biting his lower lip. "We could make the attempt to repair the gash, but there's no guarantee it would work. Judging by Pattie's findings, I doubt that it would."

Gold looked to Tev and to Gomez. They had presented their findings, and there was nothing more to say. "Very well," he said, "I'll send a preliminary report to Starfleet requesting the evacuation of Kharzh'ulla IV. Dismissed."

Gomez nodded and stood. She stepped to the threshold and stopped. Tev continued to sit, as if lost in thought. "Tev?" she said.

Tev looked up at Gomez. "What if there's another way?"

"What've you got, Tev?" asked Gold.

"Our problem is that the elevator will collapse. Nothing we do can stop that." Tev paused. "What if that's the solution? Allow the elevator to collapse, but a controlled collapse."

"And the Ring?" said Gomez.

Tev shook his head. "Irrelevant. At a geosynchronous orbit it will stay in place, and it will hold the elevators up. But the damaged elevator, if we detach it from the Ring and let it fall, won't pull the rest of the Ring down onto Kharzh'ulla."

"The problem *is* the solution," said Gold quietly.

Tev shrugged.

"Captain," said Gomez, "it's worth a shot. It's not as if we have anything to lose."

Gold nodded slowly. "I see one problem. A big problem." He looked straight at Tev. "If I know Tellarites, they won't like an outsider telling them how to do things."

Gomez hastily resumed her seat. She spoke quickly, excitedly. "But it would save their world. First Minister Grevesh would see that. Minister Eevraith would see that. It's the best possible solution."

Tev spoke, his voice low and hushed. "The captain is correct. The Kharzh'ullans wouldn't accept the idea, not if we proposed it to them. Pride defines Tellarites, just as honor defines Klingons, creativity defines humans, and logic defines Vulcans. It is part and parcel of who we are and how we see ourselves. Tellarite pride kept the Kharzh'ullans from asking for help a year ago. Tellarite pride would keep them from seeing the rightness of our solution to their problem." Tev shook his head. "No, we cannot tell them how to save their world."

"What are you suggesting, Tev? That we take it on ourselves to just drop the elevator without telling them?" said Gomez. "I somehow doubt they'd appreciate that."

Tev locked eyes with Gomez. "The Tellarites have to tell *us* how to save their world."

CHAPTER 7

Eevraith looked up into Kharzh'ulla's night sky. It was rare for the Ring overhead to be visible at night—unlike a moon, the Ring was too close to the planet for it to ever leave Kharzh'ulla's shadow—and tonight proved no exception. To the east and west, however, close to the horizon where the Ring's arc still fell in sunlight, the Ring shone bright and silver against the dark sky. One of his first proposals as transportation minister was for running lights to be mounted along the Ring's edge, to make the whole of the Ring visible day and night, but cost-benefit analysis found no practical use for such a system. Perhaps when Grevesh retired, and he took the reins of government as Grevesh's chosen political heir, then things might be different.

Prelv's streets were largely deserted as he walked through Old Town. This section of Prelv had once been the original settlement, and around it the apparatus of government and industry had developed. But cities, when given space, grew outward, leaving behind buildings out of date and no longer needed, and such had happened with Old Town. One of the proposals Grevesh had put forth when he ran for first minister fifteen years before had been to turn the area into a memorial museum and park devoted to those early days, and on that platform the masses elected him.

Eevraith did not much care to mingle with the common folk—too low-class for his tastes, and too prone toward sentiment for the old ways—but he recognized their value to his chosen career; had it not been for them, Grevesh might still have been an academic, and Eevraith might have been a mere councillor, not transportation minister.

Still, had he not urgent business in Old Town, Eevraith would not have been there, not at this hour. He would rather have been home, in bed with his wife, and not on an unknown errand at the behest of a cryptic message: "As you value your career, meet me tonight at two bells at the Chrainolga." The Chrainolga was a cathedral, built in service to one of Tellar's ancient religions, one relating to ancestor worship. He stood before the building, an imposing structure that dated back to the colony's earliest days, and the only building in Old Town still used for its original purpose. Three towers rose above the building's vast sanctuary hall, and Eevraith mounted the steps to the Chrainolga's massive doors. He had been here only twice before, both times for Grevesh's political appearances, and certainly for no personal or spiritual reasons of his own.

Atop the steps stood a robed Tellarite. Eevraith had seen the type before, clerics of the religious priesthood. They had never been a factor in past campaigns, and they generally asked for nothing from the government, so he gave the cleric no attention as he strode up to the doors. He took the brass handles in hand and gave them a hard pull. Nothing. The doors were bolted from within.

"What do you seek?" he heard from behind him. Eevraith turned. The cleric. He was short, his voice deep, his head and body covered by the white robe he wore. Eevraith couldn't place his accent. One of the southern continents, perhaps.

"I was to meet someone here," said Eevraith. He shook his head. "It doesn't matter, it was probably of no importance." He turned and started back down the steps.

"Wait," said the cleric. Eevraith turned, and the cleric held before him the key to the sanctuary.

He looked past the cleric and nodded toward the doors. "There's someone within?"

The cleric nodded. "Perhaps even the answers you seek."

Eevraith chuckled silently. "I have no questions."

"None that you have asked."

Eevraith closed the space between them. "Are clerics always so cryptic?"

The cleric ignored the question, and turned and unlocked the sanctuary doors. Eevraith pushed him to the side, took the brass handles, and pulled the doors open.

Inside the sanctuary was quite dark, with only the lit candles along the walls and at the pulpit providing any illumination. Eevraith slowly stepped inside.

He walked halfway up the central aisle, his footfalls on the polished stone echoing loudly in the silent chamber. He looked back over his shoulder twice toward the doors, hoping to see the cleric, hoping for some reassurance that there was some meaning to this midnight rendezvous, but the cleric had vanished, and Eevraith continued onward alone.

He heard footfalls, and turned. Framed in the door, backlit by the street lamps outside, was a Tellarite. From his distance, Eevraith could judge nothing—height, age, even gender. "Who are you?"

No answer. The newcomer took a few tentative steps into the Chrainolga's sanctuary, then stopped.

"Come no closer!" shouted Eevraith, and his voice reverberated off the carved stone walls. "I'm armed."

The newcomer took something from his side—perhaps a weapon—and held it up.

"What are you doing?" said Eevraith, his voice rattling.

A brilliant light blinded him, and Eevraith clutched his eyes in pain. The footfalls began again and came closer, and Eevraith fell to the ground in pain and fear. "Who are you?" he cried again.

The footfalls stopped, somewhere near his head. "Eevraith?" he heard.

He opened his eyes. Purple afterimages filled his vision, and his eyes were unable to focus. "Tev?" he said, half-recognizing the voice. "Tev, what's the meaning of this?"

Rough hands grasped his shoulder and yanked him up off the sanctuary floor, then shoved him into a seat on a wooden bench. "You could hurt yourself like that, Eevraith."

"Tev, you blinded me with that light!" Eevraith shouted. His vision had begun to clear, but the interior of the sanctuary and Tev still appeared murky to him. Tev took his torchlight and set it atop a table pointing upward, and the interior was bathed in twilight as light reflected from the high ceiling.

"How was I to have known you would look directly into my light?" Tev took a seat on a bench opposite Eevraith and propped his head in his hands.

Eevraith rubbed his eyes. "What do you want, Tev? I haven't the time for this. I have a meeting of some sort." Realization dawned on him, and he looked up at Tev through his bleary eyes. "The meeting. It was you. This was all your idea."

"I knew I could appeal to your baser natures—curiosity and your career. Who would send you a cryptic note, asking for a clandestine meeting at a little-visited location at an inconvenient hour, offering to further your own political ambitions? You had to know. You wouldn't have been you if you hadn't come."

Eevraith's head hurt. "We're not children anymore, Tev." He paused and looked at Tev. "How did you get that message into my office?" Before Tev could answer, he realized the answer. "The transporter. You beamed it into my office, onto my desk."

Tev shrugged. "Not onto the desk. *Above* the desk. Six centimeters, to be precise, and gravity took its course."

"You're too insufferably pleased with yourself."

Tev said nothing, and they sat together in silence as Eevraith's eyes cleared somewhat.

"How is Biyert?" asked Tev.

"Fine," said Eevraith, caught off-guard. "She's fine. She dotes on our daughters too much for my taste, but that makes her happy." He shrugged. "She wants another child, but I don't know that I love her that much anymore. If I ever did." He looked at Tev and scowled. "Why does this even matter to you? The two of you weren't going to be together, not the way you wanted to be. Her family would never have approved. How would it have looked to have the granddaughter of the rising leader of the ruling party marry an off-worlder? By Phinda, Tev, that would have cost the party more than an election—it would have cost it *power* for a generation." He paused. "Is that what you really wanted? To destroy everything your father worked so long and so hard to achieve for Grevesh and the party?"

"Leave my father out of it," Tev said, his nostrils flared in anger. Eevraith said nothing. Finally, Tev said, "Did you at least tell Biyert I had returned?"

Eevraith shook his head. Reading the expression on Tev's face, he said, "I didn't even know until I saw you in the palace that you were aboard the *da Vinci*. Had I known, I would have asked Starfleet for another ship."

Tev nodded. "Starfleet thought, in light of my history here and my experience with the Ring, that the *da Vinci* was the ship best suited for this mission."

Eevraith blinked a few times, his vision very nearly returned to normal. "Under other circumstances, I might agree," said Eevraith quietly.

Tev looked down, following Eevraith's gaze, to the padd in his hands. "I have the mission report." He paused. "It's as I feared. The elevator cannot be repaired."

Tev held out the padd. Eevraith considered it for a moment, then reached out and took it. He looked down at the screen, weighing whether or not he should read the report. He wanted to read it, had to know what it said, what the options were, but there would be time enough the next few days for that. "The elevator," said Eevraith at last. "You can't repair the damage."

"No," said Tev quietly.

"The dampened oscillation from the structural integrity fields."

Tev nodded. "The shell was held too rigid. At the edge

of the structural integrity fields, the shell stressed more than it should have."

"You wanted to gloat," Eevraith said, his voice neutral, his statement flat. "You always had to be right. You always had to know more about the Ring and the elevators than anyone else. This is your payback, for all the perceived slights of twenty years ago." He stood, his face flushed in anger, and threw the padd onto the stone floor. "Did you do *any* legitimate work? Or did you and your team work from a preconceived notion that Kharzh'ulla would have to be abandoned out of your misplaced sense of spite?"

Tev spat on the floor in front of Eevraith, then looked up into Eevraith's eyes with a look of cold fury behind his own. "Don't *ever* insult my work again, Eevraith," Tev said, his voice low. "Forget that at your peril." Tev paused as Eevraith stumbled back to his bench. "You owe me a favor. I left you in peace twenty years ago. I did nothing to derail your personal and political ambitions when you know damn well I could have."

He stood, walked across the chamber, picked up the padd Eevraith had so carelessly thrown, and held it out to him. Eevraith looked up at the proffered padd through bleary eyes.

"The solution," Tev said. "How to save Kharzh'ulla without evacuation." He paused and looked meaningfully at Eevraith. "How to save your career and further your ambitions."

Eevraith looked at the padd held before him. He thought about taking it in his hands again. "The elevator will collapse," said Eevraith, his voice tired and heavy. "What else is there to say, other than evacuate Kharzh'ulla?"

Tev bared his teeth. Eevraith found this disconcerting. "Accelerate the collapse," Tev said.

"You look tired, Gomez," said Gold.

They walked together through the *da Vinci*'s corridors toward the bridge, their morning ritual.

Gomez smiled wanly. "Late night, sir."

"Work or pleasure?"

She made a *pffft* sound and shook her head. "Work. Strictly work." They reached the turbolift, stepped inside, and took up positions on opposite sides.

"I heard you approved some sightseeing trips to the surface," Gomez said.

Gold nodded. "I've thought of going down myself. The Ring is impressive enough from orbit, and I'm told it's spectacular from the surface."

Gomez gestured, her hand cutting an arc through the air in front of her. "You should see how the sunlight catches the Ring."

"With luck, I'll have the chance before we leave."

Gomez nodded. "How long will a planetary evacuation take, do you think?"

Gold exhaled loudly and frowned. "Six months, for a population this size. The real problem is whether or not the Federation has the resources for an evacuation." He paused. "I don't know that they do."

"The Dominion War," said Gomez.

Gold nodded. "The rebuilding is part of it, certainly. There's also the question of political expediency."

"How so?"

"Tellar is a Federation member world, but Kharzh'ulla isn't. As a political entity, it's aligned with the Federation, hence their offer to allow Starfleet to use the Ring as a staging area for the fleet during the war. But their acquiescence to the request was grudging, and Starfleet, which would be the one to handle any evacuation, is likely to remember that."

"Even with lives at stake?"

"It would depend, I think, on the urgency of the situation. How close is the elevator to collapse? How long can the Kharzh'ullans' temporary solution hold the elevator in place? How many people can the Kharzh'ullans evacuate themselves? Starfleet would take those three questions into account, and if in their opinion the elevator can remain stable for three or five years, any evacuation might not happen until a few years down the road." He paused. "There are planets who contributed more to the war effort and who suffered more than Kharzh'ulla."

The turbolift doors opened onto the bridge. Gold and Gomez had arrived early for their shift—gamma shift hadn't yet gone off duty, and alpha shift hadn't yet arrived.

Tev turned in the command seat to the turbolift doors and stood as Gold and Gomez stepped onto the bridge. "Good morning, Captain," he said.

"How was the mission to the surface?" asked Gold as he took his seat in the command chair.

Tev shrugged. "The Kharzh'ullans have their choice now—abandon their world, or collapse the elevator to save the Ring."

"And it's up to them to decide which path to take," said Gomez.

"Which way do you think Eevraith will go, Commander Tev?"

"Eevraith will do what is best for Eevraith. Saving Kharzh'ulla saves his career."

Gold nodded. He turned to Gomez. "If the Kharzh'ullans accept Tev's plan, how long would it take to implement it?"

Gomez looked to Tev. "A day. Maybe less." She paused. "We'd have to evacuate some of the Ring and the elevator base, and then place detonators near the base of the elevator."

Gold leaned back in his chair and sighed. "Now begins the waiting." He turned to Tev. "You're dismissed, Commander. Get some rest."

"With all due respect, sir, I would prefer to remain on the bridge."

Gold nodded. "As you wish."

Alpha shift came on duty—Haznedl at ops, Wong at conn, Shabalala at tactical. Gomez and Tev reviewed reports, but there was little to be done unless or until the Kharzh'ullans accepted the idea of collapsing the elevator.

"Sir," said Shabalala, "we're being hailed. First Minister Grevesh."

Gold nodded. "On screen."

The viewscreen changed from Kharzh'ulla and the Ring to the interior of Grevesh's ministerial office.

"First Minister," said Gold as he rose from his command chair and approached the viewscreen, "this is an unexpected surprise."

"Captain Gold," said Grevesh, *"I bid you a happy morning. Is your Commander Gomez there?"*

Gold nodded, turned, and gestured to Gomez. "She is, yes."

Grevesh nodded. *"I wish her advice, Captain. I trust you do not mind."*

"Not at all, First Minister." He nodded to Gomez, and she took Gold's place before the viewscreen.

"First Minister, what can I do for you?" Gomez asked.

Grevesh smiled. *"Minister Eevraith came to me this morning with a most unusual proposal, and I wished to solicit your opinion."*

"If I can help, of course."

"I thought his idea mad, but if he says it can be done, perhaps there is some truth to it. He tells me that the elevator cannot be repaired, and that our only option to save Kharzh'ulla and the Ring is to allow the damaged elevator to collapse."

"Collapse?" said Gomez with a hint of skepticism in her voice. "Wouldn't the elevator's collapse bring the Ring down on Kharzh'ulla?"

"Indeed," said Grevesh. *"I thought much the same. But Eevraith tells me that if we separate the elevator from the Ring and allow* just *the elevator to collapse, the Ring will remain fixed in place."*

Gomez crossed her arms and stroked her chin pensively. "Collapse the elevator, but allow the Ring to remain in place?" She paused. "First Minister, could I discuss this with Captain Gold and Commander Tev?"

Grevesh nodded. *"Please, Commander Gomez, take your time."*

Gomez smiled. "Just a few moments, First Minister." She made a throat-cutting gesture to Shabalala.

"The channel is mute."

Gomez looked at Tev. "Eevraith presented your plan as his," she said.

Tev nodded. "Of course."

"Doesn't that bother you?" said Gold.

"If it saves Kharzh'ulla," said Tev, "I do not care what Eevraith does."

Gomez nodded. She knew Tev's sense of pride from personal experience. She could only imagine the sense of pride Eevraith had to be the politician that he was.

She returned to the center of the bridge. "Tony, reopen the channel."

Shabalala nodded. "Channel open."

"First Minister Grevesh," said Gomez, "I've consulted with Captain Gold and Commander Tev. They're skeptical of Minister Eevraith's plan, but they're willing to look into whether or not it will work."

"Minister Eevraith assures me that it will."

Gomez nodded. She turned and looked at Tev, hunched over a computer terminal. "Commander Tev?" she said loudly.

Tev looked up. "Commander, I believe Eevraith's plan will work."

"Did you hear that, First Minister? Tev has run a simulation of Minister Eevraith's plan."

On-screen, Grevesh smiled. *"I thought Minister Eevraith mad. This reassures me that his idea was not."*

Tev rose from his seat and came to Gomez's side. "Commander," said Tev, "Eevraith's plan is a simple one. We could implement it within six hours."

"Six *hours?"* repeated Gomez. "So soon?"

Tev nodded as he looked directly at Grevesh on the viewscreen. "Yes, Commander. We need only detach the elevator from the Ring, and if we were to detonate explosive charges near the elevator's base the elevator would collapse into the ocean."

"Or," said Gold as he joined Tev and Gomez in the center of the bridge, "we could use the *da Vinci*'s tractor beams to pull the elevator into deep space, so as not to pollute Kharzh'ulla's oceans."

Grevesh nodded. *"Very clever, Captain. And very wise."*

"If the minister approves," said Gomez, "shall we make the attempt today?"

"I am not by nature a hasty person, Commander

Gomez, but we have delayed enough with the elevator. Time may not be essential, but I would feel more secure with the knowledge that the threat of the falling Ring had been resolved, as would all Kharzh'ullans."

Gomez smiled. "Then we shall begin preparations here to collapse the elevator, First Minister. If you and Minister Eevraith would care to beam aboard, we would be glad to have you aboard to witness the elevator's collapse."

Grevesh nodded. *"I would very much like that, Commander Gomez. I hope to give you an answer soon."*

"Of course," said Gomez. "*Da Vinci* out." The viewscreen went dark.

"Well," said Gold with a sigh, "fine acting job, both of you."

"Thank you, Captain," said Gomez.

Tev said, "What is your plan?"

"We'll place detonators on the elevator shaft as soon as Grevesh gives the word. We'll also need to coordinate an evacuation of part of the Ring and the elevator base with Kharzh'ullan authorities."

Gold rubbed his chin. "That could take some time, Gomez. There's no need to rush this."

Gomez nodded. "I agree, Captain, but collapsing the elevator will be simple and straightforward." She turned to Tev. "Grab a quick nap, Commander. You'll need it."

CHAPTER 8

Tev materialized in space, alone. Tev, Gomez, and Pattie were beamed to locations one hundred twenty degrees apart around the damaged elevator shaft, two hundred kilometers above the base. There they would await the transport of antimatter charges to be clamped magnetically to the shaft's outer surface.

He opened his eyes, which had been closed tightly before he dematerialized aboard the *da Vinci,* and ten meters in front of him was the elevator shaft casing. "*Daokhra!*" he exclaimed as he lost his equilibrium in the zero gravity environment.

The elevator shaft dominated his view, filling his vision as far as his eyes could see in any direction. The shaft was ten kilometers in diameter at this point along its length, and from Tev's perspective the curvature was so slight that the shaft appeared to be flat, not curved. Had he been able to look down in his environmental suit he would have seen Kharzh'ulla two hundred kilometers beneath his feet. Tev felt queasy in his stomachs.

He heard Gomez's voice in his ear through the open comm circuit. *"Tev, can you read me?"*

"I . . . I read you, Commander," he said, his voice quiet and hoarse.

"Are you all right?"

Tev squeezed his eyes shut. His breathing went ragged. "Fine, Commander. I'm fine."

"Tev, I need you to focus."

Tev's breathing became shallow and fast. *"Tev!"* he heard, but as he began to hyperventilate in his environmental suit he couldn't answer Gomez. His breathing slowed, he began to pant—the suit's atmosphere changed, recirculating carbon dioxide and decreasing the oxygen content.

He caught his breath and began to breathe deeply. Lancing pain sliced through his eyes. Distant voices sounded over the comm channel, probably Gomez and the bridge, but he couldn't focus on them. Despite the head pains, despite the confusion his body felt at the zero-gee environment of open space, he felt peaceful. Calm.

"Commander," he said, after several seconds, "I'm all right."

"Tev," he heard, recognizing Captain Gold's gravelly voice, *"what's your status?"*

"A touch of space sickness, sir."

He heard in the background what he thought was Dr. Lense's voice. *"Tellarites don't handle null gravity well. Upsets their equilibrium. We might want to beam him back, have someone else place the detonation charges."*

"I will be fine, Doctor," Tev said. "Might we continue with the mission?"

"I agree with Tev," said Gomez. *"If he says he's fine, I'll take him at his word,* then *expect him to visit sickbay once he's back aboard. But he's in place now, so let's move on."*

Moments later a detonation charge materialized silently between Tev and the shaft. It was large—a circular based cone two meters around and five tall. Within the cone was an antimatter pod and a remote detonator to collapse the antimatter containment field, causing an annihilation capable of destroying the elevator shaft.

Tev touched the maneuvering thruster control on his right arm and moved slowly toward the charge. "Contact," he said as he grappled with the handle at the end of the cone.

"Contact," Gomez said.

"Contact," said Pattie a few moments later.

Using the maneuvering thrusters, Tev pushed the cone toward the elevator shaft. A minute later he felt a slight jolt as the broad base of the cone made contact with the shaft, and he cut off the thrusters. He ran his hand along the side of the cone, touched the maglock control, and locked the cone to the side of the shaft.

"Cone in place, Commander," he said.

"I copy that, Tev."

He let go of the cone and floated in space beside it. He closed his eyes, touched the maneuvering thruster control by memory, not sight, and oriented himself with his back toward Kharzh'ulla. He opened his eyes to look straight up the length of the elevator shaft. He took a deep breath, taking in the sight of the shaft dwindling into infinity. It had stood for thousands of years, and by his actions it wouldn't stand even another day. He felt his eyes go moist, and his breathing became choked. He wanted to look down, down to Kharzh'ulla, to the places he had known so well as a youth, but he couldn't bring himself to do so. He had always looked up. When his mother died, he looked up. When he declared himself for engineering at the university, he looked up. When he left Kharzh'ulla, his career in disgrace, he looked up.

As the transporter beam took him, he looked up.

"I'm *fine,*" said Tev, his arms crossed, his brows knotted.

Lense frowned. "That's my determination to make, not yours." She picked up her medscanner off the worktable. "Now, lie down on the biobed."

Tev sat resolutely on the biobed. "Doctor, it was the merest case of zero-gee discomfort." He looked to Gomez standing near the sickbay doors. "Commander Gomez will attest to that."

Gomez held up her hands in a don't-look-at-me gesture.

"Discomfort?" repeated Lense. "The med sensors in your suit showed your heart rate up, your blood pressure up, and you were hyperventilating." She paused, taking in Tev's defiant expression. "I can have you medically relieved from this mission, Tev."

Tev flared his nostrils and narrowed his eyes. He flopped backward onto the biobed in exasperation. "Very well, Doctor. Run your tests."

Lense smiled sardonically and shook her head.

"Well," said Gomez, "if the patient's in good hands, I'll be in the transporter room meeting First Minister Grevesh and Minister Eevraith."

Lense nodded, then turned back to running her medscanner above Tev's body. The last thing Gomez heard as the sickbay doors closed behind her was a snort of derision from Tev.

Slumped in his antigrav chair, Grevesh looked frail. Gomez thought he hadn't looked particularly strong on the surface, but under the *da Vinci*'s higher gravity, he seemed to wilt. "First Minister, are you all right?"

Grevesh blinked his eyes a few times, as if to clear them, and Eevraith knelt down on the transporter platform beside him. "First Minister?" Eevraith said.

Grevesh pushed Eevraith away, and he inhaled loudly and deeply. "I feel heavy," he said, his voice weak. He smiled when his eyes focused on Gomez.

Gomez nodded and smiled. "You feel that way because, in essence, you *are* heavier. But as your body becomes accustomed to the higher gravity aboard ship that feeling will pass." She stepped up onto the transporter platform and knelt at Grevesh's knee. "Welcome aboard the *da Vinci*."

Grevesh patted Gomez's hand. "Thank you, my dear."

Eevraith and Gomez rose, and Grevesh's chair floated off the transporter platform and out into the corridor. Two security guards led the way as they walked to the turbolift.

"How much preparation has your team done, Commander?" asked Eevraith.

"We've placed the detonation charges, and now we're moving on to the next phase—detaching the Ring segment westward of the damaged elevator."

"How?"

"The Ring consists of segments a few hundred kilometers long. What we're doing is simply 'breaking' the Ring at one of the joints with explosive charges, then using focused phaser bursts if needed."

"Clever," Eevraith said. "How long until you 'break' the Ring?"

Gomez shrugged. "Within an hour, once our engineering team reports back."

The turbolift doors parted, and Grevesh, Eevraith, and Gomez entered the cabin. The doors slid shut, and Grevesh looked up at Gomez standing on his left. "What of the people living in the Ring?" The Ring was inhabited along much of its length. The section above the damaged elevator had a large population due to its proximity to the elevator that serviced Prelv. The Ring segment east of the elevator's terminus had been abandoned after the Jem'Hadar attack, but to the west twelve thousand Kharzh'ullans called the Ring home.

"Fortunately," she said, "we've moved only a thousand Kharzh'ullans."

"The rest of that Ring segment won't be affected?" Eevraith said.

Gomez shook her head. "We wanted to remove the parts of the Ring that were most affected by the stresses the SIF on the elevator caused. Only a few hundred kilometers."

"We evacuated the elevator base of the repair and construction teams this morning," said Eevraith.

Gomez nodded. It was a wise precaution if the elevator shaft fell onto the base as the *da Vinci* attempted to pull the shaft away from the planet.

Grevesh patted Gomez's hand as the turbolift doors opened onto the bridge. Grevesh's chair floated forward onto the bridge, and Eevraith and Gomez followed closely behind.

Grevesh's eyes were transfixed by the image on the viewscreen. From the *da Vinci*'s vantage point high above the elevator terminus the Jem'Hadar-inflicted damage to the Ring was clearly visible—the shattered Ring dominated the viewscreen, with Kharzh'ulla IV as a backdrop.

Grevesh's eyes watered and grew heavy.

Eevraith knelt beside him. "First Minister . . . ?"

Grevesh waved him away. "Every morning I go out onto the balcony and look up into the dawn sky. Every morning I see the break in the beauty and order of the Ring." His voice grew quiet. "I saw it happen. I watched the battle. I saw the lights dancing in the night sky." Then his voice hardened in anger. "I saw the explosion as the *grelvan* Jem'Hadar destroyed the Ring." Looking to Gomez, he bowed his head slightly. "I apologize. My feelings are strong. I meant no disrespect."

Gomez smiled, uncomprehending. "*Grelvan*" must have been a strong Tellarite curse. She would have to ask Faulwell about that. "No apologies necessary, First Minister. May I present Captain Gold?" She gestured to Gold, standing at his command seat just beyond the bridge railing.

Grevesh nodded, and his chair came around the railing and into the center of the bridge. "Captain," said Grevesh, "I had not seen the damage from space before. Thank you for the opportunity." He smiled, and his hairless face seemed to brighten. "Now we can save our future."

"How did you even find this place?" asked Carol Abramowitz.

Fabian Stevens leaned back in the chair at the open-air café and shrugged. "Just playing tourist." The café sat along Prelv's waterfront, and from their table Stevens and Abramowitz had an excellent view of the ocean and of the elevator that rose to the southeast.

"I'd have thought they'd be busier," she said. She took a sip from her glass of *obrie,* a local fruit wine, and scrunched her eyebrows. It had a stronger bite than she expected; she wondered idly what the *trema* fruit tasted like, if the fermented juice was so strong.

Stevens turned and looked into the restaurant behind them. A dozen patrons milled about inside. "Seems busy enough to me."

Abramowitz shook her head. "No, I would have expected to see more Kharzh'ullans getting a good view of the elevator's collapse."

Stevens glanced at his wrist chrono. "That's not for several hours yet."

"Then why . . . ?"

"Why are we here?" finished Stevens. He shrugged. "Why not? Get good seats? Get lunch?" He smiled. "Maybe even both."

Abramowitz looked up into the sky. Stevens was right—they had a fantastic view. The sky was relatively cloudless, save for a bank of cumulus clouds off to the far south. The sky had a deep blue color, almost cobalt. Kharzh'ulla's sun, while not directly overhead, had fallen slightly to the southwest, and sunlight glinted off the Ring. The damaged elevator rose in the south, a straight line rising from beyond the horizon to the Ring high above, looking perfectly serene. Even the smell of the ocean salt put Abramowitz into a quiet, reflective mood. Sometimes, she realized, there was a value to playing tourist.

The waiter came by with their lunch order. Abramowitz

had ordered a vegetable platter, but to her eyes the Kharzh'ullan vegetables had the wrong color. What might have been green on Earth was nearly black in hue, and things that might have been tomatoes were blue instead of red. She looked at Stevens's order, a native meat of some kind.

"Are you sure that's wise?" she asked.

"Hmm?" said Stevens as he took a bite off his fork.

"Eating that," said Abramowitz as she pointed at Stevens's lunch with her fork.

Stevens followed the line of her fork and looked down at his plate. "This?" he said with a slight frown. "Looks fine to me." He shrugged. "Even if I couldn't pronounce it." He took another forkful, shoved it in his mouth, and began to chew.

Abramowitz rolled her eyes and shook her head. "Don't blame me," she said, "if you end up in sickbay, eating something you shouldn't have."

"From lunch?" He crinkled his nose. "Not going to happen. Not with my cast-iron stomach."

A Kharzh'ullan came running along the boardwalk toward them. He ran past the café's outdoor tables. Stevens paid him no attention, but Abramowitz turned and followed him with her eyes as he continued down the boardwalk. He stopped and looked up into the sky. She nodded slowly—the elevator was sure to be in everyone's mind today—and turned back to her lunch.

"That was odd," she said quietly.

"Hmm?" said Stevens. She hadn't realized she had spoken loud enough for Stevens to hear her.

"That Kharzh'ullan that ran past us." She turned back and gave him another look. Where he stood, there now had gathered a crowd. "He was in too much of a hurry. The elevator won't be collapsed for another few hours."

Stevens nodded. He glanced up at the elevator shaft.

"Carol," he said. "Turn around. Take a look."

"What?" she said as she turned in her chair.

Her gaze followed Stevens's.

The elevator shaft was listing.

What had been a straight line from horizon to sky was now bent, and far above the terminus was detached from the Ring.

"Fabian," she said.

He stood. "I think we have a problem." He tapped his combadge. "Stevens to *da Vinci.* What's going on up there?"

CHAPTER 9

"Gomez!" exclaimed Gold as he rose from the command seat. Red alert sirens screamed. "What happened?"

Gomez turned from the rear science station and took in the sight on the viewscreen. The elevator terminus appeared to have risen above the Ring in its geosynchronous orbit. Eevraith huddled over her shoulder and fidgeted nervously. "The elevator shaft decompressed when we detached it from the Ring." He nodded toward the viewscreen. "The decompression caused premature detonation of the charges we planted five hundred kilometers above the base."

Gold came to the railing and looked to Gomez. "Decompression? Explain."

Gomez frowned as she tried to put her thoughts into words.

"I can explain, Captain," said Eevraith.

Gold said, "Go ahead, Minister."

"The structural integrity fields we used to keep the elevator intact. In keeping the elevator shaft too rigid, we may also have made it too heavy."

Gomez nodded. Structural integrity fields could make matter artificially as dense as neutronium, increasing its weight temporarily. "That could be why the Ring was stressed by the SIF. It wasn't holding the elevator shaft up. It was holding it *down.* When we detached the terminus from the rest of the Ring, it would bounce up like a coiled spring."

"Precisely, Commander," said Eevraith. "By 'springing' up, the elevator could have jarred the charges enough to cause them to detonate prematurely."

Gold nodded.

"Captain," said Shabalala, "Mr. Stevens is hailing us. He wants to know what's happening."

Gold sighed. "I want to know that myself. Tell Stevens to stand by." He turned to Songmin Wong at the conn. "Position us above the elevator terminus, Wong." The lieutenant's hands danced across his console. "Engage," said Gold.

The *da Vinci* was thousands of kilometers out of position. The plan had been for the *da Vinci* to make a tractor lock on the elevator terminus, then detonate the charges. Now that the elevator was in motion, Gomez wondered, would the *da Vinci* be able to prevent tragedy?

"I'm needed on the bridge," said Tev as he sat up on the sickbay biobed. Red alert sirens screamed in the corridors and they could be heard in sickbay.

Lense moved to block him from leaving as he stood.

"No," she said, putting her arm across his chest, "not until I say you can."

"With all due respect, Doctor," said Tev, his voice low, "if something has gone wrong with the elevator or the Ring, there's no one aboard better qualified than I to deal with it."

"Commander Gomez? Minister Eevraith?"

Tev snorted.

Lense took a step back and folded her arms. "If I give you permission to leave, you'll be back once the crisis is over?"

Tev considered this for a moment. "You may have Lieutenant Commander Corsi send a security detail to drag me back."

"I'll hold you to that." Lense gestured to the sickbay doors. "Go."

"In position, Captain," called Wong.

Gold resumed his seat and nodded. "Very good."

Grevesh's chair came up to Gold. "Captain," he said fretfully, as he looked back and forth between Gold and the viewscreen. "Can you save the planet?"

"If we don't, it won't be for lack of trying, First Minister," said Gold. "But these people haven't let me down yet." He looked at Grevesh, then looked squarely at the viewscreen. The terminus of the elevator had shifted from its earlier position. Where before it had risen above the Ring's geosynchronous orbit, it now had fallen back to its earlier height and out of its equatorial position. "Where's she falling, Gomez?"

Gomez looked to the sensor console, then looked up at the viewscreen. "The elevator is angling to the south by four degrees." She paused. "Given its height, if it continues to fall in that direction, it will wrap around the planet."

Gold rose and came to Haznedl's console. He planted his hand on her shoulder. "Can we get a tractor beam lock on the terminus?"

Susan Haznedl's hands played across her console. She frowned, and looked up at Gold. "We'll need to move in closer because of the weight of the elevator."

Gold looked to Wong. "You heard her. Do it."

Eevraith rushed to Gold's side. "Captain? We haven't much time."

Gold looked up into Eevraith's blurry red eyes. "We can't make the time, but we can steal it where we can."

The turbolift doors opened, and Tev stepped out. Gold, Gomez, and Eevraith all turned. Tev took a long look at the viewscreen. "I apologize, sirs," he said. "I was delayed."

A crowd had begun to gather near the waterfront, more than just the few that had gathered at the end of the boardwalk minutes before. From the shop next door to the restaurant, Kharzh'ullans poured outside and began to look up into space. Stevens imagined that the local broadcast networks were covering the impending collapse of the elevator.

A Kharzh'ullan ran up to Abramowitz and Stevens. He towered over them both; he stood nearly three meters tall. "You're from the Starfleet ship. The one sent to repair the Ring." He looked up into the sky at the elevator and the Ring. "What have you done?"

"I don't know what's going on," said Stevens.

"Fabian," said Abramowitz, "I think the elevator is starting to sway."

Stevens scowled. To him, it appeared as though the elevator were stationary and straight, albeit with a kink near the horizon. At the Ring, however, the elevator was no longer attached; where he could see the break to the east where the Jem'Hadar had destroyed the Ring during the war, he could now see another break to the west of the terminus. He only wished that the *da Vinci* had given him more to go on than Tony's terse "stand by."

Stevens looked up at the Kharzh'ullan. "The *da Vinci* is doing what they can. What they planned on doing."

The Kharzh'ullan looked skeptical. "I thought they were not collapsing the elevator for several hours yet."

Stevens shrugged. "We probably had the time wrong." He looked past the Kharzh'ullan at the elevator. It wasn't swaying, as Abramowitz had thought, but it did have a pronounced list.

Abramowitz pointed up at the elevator's terminus. Stevens and the Kharzh'ullan followed her gaze. "Fabian! The elevator is starting to fall!"

"Tractors!" ordered Gomez.

Shabalala nodded as he touched the tractor beam control. "Tractor beams engaged."

"Take us to a higher orbit," said Gold.

"Aye, sir," replied Wong.

The bridge lights flickered momentarily, and the usual smooth engine hum was replaced by a grating whine. Gold frowned.

"Captain," said Tev from the engineering console, "engines are showing strain due to the tractor beam."

Gold rose and looked at Tev. "Already? We've only just engaged it."

Tev nodded. "It's the elevator's size, sir. Its length and its mass, now increased due to the structural integrity fields. The tractors simply weren't designed for it."

Gold looked to Shabalala. "We're holding the elevator in place, Captain," he reported. "I could be wrong, but it looks like the bottom of the shaft may have fallen into the ocean."

"Damn," said Gold as he returned to his seat. He looked to Grevesh at his left. "We're doing what we can."

Grevesh nodded slowly and put his withered hand on Gold's knee. "I know, Captain. I know."

"Captain," said Gomez, catching his attention, "I have an idea. What if we broke the shaft in two with a photon torpedo?"

Shabalala shook his head. "With all due respect, sir, we'd never get a firing solution. Not from where we are."

Tev came to Shabalala's side and looked to Gomez and Gold. "The lieutenant is correct. Positioned above the terminus as we are, we could not fire on the elevator's base, nor at any point along its length, with any accuracy. But if we were to drop the tractor beam and maneuver to a lower orbit, we could accurately target any point we wish."

Eevraith put his hand on Tev's shoulder and shook his head. "We haven't time for that, Tev."

Tev brushed Eevraith's hand away. "Captain," he said quietly, "we have the time. We need only go down and away, as quickly as we can."

Gold looked from Eevraith to Tev and back. He scowled.

"Shabalala," Gold said at last, "load torpedo bays." He turned to Wong. "You heard Tev. Down and away, your discretion."

The conn officer nodded. "Course plotted, Captain."

Gold took a deep breath. "Wong, as soon as the tractors disengage, full impulse."

Wong swallowed hard and nodded. "Aye, sir."

Leaning back in his command chair, Gold said, "Shabalala, disengage the tractor beam. Wong, go!"

The engine whine ceased as Gold felt himself pressed back by inertia into his command seat as the inertial dampers worked overtime.

"We're in position, Captain," said Wong.

On the viewscreen was the elevator, running from top to bottom of the screen. Behind it, curving away, was the Ring as it passed behind Kharzh'ulla and dwindled in the distance.

Gold looked to Tev. An unspoken communication passed between them. Tev nodded.

"Fire," said Gold.

Dark clouds had begun to roll in from the south. Abramowitz paid them no attention, save to note their obscuring of the elevator at the horizon.

"The elevator looks as though it's toppling," said Stevens.

Abramowitz nodded. The terminus had fallen significantly away from the Ring by ten degrees of separation. Whether the separation was due to the elevator falling toward Kharzh'ulla or away from them in Prelv she couldn't tell from her vantage point.

A bright flash in the southeast sky caught her attention. A shuttlecraft, the sunlight glinting off its side? No, something else.

"Those are photon torpedoes," Stevens said.

Overhead bright lights streaked across the sky and made contact with the elevator above the cloudheads.

Above the point where the torpedoes struck the elevator, it began to list significantly. Abramowitz even thought the elevator might have been broken in two.

The *da Vinci* sped back to the elevator terminus. In the minutes since the torpedo detonation it had fallen closer to Kharzh'ulla's surface—not by much, only a few dozen kilometers.

"Engage tractors," ordered Gold.

Shabalala nodded and touched his console. "Tractors engaged." The engine whine, while not as harsh as earlier, was still louder than Gold would have wished.

"Captain," said Tev, "the lower portion of the elevator will fall into Kharzh'ulla's ocean."

"Impact?" Grevesh asked, his hands trembling.

Tev took a deep breath and sighed. "The section is three hundred kilometers long. In its impact path there are no landmasses. At a guess, waves five meters high might come ashore in Prelv."

"What's the distance from the base to Prelv?" asked Gomez.

"Three thousand kilometers. By the time the waves reached Prelv, they would be largely spent of energy." He looked meaningfully at Gomez. "That would be hours from now."

Gomez nodded.

"Captain," said Wong, "we are pulling the elevator shaft into orbit."

Gold nodded. He looked at Grevesh and patted the back of his hand. "We're saving your planet, First Minister."

Grevesh smiled and nodded contentedly.

"Captain," said Tev, "the lower portion of the elevator broke into three pieces. They have all landed in the ocean."

Gomez looked up from the computer console at her side. "Captain, sensors show the Ring is stable in its geosynchronous orbit."

"Good job, Gomez."

"Captain," said Wong, "we're now passing two hundred thousand kilometers. If we disengage tractors, the elevator shaft will fall into Kharzh'ulla's sun in about four months."

Gold turned to Grevesh. "It's your call, First Minister."

Grevesh looked at the viewscreen. Kharzh'ulla had receded into the distance, and the Ring was prominent, but the elevators were invisible against the blackness of space. The elevator shaft—now twenty-five thousand kilometers long—trailed behind the *da Vinci,* the tractor beam an electric blue against space. "Let it drift," he said, his voice suddenly strong.

Eevraith rushed to his side and stood between Grevesh and the viewscreen. "First Minister," said Eevraith. "Don't be hasty. We can use the elevator as the building block of its replacement. We needn't toss it away."

Grevesh looked up at Eevraith, a hard look in his eyes. "If we rebuild the elevator, we do it on our own terms. We rebuild because we can, because we have the knowledge and understanding to do so. For two centuries we rode on the back of a long-dead civilization. We used what they left behind and made it part of our culture, without understanding what it was and how it worked. The Ring and the elevators were a gift, but an unearned one." He turned and looked at Tev standing near the tactical console. "If the Ring is to be our destiny, we must learn how to make it our destiny on our own terms. Not on history's terms."

Grevesh's chair moved forward, and Eevraith stepped gingerly out of its path. The chair came around the bridge railing, and the eyes on the bridge followed. Around the tactical console Grevesh came, and he stopped before Tev. "I have shamed you, Mor glasch Tev. I accused you of not being a Kharzh'ullan, and I should not have done so. Your thinking saved our world. We can make a future together."

Tev knelt at Grevesh's knee and took Grevesh's weak hands in his. "No forgiveness is needed, First Minister."

Grevesh smiled. "Your father would be proud of you today, Tev."

The chair backed away, and Tev rose. Grevesh stopped at the turbolift doors, took one last look at the sight on the viewscreen of the elevator shaft still under the *da Vinci*'s tractors, then turned and entered the turbolift car.

Gold thought he seemed content.

"Cut the tractor beam, Shabalala," he said.

"Aye, sir," the tactical officer said with a smile. "Tractor beam disengaged."

The electric blue glow faded, and the elevator shaft drifted in space.

"Thank you, Captain Gold," said Eevraith.

Gold jerked a thumb in Tev's direction. "Tev's the one you should be thanking, Minister."

Eevraith's brows knotted. Tev said nothing.

"We know whose plan it was that saved Kharzh'ulla, Minister," said Gold slowly. "Perhaps the first minister doesn't, and it doesn't concern me especially whether he does or not. But on my bridge, *we* know. You can make that right, here and now, or you can't. The choice is yours, and I won't belabor it."

Eevraith looked hard at Gold, then at Gomez. A scowl crossed his face. "I haven't any idea what you're talking about, Captain Gold. If you're accusing me of something, I would expect something more than a vague threat."

Gold leaned back in his chair and spread his hands wide. "I'm neither accusing nor threatening, Minister. Merely stating."

Eevraith rose from his chair. His eyes narrowed, and he looked quickly to Tev standing next to Shabalala at the tactical console. Tev kept a neutral expression, his eyes locked on the viewscreen. Eevraith frowned. "I'll be in the transporter room. I have business to attend to in Prelv."

Eevraith turned and hurried to the turbolift.

As the turbolift doors snapped shut behind him, Gold stood and looked at Tev. "I'm sorry, son. I thought he'd have been a big enough person to admit that he wasn't who he thought he was."

Tev shook his head. "No need to apologize, Captain. Eevraith is who he is, a creature of politics and necessity."

Gomez stood and nodded. "Well, gentlemen, we still have personnel on the surface."

"Wong, take us back to Kharzh'ulla IV. Standard orbit," Gold ordered.

* * *

Abramowitz and Stevens huddled with several Kharzh'ullans beneath the canopy in front of the restaurant against the pouring rain. The storm had risen suddenly, the black clouds moved in from the south as the elevator fell, and a sudden thunderstorm erupted. They would have gone into the restaurant to ride out the storm until the *da Vinci* beamed them back, but the Kharzh'ullans crowded the interior and there was no more room.

Stevens thought he heard another thunderclap, but when Abramowitz pointed at the pier, he saw three human shapes take form in a transporter effect. He could barely make them out—Domenica Corsi and two security guards—and as they materialized, they raised their hands above their heads in a futile effort to block the rain and ran toward the restaurant.

"You took your sweet time!" shouted Stevens over the sound of the rain.

Corsi stopped in front of him, and Stevens thought he detected a sardonic smile cross her face. "You're all wet," she said.

"So are you," he retorted feebly.

"Why didn't you just beam us back?" asked Abramowitz.

Corsi nodded. "The captain wanted us to beam down and see if everything was all right."

"It is, except for this storm," said Abramowitz.

"Tev says it's because of the elevators that fell into the ocean," said Corsi. "They evaporated the water when they hit, and now you've got the rain."

That made sense to Stevens. The storm clouds had come in from the south, just as the elevator fell.

"Corsi to *da Vinci,*" she said as she tapped her combadge. "Five to beam up."

"Domenica," said Stevens.

"Yeah, Fabe?"

"I don't feel so hot."

Corsi frowned. "Stand in the rain, you catch a cold. That's what my grandfather always said."

Abramowitz laughed as the rain fell. "I think it's more that he ate something he shouldn't have."

Corsi shrugged as the transporter effect took them. "Why am I not surprised?"

CHAPTER 10

"We're being hailed, sir," said Lambdin, the *da Vinci*'s gamma-shift ops officer. He turned in his seat back toward Tev. "It's a private communication for you."

Tev snorted. "From whom?"

Lambdin's fingers played across his console. "Sender identity not disclosed. But the message is tagged as coming from the palace on Prelv."

Tev stood. He began to move toward the conference room doors, then stopped. "On screen," he said to Lambdin.

"Sir?" said Lambdin, confused.

"On screen," Tev repeated as he returned to the captain's chair.

Lambdin raised his eyebrows, and the image of Kharzh'ulla on the viewscreen was replaced with Eevraith.

"I thought this was a private communication," said Eevraith.

Tev flared his nostrils. "Look about, Eevraith. There are but four of us on the bridge." Tev, Lambdin, Winn Mara at tactical, and Martina Barre at conn. "Whatever you say will remain here."

Eevraith nodded slowly. *"I wished to thank you, Tev."*

Tev said nothing.

"Did you hear me? Thank you."

"I heard you, Eevraith. What do you wish me to say? That I appreciate your gratitude?"

Eevraith snorted. *"Is that what you want, Tev? An argument?"*

"I want nothing, Eevraith."

They fell silent, the only sound the hum and chirp of consoles about the *da Vinci*'s bridge.

At last Eevraith spoke. *"You should see the celebration. Fireworks over Prelv, now that the rains have subsided, the crowds at the waterfront. It's momentous, Tev, to put away a year of fear, to open a new door to the future."* He paused. *"Some of your crew are there. You should be there, too."*

"I did all that was needed."

"Biyert asked about you, earlier today."

Tev's nostrils flared. "I don't believe you."

Eevraith frowned. *"You know me too well."* He paused. *"I thought if you believed . . ."* His sentence trailed off, incomplete.

Moments passed with neither saying a word. Tev sat impassively in the captain's chair, while Eevraith fidgeted behind his office desk.

"Will there be anything else, Eevraith? Or should I close the channel?"

Eevraith sighed. *"No, I suppose there's not,"* he said

with finality. *"I had hoped . . ."* The sentence trailed away. He looked down at his desk, away from Tev.

"Gersha gorva orga," said Tev in Tellarite. *May your life prosper.*

Eevraith looked up at Tev. His eyes narrowed, his brows tightened, and the corners of his mouth turned upward. He smiled, a most un-Tellarite gesture. *"Thank you, Tev."*

Eevraith's office disappeared from the viewscreen, and the image of Kharzh'ulla, centered on Prelv, returned to the screen. Above Prelv bright flashes could be seen, the fireworks of the Kharzh'ullan celebration. The elevator that had risen from the ocean to the city's south now drifted in space, but the city and the world would live to face the future.

Tev felt, for the first time this mission, content.

Bart Faulwell touched the door page. Sonya Gomez answered, her uniform jacket undone, her hair askew.

"I am not interrupting anything, Commander?"

Gomez shook her head wearily. "Not at all. Just working on the post-mission reports. Come in." She gestured to her worktable. "Care for anything to drink?"

Faulwell took a seat at the table in Gomez's cabin, setting his padd in front of him. "Thanks for the offer, but no."

Gomez nodded. "Earl Grey tea, hot," she told the replicator. A steaming mug materialized, she took it, and took the other seat at her table. "What do you have for me, Bart?"

He pushed the padd across the table to Gomez. "Believe it or not, the answer to your little puzzle."

Gomez stared at Faulwell. "You said it might take weeks. . . ."

Faulwell smiled. " 'Might' being the operative word. In actuality it took two days."

"Two *days*? How?"

"No one but a linguist with anything less than a passing familiarity with Tellarite, Federation Standard, and another language would have noticed or even known what to look for. The universal translator would have been insufficient and would have hidden the evidence."

"How so?"

Faulwell shrugged. "The UT lacks a sense of humor. Don't misunderstand me, Commander—it's a fabulous tool, and it makes *my* job easier, but it doesn't have an understanding of the subtle nuances of language. Puns and wordplay are beyond it. Commander Tev's dissertation—"

"It *is* Tev's writing?" Gomez interrupted.

Faulwell nodded. "No doubt whatsoever in my mind." He paused. "Have you noticed that Tev curses in Romulan?"

A puzzled look crossed Gomez's face. "No, I always assumed he was speaking Tellarite."

"You'd think that, unless you knew Tellarite *and* Romulan. He'd been aboard a good two weeks before I noticed. I can't say how or why he does, only that he does. And, curiously enough, Romulan curses turn up in the dissertation."

"You're kidding."

"Nope. The curses as transliterated match with actual Tellarite words, and fit the context of the work. There are twenty-seven examples of Romulan curses in the document, the most frequent one being *hviehti ifv swuihsywhilluei,* which means roughly 'Klingon vermin dung.'"

"But the phrase isn't written that way, is it?"

Faulwell shook his head. "It's a transliteration of the Romulan words into the Tellarite alphabet arranged into Tellarite words. In Romulan the phrase 'Klingon vermin dung' is three words long, while the Tellarite phrase used time and again is written in six words—*hveet tiv swih sih il li*—meaning 'torque of the turning gears.'"

"Coincidence?"

"I doubt it. The phrases used come across as awkward and ungrammatical and don't fit the style used in the rest of the dissertation. He could get away with it for two reasons. First, he wasn't a native and didn't speak the Kharzh'ullan dialect. Second, the only way to catch the Romulan curses would be to read the dissertation aloud."

"You didn't—" Gomez began.

Faulwell shrugged. "The computer has a fine reading voice, Commander. It wasn't as if I had anything better to do this mission."

"But you did, Bart. You could have gone on one of the tourist parties."

Faulwell shrugged. "Believe me, Commander, I'm glad I wasn't on Fabian's restaurant tour of Prelv."

Gomez laughed. She'd heard how Stevens landed in sickbay after beaming back to the ship. Kharzh'ullan cuisine didn't sit well with the *da Vinci*'s tactical specialist.

"Thank you, Bart. I owe you for this."

"We'll worry about that another day," he said as he stood. "Get some sleep, Commander. You look like hell."

"I will, later, once these reports are out of the way."

She smiled. "You'd better get back to that book I interrupted. Anthony would never forgive me for keeping you from it."

As the doors to Gomez's cabin opened, Faulwell nodded. "Good dreams, Commander."

Gomez reclined on her bunk. She needed a change of pace from the traditional post-mission stress and began reading Faulwell's report on the dissertation. Ten minutes later she fell asleep, exhausted.

In the center of the mess hall Tev again sat alone, a plate of those twigs—according to Lense, it was called *coun'unr,* and it aided middle-aged Tellarites like Tev with their digestion—in front of him and padds scattered across his table. Gomez went to the replicator and asked for chicken teriyaki and rice. The plate materialized, and she walked to Tev's table and took a seat across from him. "Mind if I join you?"

"I was attempting to work, Commander," said Tev. He fingered the *coun'unr* on his plate, and plucked one of the dried leaves in his mouth. He indicated the padd before him. "Captain Gold asked for the mission reports at 1500 hours, and I have much work yet to do."

"If you wanted to work, you wouldn't do it in public," said Gomez with a smile.

Tev glared at her. "Perhaps." He shrugged.

Gomez paused. "I want you to take a look at something." She proffered a padd to Tev.

He looked at it, then at her, and finally took it. "What is this?"

"Something I had Bart research for me."

"Why should I care, Commander?"

Gomez shrugged. "I don't know, Commander. You might find something of interest in it."

He flared his nostrils in annoyance, called up the file loaded on the padd, and began to read. He thumbed through several pages, his eyes ranging back and forth across the text. He glanced up at Gomez from time to time, shook his head, and read more. Reaching the end, he sighed, snorted, and handed the padd back to Gomez.

"*Aetiu khieth,*" he said.

"Romulan?"

Tev nodded. "Roughly translated, *aetiu khieth* means 'damned to the seven hells.'"

Gomez smiled sardonically and shook her head wearily. "How did you ever learn Romulan curses?"

He shrugged. "Kharzh'ullan society can be rather . . . conservative, so I turned to Romulan curses to express myself, as the Kharzh'ullans wouldn't understand what I said, but I could express what I really felt."

"But you could have used *any* language—Vulcan, Klingon, Andorian. But Romulan, though—why?"

Tev sighed and scrunched his nose. "Why not?"

"What did you do, Tev? Sit in your room and study Romulan on your own?" She shrugged. "That seems rather dull."

"Perhaps." He paused and looked meaningfully at Gomez. "I had few friends in my youth. Eevraith was one of them. I needed . . . hobbies . . . to keep the mind occupied. Math and science provided little challenge for me. Language, however, proved more difficult, and why not Romulan, a language that few knew? I must commend Bartholomew for his detective work. I hadn't thought the evidence would be so transparent."

Gomez leaned back in her chair. "If it's any consolation, I thought he would do a simple style analysis on the Ring dissertation. It never occurred to me that there might be hidden messages within the text."

"Blame it on the cleverness of youth, Commander."

"Then the paper was, in fact, yours?"

Tev's nostrils flared. "Of course. We wouldn't be having this conversation otherwise, would we?"

Gomez shook her head. "No, I suppose we wouldn't."

Tev nodded slowly, but said nothing.

"Why, Tev? Why allow everyone to believe the paper was his and not yours? You could have exposed him as a fraud at any time in the past few days. You could have even exposed him twenty years ago. Why remain silent, when he has the life that could have been yours?"

Tev sighed deeply and rocked back and forth slowly in his chair. His eyes narrowed and focused somewhere beyond Gomez, almost as if he was looking past her into the memories of the past.

Finally, Tev spoke. "Do you remember our first meeting with First Minister Grevesh? How he said I would never be a Kharzh'ullan, only a Tellarite?"

"Yes," said Gomez. "I thought that was rather insulting."

"Such is the attitude my family faced for the entirety of our time on Kharzh'ulla. I was born on Tellar, spent my first decade there. Tellar is a cold world, a wet world. Tellarites lead their lives in a state of constant fog and mental oppression. Our eyesight is poor. Our digestion is terrible. Gravity makes us short and stocky." He paused, took a deep breath, and then continued. "Kharzh'ulla, on the other hand, was everything that Tellar was not. The weather was mild, the climate warm. Gravity was much lighter than the norm, and our bodies adapted to the new environment. Even though immigration from Tellar continues to this day, off-worlders are looked upon as outsiders and never as part of the community. Had I accused Eevraith of stealing my dissertation, nothing would have happened to him. The Kharzh'ullans expect such behavior on the part of off-worlders, never from one of their own."

Gomez nodded. "You hate him, don't you? Eevraith?"

Tev shrugged. "Hate? I stopped hating him long ago."

"Why?"

"There was a time when I thought I wanted the life Eevraith has now. When my first attempt at an engineering career ended so abruptly, my father secured an appointment to Starfleet Academy, despite my being in my mid-twenties, and I discovered that I liked what I did in Starfleet. Do I have regrets? Certainly. But I have seen more and done more in my tenure with Starfleet than I would have if I had remained an outsider on Kharzh'ulla. So, no, I don't hate Eevraith anymore. He has a politician's instincts. I do not. Were it not for him, I would not be here now."

Gomez smiled. "That's very enlightened, Tev. Very philosophical."

"Merely a statement of fact, Commander."

"I'll leave you to your work, then," said Gomez as she stood.

"One thing, Commander," said Tev.

She nodded perfunctorily.

"If this matter could remain between us . . . ?"

"Of course, Tev. Well, between you, me, and Bart. And I think we can trust to his discretion."

Tev nodded. "Thank you."

She turned and walked to the mess hall doors. She turned and looked at Tev. "Good work on the mission, Commander. Thank you."

Tev nodded, made a grunting sound, and turned back to his padds. Sonya Gomez smiled as she stepped through the mess hall doors. She had often heard the saying, "you can never go home again," but until this mission it hadn't occurred to her that it was more often a case of "you wouldn't want to go home again."

ORPHANS

Kevin Killiany

CHAPTER 1

Eve of the Quest

Naiar stroked Striver's arching neck, following the rough pull of the currycomb with a soothing palm. His mount's blue-black coat already glistened in the source light streaming through the stable's doorway, but youth and beast enjoyed the ritual.

"Tomorrow," he murmured, Striver's ear twitching at the sound of his voice. "Tomorrow, the quest."

The riderbeast seemed unimpressed, but the creatures were not known for their sense of adventure. Naiar set the grooming tools on the shelf and checked the level of the feed trough. With a final pat for his mount, he let himself out of the stall.

In the stable yard he paused, his eyes following the curve of the world up and up until it was lost in the haze of the sky. Some mornings, just as the source breached the Dawn Mountains, Naiar knew the fabled lands above the sky could be seen, just for a moment, in the morning glow.

Until three fours of days ago, he had thought his destiny lay there, above the sky. That had been the goal of his proving quest.

But then the gnomes had appeared, stumbling out of the mountains near a fallen hollow. Strange creatures, shaped much like People, but short and hairless, or mostly hairless. Strangest had been their faces, with eyes above the nose, squeezed down toward the bottoms of their heads.

They had stayed awhile in his father's House, though they ate nothing they had not brought with them and drank only water, and that after they had added strange herbs of their own. The Doctors believed the gnomes feared some binding curse that would hold them to the land of the People, but Naiar, who had nearly choked when he tried a bite of their food, suspected the gnomes simply did not eat as People did.

The gnomes had said, in the days before they lost their speech, that they were seeking access, though to what was not clear. They had been fascinated by the stories of the hollows of the Builders and made much of the mirrors purchased from the Barony of Atwaan. The two who might have been female had listened for hours as Nodoc recounted the histories of mad giants and children who had wandered from the depths of the world generations before.

When they could no longer speak as People—their powers, the Doctors said, fading in this world—the gnomes had left the Tetrarchy and the borders of the known world. They had followed the direction of the source—duskward, away from the mountains—seeking the origins of the old stories. His father had given them writs of safe passage, though how far that would carry them in the wilds was uncertain. Not every House and Hold loved the Tetrarchy when the Tetrarch's armsmen were not present. Most thought the gnomes to be mad, but Naiar knew now his destiny was to follow them, to learn the secret of this access.

The lands above the sky had always been there. They would be there still for him to explore when he returned from his proving quest. Though he was heir in his brother's stead, it would be many fours of seasons before his training in governance became intense. Time enough to pursue his dreams.

Turning away from the main compound, he made his way to the clan's birthing pool, sheltered in a hollow far from casual eyes. Ignoring the inviting scent of the water, he circled the pool to the memorial field beyond. The stones of the stillborn were unmarked, but he had long ago decided which were those of his clutch brothers.

"Tomorrow I go on my quest," he told the three stones slightly apart from the others. "I know it is a shadow of the great Journey the People are on. Less than a shadow of your journey. But . . ."

He paused, not sure what to add to that. After a moment's thought, he pulled a leather pouch from his belt. Transferring his flint and tinder to his tool pouch, he scooped a thick handful of soil from the center of the triangle of memorial stones and filled his fire pouch.

"I'll bring it back," he said, "and you'll see where I've been."

The source was nearing the end of its journey. Soon darkness would come. Already the hollow of the birthing pool was deep in shadow and a chill wind, working its way among the rocks, ruffled the sleek hair of his neck and arms.

"Tomorrow," Naiar promised again, and turned toward the house.

The yard in front of the great house was abustle with grooms and servants unloading the packbeasts of a modest caravan. Naiar recognized the sigil of Tolan, the second house of the Tetrarchy, and quickened his step. To see Miura before his proving quest . . .

"Ho!" The shout brought him up short at the threshold.

"Uncle!"

"No rush, son." The older man slapped his rounded shoulder, propelling him the rest of the way into the hall. "She's not with me this night."

Naiar lidded his eyes for a moment, embarrassed he'd been so transparent. Uncle Tolan laughed as he shed his heavy coat.

"No coat, boy?" he asked as a servant took his. "You'll catch your death yet."

Naiar shrugged; the remark was not worth comment. Everyone knew the young, those who survived their birth and avoided the withering, did not feel the cold the older generations complained so much about. Still, he never met a relative who did not comment on his light jerkin and vest within a minute of their greeting. He hoped he'd be less predictable in his old age.

Torches lit the hall, though the source was not yet gone. The traditional quiet evening with close family before the quest was being replaced with a hasty feast in honor of his uncle's visit. Naiar minded not in the least; he greatly preferred hearing news of other households to the lecture on his House's history and their expectations of him as heir that he'd been dreading.

Miura across the table, her down golden in the torchlight, would have made the evening perfect.

At the moment the feast table was still being assembled, trestles and planks added to the everyday sideboard. Naiar suspected the kitchen was frantically adding fruit dishes and quickbreads to the modest feast prepared for the family of the House. Uncle Tolan would not care, knowing how close to dinner he'd arrived, but Cook would never let it get back to Tolan House that Nazent House had not excelled at a moment's notice.

Two servants entered from the family door, bearing a padded chair between them.

"Nodoc!" Uncle Tolan cried out with the same joy he'd had at the sight of Naiar. He towered over the tiny gray form of Naiar's older brother nestled in the chair, but seemed unaware that anything was amiss.

The servants lowered the chair, and Uncle Tolan dropped casually to one knee to be eye to eye with his cousin's oldest son.

"You've tales to tell, I'll wager," he said. "Consorting with gnomes, from what I hear."

"We all consorted," Nodoc countered cheerfully. "Many spent as much time with them as I."

"But none have your keen eye and wit. I'll have the whole story from you before the evening's out. And a tale of my own to trade," Tolan added, glancing up at Naiar to include him in this last.

"What sort of tale?" Nodoc asked. "We've time before dinner."

Tolan cast his eye about the hall, gauging the state of readiness, and nodded. Naiar hooked a basket with his foot, overturning it to make a stool. The stream of servants flowed around their island without comment.

"A beast, a magical beast, by all accounts," Tolan said, "has been seen in the foothills of the Dawns."

"Near the Fallen Hollow?" Naiar guessed.

"At first," their uncle said, "though it's been seen elsewhere since, following the path of the source."

"How is it magical?" Nodoc demanded.

"It is very like an insect, but blue as an ice flower, with only eight legs."

"A blue insect is new, not magical," Nodoc said.

Naiar nodded, content to leave the conversation in the hands of his learned brother. The insect, hardly a beast, did not sound too remarkable to him.

"Even an insect that cries out in a voice like ringing bells?" Tolan asked.

"That we've never seen an insect with a voice does not mean all insects are silent," Nodoc answered. "And missing a four of legs could merely mean an injury."

"Did I mention," Tolan asked innocently, "that the beast is the size of a packbeast colt?"

"You did not!" accused Naiar.

"When you say it cried out," Nodoc asked, his mind leaping to another trail, "did it merely give voice or did it attempt to speak?"

"On that our witnesses are divided," Tolan admitted. "But—"

"Tolan!" Nazent's voice cut through the industrious murmur of the hall. "Where are you?"

"Here." Tolan rose. "The slackness of my host forced his sons to hold court in his stead."

"Ha. Then you are in good hands," Nazent said. "I can retire in peace."

"Not before we eat!"

The cousins linked arms, making their way toward the head table, which was arrayed with an overabundance of food. No doubt the Householder had delayed his entrance to give Cook time to present this feast. Thus is the loyalty of servants earned.

As Nodoc, borne in his chair, followed, Naiar made a business of righting the basket and returning it to its place.

A magical beast, perhaps following the gnomes? If friend, a valuable ally. If foe, a worthy opponent. By the time he reached the sideboard, the nature of Naiar's proving quest had undergone another change.

CHAPTER 2

Four fours of days before the Quest

The *da Vinci* was spiraling madly.

Centered on the main viewer was a dark blue-gray cylinder, nearly invisible to the naked eye against the blackness of space. With nothing to provide scale, its size was impossible to determine, but there was an unmistakable sense of mass. The thing was huge. Beyond it the field of stars was a sheet of diagonal streaks. At irregular intervals the image of the cylinder would jerk minutely and the streaking stars changed angle as the *da Vinci* altered orbit.

Captain David Gold sat in his command chair and tried to convince his inner ear that the spinning sensation was all in his imagination. By trial and error he had determined this was most successful when he remained seated.

"Sensors are still unable to penetrate beyond the outer levels," Lieutenant Commander Mor glasch Tev announced from one of the aft science stations. "We'll have to get closer."

Gold could tell from the set of his shoulders that Songmin Wong did not like the idea. He didn't blame the conn officer; he knew enough about piloting to appreciate the concentration needed to hold the *da Vinci* in a circle less than a light-second in diameter at warp one.

"What will that gain us?" he asked his second officer.

The Tellarite stifled an impatient sigh. Gold doubted Tev would ever lose his arrogance—he'd earned it honestly—but it was good to see him learning to curb expressing it.

"It will not be possible to determine that until we have gotten closer," Tev replied. "But based on our last course adjustment, sensor efficacy should increase by four percent."

"Wong?"

"We're near tolerances now," the young lieutenant replied, leaving the implications hanging.

"You recommend?"

"Pulling out to sixty-three thousand kilometers," Wong answered promptly. He'd clearly been giving the matter a lot of thought while fighting to hold the *da Vinci* in place.

"Faugh," said Tev. "That's no better than leapfrogging."

Gold sat for a moment, considering the four percent. They needed more information; he wanted to have at least the outline of a plan in hand before the others arrived. But it would do him no good if he damaged his ship getting it.

Perversely, his left hand itched. It had been doing that when he was frustrated ever since he got the biosynthetic replacement after Galvan VI. Knowing it was psychosomatic, and knowing it was a common experience with prosthetics, did nothing to make the sensation go away.

"Your choice," he said to Tev.

"Continuous scans offer the best chance of penetration."

Gold nodded. "Wong, take us out to sixty-three thousand kilometers and continue spiral." He stood up, resisting the urge to scratch his prosthetic hand as he made his way to the turbolift. "I think everyone's had a chance to chew on the data. Haznedl, notify the team we'll be meeting in ten minutes."

"Captain!"

The urgency in the tactical officer's voice brought Gold up short.

"What is it, Shabalala?"

"There's a Klingon"—he paused for a moment, evidently rechecking readings on his board—"warship approaching at warp five. It has not responded to hails."

"Better make that fifteen minutes, Haznedl," Gold said as he returned to his chair. "And call Gomez to the bridge. It seems the other half of our team has arrived ahead of schedule."

"Faugh," repeated Tev.

"Let's not make them try to match orbits, Wong," Gold said. He was aware of the turbolift opening and Commander Sonya Gomez, the ship's first officer and leader of the S.C.E. team, taking up station behind him. "Jump five light-minutes ahead of the colony vessel and drop from warp."

On the viewscreen the spinning star field executed a jarring pinwheel and righted itself. For a moment the streaks of starlight radiated in comfortingly straight lines from the center of the screen as the *da Vinci* leapt ninety million kilometers in a matter of seconds. Then, for the first time in what seemed like months to Gold, the stars became steady points of distant light. They were in normal space.

"Let's see who the Klingon Empire has sent us, Shabalala," Gold said.

The image on the viewscreen shifted, and for a moment the bridge was silent as the crew regarded the ungainly shape bearing down upon them.

"Haznedl," Gold said at last, "is there anything in our database about pregnant D-7s?"

The operations officer tore her eyes from the bizarre ship and rapidly tapped her console.

"Nothing fits that specific configuration, sir," she reported at last. "But that does seem to be a modified D-7 attack cruiser."

"Shabalala?"

"Sensors indicate the ship is constructed from components of various ages, evidently from other vessels." The tactical officer paused, considering his readings. "The flattened oblate spheroid under the engineering section is a troop transport module. Those were never used on attack vessels."

Gomez frowned. "That looks a lot stubbier than the D-7s I remember."

"You remember D-7s?" Gold asked. "I would have thought they were at least a century before your time."

"From the Academy," she said. "History of ship design."

"Ah."

"Obviously, the mass of the troop transport module alters the dynamics of their warp field," Tev said impatiently. "They shortened the central pylon by twenty percent to compensate."

The moment Tev said it, Gold saw it was true. The central pylon, what he thought of as the "neck" of the ancient Klingon cruiser, was indeed shorter than it should have been. Combined with the "flattened oblate spheroid"—which looked to him like nothing so much as a huge loaf of pumpernickel—it created a silhouette unlike any ship he'd ever seen. No wonder the database had not been able to identify the vessel; he was impressed it had recognized it as Klingon at all.

"Any response to hails, Shabalala?"

"No, sir, they're—"

"What the hell?" Wong's exclamation cut him off.

On screen, the Klingon cruiser swung about in a leisurely arc and took up position off the huge cylinder's beam. Wong brought up an inset tactical display that showed the Klingon's warp field in place as the pair passed the *da Vinci.*

"Refresh my memory, Wong," Gold said. "What is the minimum speed of a ship at warp?"

"Lightspeed, sir."

"And they are at . . . ?"

The tactical inset flickered as Wong reset the sensors. They flickered again.

"Point seven six light," he said at last.

"Theories, Tev?"

"They are violating several physical laws," the Tellarite growled. "And ignoring fundamental warp mechanics."

"So noted," Gold acknowledged. "Haznedl, pipe this information down to engineering. Tev, I want you and Conlon working on figuring out how they do this."

"Why?"

"Because these are Klingons," Gold said. "Unless we can prove we're at least their equals, they're going to ignore us."

"Why not let them?" Tev demanded. "The object is heading into Klingon space, that's why they're here. Why not leave and let them handle the situation?"

Gold tapped his fingers lightly on the arm of his command chair as he watched the mismatched pair of ships on the screen. "Because I'm not altogether sure I'd like the Klingon solution to the problem of a giant colony vessel on a collision course with Qo'noS."

CHAPTER 3

By now, Nancy Conlon had steeled herself against Tev's appearance in her engine room. Within the first few weeks of his arrival on the *da Vinci,* she came to realize that he would never recognize that he was in *her* domain. From Tev, she would get no courtesy, nor would she even be treated as a colleague. True, he had more experience and a higher rank, but it was still *her* engine room. Tev's predecessor, Kieran Duffy, had always treated Conlon's predecessor, Jil Barnak, with due deference whenever he came down here, and Barnak as a result gave Duffy a fair amount of latitude in the engine room. Tev, though, acted as if Conlon owed him that latitude.

When she stood to greet him, therefore, she expressed no surprise when he came around her desk and took her chair without comment as though she'd relinquished her position. He briskly cleared her screens without glancing at them, not noticing the relevant data she'd organized nor her preliminary sketches, and without a word of greeting, launched into a summation of the problems facing them as though she were a classroom full of freshmen.

"What the Klingons appear to be doing is impossible," he pronounced, busily adjusting her screens and pulling up some of the same data he'd just removed. "Therefore what they are doing is not what they appear to be doing."

Conlon listened with half an ear as he ran through a list of warp and physical principles which precluded a stable warp field at sublight velocities. Moving to an auxiliary panel, she called up an inventory of ship's stores. It took her a matter of moments to locate the components she wanted and flag them. With a few quick taps, she routed her list and orders that they be brought to engineering ASAP.

"What makes the Klingon feat look impossible is the limitations of human perception," Tev's lecture broke in on her consideration of necessary parts they didn't have. "And instrumentation that assumes the observer is human."

He was focused on her desktop display and she realized he was drafting a diagram as he spoke. Though she couldn't see the image, his gestures were quick and sure. Despite herself she was impressed with his ability to multitask.

"Human senses perceive any event which takes less than a fifteenth of a second as instantaneous," he explained. "Tellarites can discern events as brief as one twenty-fourth of a second."

And Klingons a thirtieth of a second, Conlon added mentally, *and Vulcans something just under a forty-third of a second.*

"As soon as I saw real-time data—numbers, not images—I realized what was happening." Tev spun her desktop display around so she could see his diagram.

She was not surprised to see it was very similar to her own. There was no getting around the fact that for all his pomposity the Tellarite knew what he was doing.

"Not bad," she said. "But it's clear you're not a ship's engineer."

"Oh?"

If she had been less sure of herself, the frozen tone of Tev's single syllable would have stopped her.

"You've got the theory," she said, tapping contacts on the auxiliary board, "but your design assumes unlimited matériel and ideal efficiency."

With a grin, she rotated her screen, showing him the schematics of her own design.

"We have components for three complete assemblies, which my people are already working on," she exaggerated slightly. "If you have some ideas on what we can substitute here and here"—corresponding points highlighted—"we can have a fourth."

Too late she kicked herself for not having a visual recorder going. Tev's stupefied expression was priceless.

CHAPTER 4

Bart Faulwell was literally two steps from the observation lounge when the meeting was announced. So far there was no need for a linguistics or cryptography specialist on this mission and he'd been prowling, pen and paper in hand, too restless to sit as he worked on his latest letter to Anthony. The process had become more protracted over the years, which suited him fine. The longer he took, composing the letter by hand the old-fashioned way, then recording the actual subspace message, the longer he could hold on to the feeling of spending time together.

He considered a quick dash to drop the pen and paper off at his cabin, but it didn't seem worth the trip. Besides, he couldn't remember the last time he'd been the first one to a staff briefing.

He expected Tev to be next, but it was in fact Soloman. The Bynar favored him with a preoccupied nod before settling down and focusing on a padd of his own.

Domenica Corsi and Fabian Stevens arrived together, and Faulwell was startled by a sudden stinging of his eyes at the sight of them separating at the door. It took him a moment to realize it had reminded him of Kieran Duffy and Sonya Gomez holding hands under the table in staff meetings—one of their near-comic efforts to keep their romance under wraps.

He shared the incident and his feelings with Anthony, knowing his partner would understand. When he looked up from his writing, he was surprised to see everyone but Tev had arrived; Pattie was just sliding onto her specially made chair. Across from him, Elizabeth Lense met his startled gape with a smile.

Captain Gold opened the meeting. "All right, people, we've had two hours, but now the other team has arrived. What have we got to show for our head start?"

"A multigenerational deep space vessel of classic cylindrical design," Gomez recited briskly. "Propelled by a very basic ion drive. Nuclear rockets rotated the ship, the angular acceleration providing ersatz internal gravity. Right now neither is working; it's coasting and spinning on momentum."

"'Coasting' at two hundred and twenty-eight thousand kilometers a second," Stevens said. "With that technology, attaining point seven six lightspeed required centuries of acceleration."

Faulwell knew that maddening velocity, over three times full impulse but well short of lightspeed, had created a navigational nightmare for the *da Vinci*. They had spent an hour repeatedly jumping ahead of the colony ship at warp and scanning it as it passed. Then for the last hour and a half they had been corkscrewing insanely around the axis of its course at warp one to stay abreast.

"Also considering the technology," Pattie chimed in, literally, "at least a century went into its construction as well." She touched a few controls. A schematic diagram of a circle comprising several interlocking rings appeared on the main screen. As she spoke, several sections of the diagram lit up. "The outer hull comprises several hundred meters of fused nickel-iron, probably an aggregate of asteroid material. This is reinforced by a gridwork of dense alloy similar to duranium but with an odd spectral signature." A molecular model, with a few gaps, and a matching spectral band appeared below the schematic. "The decks we can scan below the outer hull"—Pattie interrupted herself with a crystalline sound of amusement—"or, from their perspective, *above* the outer hull, are of similar construction and appear to be filled with myriad large, inert items. One would guess long-term storage. The weight distribution problems in spinning something this size are enormous." The schematic rotated and elongated, becoming a side view of the huge cylinder. Pattie continued to tap controls as she spoke, an apparently random pattern of bright green dots spread across the image. "The builders dealt with it by installing over one thousand nuclear rockets to govern rotation. They seem to have simply been mounted on the surface of the completed ship. Notice spacing is not uniform; their placement reflects internal mass."

Pattie paused and on the screen green dots began to go dark. "At least five hundred years ago the system began to fail." She looked to Gold. "Commander Tev was investigating how and why."

"He's working with Conlon on something," Gold said. "Is his input essential right now?"

"No," Pattie said. "Just curious."

She turned back to the panel and tapped a few more commands. What Faulwell took to be stress or force calculations appeared along the top and bottom of the screen. Lines connected the equations to points along the length of the ship that glowed an ominous purple.

"Without the balancing thrust of the rotational rockets, the entire system is unstable. At this scale something as slight as a point-zero-one difference in density between sections could cause dangerous torque shears." Pattie paused for a moment, her good humor of a moment ago gone. "Without more complete structural data I cannot say precisely when, but sometime in the next year at most. . . ."

The numbers bordering the image changed as the purple points became a network of jagged lines. With surprising speed the image of the ship broke apart.

No one spoke for a moment.

"What makes that important right now is the interior," Gomez said at last. "Based on what we could scan through the ends of the cylinder during our initial leapfrogging, the inner surface is designed to emulate a Class-M planet."

"The whole thing can't be full of air?" Faulwell asked.

"No," Gomez assured him. "Angular acceleration keeps the atmosphere within a kilometer or so of the surface."

"A kilometer or so," he echoed. "Exactly how big is this thing?"

"Computer models indicate there are just under twenty-six hundred square kilometers of planetary surface in there."

Faulwell's mind boggled slightly at the figure.

"Inhabited?" Gold asked.

"We *think* so." Gomez nodded to Lense.

"Analyzing the life readings, I've definitely identified half a dozen animals analogous to Terran mammals," the chief medical officer said. "Their groupings and proximity would indicate some are domesticated animals and others are the domesticators, though that's conjecture."

"Conjecture you think is accurate," Gold said.

Lense nodded, then glanced around the table at the others. "Extrapolating from what we saw through the bow, there are anywhere from thirty to sixty thousand colonists aboard that ship."

CHAPTER 5

Three fours of days and two before the Quest

Terant, son of Terant, grandson of Terant, Baron of Atwaan, pretended he did not notice Rajho and Vissint enter the Hall of Memory. He knew they would indulge him this rudeness in his grief.

Through glassless windows above him the source light streamed in golden shafts to illuminate the brass marqued tombs set in the far wall. He could hear faintly the bells of mourning and the choir of Doctors chorusing a song of comfort. The sounds were of another world. Closer above him he heard the chirp and rustle of birds for whom the rafters of this hall were home. From them he gained greater solace.

This hall had been one of the first great works of his grandfather. The first Terant had conceived of it as both monument and audience chamber for conducting ceremonies of state. From the rafters hung banners, faded slightly now with dust, of the Houses and Holds that had sworn the new baron fealty.

Terant the eldest was known to have seen the future and to have been the first to realize access to the hollows meant power. When he, a mere border warden, had deposed the old baron, it had been widely accepted that the blessings of the Giants, and perhaps through them the Builders themselves, had rested upon him. He had gathered others to his banner with promises of wealth, and gained control of all the hollows between the Wilderness and the Great River.

Terant's able government and shrewd business skills had brought prosperity to Atwaan. His armsmen—the best paid duskward of the Tetrarchy—provided protection from dangers within and without. In exchange for their comfort and security, his subjects rendered the baron and his son and now his grandson their complete obedience and their lives.

There was no dust on the trophies, Terant noticed idly, nor droppings from the birds above. For all its air of abandonment, someone kept the hall clean. He wondered who had ordered that.

Along this wall, in niches and on pedestals, were treasures of uncertain value, oddities no one could identify wrested from the hollows of the Builders. The barony's wealth sprang from the trade in these curios; treasures of the Builders were highly prized as art and jewelry and even talismans. In the days of pomp, the crowds had kept to this side of the hall, avoiding the misproportioned sepulchres along the farther wall.

There were no court functions here these days. Terant now did as his father had done and held audience like any Holder, before the house where all who had business could see and approach. His grandfather's hall was a disused monument, a mausoleum that did nothing to calm his spirit.

He rested his hand for a moment on the throne of the Builders, a plain chair of massive scale, far larger than his grandfather's ornate seat atop the dais. Only his grandmother had not been foolishly dwarfed by its dimensions.

As a child he had explored the Hall of Memory seeking mystery, thrilling himself with the fear of ghosts. Now again he came seeking . . . something. And if there be ghosts, he would be glad for the comfort of their company.

But there was no comfort here; even the air smelled dead.

He'd had too much of death.

Rajho and Vissint were still waiting, carefully just beyond the edge of his vision. The Doctor General and Chancellor of State would not impose lightly on his solitude, and the two coming together boded something pressing, something that needed his attention. Stifling a sigh, he squared his shoulders and turned to face them.

Both nodded deeply, not the bow his grandfather had required, but the chin to chest of his father, not breaking eye contact. When authority is absolute, one need not add debasement to obedience.

"What news?" he asked.

Rajho looked to Vissint, who nodded for him to proceed.

"Baron, your wife is in good health," the Doctor said. "The water of the pool is pure, the herbs and unguents fresh and free of poisons."

"Wherein then lies the fault?" Terant asked.

"Perhaps"—Rojha hesitated—"something occurred during the pregnancy?"

"That—" Terant shouted, then stopped himself, biting back the next words. A deep, cleansing breath; a second. "That is what you said last time," he said, aware that the preternatural calm of his voice was more terrifying than any rant. "And the time before that; and the time before that."

He stepped toward the Doctor. To his credit the smaller man did not shrink back.

"In four attempts to conceive an heir we have followed all of your directions. Tell me"—his smile was slight and cold—"what have we to show for your advice?"

Rajho wisely said nothing.

"Sixteen memorial stones," Terant answered his own question. "Sixteen stones in three years. Is this not remarkable?"

"Baron?"

Terant's eyes snapped to his chancellor. Vissint understood he had thrown himself between Rajho and a spear. A bold move by a good man. Somewhere beneath his grief and rage, Terant recognized these men were not his enemies. He made the effort to modulate his voice.

"Yes, Chancellor?"

"I wish with all my heart your tragedy was unique," Vissint said, "but it is not."

"How do you mean?" The anger was shocked back into Terant's voice. "Four pregnancies have ended in death—four fours of my children are dead—and you say this is not unique?"

"There have been no live births in all of Atwaan," Rajho blurted in a rush, then flinched under the baron's glare.

"Is this true?" Terant demanded. Then, when neither man spoke: "Is. This. True?"

"Yes, Baron," Vissint answered. "No infant has been born alive in over a year."

Terant paused, remembering the crowds, neat and orderly about the pavilion, picturing in his mind the populace. When was the last time he had seen a family with a clutch of infants? Not a four, no, not in the years since the withering had begun; but three or two or even one? He could not remember. There had been no babies. . . .

"And I was not told?"

"We sought a cure," Rajho answered. "And forbore to tell you until we were successful."

"And you did not warn me? Did not warn my wife?"

"We thought that of all the People," Rajho said, "you would be spared."

Terant raised his hand, forestalling words. He knew the Doctor was not flattering him idly.

Along the opposite wall, half concealed by pillars, were the sepulchres of the Giants. Mad, they had been, and dying, but they had caused all that was now Atwaan to be. Had caused *him* to be.

His grandfather had been young, newly made a border warden for the barony, when the Giants had emerged from the hollow of the Builders. His grandmother had been among them, a girl on the threshold of womanhood, the only one to survive the killing fever.

Young Terant the eldest had married her when she was of age. She had been head and shoulders taller and half again as broad as the brawniest champion, beautiful despite patches of skin left bare by the fever, and he had loved her. As their son Terant had been devoted to her and as he—who remembered his grandmother as a great, looming gentleness—had adored her.

No one breathed it aloud, but in their hearts the People believed the Giants were descendants of the Builders. And on the strength of her blood in his veins, the Doctors had conspired to keep from him a tragedy that scourged his people.

Journey! Had they thought to find the cure in his children?

"Dispatch riders," he said. "Dawnward and duskward, upwater and down. Under my marque inform them of our plight—"

He caught himself.

"Do not reveal its totality, but hold back no medical detail. Inquire of their Doctors for any theory of cause or program of cure." He raised a finger. "Make clear to them that there will be a reward commensurate with the usefulness of their information."

"At once, Baron."

Terant did not acknowledge the parting salute. His eyes, narrowed in calculation, were fixed on the sepulchres of the Giants.

CHAPTER 6

Three fours of days and three before the Quest

Conlon wrestled the two-meter section of power transfer conduit around in the much-reduced free space of the engine room. There really was no other place for the assembly. Her staff had rerouted everything that could be rerouted to auxiliary panels and were keeping as much out of the way as possible. When completed, the plan allowed sixty centimeters of sidle space along either side, but for now the entire central floor area was occupied.

The PTC looked deceptively light, but it was constructed of six phase-transition welded layers of tritanium and transparent aluminum; the mass was considerable. She wished there was room for a null-grav grapple as she muscled the conduit into its coupling. Bracing it in place with her shoulder, she triple-checked the fit before engaging the molecular seal.

The assembly was low-tech but complex. Not a combination that inspired confidence, but it was the best they could do outside of a shipyard.

A transfer shunt directed the plasma that would have gone to the nacelles into the rotating secondary attenuation chamber. The rotating chamber matched up with each of three constrictor segments, which magnetically narrowed—and intensified—the plasma stream. The constrictor segments each connected sequentially with one of four lengths of PTC, rotating like the barrels of a Gatling gun. At the far end was a collection chamber that split the flickering energy into two fixed PTCs—or would when she got them in place. These two longer bypass conduits carried the twin streams back to the nacelle channels.

With gross mechanical rotation, exact alignment was always a problem—nearly an impossibility when tolerances were measured in microns. Tev had earned them an extra margin of error by devising ablative stents for the floating couplings. Any flash would vaporize the sleeves harmlessly without refracting back into the peristaltic field. Their elegant practicality almost made her take back her remark about his not being a ship's engineer.

Almost.

At the moment Tev was checking her work on the constrictor assembly. She heard his surprised grunt at the first readings and listened as he recalibrated his tricorder and tried again. This time his grunt was approving.

Conlon smiled grimly as she tightened the duranium collar around her latest connection. In operation the system would be surrounded by a containment field running off the impulse drive. At this level of energy—and risk—she was going for every scrap of protection she could.

Turning, she was surprised to find the first section of bypass conduit at her elbow. Actually, it was only one end of the conduit; the other, some three and a half meters away, was in Tev's hands.

Humanly impossible, she thought as she grabbed the conduit.

"Work will proceed faster," Tev said, "if we dispense with the progressive assessments."

Conlon loose-fit the PTC into the collection chamber without comment and waited while Tev made his connection before beginning the sealing process.

"Dispense with the progressive assessments," she thought, her smile grim. *Not checking my every move is probably the highest compliment in that prig's repertoire.*

CHAPTER 7

Three fours of days and two before the Quest

This time Faulwell was not the first to the meeting, he noted as he slid into the chair beside Carol Abramowitz. Tev and Nancy Conlon were by the main viewscreen, which showed an animated tactical schematic of the Klingon cruiser taking position alongside the colony ship. Scuttlebutt had it the Klingons had moved back and forth over the entire cylinder at close range before taking up position near its leading edge. This was a subject of some annoyance to those still trying to discern the colony ship's secrets from a maddeningly corkscrewing distance.

"The point, of course," Tev was saying, "is that no stable warp field can do what the Klingon field seems to be doing."

"Which means it can't be a stable warp field," Gomez said.

"Right," Conlon said. "Their warp bubble is blinking on and off twenty-four times a second."

"They are actually at warp less than half of each second," Tev said. "But because they only move minutely with each warp, the net effect appears to be that they are moving through normal space at point seven six light."

Stevens looked like someone had spit in his soup. "Hang on, a single warp drive can't strobe on and off that fast."

"It's a series of warp fields." Tev adjusted the screen, and the Klingon's warp field began cycling rapidly through a rainbow of hues. "But not separate warp drives."

"The warp signature clearly shows a single core," Conlon said. A wave pattern appeared across the bottom of the screen. "But with a variety of harmonics."

"Six of them," Tev added.

"What they are using is six separate actuation assemblies," Conlon said, "shunting between them in rotation."

Faulwell wondered if he was the only one fighting off the impression that Tev and Conlon had become Bynars.

"How?" Gold asked.

"Imagine six parallel sections of primary plasma transfer conduit, each with its own constrictor segment," Conlon began.

"Power is routed through each sequentially," Tev took up the thread. "But just as it fully engages; the plasma is shunted to the next."

"They're riding the clutch," Gomez said.

"Right." Conlon grinned at the first officer. "But to do

it without frying their transfer plate, they have to use six separate clutches."

Faulwell shook his head. Every time he thought he was up on his engineering terms, at least enough to follow the conversations in this room, somebody would go and raise the bar on him. He didn't understand a word Conlon or Tev had said.

"Why doesn't everybody do this?" Gold asked.

Gomez answered this one. "Because eventually the on/off cycle will crystallize the plasma injectors."

"Exactly," Tev said.

Gold frowned. "Define *eventually.*"

"Two hundred hours, maybe more in a pinch," Conlon answered. "And with anything over a hundred and sixty I'd want everything checked out by a starbase before we went on any long journeys."

"You say we can do this?" Gold arched an eyebrow. "You've already set this up?"

Tev and Conlon practically beamed at each other.

"Chief Engineer Conlon devised the original design," Tev said.

"Lieutenant Commander Tev figured out how to make it work," Conlon interrupted.

"A detail," he said modestly.

Faulwell saw Gold and Gomez exchange glances as others around the table straightened slightly.

"The engineering staff is conducting final tests now," Tev added. "Though this is a formality. Chief Engineer Conlon and I assembled the system ourselves."

"First Corsi and Stevens . . ." Abramowitz said under her breath.

A single bark of startled laughter escaped before Faulwell caught himself. He was just able to muster an expression of polite inquiry by the time everyone else in the room looked his way. He tried to kick Abramowitz under the table, but she had shifted her legs to the other side of her chair.

"We had four matched sections of PTC in stores," Conlon went on after a slight pause, "but only three constrictor segments, which was a problem because at least four assemblies are needed to make the system work."

"Three plus the existing drive . . ." Gomez began.

"I didn't want to use ship's primary systems any more than absolutely necessary."

"Of course."

Again, Conlon smiled. "Lieutenant Commander Tev solved this by putting the constrictor segments and PTCs on separate rotations."

"So we'll be strobing in three/four time?" Gold said.

"Exactly."

"How long until you're ready?"

"Thirty minutes," Tev said. "The conn officer will need to be briefed on navigation under these conditions."

"We'll need to drop out of warp for eighteen of those minutes," Conlon added, "to switch from the primary plasma transfer assembly to the strobe device."

"Let's get to it," Gold said. "Everyone else get your ducks in a row. We meet the Klingons in forty minutes."

"Steady, Wong."

On the screen the colony ship and its Klingon escort bore down on the *da Vinci* at three-fourths the speed of light. Intellectually Gold knew the image was enhanced, altered to suit human eyes. At this range the dark-gray-on-black vessels would have been invisible. Even visible, their velocity would have distorted their shape to human eyes. But to Gold the sight of the mismatched pair was real enough.

They'd jumped five hundred and forty million kilometers, half a light-hour, ahead of the colony vessel to prepare for this rendezvous.

"Conlon, everything still go?"

"Spindizzy's running hot and true, Captain," came the instant reply over the intercom. *"Ready when you are."*

The corner of Gold's mouth quirked at the chief engineer's nickname for the . . . well, what was a proper name after all? He envisioned the rapidly rotating lengths of plasma conduit interlocking sixty-some times a second, with constrictor units spinning independently at some ungodly speed of their own. "Spindizzy" seemed as good a name as any.

"Then bring Spindizzy online at your discretion, Conlon."

"Engaged." A pause, then: *"All readings nominal. We're good to go."*

"Come about," Gold said to the conn officer. "Match speed and take up position on the opposite beam. Show them what we can do, but don't make a challenge out of it."

"Matching course and speed, mirroring position, aye," Wong said.

The *da Vinci* arced gracefully into its new heading. Gold saw the stars streak briefly as Wong held the warp field stable, interrupting the flicker for a fraction of a second to accelerate into position. A moment later they took up station on the colony vessel's port beam, or port beam relative to its course, Gold amended mentally: neither ahead of nor behind the Klingon ship.

"We are being hailed," Shabalala said almost immediately. "They say prepare to be boarded."

Gold didn't need to consult his granddaughter's Klingon fiancé to know that was imperious even for Klingons.

He did not for a moment think their coming to him was meant as a courtesy. They wanted to see his ship without showing him theirs. He considered refusing, but keeping them out would require him to raise shields, something that could only devolve into a confrontation. Though some military historians might be interested in how a modern *Saber*-class starship would fare against a heavily modified, but still ancient Klingon ship of the line, he couldn't imagine how that would help the colonists they'd come to save.

"Haznedl, have all personnel directly involved in the mission report to the observation lounge," Gold said, heading toward the turbolift. "Shabalala, transmit the coordinates of our transporter room and tell them they will be welcome in five minutes. Then tell Corsi to send some people to transporter room one and warn Poynter that we're about to have guests."

"Aye, sir."

"Oh, and tell Corsi to have Blue's chair removed from the observation lounge. I don't want to insult their captain by not putting him on an equal footing with me."

Shabalala smiled. "Understood, sir."

CHAPTER 8

Kairn looked about with interest as the Federation vessel's transporter room materialized around him. He was careful to betray no excitement, of course, emulating the weary professionalism of Captain Kortag. The captain made this seem completely routine, which, as far as Kairn knew, it might be.

Not so Langk, ostensibly second in command of the engineering team Kairn led. Head and shoulders taller than the others, Langk stood like a chieftain taking possession of a prize.

Langk was of the powerful House of K'Tal and destined for greater things—chief engineer of the *Sword of Kahless* within the decade, to hear him tell it. He obeyed as a warrior should, but let no one forget his social status. Where Kortag's uniform was supple with years of service, Langk's was polished to high luster, squeaking with his every movement.

Kairn hoped that whenever the young warrior managed to make a complete fool of himself, he'd do it without dishonoring the Empire.

For his own part, Kairn wore more cloth than leather, his only badge of status the Master's dagger across his heart.

Facing them now were four humans, one male and three female.

The captain was instantly apparent; though not as grizzled as Kortag, he was just as gray. The practice of giving nursemaid tasks to senior warriors whose honored prime was past seemed common to both cultures.

The gray human surprised Kairn by speaking in precise, if heavily accented, Klingon. "I am Captain Gold. The *da Vinci* is my ship."

"Kortag, captain of the *Qaw'qay'*," Kortag answered. Then, not to be outdone, he continued in the Federation's language. "Commander Kairn, leader of the engineers, and Lieutenant Langk, his second."

Kairn nodded in acknowledgment; Langk raised his chin a notch.

Captain Gold indicated the darker-haired female, then the golden one. "Commander Gomez, leader of the S.C.E. team. Lieutenant Commander Corsi, chief of security." Then he indicated the woman behind the transporter console. "And Transporter Chief Poynter."

That surprised Kairn; a mere technician would never be introduced to officers. Kortag grunted in unsurprised acknowledgment, evidently familiar with human custom. Langk turned his shoulder to the technician.

"If you will accompany us to the observation lounge," Captain Gold was saying, "we can discuss strategy."

As he stepped from the transporter platform behind his captain, Kairn stole a quick glance at the light fixtures and another at the fit of the control console. The technician caught his eye and smiled, recognizing the professional appraisal.

Kairn cocked an eyebrow, engineer to engineer, before falling into step with the human engineer.

As they walked side by side behind the captains and ahead of Langk and the security officer, Kairn was very aware this was the first time he had been so close to a human. He clasped his hands behind his back to avoid accidental contact, content in her apparent decision to walk in silence.

His senses heightened by stress, he noted the air lacked the scents of a living ship. Shifting his eyes but not his head, he saw an overabundance of ventilation fixtures, though he felt no breeze. His fingers drummed idly on the hilt of his Master's dagger as he calculated the volume of air they must be moving.

Behind him Langk cursed. Kairn turned to see the warrior staring, his hand on the hilt of the *d'k tahg* at his hip. A huge blue arachnid stood on the threshold of a cross corridor. However, Kairn noted that a Starfleet communicator was attached to the apparition's upper body. The beast must be a member of the crew.

"I have heard of Nasats," Kortag's voice carried from behind him. He and Captain Gold had also turned at the sound of Langk's curse.

"Pleased to meet you, too," said the creature in a voice like crystalline bells.

"This is P8 Blue," Commander Gomez introduced. "She's our structural engineering specialist."

Langk compensated for his first reaction by nodding to Pattie as an equal. Every now and then he surprised Kairn into thinking there might be hope for him.

The Nasat mirrored the nod solemnly, curling its—

her—antenna nearest the humans. As the group resumed its way to the observation lounge, she fell in beside Kairn.

"What do you make of the energy source?" she asked conversationally.

"Energy source?"

"Large source of radiant energy." She took his obtuse question in stride. "Appears just below the forward hull every seventeen or so hours, then seems to fade."

Kairn considered for a step. Much of this was to be discussed openly in a few moments, so there was no point in secrecy on this issue.

"An apparent artificial sun," he said neutrally. "It takes just over eight point five standard hours to traverse the interior of the vessel from bow to stern."

"I was afraid of that." P8 Blue made a sound like a breeze through copper wind chimes. "A seventeen-hour day will play hell with our sleep cycles and won't convert easily at all to standard time. We're going to spend a lot of energy wondering what time it is."

Kairn was still considering whether this was Nasat humor when they entered the observation lounge.

There were a half-dozen other Federation personnel already there, standing to greet the visitors, but Kairn barely registered their presence. His attention was completely captured by the huge windows. He doubted there was that much transparent aluminum aboard the *Qaw'qay'*. How complex must their structural integrity field parameters be to compensate?

Kairn did not consider the effect of using his dagger until it registered that the Federation engineers were suddenly silent. He'd meant to work quickly while they were distracted with being presented to Kortag, but the glint of his blade extended before him had drawn every eye in the room. He slowly lowered his hand until the blade was flat across his stomach.

Langk snorted derisively. Kairn saw Kortag's hand move, perhaps a centimeter, enough to silence the young warrior. He thought he saw a faint glint of amusement in his captain's eye, but no help. It was his blunder to deal with alone.

The Federation structural engineer saved him from having to speak.

"May I?" she asked, extending one of her hands.

Kairn paused. One did not surrender one's dagger lightly. On the other hand, one did not wave a blade—even a Master's dagger—in another's house without explanation. He offered it to her hilt first.

The Nasat peered closely at the dagger for several seconds, turning it over several times as she studied the blade. The other engineers seemed content to wait as she made her examination, Kairn noted. Professionals waited for information before they acted. He hoped Langk was taking notes.

Kairn knew P8 Blue had deduced the dagger's purpose when she extended her arm and began waving the blade experimentally before her. She laughed, a delightful tinkle of glass.

Turning from the window, she extended the dagger toward a stocky officer near her captain. Kairn realized he was more powerfully built than a human, with a commanding, aggressive mien: a Tellarite.

"Commander Tev, you are—" She stopped herself. "No, that can't be right." She considered the blade a moment. "Of course," she turned to Kairn. "This is made to your dimensions."

"Every Master Craftsman fashions his own," he said neutrally.

She peered at the edge, turning it so the etchings along the flat of the blade caught the light.

"My Klingon is not good, but this is a scale, and these conversion factors, while *this*"—she flipped the dagger and sighted at an angle along the opposite side of the same edge—"handles proportion and ratios."

She looked around the lounge at her teammates and seemed to realize she'd lost them.

"It's a measuring tool," she said. "Depending on which edge he uses and what angle he holds it at, Kairn could use this to tell you how many square centimeters of fabric are in your uniform or the displacement of the *da Vinci*."

She reversed the blade, offering Kairn the hilt.

"Before we part company," she said, "would you instruct me on fashioning one of my own?"

Kairn's hand hesitated midmotion. He knew Captain Kortag's heart; there was little chance the two ships would part on friendly terms. He lacked the guile to smile as he retook his dagger.

Commander Gomez presented the remaining Federation engineers, introducing four more humans, a lone Bynar, and the Tellarite. Though Kairn did not retain names, he was impressed by the range of specialties included. What role would a cultural specialist or a physician play in engineering? This team was obviously intended to deal with a wide range of situations without support.

He introduced himself and Langk when she finished. Captain Kortag had already identified himself to the only person aboard the Federation vessel who mattered.

The courtesies attended to, Kortag took the proffered seat, identical to the Federation captain's facing him from the opposite end of the table. Langk and Kairn sat at either side of him as Gomez and the Tellarite flanked their own captain.

In Federation fashion the others attempted to leave the visitors enough space, crowding toward their end of the table. However, even with their security chief standing by the door, there simply was not enough room for formal separation. Kairn found himself elbow to elbow with the Nasat, which, he decided, he did not mind at all.

For the next forty minutes the technical data flowed freely. The Federation engineers had done a thorough job of modeling the alien vessel. They had missed the entry ports, but their deep scans revealed much of the structure that had eluded the *Qaw'qay'*.

Even Langk was not immune to the spirit of cooperation, questioning the Tellarite's assessment of some detail, then conceding the point. Kairn could not remember the last time that had happened.

Kairn found himself comparing the two captains. Both followed the multiple conversations with evident interest and comprehension, but offered no comments of their own. Clearly each was comfortable with letting the specialists under their command work in their own way. The two looked to be of an age, but he knew nothing of how human longevity compared to that of Klingons. For all he knew, Captain Gold was twice as old as Captain Kortag, or had only half his years.

When his captain shifted slightly in his chair, Kairn knew the period of conviviality was about to end. Langk realized it, too, straightening in his seat and resuming his imperious warrior's air. The others, of course, noticed nothing.

"Have you determined their point of origin?" Kortag demanded.

"No," the Tellarite, whose name, Kairn r... was Tev, said shortly.

"No," Kortag echoed, and waited.

Kairn knew his captain understood
been unable to discover the colony ship
He wondered whether Kortag though
was withholding information or simp
as a pretext for confrontation. Both s

"From its current heading, we
passed through the Dancido syster
years ago," the Tellarite said. "W
apparently over a protracted p
Dancidii."

"Six hundred years ago?" as
female. The cultural specialis
rectly. "That was during the
hardly had space flight the
have been—"

"Primitive nuclear missil

The image of the colon
tated, shifting from a sc
representation. Centere
trench about a third o
edge of the cylinder. K
even collar ringing half the
eral craters of various sizes were g
trench.

"There was apparently a structure here which
Dancidii took to be the control center," Tev said. "It was the target of at least fifty low-yield nuclear warheads."

Kairn knew from their analysis of the rotational rocket control network, something invisible to the Starfleeters' distant scans, that the Dancidii had been right. He did not need to look to his captain for guid-

"To work *with* us," Gold said. "This is a joint mission."

Kortag gave no sign he heard the words, much less granted their validity. He stepped forward.

"Our intent is to save the thousands of beings aboard that vessel," Gold stated flatly. "You are welcome to ei
ther help us do that or get the hell out of Federati
space."

The human's voice lacked Klingon heat, but s
knife blade.

Kortag whirled at the threshold, his ey

Langk and Kairn stepped clear, but their
charge. Instead he stalked back to st
chair at the head of the table.

"The Klingon Empire does not
peoples," he growled; his raised
sponse. "Do not insult me by de

"Your choice, sir," Captain
tone. "Do you go or stay?"

Kortag swept the Fede
coming at last to the S

"We have a comm
you propose?"

problem." He s
gons will deal with it."

"The ship is in Federation space,
pointed out. "And will be for eight more days."

"Your Federation *asked* us to come."

CHAPTER 9

Three fours of days before the Quest

I've done this before, Fabian Stevens told himself as he watched the giant cylinder rising under his feet. *This is no different from landing on the Plat.*

On the other hand, the Kursican Incarceration Platform had been spinning in orbit, not streaking through deep space at some ungodly fraction of the speed of light. And he had approached it, not hung in front of it like a Lilliputian matador taunting a planet-sized bull. Well, maybe *hung* was not the right word. He—along with Kairn, Tev, Soloman, Carol Abramowitz, Pattie, and Lauoc—had been beamed into space directly in front of the colony ship moving at exactly the same speed. The plan was to slow down just enough to soft-land.

Stevens found it hard to brake; far too easy to imagine himself smashed to a monomolecular film on the spinning surface. Forcing the remarkably vivid mental image aside, he focused on aligning his flight with the garish, eight-pointed star that had been beamed to the center of the twelve-kilometers-wide plain of metal.

The visual target was intended to provide both orientation and a sense of scale to help them judge their descent. For Stevens the kaleidoscopic effect also added motion sickness, but now did not seem like a good time to bring that up.

Stevens cringed at his own unconscious pun.

Kairn seemed to have no qualms about colliding with the gigantic ship. Stevens could see the coal black Klingon environmental suit "below" him and to his left, plummeting with apparent disregard for danger.

Tev's white Starfleet suit, stockier than the usual cut, was perhaps a heartbeat behind. Stevens was glad to see the others—including Lauoc—matching his cautious approach. At least some of the away team was sane.

Lauoc Soan was their security contingent. Stevens didn't know him well, but he was glad the Bajoran was along. Not that he was concerned about any possible danger from the colonists—or would they be "natives" on a ship so large? Tev was already showing signs of not adjusting well to being under Kairn's command. The two might need a referee and he wasn't up to it.

Domenica had wanted three security officers on the mission: herself, Lauoc, and Rennan Konya. The Klingon captain had rejected Konya out of hand; he didn't want a Betazoid "mind reader" near his officers. Nor had he liked the idea of a security officer who outranked the mission leader being along.

But Lauoc, chin high on most people and muscled like a piece of beef jerky, had impressed the old Klingon. Part of it had been the web of scars from a Breen neural whip rising from his collar to just below his left eye, and a lot of it had been that Lauoc had served on the *Abraxas,* but it was the way he didn't blink when Langk had threatened him that earned him the nod.

In fact, when the big lieutenant had scoffed at the idea of a Federation runt coming along to protect him, Kortag had surprised the hell out of everybody by pulling him from the mission. The warrior had started to puff up in protest, but the look in his captain's eye had deflated him pronto. Stevens had the impression he'd be scrubbing induction coils by hand for the foreseeable future.

The second surprise had been Kairn's tapping Pattie instead of one of his own to fill the vacancy. Except for that big guy, these Klingons were not running true to type.

With a start, Stevens realized he had daydreamed his way to within a hundred meters above the spinning nose of the giant ship. Wouldn't do to meet oblivion mid-musing. He tapped his nav boosters lightly, slowing his rate of approach a bit.

The rotation was slowest at the center, but it was still enough to send Stevens stumbling as he touched down. He noted only Pattie and Lauoc seemed oblivious to the spin. In fact, the Bajoran seemed to land mid-stride on his way to the center of the target. With a few quick motions he erected the homing beacon.

"Da Vinci *to away team.*" Shabalala's voice crackled in his helmet.

It should not have crackled at this range. Instinctively Stevens looked for the *da Vinci,* but quickly looked down. The spinning canopy of stars was impossible to look at. He made a mental note to keep his eyes on the ground as much as possible.

Hull, he reminded himself, *not ground.* Though it was hard to think of a surface a dozen kilometers across as anything but the ground. It was a dark gray-blue he noticed, now that he was looking at it, and pebbled, with wide, feathery arcs of light gray and white.

"Boarding party here," Kairn said.

"You're about four kilometers from the entrance," Shabalala said. *"Bearing one four seven."*

The bearing was of course relative to the homing beacon. The spinning surface made any objective reference system irrelevant.

Without a word, Kairn strode in the indicated direction, clearly expecting the others to follow.

One thing about Klingon leadership, Stevens thought, *they don't micromanage.*

Abramowitz exclaimed suddenly.

"Problem?" Tev demanded.

"Footprints," she said with a shaky laugh. *"But they're ours. I thought the gray was part of the hull material, but it's dust."*

"Micrometeorite debris, held to the surface by the vessel's forward motion," Pattie said. *"The spiral drifts are caused by its rotation."*

"Restrict transmissions to mission specific information." With that, Tev ended the conversation.

Tellarites, on the other hand . . . Stevens did not complete the thought.

For the next twenty minutes he heard nothing except his own breathing and the almost subliminal whine and clank of his suit's magnetic servos as the away team trooped across the metal plain. At first he divided his attention between watching where he put his feet and the directional readout, but that quickly paled.

These things should come with libraries, he thought. Then, being an engineer: *Okay, wise guy, where would you put it?*

He began running a diagnostic, more an inventory than anything else. These suits were so well thought out, finding space for a library without redesigning . . .

"Sir?" he said abruptly.

"Yes?" Tev and Kairn chorused.

Stevens paused for a moment, waiting for one or the other to say something else. When neither did, he went on: "My suit is using more power than it should." He double-checked his figures on the heads-up display inside his helmet. "Every task is using about four percent more power than normal."

"Your suit is malfunctioning?" Kairn asked, his voice ominously neutral.

"No, sir." Stevens bet Klingons regarded their suits as part of their arsenal; failure to maintain a weapon probably carried the death penalty. "I can't localize it, but the drain is coming from outside my suit."

"Halt," said Kairn. *"Suit diagnostics."*

Soloman was the first to answer. *"Confirmed. My suit is also experiencing an additional drain on all systems."*

"My suit is fine." Pattie's chuckle was crystalline.

Abramowitz snorted and Stevens grinned as he shook his head. Impervious to vacuum, the Nasat engineer was of course naked to space.

"However," Pattie added, *"my utility harness seems to have lost about eight percent of its reserve power."*

Stevens frowned. Her harness, which included the vibration microphone which allowed her to speak and magnetic boots along with a selection of potentially useful tools, used only a fraction of the energy a full environmental suit did. On the other hand, most of that energy was used in highly active systems.

"Double-check, everyone," he said. "Is most of your loss through active systems or storage?"

His theory was quickly confirmed as everyone reported active system drains.

"Energy collectors," he said. "Or maybe just one big one. Something that sucks power out of active systems. That's why our communications are breaking up."

"Aceton assimilators?" Kairn suggested.

Stevens shook his head. "Aceton assimilators project the energy they steal back at the source as deadly radiation. Ambient radiation levels are unchanged."

"On the other hand," Pattie said, *"either we've traveled six hundred kilometers, or the beacon's signal is being absorbed as well."*

"The pull of such accumulators is usually exponential," Tev said. *"High projective energy devices such as tricorders should be used sparingly."*

"That means our phasers are probably useless," Lauoc said.

Stevens nodded inside his helmet. Tkon accumulators absorbed phaser fire so rapidly the beams never reached their targets.

"We should go to minimum power levels," he said, "to reduce drain."

"Agreed," said Tev.

There was a pause as everyone made their adjustments.

"Tactical systems specialist," said Kairn.

"That's me," Stevens answered.

Kairn grunted and resumed his march toward the entrance.

Effusive in their praise, these Klingons. Stevens trudged behind. *I'll try not to let it go to my head.*

With a final twist, Stevens activated the pattern enhancers.

Without waiting for a system check, Kairn gave the order: *"Transport now."*

"Transporting," Shabalala confirmed.

A shielded generator appeared, gravimetric grapple already engaged to grip the spinning surface.

If we had beamed one guy down with a pattern enhancer, Stevens thought as he helped Lauoc break the framework back down again, *the rest of us could have beamed straight to the surface without risking our necks on the landing.*

"Recharge." Kairn was speaking to Pattie, who was being held to the surface by Tev and Abramowitz.

"Gladly." The Nasat tethered herself to the generator before connecting the power feed. Almost immediately her boots clicked firmly to the surface.

Two kilometers from the edge, "forward" had become distinctly "down," and they'd had to engage gravimetrics to keep their footing. Pattie's harness, using a larger fraction of its smaller power reserves, was almost completely depleted.

"How is the power drain, Specialist?" Tev asked Stevens.

"About three percent of what she draws is disappearing." He watched the readout for a moment. "Now it's four percent. I don't think we have much time."

Each of the others recharged their suit's systems in turn. Kairn was last, and by the time he hooked to the generator, less than ten percent of its energy was going into his batteries. The rest went . . . elsewhere. Stevens still could not determine how the siphoned energy disappeared.

The generator shifted position as Kairn disconnected.

"It's losing its grapples," Stevens said. "Better get it out of here."

"Let it go." Conlon's voice was barely recognizable through the static over the communication from the ship.

"Huh?" he asked brightly.

"Chief Engineer Conlon is correct," Tev said. *"If the energy tap has locked on to the generator, beaming it aboard the* da Vinci *might enable it to access ship's systems."*

They stood back as the massive device began sliding along a curving path toward the edge of the ship, two kilometers distant. It was lost to sight in moments.

A blue-gray wall, six meters by six meters, jutted abruptly from the surface, blotting out a section of streaking stars. Between them and it was a hole, also six meters square, discernable only as a featureless blackness against the dark blue-gray of the surface.

What sort of culture would make the entrance to their world a simple tunnel open to space? Stevens wondered. Then again, he had to admit, they had no idea what might be waiting just inside. He was fairly certain that once they crossed the threshold, the energy-absorbing field would block all communications with *da Vinci.*

Well, the mission design did call for them to be completely on their own for six days on the inside. With luck, sufficient time to survey possible locations for the control center. It would be at least that long before anyone called them, anyway.

By now, "down" was emphatically toward the outer

edge. The danger of the hole was not falling in, but loss of contact that would fling them into space. They gave the square void a wide berth, approaching the wall from the side. Stevens noted it was only about ten centimeters thick and wondered if it could support them. A simple tricorder scan would have told, but might also have drained its energy. Best to save active scans for something more critical.

Kairn evidently had similar concerns. He used hand signals to order the others to remain, then stepped onto the wall alone. He stood for a moment, horizontal from their perspective, then gestured the others to join him.

Stepping to a perpendicular surface was awkward, but it was a relief to Stevens to reorient himself as they set his boots down onto the structure. Instantly the forward drag he'd been fighting disappeared as the wall became a ledge, "down" now firmly and comfortably toward the soles of his feet. The surface they'd traversed was now a wall stretching endlessly above them, while the stars . . .

Stevens turned quickly back to face the ship.

"Magnets," said Kairn.

He paused as everyone switched off their high-energy gravimetrics, then entered the tunnel. With their suit lamps at the lowest setting, the away team followed him into the darkness.

CHAPTER 10

Ahrhi uncoiled from the crouch, sword hand bracing her shield as she thrust upward with all the power of her thighs and back. The heart of her shield slammed her opponent's elbows and its metal bezel caught his wrists, interrupting a double-handed down stroke meant to split her in half. The raider reeled backward, the broadsword flying from his ruined grasp.

The second raider lunged from her right, but he was a step too far and out of position, his shortsword still raised to hack down on her crouching form.

At the top of her leap, her weight barely on the balls of her feet, her belly floating free, Ahrhi spun to her left, away from her attacker, and reversed her sword. There was a moment's thrill of terror as the hilt spun freely about her lower thumb, but she caught it firmly, blade now flat along her forearm, as she came down.

She dropped to one knee, bending all the energy of

her fall to thrusting her sword upward and back. Her heavy belly threw her balance off, but she jammed the point of her shield into the dirt, bracing herself as the bandit threw himself on her. She felt her sword pierce his unoiled leather armor with a corn-husk crackle, the impact rocking her painfully forward against her shield and stomach. His weight fell across her back, one limp arm flailing across her shoulder to fling his sword into the dust before her as his face bounced against the crest of her helm.

Twisting her blade, she pulled and spun, rolling the corpse from her as she stood to face the third raider. Again her unaccustomed weight threw her off and her sure stance was flawed by a momentary stumble.

But the last of the border raiders was retreating, his back to her and his weapon undrawn as he labored the driver's switch to hasten the laden packbeasts down the trail. If he hadn't insisted on taking the plunder with him, she'd have been inclined to let him escape. As it was . . .

To her left her first opponent was struggling to gather up his sword, at least one arm clearly shattered, and scuttle to whatever cover the hillside provided. She left him to a lingering death and loped after his fleeing comrade. Her light shield swung from her forearm as her right arm cradled her belly.

Suddenly from behind her came the thud of rider-beast hooves galloping on the dirt trail. She turned, expecting to see Joac or even Lithal in the livery of Rowath Hold.

Instead a fourth raider, mounted on a rangy rider-beast of the lowlands, bore down upon her. Their rear guard. He had stayed concealed beyond the same out-crop of rock that had allowed her to catch the others unawares, waiting until she was exposed on the trail before charging. He wore not armor but peasant's homespun—evidently a disguise, for the deadly steadiness of his leveled longsword marked him as a practiced warrior.

Part of her brain noted she was not the only left-handed fighter on the trail this day as she assessed her situation. Here the pass was too narrow to evade him and cover was too many steps behind. Her only choice was to meet his charge. She stood tall, feet planted wide with sword hand again braced behind her shield, the blade angled down and to her right, clearly prepared for his frontal assault.

The rider thundered straight toward her, bent low over the pommel of the saddle, his sword aimed like a lance. For a long breath the classic cavalry charge against the classic foot defense seemed to play itself out in the morning source light. In the last heartbeat the outlaw stood in his stirrups, swinging the sword above his head, ready to slash down from over and behind her shield.

Timed as though they had rehearsed this moment a hundred times, Ahrhi leaned right, left leg straight as right bent low, and raised her right arm above her head. Her sword was slashing low and wide even as his split her shield. A backhand swing in the direction of the horse's charge did not carry as much force as a frontal blow, but it was a cut impossible for a rider in motion to block.

The riderbeast screamed as the sword tip sliced a shallow furrow along its ribs and the severed stirrup flew to clink metallically off the stone wall of the trail. The rider's foot landed with a more meaty thump just beyond. Screaming his own agony, the rider was barely able to cling to his mount's mane as the terrified animal plunged down the trail.

A wave of fatigue swept over her, and for a moment the narrow pass swam about her. She swayed, catching her fall by jamming the point of her sword into the dust of the trail, and stood for a moment, belly pressed to sword hilt, right arm hanging limp.

Chin to chest she saw her dangling shield was beyond repair. The bezel was bent, nearly broken, and the polished leather flapped loose from the splintered wood. Dosar had made her this shield, fashioned it from stout *tayr* wood and armorbeast hide the season before his death. Last season, when the trees were in bud. For that memory she roused herself and reslung the shield across her shoulders.

Rowath, the Holder, had allowed her to stay in the married quarters after Dosar's death. He had hopes, more than she had, for the outcome of her pregnancy; he said she would need the room for her children. Until he moved her back to the barracks, she had a hearth and a place to hang this shield. A place of memory.

She was not surprised to find the line of packbeasts abandoned. The lone able-bodied raider had apparently made good use of his mobility, for she saw no sign of him. Dosar would have known where he had gone; Dosar was the tracker. Then again, Dosar's longbow would have brought the four raiders down before they'd known a warden was about.

The animals came easily to hand, having no more objection to retracing their steps uphill than they'd had to following the trail down. They were loaded, she saw, with ingots from Domat's mine, but not overloaded. The raiders had planned a long journey before finding a market for their booty.

No mystery there: this trail branched either duskward, past the lower birthing pool to Atwaan, which had mines enough of its own, or dawnward to the Tetrarchy. The Four Houses would use this little bit of metal in a day and had the wealth to pay twice its worth without blinking.

Come to think of it—and she did stop to think, peering first back down the trail, then up to the hills on either side—this was not enough to warrant a journey through the wilds to the Tetrarchy. These few must have been but one cell of a larger group of raiders. She wondered how many Holds were being raided today.

Had they known, she wondered as she continued up the trail toward Domat's outpost at the downwater edge of Rowath Hold, that the warden for these trails was dead? Their small number and the openness with which they'd moved indicated they had expected no opposition.

Certainly not to be brought down by a pregnant shield maiden in single combat. Even in her dark mood, that thought made her smile.

She had been proud to be a shield bearer, to excel in a craft dominated by men. She was a defender, sworn to protect others. For many years she had defended Dosar, guarded him against assault and ambush as he patrolled, searching out raiders and renegades.

It was a familiar partnership; no longbow man could protect himself in close combat and often no armsman with sword or crossbow could engage thieves and brigands before they escaped. Though, and again despite her mood Ahrhi smiled at the memory of Dosar's amusement, it was very rare for a warden to marry his shield bearer.

But she had been poor defense against a raider with a

longbow. No guardsman could protect another against the shaft of a longbow. They came from too far to be seen, flew too fast to see. No one held her at fault for her husband's death but her.

She jerked the lead packbeast's halter more savagely than the poor animal deserved when it tried to snatch a bite of trailside grass. She murmured an absent apology, and the creature tossed its head, rejecting it out of hand.

There was no marque of House or Hold on the arrow she now carried in her bedroll, but she knew the arrow-head. It was the narrow lozenge of dense black metal that came only from the foundries of Atwaan, though some said from the Halls of the Builders themselves. She doubted that last, but knew that when she was able to travel, it was to Atwaan she would go. When she found the mate to the arrow she carried, she would avenge her own.

Within her, her babies stirred. Hers and Dosar's. The shifting was not much, only enough to remind her. Enough to add a new depression to her dark thoughts.

The Holder's generosity did not extend to Doctor's price, and she had no friend or family to stand midwife. She would go to the birthing pool, and sooner than she wanted, alone. That was traditional. That was the way it had been done for generations. And yet . . .

She did not share the Holder's optimism about her pregnancy. She did not relish the thought of being alone when the last remnants of Dosar died within her, as every infant had died in childbirth in the last four seasons.

Her certainty of their children's deaths had placed Ahrhi on this trail this morning. She had come not seeking thieves, but the smoky pink quartz stone that caught the source light along the ridge above. Dosar had admired those rocks and had often come out of his way to watch the display of prism light they splayed across the cliff face.

As she stooped to retrieve her satchel and the memorial stones she had cut, she paused, struck by another thought. If, in the heat of combat, she had remembered the sorrow that lay before her, would she have dodged the mounted raider's charge?

CHAPTER 11

His breath plumed, condensing almost to ice before the wind whipped it away. Stevens shivered. Four airlocks and a tunnel had brought them to a rocky ledge that appeared to be high on a mountain. However, it had an atmosphere, so they were no longer reliant on environmental suits that were losing power at a distressing rate.

Before them a steep landscape of heather and copses of twisted trees fell away to a rolling landscape. Stevens could make out tilled fields and cleared pastures among the rocky dales and forests.

Pretty much answers the colonist question.

Behind him a tricorder warbled. To reduce the loss of power to their tricorders, only one was being used at a time. Right now Abramowitz was taking a comprehensive scan as quickly as possible. She'd analyze the data after cutting off the energy-hungry sensors.

From this height Stevens could make out the curvature of the world inside the cylinder. Though the natural setting strove to emulate a wide valley, the slight inward tilt of trees at either extreme ruined the illusion.

Above there was nothing. No clouds, no blue sky, only white haze that looked close enough to touch. He said as much.

"We are near the upper edge of the atmosphere." Kairn spoke as though that explained it. He shook his head. "The stench of carbon dioxide will only grow worse as we descend."

Stevens made a mental note that Klingons could smell carbon dioxide. Why being near the edge of an atmosphere would cause haze instead of, say, asphyxiation remained a mystery.

Abramowitz confirmed Kairn's assessment. "Carbon dioxide two point four percent, oxygen only eighteen percent—don't try any heavy exertions—and various trace elements, some radioactive, but nothing immediately dangerous."

"That merely confirms our external readings," Tev said.

"Always a good idea," Abramowitz answered with a smirk.

Kairn grunted with apparent amusement, and Tev chose not to answer.

"Ambient radiation is high but manageable." Abramowitz continued to read off the tricorder's display. "However, heavy metal levels in the vegetation are lethal to Tellarites and humans, toxic for everyone else. And the water . . ." She made a sour face and snapped the tricorder shut. "Drink only in an emergency and only from a swift-flowing source. It won't kill quickly, but the uranium and plutonium content is cumulative. Looks like we'll have to carry those ration packs after all."

"The math is beautiful," Soloman said suddenly.

"Oh, yes," Pattie agreed.

The two were standing at the edge of the ledge, looking out over the forest and farmland.

"What math?" Stevens asked.

"Don't you see it?" Soloman asked. "There. And there."

He pointed to a rocky ridge that ran perpendicular to their apparent mountain range, then a densely wooded bowl-like valley. Both looked completely unremarkable to Stevens.

"He is speaking of the geometric balance," Tev said. "The distribution of materials."

"The use of apparently random natural features to create the illusion of a real world while maintaining symmetry," Pattie agreed. "It's really quite elegant."

"Hmmm," said Stevens, still not sure what they were seeing. He guessed he wasn't seeing past the "apparent" randomness of the design.

"Here," Abramowitz handed each of them an oblong case about twelve centimeters by twenty-four.

"What's this?"

"Generic emergency radiation kits, complements of Dr. Lense," Abramowitz said as she handed a blue case to Pattie and a red one to Soloman. "For your self-medication pleasure we offer hypo ampoules of hyronalin—daalisan for Pattie—triox compound, and species-specific cocktails of vitamins, nutrients, and appropriate goodies for hemoglobin production, tissue regeneration, and general damage control."

Stevens turned the kit over until he found the clip and attached it to his belt. He noticed Kairn had attached his to a loop high on his vest and wondered what normally went there. The hanging kit covered the hilt of the dagger that Pattie liked so much.

"Is the darker vegetation along rivers?" Abramowitz asked, looking out over the view as the others attached the kits to their utility belts.

"Usually," Tev replied.

"Then why are all the rivers parallel?" she asked.

These Stevens did see. Remarkably regular strips of blue-green vegetation running across their field of view which seemed to start and stop at random intervals.

"Ship's rotation." Tev didn't actually say "obviously," but it was in his voice. "Inertia and angular acceleration would dictate any sizable volumes of water flow against the ship's spin. Prevailing winds will do the same."

"We will learn nothing more up here," Kairn said.

He stepped off down what might have been the merest trace of a trail without a backward glance.

Not my idea of sitting this one out, Faulwell thought as he set the anchors on the Klingon pattern enhancer pylon. Of course it was bigger and more massive and more awkward than the Federation model. *But they got here first, so we use their equipment.*

The *Qaw'qay'* had hard-landed two dozen locator beacons on the colony ship's hull during its first survey while the *da Vinci* was still orbiting. When the repair phase began, they used the beacons as transporter targets, beaming their first wave of engineers directly to the spinning surface. ("Must have felt like a near-warp transport," Conlon had said.) Those pioneers had then set up pattern enhancers that allowed others to beam over with much less drama.

The problem was, there were nearly three thousand square kilometers of outer hull and far too many trouble spots to keep using the "shoot and jump" method. Pattern enhancers had to be preset in strategic locations. This meant personnel not essential to the nuts-and-bolts repairs lugging enhancer grids across the surface of the ship and setting them up while the engineers worked. Since the mysterious power drain seemed limited to the leading face of the ship, the enhancers could be set up to await remote activation whenever a team needed to use them.

"Why not just beam the enhancers where you need them to be?" Faulwell had asked when his new job was explained to him.

Gomez had just given him that weary smile engineers reserved for particularly naive questions from soft scientists and handed him his itinerary.

It was probably a perfectly good suggestion. Faulwell tightened the straps on the Klingon null-grav sled. *They just didn't want to admit they hadn't thought of it.*

Fortunately, the Klingon beacons were positioned so that every point on the surface could be triangulated. And moving from place to place consisted primarily of lifting clear of the ship, but not out of range for the gravimetrics, and letting it rotate beneath you. Hardly difficult, but definitely monotonous. He strapped himself into the driver's seat and double-checked the next destination against the Klingon beacon grid. Muttering an Algonquin curse, he punched the actuator and the sled leapt free of the surface.

CHAPTER 12

"What do you think?" Tev asked, eyeing the lacework of ceiling cracks emanating from the pile of rubble blocking the stone corridor.

Pattie measured the wall's lean with an improvised plumb line. "If this were a planet, I'd say quake damage. As it is . . ."

"Could the exterior bombardment have been responsible?" Soloman asked.

"There's nearly a kilometer of metal and rock between the surface and this tunnel," Pattie said. "It's doubtful even quantum torpedoes would have done this level of damage." She backed toward the opening of the artificial cave, taking in every detail. "No, something inside this mountain shifted."

"An explosion?" Kairn asked.

"Or a structural failure."

Stevens looked out over the rolling countryside

below them. The cave opening was perhaps a hundred meters above the valley floor, and at this level the curvature of the ship's interior was not apparent. The ersatz sun had moved a considerable distance during their climb down, and the shadows of trees and ridges stretched toward them across meadows of heather.

"Hard to imagine a structural failure with this level of craftsmanship," he said.

"An explosion," Kairn said.

"Perhaps." Pattie sounded unconvinced.

"A damaged area near the front of an out-of-control vessel," Stevens said. "If it weren't so easy, I'd guess we found the control room first try."

"How human of you," Tev said dryly.

"Huh?"

"Humans expose their bridge atop the leading section of their vessels," Tev said, then added without looking toward Kairn, "as do a number of other cultures. But the great majority of spacefaring peoples follow the Tellarite example, placing it sensibly at the center of mass." He gestured out over the valley. "We can't pretend to understand the logic of a people who would spend a century building this. The control center could be anywhere."

"Anywhere including the very front of the ship," Stevens countered. "We need to check this out."

"We need to check out every possibility," Pattie said.

Kairn cut off Tev's reply. "P8 Blue and Soloman, you will explore the tunnel beyond the rubble."

"Why them?" Tev asked. "As a generalist—"

"You are less qualified than a structural specialist and a computer specialist to assess damage and evaluate control systems," Kairn finished. "Also, they can fit through the opening without further excavation."

Stevens braced himself for pyrotechnics, but to his surprise Tev remained silent. He wondered whether the Tellarite's restraint meant he recognized Kairn's wisdom or he remembered that the traditional Klingon response to insubordination was lethal.

Without further ado, two hundred meters of monofilament was affixed to each of the explorers. Lauoc presented them with torches made from stout branches he had flayed with a wicked-looking knife Stevens knew wasn't Starfleet issue. Tev surprised him again by producing a chemical lighter.

"We knew we were entering a primitive environment," Tev said in response to Stevens's startled expression.

Stevens bet himself that Lauoc and Kairn carried flint and steel. If he ever needed a fire, he'd have to find two dry sticks and trust to racial memory.

Pattie went first, without a torch, so all hands would be free as she explored the far side of the rubble pile with only the light of the opening. Stevens held her safety line, letting it play out over his palms as she explored. As it went slack, he pulled it slowly in, hand over hand, so she wouldn't get tangled on her way back. At last she reappeared and pronounced the climb safe and the floor on the far side solid.

"The air is a little dense," she added. "A lot of dust. Musty but breathable."

She took two torches, securing one to her harness, before scurrying down to give Soloman room to follow. He was decidedly less sure of himself as he picked his way up the pile of rocks. Stevens guessed spelunking was not a popular pastime on Bynaus.

"How do you work this lighter?" Pattie called from the other side.

"Grip the safety," Tev called back. "Depress the gas release with your thumb, then trigger the ignition with your—"

He paused as Pattie's crystalline laughter cut him off.

"In my case, use more than two hands," she said. "Back up a second, Soloman. I need the daylight to find a place to prop my torch."

Soloman backed out of the opening, Lauoc reeling in his line deftly.

"Okay," Pattie called out. "Got it."

A great hand swatted Stevens backward.

He staggered, barely keeping his footing as the ground rose and fell. Something slammed into his temple; pain brought him to his knees. He tried to rise, but a second shockwave of choking dust knocked him to the ground. He had a vague impression of Soloman blown out over their heads like a kite on a string as his vision faded from red to gray.

For an instant he was leaning over the hatch above a narrow access ladder, his eyes locked with Eddy's as the *da Vinci* died around them. Below her a gush of molten hydrogen from Galvan VI's atmosphere filled the shaft, melting Lipinski and boiling upward. Before he could move, before he could shout, Eddy calmly shut the emergency bulkhead between them; saving him and dooming herself.

No! He fought up out of the blackness, his body thrashing to action before his mind was clear. *Not this time!*

Desperately Stevens hauled on Pattie's safety line still clutched in his hands. The hot polymer burned his flesh, he could smell it, but he ignored the pain, ignored the weightlessness of the line, trying to get her out before the corridor collapsed completely. He grabbed empty air before he realized the polymer had melted through.

Kairn violated his own order, scanning the cave-in from where he lay.

"Solid for at least twenty meters," he reported. "Beyond that . . ."

He stood and adjusted his settings, then scanned again. At last he shook his head, shutting down the tricorder.

The sound of Eddy's body thudding hollowly against the bulkhead echoed in Stevens's ears.

CHAPTER 13

"I'm not a doctor," Abramowitz said for the third time, "but I think that should hold until we get back."

Lauoc's grip on the safety line had prevented Soloman from flying over the ledge and down the mountainside, but the Bynar had landed hard. He'd fractured a set of bones analogous to a human's collarbone—a quick fix with an osteostimulator, if they'd had one. Instead Abramowitz had made do with a spray cast from the medkit, immobilizing his neck, right shoulder, and upper arm.

Stevens suspected getting Soloman back in his environmental suit would present a problem, but decided not to say anything until he had worked out a couple of possible solutions. Instead he focused on redistributing the supplies from Soloman's and Carol's packs among the other four.

Lauoc joined him and began transferring items from

Pattie's smaller pack. He nodded in grateful acknowledgment; he wasn't quite up to dealing with Pattie's pack yet.

"We cannot effect rescue with our current resources," Tev said, "even if—"

Kairn cut him off. "Agreed."

Stevens wondered for a moment if he'd just seen proof Klingons were more sensitive than Tellarites. More likely Kairn was just heading off another of Tev's expositions on the obvious.

"Natives will be here soon to investigate the explosion," Kairn added. "We need to move before they arrive."

"Natives are arriving now," Lauoc said quietly.

"What?" Tev demanded.

Lauoc tapped an ear. "Iron-shod animals on a stone road."

"*Khest'n* carbon dioxide stench," Kairn said. He sniffed the air for a moment, then pointed. "Sixteen individuals, perhaps a hundred meters distant."

Without a word the four men slipped into their packs as Abramowitz helped Soloman to his feet.

Stevens noted Tev had found time to fashion a quarterstaff. Kairn's hand rested on the hilt of the *d'k tahg* at his belt; no doubt he did not consider the engineer's stiletto at his breast to be a weapon. Lauoc's hands were empty, but Stevens knew the Bajoran had that wicked knife concealed somewhere.

Unarmed, he moved closer to Abramowitz and Soloman, ready to assist in any rapid retreat.

"Left the road," Lauoc said.

Kairn grunted as eight riders cleared a copse of trees below and split into two groups, moving to surround them.

Their clothing was a mixture of quilted fabric, leather, and metal, enough alike to suggest uniforms, and they were variously armed with swords and lances. Narrow shields hung from every saddle, and two riders had crossbows slung across their backs. The animals were enough like horses to pass for distant cousins.

"A fourteenth-century Europe analog?" Stevens estimated, gauging the sophistication and fit of the weapons.

"Twelfth to eighteenth," Abramowitz countered. "Don't get too narrow until you've seen how they live."

Stevens wondered for a moment where the others were, then realized eight riders on eight mounts made sixteen. Once Kairn learned to tell the smells apart . . .

His thought broke off as the newcomers came level and their size registered. The stirruped boots were at his eye level and he could not have touched the smallest animal's withers without jumping. It was more difficult to judge the riders while they were mounted, but he estimated that their heavy belt buckles would be even with his shoulder.

If the mismatched sizes bothered Lauoc, Tev, and Kairn, they did not show it. Stevens did his best to emulate them, standing tall between Abramowitz and Soloman and the newcomers.

For their part, the two groups of riders pulled up, perhaps twenty meters distant and stared. Better than simply killing them outright, Stevens reflected, which would have been more in keeping with the European model.

"What's the temperature?" Abramowitz asked abruptly.

"Twenty-two, twenty-three," Stevens guessed. "Why?"

"Heavy clothes indicate cold weather," Abramowitz said. "Could be part of the breakdown."

"Why no gloves, I wonder?"

"Their hands will be webbed," Tev answered over his shoulder. "Ill adapted to wearing gloves."

"Webbed?" Abramowitz asked. "How can you be sure?"

"Note the facial features are in the top third of their heads." Tev did not turn his own face from the natives. "The eyes and nostrils aligned just below the brow line."

He paused a moment, evidently expecting the light to dawn. When Abramowitz and Stevens continued to remain silent, he snorted in disgust.

"Surely you're familiar with McCoy's *Comparative Alien Physiology*?" he demanded. "Low profile above the waterline."

Abramowitz shrugged, which Tev must have sensed.

"These mammals are semi-aquatic," he explained. "In Earth-specific terms: Your ancestors were lemurs, theirs were otters."

At this point the natives, whom Stevens resolved not to think of as "otters," evidently decided they'd learned all they could from a distance. Without apparent signal, the riders moved forward.

As they drew close, the two groups rejoined to form a semicircle, not so close as to be immediately threatening, but too close for casual escape. Though the swords were sheathed and the lances pointed skyward, Stevens had no doubt their weapons could be brought to bear instantly.

Without haste, Tev activated his combadge. Kairn nodded, but made no move toward his own. Stevens understood. One combadge's universal translator was sufficient to decode the native's language. As its power failed, another could be activated and the language downloaded. Depending on the energy drain, they should be able to communicate for days.

This close Stevens could see that their forearms and the backs of their hands were covered with sleek fur. Even their faces had short, down-like growth. Their eyes and nose were indeed high on their heads, but any ears they might have had were covered by leather helmets.

One native—perhaps the leader, though Stevens could see no sign of rank—spoke. His voice was a beautiful, operatic baritone and—though it was always dangerous to guess the significance of voice tone in an alien culture—he seemed more curious than threatening.

"I am Kairn, engineer in service to the Klingon Empire." Kairn answered the most likely question. Then, pointing to each of the others in turn, he gave their name, occupation, and planet of origin.

Stevens wondered at the Klingon's uncharacteristic eloquence. Then he realized Kairn was encouraging the other by example to speak at length for the benefit of the universal translator.

The native leader spoke again, first tapping the side of his head, then indicating each of the others with an open hand. Stevens noted he had four digits, two long fingers between what seemed to be two thumbs at either side of his palm.

Introductions apparently out of the way, the leader pointed to Soloman, again asking a question.

"Soloman was injured in the explosion," Kairn answered.

The leader motioned the two riders at the left end of the semicircle forward. One dismounted, towering even taller than Stevens had expected, and bowed to Soloman in what appeared to be respect. Then, too quickly for the others to react, he picked the Bynar up and handed him to the mounted rider.

With a gesture to the rest of them to follow, the leader turned his mount and the riders headed back the way they had come at a slow walk.

"It seems we've been invited to join them," Tev said dryly.

Kairn grunted.

With no choice, the party followed the horsemen.

Lauoc hung back and Stevens turned to see the Bajoran hastily arranging stones in an arrow that pointed in the direction the natives were taking them.

He did not ask who it was for.

CHAPTER 14

Domenica Corsi kept her eyes fixed firmly on the job in front of her. Just at the edge of her vision, the stars shot so quickly over the horizon she expected warp streaks. It was difficult enough to work with tools that wanted to fling themselves into space without having to cope with her own vertigo.

Though the Klingon beacon network told her exactly where she was—and that there were a dozen other workers within sight of her—over three thousand square kilometers of curving metal hull could be overwhelming. It was easy to imagine herself alone on a blue metal plane beneath an endlessly rolling sky.

She set her spanner too near the edge of the gravimetric bubble and it began to slide toward the horizon. She caught it with the absentminded skill of long practice, setting it near the personal generator without taking her eyes off the open junction panel.

This phase of the job was simple, and dangerously monotonous in its simplicity. Someday when she had the time, she'd compute the odds on a culture that had never developed active scanning technology choosing hovinga iridium to insulate their conduits. For now, the sensor-blocking compound meant all available personnel—i.e., anyone not already pulling a double shift trying to get the colony vessel's engines working—had to be on the surface checking tens of thousands of hardwire connections by hand.

Fortunately, ninety-nine percent of the navigational and control network was sealed within the duranium hull, intact except for the region the Dancidii had blasted. The network itself was integral to the hull, laid out before the builders had known where the rockets would need to be placed to balance the ship's rotation. Each unit was simply mounted on the surface and plugged into the network. That meant external junction boxes at each of the twelve hundred rotational rockets that had to be inspected.

Having external junction boxes on a system like this made no sense to Corsi. On the other hand, sending thousands of people on a two-thousand-year journey inside a tin can because there just might be a habitable world at the other end made even less sense. There was probably some perfectly logical engineering reason for the setup. Like maybe they just came that way.

Green, green, green, green, green, green, green, purple, she read the telltales. *Damn.*

"Corsi to *da Vinci.*"

"Go ahead, Commander." Haznedl's voice came crisp and clear. This far from the bow, there was no interference at all.

"I've got a break between thrusters nine-sixteen and,"

she checked her padd, "seven-two-nine." She stood and, blocking the view of the horizon with one hand, surveyed the hull as far as she could. "No visible surface damage," she reported.

"Confirmed," Haznedl replied. *"Disconnects have been reported between unit seven-two-nine and units seven-one-one and three-oh-six as well."*

Corsi consulted her padd again, this time checking the inspection schedule. Thruster seven-two-nine was scheduled to be checked by a Klingon team in thirty-six hours. The next step was obvious, but in any cross-cultural cooperative effort it was best to be sure everyone agreed what obvious meant.

"Bridge, seven-two-nine is less than a kilometer from here. Please ask Commander Gomez to advise the Klingons I wish to divert from scheduled pattern and check thruster seven-two-nine. Be sure to explain why."

"Understood." There was a hint of chuckle to Haznedl's acknowledgment. Then she broke the formal protocols of the open-mike comm system: *"Hang on a sec."*

Corsi retrieved her spanner and secured the cover of the junction box while she waited.

Who thought sixteen-sided nuts made sense?

People who think exposed junction boxes on hundred-kilometer-long colony ships make sense think sixteen-sided nuts make sense, she answered herself. She had her tools packed by the time Haznedl got back to her.

"Commander Gomez has consulted with the Klingon engineers." The ensign was once again the model of bureaucratic propriety. *"Your diversion has been approved, Commander."*

Corsi snorted at the ensign's choice of words, imagining Faulwell's—or even Fabe's—turning it into a quip.

She double-checked the coordinates for booster seven-two-nine and jumped clear of the hull.

She used her steering jets to move toward the left as her gravimetrics kept her lightly in touch with the ship spinning beneath her. In normal circumstances, she would have looked ahead for her destination, but motion sickness inside an environmental suit was no joke. She kept her eyes off the horizon and watched the blue metal plane slide by directly below.

When the rocket vent appeared, she toggled her gravimetrics, pulling herself down to the hull. She landed beyond it, of course, and had to walk back. She saw the problem while she was still a dozen meters away.

"Bridge, this is Corsi," she said. "Looks like it took a rock. Half the junction box is missing."

"Tell her to let that one go," Sonya Gomez told Ensign Haznedl. "The structural integrity field will cover it."

She glanced over at Klath as she closed the connection. The Klingon engineer nodded his agreement. The two turned their attention back to the schematic diagram on the display screen.

The reconstruction command center was a standard Federation environmental hut that had been beamed piecemeal to the colony ship's hull at the edge of what the S.C.E. team had dubbed the Dancidii Trench. Designed to house a dozen Spacedock workers and their equipment, it gave Gomez and Klath plenty of room to work.

They were fine-tuning the network of field generators that would act as stitches, holding the damaged section of ship steady when thrust was applied. She would have liked about a dozen more generators, but as Klath pointed out possible alternatives, Gomez had to admit they'd done an excellent job with what they had.

At first she had been irritated by the Klingon habit of rigging whatever was immediately available to do a job even when the parts they needed could be easily gotten from stores or fabricated on a replicator. But now she had to admit the Federation practice of using the best available first, then devising alternatives as those ran out would have left them farther behind at this point. As it was they were coming in ahead of schedule. She thought even Captain Scott would be impressed.

Probably surprised as well, Gomez thought; she had been. The Klingon engineers had proven to be remarkably adept and patient: craftsmen who took pride in quality workmanship. Not at all what she had expected.

Some things ran true to form, of course. Like Klingon workers not mentioning dangerous situations, or staying on the job until the last reserves of their environmental suits were exhausted. One technician had finished his shift without informing anyone he had been injured. If Gomez had not noticed the field repair to his environmental suit, he would never have reported it.

She had also had her entire team model complete and redundant communication for every action or change of plan, such as the multistep conversation she'd just had with Domenica. The Klingon practice of each individual simply moving on to the next task that caught his or her eye without informing anyone else had led to some confusion—and one potentially explosive confrontation—in the first day of combined operations.

Despite this, or perhaps because of it, external repairs were proceeding without a hitch. Only the density of the hull material made the work difficult, requiring the workers to pause frequently for equipment recharges and recalibrations. Otherwise, it was straightforward engineering at its best.

Even with their best efforts, however, it was unlikely the damaged giant could survive making the skew flip its designers had intended. Rather than reverse the vessel and restart its ion drive to slow it down, the Klingons intended to attach impulse engines to bring it under control.

But that was a job for years from now.

The immediate task was to repair native systems and attach structural integrity field generators at key points. Their goal was simply to make the ship stable and provide its inhabitants with a viable environment until a more permanent solution could be found.

Unfortunately, even though they'd located over two thousand unused connection ports for the network linking the external thrusters, the system was not set up to accept external commands. And, despite exhaustive searches and scans, they had found no entrance to whatever drive or control systems lay beneath the surface. If they were going to find a way to get the ship under power again, it was up to the away team on the inside.

She glanced at the chronometer mounted on the bulkhead. One hundred and six hours since Tev and the others had disappeared inside the ship; thirty-eight until any communication was expected.

She wondered what she would be doing thirty-nine hours from now.

CHAPTER 15

Suspended in the blackness, Pattie could not decide whether she was blind or the tunnel was completely dark. The question had vexed her off and on over the last several hours. Or perhaps days; she had been wandering alone for so long she was no longer sure.

Even though she knew the outcome, she repeated her ritual. She closed her eyes and waited a hundred heartbeats before opening them. The hundredth or three hundredth time she had tried that. Nothing. No difference. Either she was blind or there was no ambient light whatsoever.

She was going to have to proceed on touch. Which was what she had been doing. The last thing she had seen was that nimbus of blue flame rising from her lighter to the huge, spongy mass against the ceiling.

She'd had a long time, while feeling along walls and bumping into objects and taking chances on empty expanses of floor, to think about what had happened. The heavy mustiness she had smelled had been a cloud of spores from the lichen, or whatever it had been, filling the gaps and covering the ceiling. Just as centuries ago on Earth sparks igniting airborne flour dust had blasted mills to oblivion, the open flame of the lighter had triggered an explosive combustion of the spores.

Reflex had curled her into a ball before the biomass exploded; she never saw the fireball that singed her shell and melted most of her utility harness. The thermal shockwave had bounced her down the tunnel like a cork in a flood. If it had been a natural cave, she might well have been dashed to death against jagged rocks. As it was, the smooth walls of the corridor had scraped and beat her, perhaps—she was not sure—even knocking her unconscious.

From what she had been able to feel of the wreckage afterward, her internal bruises and contusions were a small price to pay for having been blasted out from under the collapsing ceiling. No doubt the rest of the away team, her friends, thought she was dead.

She had rested long enough.

Standing on the narrow rung, she steadied herself against the upright and flung the buckle end of her climbing rope—woven from what remained of her harness—above her head. The third time it hit the rung above and stayed. She eased the strap upward and cautiously waved another hand in the darkness until she caught the descending buckle.

If this buckle were metal, I could use it to strike a spark. Then I would at least know. . . .

Forcing the thought from her mind, she focused on fastening the two ends together. Once buckled, her climbing rope formed a loop that hung from the rung above to about waist level in front of her.

The next part of the process terrified her; she had to will herself to make each movement. It might have been easier if she were certain this giant's ladder led to safety, but she didn't have that assurance. She only knew that after possibly days of tracing tunnel walls in the dark, this ladder going up was the only thing that held any hope of being a way out.

She released her hold on the upright, and holding the straps slightly apart with two hands, she eased a foot off the rung and onto the bottom curve of the loop. She took a deep breath and, trying not to imagine the buckle slipping, pulled herself up to a standing position.

She swung for a moment, vaguely surprised she was not plunging down into darkness, then felt above her head for the next rung. Once she had pulled herself up, she sat catching her breath and repeating the ritual check of her vision.

To her left in the darkness was something hot. She was reasonably sure it was a cluster of pipes, each as big around as she was tall, that she had felt rising out of the floor near the ladder's base. At first they had merely been warm, but the heat of whatever they carried had been increasing. There was no way to tell whether the entire column was heating up or if the contents were simply hotter toward the top.

She wished her tricorder had survived the blast. It would have been good to know what was in the dark with her.

Or where she was going.

With a sigh she pulled herself to a standing position and flung the buckle end of her homemade climbing rope into the darkness above her.

CHAPTER 16

Terant sat, wrapped in a warm sleeping robe, taking care to appear at ease. Nights had not been good for his wife since the death of their children, but there was no reason for any outside his household to know that.

Vissint entered the outer parlor of the baron's private quarters in evident haste, though he acknowledged the servant who held the door before the latter withdrew. A man who understood the reciprocal nature of loyalty.

The Chancellor of State wore the formal robes of office, but with a rumpled and distracted air. Terant deduced he was at the end of a long and difficult day.

"What news?" asked the baron. He did not offer his chancellor a chair or tea from the service at his elbow.

"The gnomes have been seen on the dawnward road," Vissint said simply.

"Ah."

Their messenger to the Tetrarchy with the news of the birth blight had returned days before with word of these gnomes. They had, during the time of her visit, lost the ability to speak the language of the People. She had gleaned that the Tetrarch's Doctors were divided on the significance of this.

News that they were coming through the Wilderness toward Atwaan was interesting, but hardly warranted the chancellor's late visit.

"And?"

"And they bear letters from Nazent of the Second House." Vissint paused, ensuring that the Baron grasped the import of his next words. "The letters request that all who meet the gnomes assist them in seeking access."

Terant's breath whistled sharply through his nostrils. The flesh across his back and shoulders tightened in alarm. He slowly took a sip of tea with a steady hand.

It had been fortune of the Journey that the Giants had emerged from the hollow by his grandfather's paddock. Their arrival had driven him to deep explorations of the hollows. His miners had discovered a refined metal too heavy and dense to be worked into anything more complex than ax or arrowheads. And of course the highly prized oddments of the Builders—the luxury trade that provided so much for the Barony.

But these treasures had not been what the warden had sought. Unknown to any but his son and now his grandson and their closest advisers, the Giants in all their babbling had spoken of control. Somewhere within the hollows, very near to Terant's holding, was a secret that would give its possessor the ability to control the destiny of the world.

If one could only gain access.

The Giants had died without describing the nature of this secret, or how it might be used. But those things Terant was willing to decipher once he held the secret in his hand.

And now these gnomes, creatures of unknown purpose and knowledge, came seeking access, seeking the secret of controlling the world. They would not ask so openly if they suspected the nature of their goal was known. For now the element of surprise was on his side. But for how long?

"Take the Household Guard," he ordered. "Capture these gnomes. See that they speak to no one. Bring them to me."

Kairn paused for a moment, allowing the others to reach him.

The stench of carbon dioxide was becoming so familiar that it was no longer an effort to separate out other scents. Still, he was aware of it and could feel it robbing his body of strength and resiliency. What must it be like for the others, to be unable to sense what was affecting them? They would die without realizing they were under attack, simply slipping into sleep.

He shuddered in horror.

"Cold, Kairn?"

He grunted at the cultural specialist, an answer that could mean anything. For a creature nearly devoid of hunting senses, the human female was remarkably perceptive.

Behind her the human male was supporting the wounded Bynar over a broken section of the trail. Seeing that Kairn had stopped, and having finally learned that his stopping signaled a rest period, the human helped the Bynar sit. They were the two least adapted to survival in this nearly tech-free environment, but they made a complementary pair.

While it was the Bynar who had noticed the intricate design of the landscape, it had been the human who deduced its purpose. The frequent areas of rough terrain, as well as the dense forests, rushing rivers, and mountain ridges that extended above the atmosphere, all combined to make straight line travel impossible. They'd not seen it, but a barrier or series of barriers prevented circumnavigating the cylinder. No one could simply walk thirty-seven kilometers upwater or downwater, as the natives called it, and end up where they'd begun.

A native, unaware of the design of the ship, would think the world much larger than it was and, given the difficulties involved, be disinclined to undertake long journeys.

But how had the designers managed to keep the colonists from building and maintaining roads for two thousand years? No doubt that was the sort of question the cultural specialist was expected to answer.

In rear-guard position, and taking the responsibility with admirable seriousness, was the Tellarite, Tev. Kortag had told him that many humans were amused by a superficial resemblance between Tellarites and a Terran animal similar in temperament to a *targ*. Kairn found little to be amused by in Tev. Of all the species he had met, and he had to admit he had met very few, the Tellarite made the most sense. Kairn suspected that Tev, like Langk, was from the Tellarite equivalent of a noble House.

A single pebble ticked off a rock to Kairn's right. Lauoc announcing his return. Unnecessary for Kairn, who had his scent, but it brought Tev's head around. Neither the humans nor the Bynar noticed.

A moment later the Bajoran appeared next to Kairn.

"Twelve riders approach," he reported. "Ornate armor, a totem bearer, and someone in what might be ceremonial robes."

"Take a dose of triox now," Kairn said. "Also any medicinals due in the next two hours."

"What happened to half rations for the duration?" the human, Stevens, asked.

"An official party that may be seeking us approaches." Kairn reflected that Defense Force protocol called for him to kill the human for making such a challenge. "We must give them no reason to doubt our strength."

Even the human did not question the wisdom of that. For the next few moments everyone busied themselves with their kits.

Kairn noticed Stevens helping Soloman to a higher position, then bracing him in place with two backpacks. He nodded at the strategy. The natives who were withered from birth were accorded special courtesies on this world. All whom they had met regarded Soloman as one such; the boarding party's treating him appropriately set others at ease.

The riders appeared in due course, rounding a curve in the trail ahead, and paused. They appeared to sort themselves out, no doubt changing from travel formation to formal greeting formation, Kairn thought. The people of this ship were too fond of formality for his tastes.

When at last the riders came on, they were spread as far to either side of the trail as the terrain allowed.

"That looks like a skirmish line," Tev observed.

Kairn loosened the *d'k tahg* at his belt. He noted Lauoc had already disappeared into the underbrush.

The rider in the ceremonial robes rode in the center of the trail, the totem bearer at his elbow. He came to a stop a dozen paces before them and made a show of raising both his hands in apparent greeting. Yet even as he did so, the outriders on either flank continued on, past Kairn's boarding party to take up positions on the trail behind them.

Kairn raised his own hand in greeting.

"Tactical assessment?" he said, looking at the rider before him.

"We are well and thoroughly caught," Stevens replied.

"Agreed," said Tev.

"Their insignia match the messenger we met at Nazent's," Abramowitz added. "For what it's worth, these are the people we came to see."

Kairn nodded. Whether or not this was the baron they'd learned of before the translators had lost power he had no way of knowing. But whoever the individual was, he represented the source of the high-tech artifacts the natives were using as decorations.

Going with these natives would bring them closer to their goal. The trick would be doing it freely and not as prisoners.

That thought had barely formed when the robed figure suddenly dropped both his arms. The ring of mounted soldiers charged.

Kairn roared and launched himself at the nearest rider, *d'k tahg* upraised. Startled, the mount shied. Kairn's slashing blade caught the rider's thigh in passing. Part of his brain registered that the rider had not tried to kill him.

Gaining a bit of high ground, he paused for a moment to assess the situation. The riders were clearly trying to capture them alive.

Abramowitz and Soloman were both already slung across the saddles of riders. Tev was wielding the quarterstaff he had fashioned earlier, but with his back against a cleft of rock, it was only a matter of minutes before he would be taken. Stevens had secured a position on a small mound and was holding three riders at bay by hurling fist-sized rocks with remarkable speed and accuracy.

The scent of native gave Kairn a heartbeat's warning. He leapt just as a massive hand dropped on his shoulder. A native on foot had snuck up on him. Twisting free, Kairn bolted down the hill away from the trail.

Or would have, but a second grab by the native snagged his backpack.

Kairn's legs churned air as the giant lifted him free of the ground. He hooked his *d'k tahg* under a strap and cut free of the pack, stumbling slightly as he hit the ground running.

The native grunted, a deep, bell-like tone, and started after him.

Kairn cut right toward what looked like a narrow ravine. The larger being could overtake him on open ground, his only chance was to find a bolt-hole too small for the native to follow.

There was a sudden shriek behind him, and the native bellowed in pain. Kairn swung about, *d'k tahg* ready, to see Lauoc and the native soldier on the ground. Apparently the Bajoran had attacked from low cover, tripping the giant.

They were out of sight of the others. There was a chance. . . .

Before Kairn was halfway back to the struggle, the native rose, Lauoc held easily in one hand.

"Run!" Lauoc shouted. "Get reinforcements."

Seeing Kairn so close, the giant raised Lauoc up over his head, then slammed the Bajoran to the ground. He stood for a moment, making sure his first captive was too stunned to get away, then started after Kairn.

Kairn hefted the *d'k tahg,* his engineer's habits double-checking what he knew. The weapon was balanced to rotate at fourteen meters, half a rotation at seven, and his opponent was twelve meters away.

Kairn gripped the *d'k tahg* by the tip of its blade and drew his arm back until it hung behind his shoulder. He needed the native three steps closer.

If he understood the threat, the giant ignored it. Weapons sheathed, buckler across his back, he closed on Kairn with deliberate strides.

The *d'k tahg* sank to the hilt just above the native's knee. The leg bent the wrong way, tendons that had to be there severed, and the giant went down, wailing in agony.

Again Kairn started toward Lauoc, but shouts from the trail told him native riders were just below the crest of the rise. The only hope of victory lay in bringing back a rescue force.

Empty-handed, without weapon, food, or water, he turned and ran for the ravine.

CHAPTER 17

Pattie gloried in her pain.

Light, wonderful light, beautiful light, filled the metal chamber and sent stabs of perfect agony lancing through her skull. She laughed and cried, her crystalline voice echoing off the silver walls as she covered her closed eyes with her arms, trying to shut out the delicious brightness.

Drunk with joy, she barely had the wit to roll clear of the trapdoor before surrendering herself completely to the wonder of letting her eyes adjust. She was not blind, she thought giddily; the tunnel had been dark.

From the sound of the echoes of her laughter, she was in a large room. From the one glimpse she had had before having to squeeze her eyes tight against the brightness, the walls were made of metal. She could hear a thrumming sound—pumps?—and the drip of liquid, and could smell metal and stone and none of that heavy mustiness that had haunted her through the tunnel.

She had been in total darkness for—how many days? She was not sure.

Briefly, fitfully, she had slept at one point, tied to the ladder in darkness, and once before that in the tunnel far below, and—she was now sure—she had been unconscious for some time after the blast. But counting sleep periods was not an accurate calendar. When one considered the effects of injuries, stress, exertion, and, she could admit it now, terror, it was highly unlikely she'd been following anything close to her normal sleep pattern.

Alone in the tunnel she had not dared dwell on her condition. With no water, food, or medical supplies it would have only served to emphasize her plight. At the moment she still had none of those things, but she had light. That gave her the courage to assess her levels of dehydration and hunger.

By the time she could discern objects around her unobscured by glare and halos, Pattie was reasonably sure it had been five standard days since the explosion. The suppleness of her injuries seemed to indicate days longer, but the constant physical activity may have accelerated the healing process.

She rose cautiously to her feet, looking carefully around her. The walls and floor were indeed metal, though a dull gray now that her eyes weren't overwhelmed by photons. The light came from polished mirrors set high along the nearest wall, reflecting ersatz sunlight.

Twelve meters away the far end of the chamber was open, revealing only the haze of the upper atmosphere. From the level of glare Pattie guessed the light source was quite close; it would be early morning in the world below.

The metal walls of the room gave way to stone for the last few meters, and the opening itself was irregular. She had no doubt it appeared to be a natural cave from the outside.

It occurred to her that if she was now level with the upper atmosphere, she had climbed the giants' ladder for over a kilometer. As near as she could tell, there was no entrance to the chamber other than the trapdoor. What sort of race considered a kilometer-tall ladder a sensible way to get from place to place?

A very tall race, she answered herself, looking at what were apparently control panels set into the walls above her head. *At least four meters tall.*

Only one panel was active: a row of lights and an analog gauge that seemed to be counting something down. Time would be the most likely guess, but Pattie knew anything was possible. Though she could not read them, the pattern of numbers indicated the builders had counted in base four.

The column of pipes she'd sensed in the darkness rose from the floor and curved to run parallel with the ceiling eight meters above. The pipes ended, without apparent purpose, at a row of boxy apparatus just inside the opening of the "cave."

Pattie's speculation on the purpose of the pipes ended abruptly as she focused on the boxes, or rather the surface of the boxes. The pipes were clearly hot, but the boxes were not, which in this moist atmosphere meant condensation: water.

The dripping sound she'd been hearing was cool, clear water dripping from the metal boxes into shallow pools worn in the stone floor.

Pattie remembered Carol Abramowitz warning of the heavy metals in the vegetation and knew enough botany to know that heavy metals in plants indicated heavy metals in the water. But metal poisoning was cumulative and five days of thirst was immediate; she did not hesitate. The water tasted dusty and metallic and was the most delicious thing she had ever drunk in her life.

Not wanting to lose all the wonderful water to nausea, she paced herself and forced herself to sit back between sips.

She was leaning back against a wall, considering a nap before making her descent from the cave, when the pumping stopped. She sat up, wondering if she could recognize a problem—or what to do about it without tools—with the alien equipment.

Above her the metal boxes groaned and clanked in unison and a deafening roar almost drove Pattie into a defensive ball. Huge columns of steam blasted from the row of pipes, shooting far out over the landscape below.

Of course, Pattie thought. *The atmosphere is too shallow for real weather. We're making rainstorms.*

Meanwhile spillage from the pipes cooled as it fell in the cave. Pattie's laughter was lost in the roar of steam as she took advantage of the long overdue hot shower.

CHAPTER 18

Again the splash and drip. Testing the breeze, Kairn scented water first, then a native, different from the baron's guardsmen, but clear, and something herbal. Medicinal? He wasn't sure. But someone, singular, was definitely bathing in a pool very close to the other side of the boulder.

Kairn pressed close to the stone and listened. No need to risk detection by peeking around the boulder; his ears told him all he needed to know of his quarry's movements. Scrubbing, the herbal scent strong, followed by a long silence. Had he been detected? He relaxed slightly when a sudden splash and gust of expelled breath assured him the native had merely submerged to rinse.

He knew that to attack while the opponent was still in the pool would be foolish. The water would slow him down, eliminating surprise and giving the other time to prepare. Also, his heavy clothing would put him at a disadvantage should the enemy carry the fight to deeper water. As would the fact that he couldn't swim.

Best to wait until the native was out of the water, preferably preoccupied with dressing, before launching his attack. Kairn felt certain there was no dishonor in taking every advantage with an adversary twice your height and three times your mass.

Particularly when one was so lightly armed. He balanced his Master's dagger uncertainly in his hand. The edges were of course not sharp; honing them would have distorted the measuring scales. But the point was sharp, and thrust with sufficient force should find some vital organ, even on a being as large as the natives. His best chance was to get to whatever blade the native carried before he did. A doubtful plan since he would not know where the other's weapons were until he'd rounded the boulder and battle was joined.

For a moment he considered retreat—finding a way around the native without confrontation. But he was not mountaineer enough to scale the walls of the gorge, and backtracking to the beginning to find another way through the barrier ridge would lead him directly into the baron's forces. He had to go forward, and forward meant through the native barring his path. He hoped it could be done without killing.

In due course the sounds of bathing became the thrashing splash of a large person wading toward shore. Kairn crouched, steeling himself for battle, and waited for the first silent step on land. He was keenly aware this was not a sporting event, not a skirmish under orders. This was solo combat. He brushed aside doubt, focusing on the sounds of his enemy, straining to judge the moment of attack.

But it was his heart, not his mind or judgment, that

chose. Almost before he realized he was moving, Kairn was around the jut of rock, the best battle cry of his career ripping from his throat as he closed on the enemy.

The native woman had four breasts.

Kairn's charge faltered a fateful heartbeat as the discovery registered. He had just processed that even the lower pair were above eye level when an open-handed blow shattered his right eardrum and sent him cartwheeling toward the water.

Left-handed, the tactical portion of his brain noted. The native confirmed his assessment by hefting a sword the size of Kairn's leg in her left hand and stalking toward him.

Scrambling to his feet, Kairn shifted his grip on his dagger and considered his options.

A pool of uncertain depth behind him, a massive stone barrier to his right, a steep slope with thornbushes to his left, and a truly enormous woman with a sword she clearly knew how to use closing rapidly from in front. Even if he managed to parry with his dagger, the sword looked massive enough to break either its blade or his grip with the first blow. Death by dismemberment seemed likely.

Then the size of the native woman registered. She wasn't just huge, she was fat; her advance was more lumber than charge. If he cut to his left, her right, he would be on her weak side. He could probably elude her first swing. If he made it up the hill as far as the first thornbushes, he could be around her and free.

Truly, he was no warrior, but in his heart he knew there was no honor in a useless death. Given a choice between dying at the hands of a madwoman and saving the lives of his comrades, even a high-born warrior of the most noble House will scramble over that hill and run.

He feinted right, then dashed left. Even as he made the move, he saw she'd anticipated him. As her sword whistled, he threw himself flat, rolling beneath its arc. Only his size saved him; she simply didn't adjust quickly enough to so small an opponent.

Coming out of the roll at the run, he felt the loose gravel at the base of the slope slip beneath his boots as he clawed at the bushes to pull himself up. The thorns ripping his flesh only spurred him on. Something heavy fanned the air behind him, snagging his mane. A step, a kick, and a heave and he was above the first stand of thornbushes. He turned right, parallel to the slope, and ran as fast as the slipping soil would let him.

Behind him, farther than he expected, the native woman bellowed in frustration and pain.

Pain?

Despite himself, Kairn pulled up, his feet slipping slightly as he straightened, and looked back.

The native woman had fallen to her knees and was leaning on her sword, holding the hilt in both hands as she moaned in evident agony. Her legs and the ground around her knees were wet with what looked like water and a rusty liquid he realized must be blood. The woman struggled to rise, but her sword tip slid in the dust and she fell forward, barely catching herself with her hands. A sob racked her body.

Comprehension dawned.

"QI'yaH," Kairn swore.

He had no idea what Kahless would have done in this situation, but his own honor gave him only one choice. Sheathing his dagger, he scrambled back down the hill.

CHAPTER 19

Day two of the Quest

Pattie would have laughed if her survival hadn't depended on silence.

Three deadfall traps, set with only minimal concealment, were ranged along the side of the stream. The hunters clearly did not expect bugs to be observant.

They were also not clear on what sort of bug they were dealing with, she saw. One of the traps was baited with a mound of flowers, another with cut fruit, and the third with what looked—and smelled—like carrion. From the wilting of the flowers she concluded the traps had been set just before dawn.

For a moment she considered tripping all three traps, but her sense of self-preservation won out over her sense of humor. Moving back into the underbrush, she made her way around the clearing.

Almost too late, she noticed the cut branches. Someone had made one route through the thicket slightly easier than the others, then made an effort to conceal their handiwork. Here was a hunter with more respect for her intelligence. She backed away from that path, having no interest in finding out what sort of trap had been prepared.

Unfortunately, this put her in the position of having to decide on a course of action when she could see no more than a few meters in any direction. On the other hand, her size placed her easily under the canopy of shrubs, making her at least as invisible as her pursuers.

Until three local days ago, Pattie had never regretted not having to wear clothes. Her exoskeleton protected her against everything from the vacuum of space to the crushing pressures of an ocean floor with equal ease. The only time a Nasat wore any sort of artificial covering was for aesthetic effect—a flamboyant taste Pattie did not share.

What her satisfaction with her natural form did not anticipate, however, was first contact with members of a primitive, clothes-wearing culture. The natives had no concept of alien life-forms, much less alien intelligence. To them a naked being who resembled one of their local insects could not possibly be anything other than a giant insect.

Or, depending on the nature of their mythology, if any, she might be regarded as a magical creature, like a unicorn on Earth. While the idea of being a unicorn appealed to her in the abstract, in the concrete—*or rather, in the underbrush*—the prospect held little charm.

In any event, her first meeting with the colonists native to this vessel had degenerated almost instantly into headlong pursuit. And after three days running without food or medicine and precious little water, she was tired. The fact that three local days was only a bit over two standard days comforted her not at all.

To her right was the stream and beyond it the trail she thought the others had followed. Even in her flight, she had been following that road without actually using it, a strategy in concealment her pursuers had evidently figured out.

That stream was a problem. In the last kilometer or so it had begun flowing faster; she was no longer sure she could ford it easily. She wondered if the natives understood how unusual a brook with a slanted surface, sloshing twice as deep along its left bank, really was. In any event, somewhere ahead of her she knew it had to either turn across her path or join a greater current flowing to her left, against the spin.

Either way, it presented a danger. Not only was crossing it problematic in her condition, she would be in the open, exposed as she made the attempt.

To her left a twig snapped. Pattie fought the reflex to flee right.

The hunters obviously knew within a few hundred square meters where she was. They were trying to herd her, trying to get her to bolt in panic in a direction of their choosing. She had to admit she was perfectly willing to comply with the bolt in panic part of their plan. The trick would be doing it successfully in a direction they did not expect.

The more she thought about it, the more backtracking made sense. They knew where she was trying to go, or at least they knew what direction she had held to for three days. And, though the concealed trail in the underbrush indicated at least one dissenting opinion, they did not have much respect for her intelligence. Doubling back now might just throw them off. She'd ford the stream farther up, above the traps where it was running slow, and move perpendicular to her course for a day or so before continuing after the others.

Her mind made up, she turned back the way she had come. She ran low, close to the ground to avoid the branches overhead. She didn't want any snapping twigs or shuddering shrubs to give away her position.

She was not following her exact route, staying a bit farther from the trail and stream than she had before, just in case there was someone following her tracks directly behind.

A native called out in musical baritone from somewhere behind her and to her right. A second answered, his voice a mellifluous counterpoint, from almost directly to her right.

I'm being chased by a humanoid opera, Pattie thought as she jigged slightly left.

When she judged she was upstream of the little clearing with the traps, she cut left and bolted for the stream. She knew she didn't have much reserves left and put everything into a flowing scurry she hoped was too close to the ground for the giants to notice.

She came up short at the edge of the undergrowth. Forty meters of open grass sloped down from her position to the water.

Perhaps sixty meters to her left, still looking downstream to where the shrubbery grew to the water's edge, stood two natives. One had what looked like a bow, easily as long as he was tall, while the other bore a shield and drawn sword.

Pattie paused, gathering her strength for a dash to

the river. She had seen natives run and knew that neither of these two could catch her before she reached the water even if they saw her break cover. Her goal was to get to the water without being seen. Her real fear was that they would catch her before she made the woods on the other side of the trail.

Taking a final breath to steady her nerves, she moved into the open, keeping as close to the ground as possible. The two natives continued to watch upstream.

She had just begun to think she was going to make it when an animal whinnied loudly to her right. On the trail, across the narrow brook, was a native she had not seen, dressed in heavy leather armor and mounted on a huge black beast. She'd been so focused on the other two hunters she hadn't even looked in this direction.

To her left the natives shouted. The armored rider drew his sword and answered, his voice sounding more angry than victorious to Pattie's ears.

For her part, closer to the water than the bushes by a dozen steps, she bolted for the water. She hoped the rider's heavy armor would . . .

Pattie's back legs slid to the right and she spun around, flat to the ground. For a fateful heartbeat she lay splayed out, her head toward the underbrush. Then she tried to rise. Pain radiated from her left lower shoulder.

She was pinned to the ground. But how? The mounted native was still across the river, the other two just now running toward her. It wasn't until she saw the bowman reaching for another arrow that she realized what had happened.

Prideful idiot, she berated herself.

She was an engineer, she knew a projectile of thin enough cross section could pierce her armor. But she had become so complacent in the superiority of her exoskeleton to the thin hides of softs that she hadn't even considered one of their primitive arrows a threat.

Now here she was, pinned (*like a bug,* she couldn't help thinking) to the ground while enemies closed in on either side.

The rider would reach her first. His mount leapt the stream that had looked so impassable to Pattie with apparent ease. She could feel the thunder of the beast's hooves as he charged toward her, leaning far out and down out of his saddle, his sword raised. Was he so eager to be the first to kill the monster?

She clenched her eyes as his sword swung forward, and braced for the blow. Dirt sprayed her face. She heard the animal grunt and the sword *swish* through the air and *ting* against . . . what?

She opened her eyes, turning her head to follow the mounted warrior as he closed with the two natives on foot.

The one with the sword and shield braced himself, ready to meet the rider's charge. At the last moment the mount seemed to prance, jumping suddenly sideways to the swordsman's weak side. Even as the man turned, the animal kicked out with its hind legs, catching him full on the shield and sending him sprawling before charging past.

The bowman ducked, clearly expecting a sword slash, then turned, his back toward Pattie as the rider brought his mount around.

The beast pranced again, a strangely delicate move, then wheeled and plunged. Pattie saw an arrow fly wide, missing the wildly dancing target just meters in front of the bowman.

The rider leaned out again, his sword raised, and

again the bowman ducked. The sword parted the air just above his head, neatly clipping the top third of the bow away.

Without a backward glance, the rider trotted toward Pattie, sheathing his weapon as he came. As he drew close he spoke, his voice lighter than the other's.

"Pleased to meet you, I'm sure," Pattie answered, straining to focus on the figure towering above her. "Excuse me for not getting up."

Through the beast's legs she could see that the swordsman continued to lie on the ground. The bowman, however, was running toward the distant underbrush. She bet he'd be returning soon with reinforcements.

The mounted native spoke again, this time raising one hand, palm up.

"Oh, you do want me to rise," Pattie said.

All things considered, compliance seemed in order, though she doubted she'd have much success. She pushed against the ground and was surprised to discover the shaft of the arrow had been lopped off centimeters above her back. She was able, just, to pull herself free.

The native spoke again.

"Oh, my lower left arm is shot, so to speak," Pattie said. "And I'll leak for a while, but otherwise no real harm done."

Stooping down, she pulled the arrow fragment from the turf. The point was buried nearly half a meter down. And the point itself . . .

"See this?" She held it up for the native to see. "No wonder it cut through me. This arrowhead is durillium. From the way it's beveled, my guess is it's an insulating tile designed to tessellate with other tiles just like it. Someone has been dismantling a nuclear reactor." She turned the arrowhead over in her hands. "I wonder if they realize that?"

"Atwaan," said the native.

"Atwaan?" asked Pattie, raising the arrow high.

"Atwaan," the native repeated, pointing in roughly the direction she—and he, she now realized—had been traveling.

Pattie could hear shouts from the woods.

"I hear Atwaan is lovely this time of year," she said.

Then, taking a risk she wouldn't have dreamed of moments before, she raised her upper arms to the rider.

"Give a bug a lift?"

CHAPTER 20

The sky above was gray and rough, but light, light was everywhere. Lights, lamps, torches . . .

His mind shied from torches. Shadows on the sky? Ceiling. The *ceiling* was gray and rough. And moving toward his feet. He was floating? Being carried, gently, by giants. Where was the tunnel? He had been in a tunnel.

"Where am I?" he asked the giant at his feet, carrying the foot of his stretcher.

"We are in a medical facility, Fabian," said the giant as it set him down on a table. A bed? But its lips hadn't moved.

"How?"

The giants left without speaking.

"Over here, Fabian."

Stevens turned his head and regarded a blank wall of the same clean gray as the sky. He considered this for a moment, then turned his head the other way.

There was Soloman sitting on a high bed. He must be on a high bed, too. But he was lying down and Soloman was sitting and surrounded by books and papers.

"What's happening?" he asked.

"I believe your hair loss and pallor indicate acute radiation poisoning in humans," Soloman said. "Are you experiencing vertigo and disorientation?" Soloman paused, then added, "Ignore that question; they would not have carried you here if you had not collapsed."

Stevens focused on ignoring the question. Soloman helped by ringing a bell.

The four of them had been guests or prisoners of the Barony of Atwaan for how many days? He was not sure. But he had slept at least twice, and it had been dark when he was on the surface at least twice. That was twice twice.

Tev he had not seen twice. Tev had been with the baron. Abramowitz had been in the tunnels, too, but not the same ones. He saw her more than twice and they talked.

Lauoc was . . . He could not remember seeing Lauoc. He was somewhere, though. Of that Stevens was sure.

He had spent most of his time underground, going as deep as he could. They, the baron's archeologists or scientists or whatever, were exploring tunnels that were clearly engineering decks. Decks designed for beings at least a meter taller than they were.

There had been great rooms of what looked like suspended animation capsules, or maybe coffins. Hundreds of them. The natives had hurried him through those to the corridors beyond.

The corridors seemed to lead somewhere. There were signage and panels and labels he could not read and which they clearly did not understand, either. They seemed to think he should. He thought he should, but though machines had to comply with the natural laws of physics, nothing he saw looked familiar.

Or everything looked familiar, but not familiar enough.

When a giant appeared, he started, then remembered he was in a hospital room. This giant, not the one who had spoken to him, had come in response to Soloman's bell.

Soloman held his hands flat in the air, indicating various heights shorter than giants. Then he held his arms wide and pulled them in. Hugging the air? Gathering together. Right.

The giant left.

"I've asked that the others be brought here," Soloman said. "I've tried that before to no avail, but perhaps they will believe this situation requires next of kin."

Stevens laughed, coughing. "Tev is my next of kin?"

"Here, he is," Soloman said. "As am I."

"I knew that."

Soloman dissolved into shadow as the walls and ceiling flowed together. Stevens sat quietly on the back porch of the Corsi house on Fahleena III until Pattie shook him awake.

"Fabe!" she shouted, sounding like Carol Abramowitz.

He laughed. That was funny.

"How'd you do that?" he asked.

But when he looked at Pattie closely, she flowed like water, turning into Carol. That wasn't funny. Pattie was gone.

He cried.

"Stop it," Abramowitz said, but not cruelly. "You're wasting water."

"What's wrong with him?" Tev's voice; his next of kin.

"Radiation poisoning, dehydration, starvation, electrolyte depletion," Abramowitz answered. "And that's just a guess, made without tricorder or medical degree."

"Why is he so ill?" Soloman asked.

"The baron is apparently looking for the same sort of access we are," Lauoc said. "He put us to work with teams exploring the tunnels. Stevens made a big show of being enthusiastic about going as deep as possible. He thought it offered the best chance at finding the control center. He said they'd found a region with warm walls. He was sure they were near the epicenter of whatever went wrong here."

Stevens nodded.

Abramowitz took his belt pack.

"Hyronalin, vitamins, everything, gone," she said. "He was keeping himself dosed to try and stay down there as long as possible."

"Foolish." That was Tev.

"Dangerous, yes, but not foolish." And that was Abramowitz. "He was taking a calculated risk to follow up on the best lead we have."

"Will my medications help?" Soloman asked. "I require far less protection from radiation."

"No, you don't," Tev stated flatly.

"Thanks, Soloman," Abramowitz answered. "I think under the circumstances if we each donated half a dose of hyronalin, we may have enough to stabilize him."

"For how long?" Tev asked.

"If he doesn't go back down those tunnels, days. Certainly as long as the rest of us. Relief should be here by then."

"Relief should have been here two local days ago," Tev countered.

But Stevens could hear him removing his medkit. Good ol' next-of-kin Tev. He drifted into darkness.

When he awoke he had a sense that he had been unconscious for some time, but the others were all more or less where he had left them. Or their shadows were; his vision was not quite clear. He reshut his eyes and listened.

"One of the advantages of being in a hospital is that medicine relies heavily on diagrams," Soloman was saying. "I think I have puzzled out what is happening to the infants."

"Obviously an effect of the buildup of radioactive heavy metals in the environment," Tev said.

"No, that causes underweight and unhealthy infants," Soloman said. "And birth defects of the sort they think I am. I'm referring to what may be a near total infant mortality rate."

"How can you see what their own doctors have missed?"

"Their doctors are unaware of radioactive metals and their effect on living tissue."

There was a rustle of stiff paper.

Stevens opened his eyes and was gratified to clearly see Soloman awkwardly holding up a heavily diagramed parchment with one hand. Of course, it was too far away for him to see what the diagrams depicted, but that didn't bother him as much as the taste in his mouth. He wished the water were safe to drink.

"I cannot judge by human or Tellarite standards," Soloman said, pointing to something on the parchment. "But from a Bynar standpoint, the native birth practices are both unusual and dangerous."

Tev grunted.

"Two uteri, each with two chambers," he said. "Quadruplets are the norm, then?"

"Apparently either identical twins or fraternal sets of identical twins," Soloman agreed. "But that's not the key. See here? It's how they are delivered."

"Is the mother underwater?" Abramowitz asked.

"It coincides with Tev's observation that they are semi-aquatic," Soloman said. "And is the very un-Bynar portion of the process. External fluids are very dangerous to us."

"Humans, too."

Tev said nothing.

"The natives apparently rely on external water to, well, irrigate their system," Soloman said. "And support the infants through the delivery process."

Stevens heard something heavy—a book?—being shifted and perhaps the flipping of pages.

"If I understand these diagrams correctly," Soloman went on, "childbirth on land is possible, but extremely traumatic and potentially lethal for both mother and infants. They much prefer underwater delivery."

"Unusual," Tev said. "And dangerous for most species. But how can what is obviously normal for them suddenly be lethal?"

"Follow the illustrations." Soloman rustled more papers Stevens could not see. "Their culture relies on the use of a traditional birthing pool, with various medicinal herbs planted about and a sheltered cave for the mother and infants to recover."

"Many cultures have stylized and traditional—" Tev broke off mid-sentence.

"What?" Abramowitz asked a half second before Stevens.

"There's no way for the water to leave the pool."

Stevens groaned.

"Fabian," Abramowitz was at his side. "You're awake. Are you all right?"

He nodded, tears stinging his eyes.

"The babies," he said.

"What?"

"The pools are fed by slow springs," Soloman said. "Hardly more than seepage from the water table. But the only way water leaves is through evaporation."

"I don't follow." Abramowitz sounded doubtful.

"The water evaporates," Tev explained, "but the heavy metals remain. After centuries of buildup, the concentrations . . ." The Tellarite's expression was strangely fierce as he faced the others. "At the moment of birth," he said quietly, "they are killing their infants with toxic shock."

"Oh." Abramowitz sat on the edge of Stevens's bed. "My God."

CHAPTER 21

There was a birthing pool ahead.

Naiar reined Striver in, standing in the stirrups to peer ahead. Yes, there was the grove of *dissel* and the shielding rock and a truly saddening number of memorial stones grouped along the gentler slope of the ravine. He let his eyes travel up the hillside, looking for the traditional fall of *myyr* vines that should screen the—

He froze, though there was no chance he had not been seen. Crouching on the trail to the nursing cave was *something*. Not a man, he was sure; not People, but . . .

Could it be a gnome?

He glanced back and down at his companion. The magical beast was too close to the ground to know what lay ahead. In a moment he would know whether the creature and the gnomes were friends or enemies.

Making a show of slipping the retaining strap from

his sword hilt, he loosened the weapon in its scabbard. His companion asked a question in its bell-like voice, but he gave no sign he heard. Instead, he nudged Striver into an easy walk toward the crouching gnome.

A glimmer of ice-flower blue at the corner of his eye told him the beast had moved to cover in the underbrush off the trail. Prudent, given its size and helplessness.

As he neared the edge of the birthing pool opposite the path to the cave, Naiar realized the gnome was not so much crouching as sitting on his heels, a position impossible for the People. He seemed at ease; wrists resting casually on his knees and what looked to be a cane lying across his thighs.

The gnome watched his approach with apparent disinterest until Striver rounded the birthing pool. Then he rose smoothly to his feet, the walking stick across his lap revealing itself to be a sword, long for his size, as he swung it out and down to let its tip rest lightly on the ground. Though he stood less than chest high, there was something imposing in the gnome's stance.

Naiar felt Striver's muscles between his thighs tremble with sudden excitement. His riderbeast, trained to combat, sensed the challenge as well as he did.

He reined in.

The gnome's sword looked to be a guardsman's duty arm, too short for combat against a mounted opponent. But as the thought formed, Naiar realized the gnome had positioned himself between a patch of thornwood and an escarpment at the top of a sharp rise in the narrow path. He would not be facing an enemy on riderback. If Naiar sought to engage him, it would be on foot, and the escarpment would limit the swing of his longsword.

Of course, he could just go by, ignore the gnome and continue on to Atwaan. Naiar looked to the path ahead and back to the gnome. If this gnome was not one of those which had supped at his father's House, it was of much the same type. He could not pass without solving the mystery of the stranger's presence.

With unhurried deliberation, he dismounted, keeping Striver between himself and a sudden assault. Lifting his buckler from the pommel, he hissed Striver's command to move away from the field of combat. With buckler lowered and sword sheathed, he stepped forward, ready to parlay, but prepared to fight if necessary.

The gnome watched him approach until he was perhaps a four of steps beyond reach. Then, with an unhurried deliberation that mirrored Naiar's, he brought the sword up and settled into a shallow crouch. Naiar did not recognize the two-handed stance, but the gnome's ease and confidence in assuming it assured him it had been tested in combat.

He reached for his own weapon.

"Take heed, armsman of the Tetrarchy!"

Naiar froze, his sword half-drawn.

A woman's voice, shouting from the nursing cave?

Looking past the gnome he saw the dense screen of *myyr* vines shift slightly and the wicked shape of an Atwaan arrowhead catch the source light. He realized she must be holding the longbow sideways to be able to draw it in a cave; awkward, but not impossible. At this short range, missing the gnome and hitting him would require little effort.

"Who speaks?" he demanded.

"A warden of Rowath Hold," the voice answered, "who came to the birthing pool with four memorial stones and despair."

There was a catch to the voice. Naiar did not wonder at her tears. His own heart was saddened to hear the birth blight was known in the remote mountain holds.

But if she was in the nursing cave . . .

"Are you—" He hesitated, not wanting to ask what could not be true. "Well?" he finished lamely.

"Two daughters live because that gnome forced the life of his own breath into them." The declaration was raw with emotion. "Harm him and all the wealth of your Tetrarch masters will not protect you."

Naiar eased his sword back into its scabbard and secured it.

"I will harm neither you nor your children, good mother," he promised.

"True."

Facing an armed gnome and a longbow, Naiar could not fault the sardonic acknowledgment. The gnome moved not at all, which made sense; he heard their voices, not their words.

"I would speak to you," Naiar tried again, trying for a light and friendly tone. "But your champion will not let me pass."

"Then heed my champion," came the quick response. "And heed me: Your best path is the one you were following, away from here."

The arrow tip wavered not at all; how long could she hold her weapon drawn? Long enough. Hand away from his hilt, Naiar took a careful step backward.

Suddenly chimes pealed in the wind. A sphere of ice-flower blue bolted from beneath the *dissel* thicket to the left and behind the gnome, and rolled toward him with incredible speed.

The woman in the cave screamed a warning, but did not loose her arrow.

Naiar had a panicked instant to think he would have to kill his companion. Personal loyalty held no place against protecting a gnome who could breathe life into the stillborn.

For his part, the gnome gave a shout of what could have been joy even before he turned to meet the charge. Throwing wide his arms, he dropped to one knee as the ball burst open to become Naiar's creature, its own arms thrown wide.

The two came together, not quite an embrace, but clearly not combat. Their voices mingled in rapid exchange, a crystal bell and gourd of gravel uttering syllables unintelligible to any but themselves.

Naiar stood for a moment watching, his own mind racing. He sensed that events had moved beyond the confines of his own personal Quest. He was certain this gnome was one of the party from his father's House and had clearly been through some ordeal that had separated it from the others. If the others still lived. The time had come to set aside the protocols of tradition.

"Good mother," he called. "I am Naiar, son of Nazent, heir to the Second House of the Tetrarchy. As our companions are clearly allies, I suggest we join forces to face whatever lies ahead."

The screen of *myyr* vines parted and a woman of imposing height stepped into the open. Her right arm steadied a sling that held two small forms to her lower breasts; her left hand held an arrow.

"Well met, noble youth," she said. "But now what shall you do for your proving quest?"

She grinned and Naiar shut his mouth. He had not meant for his realization that she'd never had a bow to be so comically clear.

CHAPTER 22

"The gnome does not eat," Ahrhi said as she accepted a joint of the *plith* Naiar had roasted over the campfire. "I don't think he knows how."

"Not know how?"

"He offered me a bit of every plant in the hollow trying to find something I would eat." She licked the grease running down her wrist. "Cut his hands to tatters making a *dissel* salad."

Naiar laughed, nearly choking on his water.

"They do eat, I saw them at my father's House," he said. "Though only food they carried with them."

"He has no pack."

"Nor does—" Naiar broke off, embarrassed. "I've been calling it 'Magical Beast,' but now I think it's neither."

"A gnome," she agreed.

"I think our food may be poison to them."

"Then it is the smell of our cooking," Ahrhi said, "and not our company that keeps them so far upwind."

Tossing the bare bone back into the flames, the mother began adjusting her infants' slings, shifting them from upper breasts to lower. Naiar averted his gaze, offering her a privacy she did not seem to need, and listened to her cooing to her children as he watched the two gnomes deep in their own conversation some distance away.

The Doctor gnome had used some unguents and potions from the purple case he wore at his chest on the . . . other gnome. It had seemed to gain some strength, and he was certain the sudden bursts of crystal raindrop sounds were laughter.

"I think this Doctor is one of the gnomes that supped at my father's House," he said at last. "But he does not seem to know me."

"How many gnomes have you met?"

"Six."

"You have met only six gnomes and are not sure he is one." He could hear the grin in her voice. "How many People do you think he has met?"

"But People are different," he protested.

She didn't bother to answer.

Striver nickered.

Naiar saw that Ahrhi's sword was in her hand as swiftly as his. The Doctor gnome was also on his feet, though he didn't bother to draw his little knife. Instead he shooed the blue gnome into a *dissel* thicket, then stood between it and whatever was coming.

And several somethings were coming. Too many riderbeasts for Naiar to count by the sound of their hooves were coming up the trail he had followed.

Ahrhi cursed and resheathed her sword. Running to

the Doctor gnome, she pulled her nursing slings over her head and handed her infants to him. Gesturing to the startled creature that he should get down behind the bushes, she turned and hurried back to Naiar's side.

Together they moved away from the *dissel* grove, out of the firelight.

Naiar heard the leading riderbeasts round the rise that concealed the birthing pool from the trail. They pulled up, allowing others to join them.

"I'll get to Striver," Naiar said quietly. "You get the others up to the cave."

"And then what?" Ahrhi asked. "Hold them at bay with my arrow? I count three fours at least. Wits, not swords, will get us out of this."

In the darkness they heard the riders spread out, clearly angling to block off any escape from the hollow. Naiar's mind raced. Knowing one had to survive by one's wits and actually formulating a plan were two very different things.

Suddenly, strange lanterns in the hands of some of the riders threw broad beams of white light across the clearing. It took only a moment for the lights to find Naiar and Ahrhi, illuminating them from a four of angles.

The light bearers held position while the others came on. As they neared, Naiar realized there was something wrong with their silhouettes. The riders were the size of children, many with strange and ungainly packs on their backs.

"Gnomes!" Ahrhi hissed a heartbeat before Naiar made the realization.

The lead gnome rode into the light: a female almost without color. She reined her mount in a four of paces distant and with one hand leveled a crossbow of bizarre design at Naiar's chest.

Naiar was vaguely aware she was flanked by a gnome maned like the Doctor, head and shoulders taller than she was, and another of her size with no hair and rich brown skin, but all he saw clearly were the alien eyes regarding him along the length of the weapon.

He heard Ahrhi sheathe her sword. Not daring to break the leader gnome's gaze, he followed suit.

The gnome spoke, her words unintelligible. A heartbeat later, the strange box mounted on her shoulder said: "[explanation/cause] should I [kill/destroy] you not?"

Naiar recognized the strangely stuttering grammar. The gnomes at his father's house had spoken thus when unsure of shades of meaning.

Before he could formulate an answer to the question, however, the crystal peal of the blue gnome's voice came out of the darkness.

The box on the leader's shoulder intoned flatly: "Because he saved my [shell/legs/life]."

The lead gnome gasped as Naiar's traveling companion stepped into the light.

"[noise/name 'Pattie']," the box said. "You look like [waste material]."

"Tactful as ever [noise/name 'Corsi']." The box did not capture the laughter Naiar heard in the blue—in *Pattie*'s—voice. "Put up your toy before you have a [glandular poor judgment]."

The leader gnome—Corsi—nodded to Naiar as she ported the weapon.

A second female gnome, this one with dark hair covering only her head, stepped into the light. She had a large backpack connected by wires to what looked to

Naiar like a flagon and a hand mirror. Ignoring everyone else, she studied the mirror while passing the flagon over Pattie's body.

"[Everything transcribers] and [unknown]," Pattie said. "How do you [source]?"

"The [source-eaters] cannot [see/feel/touch] living [source]," said the maned gnome beside the leader. "I tailored [germs/rot/sickness] into [life-source-fuel-units]."

"[noise/name 'Langk'], I'm impressed," said Pattie. Then to the dark-covered female: "[Ignore] me. There are two newborns you should examine."

"Newborns?" She looked up from her mirror. "Where?"

"Here." The Doctor gnome stepped into the light, an infant in either arm.

"[noise/name 'Kairn'], are you now a [servant/nursemaid]?" Langk's scoffing tone needed no translation.

Ahrhi's sword sang from its sheath. A single step brought her within reach, her eyes level with the mounted gnome's.

"Jest not, dwarf," she said. "My daughters live by his breath."

Langk's hand stopped halfway to what looked to Naiar like a curved blade without hilt strapped to his back. The gnome was fighter enough to realize no undrawn weapon could stop a ready sword.

"Wisdom, Langk," said the Doctor Kairn. "Now apologize to the [beatific noble-born female] before she eats your liver."

"[Waste material]," said Corsi. "I forgot the [doomed] [object] was [atop/active]."

From that point Naiar and Ahrhi found themselves caught up in rounds of introductions and explanations. Names and stories were exchanged as the translation device became more adept. Ahrhi introduced Naiar as an apprentice armsman, by her example assuring him his violation of the code of the Quest would remain their secret.

Tolan and a force of the Tetrarchy's armsmen were perhaps a day behind, and they advised the gnomes to wait for them in the hollow. The birthing pool was already within the borders of Atwaan. Ahrhi had chosen it because she had planned on going to Atwaan in search of vengeance after she had buried her four children.

The Doctor gnome Lense pronounced Ahrhi's daughters "strong as Brikars," though Kairn attributed their health to having Klingon hearts. The Doctor described Kairn's administration of potions as "overkill," which, given their survival, must have been a mistranscription by the speech boxes. She had also clearly expected Ahrhi to be somehow weak from childbirth and repeated her Brikar assessment.

Ahrhi and Langk earned each other's grudging respect sparring with their disparate weapons, while Naiar devoted himself to learning all he could of the gnomes' many devices.

As they had suspected, the stench of gnome food made the infants wail.

CHAPTER 23

Tolan won the Battle of Atwaan without leading a single charge. His victory was complete without a blow being struck.

The tales of war and battle told around campfires are things of violence and blood. Yet the story of Tolan's victory was a favorite retold for generations. Though no sword was drawn nor arrow nocked, it was a model of valor and wisdom in the face of deadly peril.

At the van of Tolan's advance onto the plain before the city of Atwaan, Ahrhi, the shield maiden of Rowath Hold, sat astride Tolan's finest charger. To her left was the Master gnome Kairn, holding the reins of her mount, for as a girl of the mountains she had never ridden. To her right rode an apprentice armsman without rank—and here the listeners would exchange smiles around the campfire—with a marvelous blue being riding the pommel of his saddle.

Behind these came the vanguard, two elder gnomes—*captains* in their tongue—flanked by four fours of battle gnomes. These wore strange and varied regalia, bristling with strange weapons and all manner of mysterious devices.

And well behind them, astride his second finest charger, came Tolan. At his back were mounted four sixty-fours of Master armsmen of the Tetrarchy with four times as many guardsmen afoot.

But it was not this show of force, nor the strangeness of the gnomes, which caused the armsmen and guardsmen of Atwaan to give ground. They fell back, opening a broad avenue to where the baron sat prepared to direct his forces at the sight of the two infants alive in their mother's arms. Not one of them would have obeyed an order to attack.

Nor would Terant have given it. Even as the invaders marshaled themselves before him, he had eyes only for the two youngest People in all the world. Tolan had to speak his name twice before he looked away.

"Gather all of the women who are with child," Tolan had said without preamble. "The gnomes will ensure their infants live. After that, we will talk."

There was more to the story, of course. Every child, and there were many children, knew how the gnomes had cleansed the water and the air and most of all the birthing pools. The gnomes had calmed the accumulator which in ways mysterious had prevented the Giants—the *crew*—from waking and keeping the world safe and rightly on its path. And the crew had awakened and the world was safe and once again upon its path.

But the gnomes had left and the giants had returned to their slumber beneath the hills and the world was again home only to the People.

And it was their heroes the People remembered. Two warlords, each at the head of a mighty army and each with cheeks matted with tears at the sight of living newborns. Two leaders and one promise: "We will talk."

On that foundation was the Alliance formed. With those words the last war of all the Journey ended.

"Do you suppose the Klingons will ever tell us how this ends?" Gomez asked.

She was standing to the right of Gold's command chair, watching the screen as the People's vessel—they had no name for it—spun in the darkness. The *da Vinci* was so close there was a definite sense of "down" to their perspective. The new navigational array swung into view, then off the screen in a matter of seconds.

"According to Kortag, it won't end for another two centuries," Gold said. "That's how long it will take the People to reach the world the Empire is giving them."

"That strikes me as uncharacteristically generous," observed Tev from the aft stations.

"No exploitable resources, no strategic value, no animal life above trilobites, and it stinks of carbon dioxide," Gold said. "It's exactly the sort of world they'd want to give away."

"Lieutenant Conlon reports that the plasma injectors are fit to carry us as far as Deep Space Station K-7," Haznedl reported. "We can get under way at any time."

"Any unfinished business here, Gomez?" Gold asked.

"Pattie?" Gomez passed the question to the structural engineer at the auxiliary science station next to Tev.

"Structural integrity fields and thruster network are both operating at optimal efficiency," Pattie answered, her dagger *ticking* against her breastplates as she turned from the diagnostic display. "Our mission is technically complete."

"Personally, I'd like to spend another month," Gomez said. "Just to solve the mystery of where the People came from."

"Spectral analysis of their artificial sunlight does not match any of the suspected source systems," Tev said with the air of one pointing out the obvious. "Occam's razor indicates they are refugees from the Luri Cloud. More precisely, a planet orbiting the sun that exploded to create the Luri Cloud."

"That would make the ship close to two thousand years old," Gomez said. "Why would they lock their descendants into a medieval culture for two thousand years?"

"You'll have to double-check with Abramowitz," Gold said, "but maybe they thought that was a viable level of technology for colonizing an uninhabited world. Once the crew got them down, they could survive on their own. A higher tech society would need support till it was established."

"Maybe." Gomez sounded unconvinced. "But it left them helpless in the face of radiation poisoning."

"The builders assumed the crew would always be on hand to deal with mechanical problems."

"They also assumed neighboring solar systems contained uninhabited Class-M planets ripe for their colonization," Tev observed. "Was that hubris or a lack of imagination?"

"More likely lack of choice," Gold said. "They were building a lifeboat, after all."

"Message from the *Qaw'qay'*, sir," Shabalala said. "They remind us we are fourteen minutes from Klingon space."

Tev snorted.

"Wong, lay in a course for Deep Space Station K-7," Gold said. "We've got work to do."

GRAND DESIGNS

Dayton Ward & Kevin Dilmore

CHAPTER 1

Now . . .

Alarm klaxons wailed across the bridge of the *da Vinci,* echoing off the bulkheads and driving directly into David Gold's skull.

"Captain!" Lieutenant Anthony Shabalala shouted from the tactical station. "Orbital Station 4 is moving out of position and beginning a descent toward the planet!"

"Kill the alarm and go to yellow alert." Gold rose from his command chair. "Shabalala, put the station on screen."

The image on the main viewer shifted and he recognized the stout, utilitarian lines of one of Rhaax III's four orbital cargo transfer platforms. It was his first time viewing one of the stations this closely. More than half the size of Spacedock, the Rhaaxan platform possessed none of the more artistic blending of form and function that characterized Earth's primary starship maintenance facility. Even from this distance, Gold could make out the numerous docking ports and cargo storage bay hatches adorning the station's outer hull.

"Hail them," he said, counting silently as contact with Orbital Station 4 was attempted. He felt his anxiety level increase with each second the link was not established. It only got worse when Shabalala shook his head.

"No response, sir."

"Tev and the away team are on that station," Commander Sonya Gomez said. "Have you tried contacting them?"

Nodding, Shabalala replied, "None of the team is answering, Commander."

Sitting at one of the bridge's rear science stations, Fabian Stevens turned in his chair. "Captain, the station isn't just falling from its orbit. It's a controlled maneuver, descending toward the planet at a constant speed and moving under its own power."

"Where the hell is it going?" Gold asked. "It'll burn up if it enters the atmosphere." What was happening over there? Already on board as part of his assigned inspection duties, Tev would have called in the moment anything unexpected occurred. Was he hurt? What about the rest of the away team?

Oh no.

It was so simple, he realized. Even though the station likely would break up as it passed through the atmosphere, killing everyone aboard, the facility's size and mass would still be enough to cause widespread damage when it impacted on Rhaax III's surface. And if some lunatic was currently maneuvering the station so that it would fall on or near a populated area . . .

"How much time until they enter the atmosphere?" he asked.

Shabalala checked his console before replying. "At their present course and speed, about twelve minutes, sir."

"Something else, Captain," Stevens called out. "Sensors are detecting a massive chemical reaction underway inside some of the modules storing oxygen and other compounds for their life support systems."

"Is it a threat to the people on board?" Gold asked.

Stevens shook his head. "I can't say just yet, sir."

"Well, find out," the captain snapped.

Though Ambassador Marshall had been standing silently at the back of the bridge to this point, Gold knew that he would not be able to hold his tongue much longer. The captain's suspicions were confirmed when Marshall stepped forward.

"How many people are aboard the station?" he asked.

"Sensors show two hundred and five life signs," Shabalala reported.

"You have to do something, Captain," Marshall said, his face a mask of anguish.

"I *am* doing something, Ambassador," the captain replied. Despite being irritated at the diplomat's observation of the obvious, Gold chose to ignore it and channel that energy elsewhere. Turning back to the viewscreen, he ordered, "Wong, move us into transporter range."

"Captain," Shabalala called out, "I am receiving an incoming hail from the station."

"On-screen," Gold said.

The viewer changed images again, this time to show a Rhaaxan male, muscled and wearing dark gray worker's coveralls. His orange features were clouded in apparent anger.

"Federation ship," the Rhaaxan said, *"our quarrel is not with you, but rather the government of our home planet. Do not attempt to interfere with us in any way. You are directed to keep your vessel out of range of your weapons and matter transfer systems. We have your officers in custody here and though I do not wish to harm them, I will kill them if necessary."*

"What do you want?" the captain asked.

"Our freedom, once and for all. Either that is granted today, or everyone on Rhaax will die."

CHAPTER 2

Three weeks earlier . . .

Sitting in his customary place at the head of the table in the *U.S.S. da Vinci*'s conference room, Captain David Gold schooled his features and put on his best smile, and with practiced ease allowed none of the irritation he felt toward Ambassador Gabriel Marshall to show.

Gold had dealt with the ambassador on infrequent occasions in recent years, but all of those encounters had taken place via subspace communications link. Most of those interactions had also been quite unpleasant. With little patience for diplomats in general, and Marshall in particular, Gold was thankful to have avoided face-to-face meetings with the man to this point. Being the captain of a vessel assigned to deep space duty helped in that regard.

Naturally, karma had therefore seen fit to bring the ambassador across space to him.

"We've been here nearly a week now, Captain," Marshall said, "and your people haven't found anything. I'm sure I don't have to remind you that the longer this process takes, the longer the approval of the Rhaaxans' application for Federation membership is delayed."

Gold knew that the government of Rhaax III was enthusiastic about joining the United Federation of Planets, having tendered their application several years ago. Though the process of admitting a new member to the Federation was anything but simple, it was not until discussions between the Rhaaxans and the Federation started that things became truly chaotic.

"Ambassador," Gold said, "my people are working as quickly and thoroughly as they can. This whole *megillah* has been problematic from the start, and even you have to admit that Starfleet and the Federation haven't made things any easier."

It was during initial talks with the Rhaaxan government that Starfleet expressed interest in establishing a base on the system's fifth planet, where a colony had been founded nearly two centuries earlier. The system's proximity to Romulan space made it an attractive location for a Starfleet facility that might serve as the base of operations for a new series of observation outposts along the border. Rhaax V, or Numai as it had been named by the colonists, also possessed rich deposits of dilithium and other useful minerals. With all of this on the discussion table, along with the government of Rhaax III's eagerness to open up trade routes with the Federation, membership and cooperation seemed a certainty.

Unfortunately, the people already living on Numai had other ideas.

"Of course I can admit that things haven't gone as smoothly as we would like, Captain," Marshall replied, "but it's because they haven't that I'm here. It's my job to see that this dispute between the Rhaaxans and their colonists is settled quickly and amicably for everyone involved."

Unable to stop himself, Gold chuckled at Marshall's bold statement. "No disrespect to your diplomatic prowess, Ambassador, but that's a goal that's easier stated than accomplished. From everything I've seen, the Rhaaxans on both planets appear to be set in their ways."

Established at great expense in money and matériel, the colony on Numai had remained an independent entity since its founding, charting its own development while maintaining ties with Rhaax III through trade of minerals, crops, and the like. Part of the original agreement between the settlers and the government was that just over a century from now, the colony would become a sanctioned state of Rhaax III, falling under its control while sharing the fruits of its development for the betterment of all. In the beginning, that had seemed a sensible and agreeable course of action.

Then, the Federation arrived.

Since learning of Starfleet's interest in establishing a base on the colony planet, the Rhaaxan government had been applying steady pressure on the colony, trying to force its early return to the fold. The colonists so far had resisted such a move. Fearing that the identity and culture they had labored to create over two centuries would be lost upon being absorbed back into the larger Rhaaxan civilization, the colony's leadership had instead made known its intent to apply for separate Federation membership.

"Let me worry about smoothing things over between Rhaax III and its colony, Captain," Marshall said. "It's only a matter of time until I steer them to an agreement."

Had he not forced himself to keep his expression neutral, Gold surely would have rolled his eyes at the ambassador's pronouncement. While the *da Vinci*'s current assignment had taken several days to become boring, tiresome, and frustrating, the diplomat had arrived with those qualities already operating at full capacity—and yet still had done his level best to improve in those areas.

However, despite any animosity Gold might feel toward Marshall, the captain knew that the diplomat was good at his job. He would have to be, from what Gold had learned in his own research into the Rhaaxan situation. The populations of both worlds had mixed feelings about how to solve their mutual problem. Polls had shown that while many citizens agreed with their governments, a nearly equal number of both planets' populations felt the colonists had earned the right to run their world as they saw fit.

The Federation had mediated several attempts to debate the issues, but in the end, neither side was willing to budge from its position. As time passed, tensions rose, rhetoric sharpened, and the rift between the two planets had grown to a chasm, a fact soon demonstrated with alarming clarity.

"This latest incident would seem to be a major obstacle to overcome," Gold said. "It was just arguing around a table until the Rhaaxan government authorized an attack on the colony."

And it had not stopped there. Rhaax III's military resources were limited, and the colonists were able to defend themselves long enough for the assault to be called off. Following that failed action, the Rhaaxan leaders had upped the stakes by threatening to unleash a biogenic weapon. Such an attack would force an evacuation of Numai. By cooperation or coercion, the government rationalized, the colonists would return to the embrace of their mother world.

"The very idea is appalling," Gold continued, "but what's even more alarming is that after all of this, we're still sitting here, considering Federation membership for these people."

For the first time since his arrival aboard the *da Vinci,* Gold saw Marshall's normal bluster falter. The ambassador leaned back in his chair, closed his eyes, and rubbed the bridge of his nose. The captain said nothing, allowing the other man a moment to collect himself.

Returning his attention to Gold, Marshall said, "Ordinarily, you'd be right, Captain. It goes against everything we represent to welcome with open arms one society willing to decimate another for its own ends. However, we caused the problems between the Rhaaxans and their colonists through our own stupidity. Our putting the cart before the horse, getting excited about the strategic possibilities this system offers, has brought these people to the brink of war. Now it's my responsibility to resolve this situation peacefully, and I can't do that without help from you and your team."

Though he was amused at the notion of how painful such an admission had to be for a man like Marshall, Gold chose not to mention it. Instead, he said, "The Rhaaxans could have chosen a path other than confrontation to solve their problems. The colonists were the ones who called for disarmament, so at least they appear to want to work things out."

The Federation had responded by sending in the *da Vinci* and its S.C.E. contingent tasked as weapons inspectors to oversee the collection and disposal of any large-scale weapons, conventional or otherwise, the Rhaaxans might possess. Commander Gomez had wasted no time putting her team of engineers to work, sending them to key facilities on both planets as well as the family of space stations orbiting both worlds that were used to transfer cargo shipped back and forth across the system.

Having apparently regained his usual smug demeanor, Marshall said, "The colony's desire for a quick resolution is precisely why I find your team's progress discouraging."

"It's only discouraging if you hope to find something, Ambassador," Gold replied. "According to Gomez, there's nothing for us *to* find. All large-scale conventional weapons were accounted for, and there's no evidence of any biogenic weapons or that there ever *were* any." The inspections had been underway for nearly a week when Gomez made the pronouncement: The threat against the colony was a hoax. When the Rhaaxan Assembly was confronted with her team's findings, the governing officials had confessed that no biogenic weapon existed, despite their best efforts to produce one.

"It was all a ruse," Gold continued. "The assembly saw it as their last chance to convince the colony to stand with them in their quest to join the Federation." Shaking his head, he added, "If that's true, and so far we have no reason to believe it isn't, then perhaps we can concentrate on working out a lasting agreement between these people."

He leaned forward until his forearms rested on the conference table. As he did so, he caught himself staring for an extra moment at the prosthetic that had replaced his left hand, lost during the tragic mission to Galvan VI. The biosynthetic hand looked real, felt real, and was superior to his original hand in every measurable sense—a triumph of biomechanical engineering that had been the best way to provide him with a replacement for the loss he had suffered.

In a similar fashion, it now fell to Marshall and the *da Vinci* crew to craft a solution here, one that was better than leaving the Rhaaxans to their own devices.

"What happens after all of this?" Gold asked. "Once we straighten this mess out, it still leaves the issue of allowing the Rhaaxans to join the Federation. You can't possibly think they're ready."

Marshall shook his head. "Perhaps not the home planet, but the colony has potential. Even after the threats leveled against them, they've handled this situation with remarkable poise and grace. There may be a bright side to this whole thing after all."

"Starfleet wanting that base on their planet doesn't hurt, either," Gold countered.

To the captain's surprise, Marshall did not refute the observation or even respond with his usual air of irritation. "I'd be lying if I said that wasn't a factor, Captain. Given what the Federation has been through, we need eyes, ears, and friends wherever we can find them."

Before Gold could comment further, the whistle of the ship's intercom filled the air.

"Bridge to Captain Gold," called the voice of Lieu-

tenant Commander Mor glasch Tev, the *da Vinci*'s second officer. *"Commander Gomez is hailing us from the surface and is requesting to speak with you and Ambassador Marshall."*

"Put her through, Tev," Gold replied, directing his attention to the viewscreen on the conference lounge's far wall. The image on the display shifted from a schematic of the *da Vinci* to the face of Sonya Gomez.

"What can we do for you, Gomez?" he asked. Though her appearance was as immaculate as always, Gold noted the shadows under his first officer's eyes and her slightly paled complexion. Gomez and her teams had been working steadily for days on their current assignment and the strain was beginning to show around the edges, but Gomez herself had also been pulling double duty as she kept Marshall apprised of the current situation. The diplomat had deluged her with his various requests, demands, and whatnot for weeks now.

Gold had wanted to step in and say something, but this mission was one of those rare occasions where the S.C.E. team's autonomy worked in Marshall's favor. Gomez and her team had received their orders on this mission directly from Captain Montgomery Scott, head of the S.C.E. back at Starfleet Command. Scott's superiors had directed full cooperation and support for Marshall's mission to the Rhaaxan system, leaving Gold and the rest of the *da Vinci* crew as little more than interested bystanders.

Gomez had taken a small away team to investigate one of the prime target areas on Rhaax III's southernmost continent, a scientific research laboratory that was one of several sites suspected of housing secret weapons development operations. Even before she replied, a twinge in his gut told Gold that for Gomez to want to talk to both him and Marshall, she must have found something noteworthy.

His instincts were confirmed as soon as he heard the commander's voice.

"Hello, Captain," Gomez said. *"I've got good news and bad news. We've found evidence of advanced biogenics research. Advanced for them, anyway. Their level of technology is roughly equivalent to mid-twenty-second-century Earth."*

"So they do have biogenic weapons?" Gold asked.

On the screen, Gomez shook her head. *"Not yet, sir, but they've been working hard to create just the type of weapon they threatened to use against the colonists. If they keep to the same track they're currently on, they'll be able to field a weapon in about eighteen months."*

Leaning forward in his chair, Marshall's brow furrowed as he listened to Gomez's report. "Commander, what do you mean by 'keep to the same track'? I take it you haven't given us the bad news yet."

Gold noted not only a distinct pause after Marshall's question, but also a fleeting look of unease on Gomez's face. Was she hesitating for some reason? Whatever was giving her doubts, she got control of it quickly before replying.

"We've scanned their computer records, Ambassador, and found a lot of data on numerous failed experiments they've conducted over the last several years. The thing is . . ."

Her voice trailed off and Gold again saw the uncertainty in her eyes. What was wrong with her? Was whatever she and her away team discovered that serious?

"Gomez?" he prompted after a few more seconds.

"Captain," she continued, *"even with the conclusions*

reached during some of these botched attempts, they got close to a solution a couple of times without even realizing it. Someone could actually stumble across a correct biogenic sequence by accident and have the makings of a superweapon in just a few months. Sooner, if they push it."

Neither Gold nor Marshall said anything as the revelation sank in. Though the Rhaaxan government had been bluffing when they had threatened the colonists with a global weapon, they had been working to create just such a device. Had the means been at their disposal, would the assembly have actually authorized its use?

Anxiety clouding his features, Marshall looked to Gold. "What do you suggest we do about this?"

To Gomez, the captain said, "Impound any research data and material you feel relevant to your discovery. Have it transported back to the ship for further analysis." Then he looked to Marshall. "Knowing just how close the Rhaaxans are might be good information to have at some point."

"One more thing, Captain," Marshall added. "I recommend that we refrain from discussing what the commander's found with anyone, not even the other inspection teams, at least until we have the situation completely under control."

Gold did not like the idea of keeping potentially vital information from the rest of the crew, particularly those involved in inspections around the planet, but he could see the ambassador's point. "I'm going to have to agree with Mr. Marshall. Pass the word to the rest of your team, and let's keep this under wraps for now."

"Aye, sir. I'll take care of it. Gomez out."

As the communication ended and the viewscreen went dark, Marshall said, "Meanwhile, your people should finish out the inspections. There's no telling what else they might find."

Gold agreed, knowing that the ambassador would use the time to continue mediating discussions between the Rhaaxans and the colonists, working to find some common ground upon which to build a peaceful, lasting solution that would eventually allow the Federation to welcome new members.

Good luck, the captain mused.

CHAPTER 3

"*The makings of a superweapon in just a few months. Sooner, if they push it.*"

Even as she reached out to silence the playback of the recorded message, the human female's voice continued to ring in Randa Palakur's ears.

Could it be true? Did mere months, possibly weeks, separate the people of Rhaax from unlocking power of a type unmatched in their history? The Starfleet engineers seemed to have confirmed it, apparently choosing to keep that information to themselves.

"Do you need to hear it again, Prefect?" A voice from the seat next to hers broke Randa's thoughts, reminding her that she was still in the meeting that Shalowon, her director of security, had requested in her private chambers.

"No, that won't be necessary," she replied. "How did you come to have this transmission?"

Shalowon leaned closer to her, his features turning smug. Dressed as he was in the normal dark green uniform of the security service, impeccably tailored to his muscular physique, and contrasting sharply with his pale orange skin, the confident smile he affected made him seem even more dangerous than Randa knew him to be.

"My people have been monitoring the Federation teams' communications since their arrival," he said. "There was little of interest until we heard this exchange just today."

"I suppose it was prudent to eavesdrop, Shalowon, given the circumstances," Randa said, "but allow me to feel a little uncomfortable that we have reached such a point with the Federation."

"I am starting to forget why we wanted them here in the first place, Prefect," Shalowon replied, straightening in his seat. "I daresay our problems with the colony might be manageable without their interference."

Randa allowed the security director his jaundiced view, despite the fact it was he who coordinated the ill-fated military action against the colony that had resulted only in a decimation of the Rhaaxan forces not equipped for such an engagement. Shalowon made no secret of his belief that Rhaaxan armies were hamstrung by the reluctance of the assembly to use all military options at their disposal, and his pronouncements of that view only served to turn a wave of popular sentiment against the leaders who authorized the attack. That led to the assembly's attempt to threaten the colony with a nonexistent biogenic weapon, a threat that was defused by the very Federation officers invited by the assembly to help mediate the whole affair. Randa knew Shalowon remained convinced that the colonists' fears of biological warfare would have led to the dissolution of the jurisdictional pact and paved the way for Federation admission.

"Prefect," another voice said from across the table, "if I may?"

Randa smiled a bit as Malik leaned forward in his chair, noticing the cool look he directed toward Shalowon. Her aide had long been a supporter of the colony's interests during discussions of the Rhaaxan Assembly. Of them all, Malik had spent the most time in person at the colony, making visits there as part of numerous official delegations. The content of his remarks would not likely come as a surprise, but Randa had grown to appreciate his perspective on Rhaaxan issues as they might relate to the colonists.

"You have been uncharacteristically silent, my friend," she said. "Please, share your thoughts."

"I think even Shalowon would agree that the objective eyes of the Federation delegation serve both Rhaaxans and the people of the settlement on Numai. It is a potentially volatile triangle of negotiation we find ourselves within, but no one side is pitted against any other."

"If the Federation is poring over our databases and preventing our scientists from reaching research goals," Shalowon countered, "that should be enough reason to believe they have sided with the colony and have lost interest in what we have to offer."

Holding out his hands in a gesture of supplication, Malik said, "Or maybe they are just protecting us from ourselves."

"Both of you, please," Randa said, hoping she could separate the men from their personal agendas for the time being. "Shalowon, the Federation is not preventing us from accomplishing anything. They merely observed that we were closer than we realized in our research. Given the circumstances, their alarm is justified. But we know they will see many things we cannot, and that benefits us more than it harms us. Their resources and technology are much greater than ours, and that is but one reason we have petitioned for membership these past years."

"Then why aren't they offering to help?" Shalowon asked. "Surely they can . . ."

"Help create a weapon?" Malik laughed derisively. "The Federation is not in the business of giving a society the means to subjugate another people."

Shalowon glowered at the political adviser. "We are *one* people, Malik, although I am sure you and the colonists think that we are some sort of oppressors waiting to strike."

"We threatened to wipe them out with a weapon. . . ."

Shalowon cut him off. "It was a bluff."

"With a *weapon,*" Malik repeated, this time with an edge in his voice, "that we seem very close to be developing for real!"

"Enough!" Randa surprised herself with the force of her outburst. "I called you here to offer me clear counsel, so set your tempers aside. I recognize now that our rush to threaten the colony was wrong. Regardless of where our research on biogenic agents may be, we have agreed to halt it. This is not the issue at hand now."

Shalowon spoke with a softened tone. "You heard the Starfleet woman as clearly as I did, Prefect. Do you not agree that the issue must be revisited? We must be on the verge of a discovery that will make the colonists seriously consider our intent to establish our authority there. Continuing our research and reviewing our studies allows us to have the option of force should we need it."

Randa paused, searching her mind once again for a means through which she could convince the people of two worlds to share her vision. She felt so close to a solution that it seemed tangible: an alliance with the Federation that would benefit Rhaaxans as well as the Numai colony, and possibly provide a way for the colony to enjoy its independent state while securing enforceable trade agreements vital to life on Rhaax.

Have we come to this?

Turning to Malik, she said, "If only I could understand why the colony so strongly opposes the idea of joining the Federation."

"You have answered part of your own question, Prefect, and you don't even realize it," Malik said and offered a smile. "Centuries have passed, yet we on Rhaax still refer to the Numai settlement as a colony; *our* colony. Look at how things have evolved there. Yes, we remain one people, as Shalowon said. Many on Numai want to honor the original pact and rejoin the fold under one jurisdiction. However, they want to do it as a union of two equals, not as one government exerting its authority over another. In a sense, a growing number of those on Numai see a Federation membership as trading one offworld ruler for another. Their world is thriving and expanding. In recent years, we on Rhaax have demonstrated only that we are growing in our dependence on them."

"We do depend on them," Randa admitted. "Their shipments of ores and energy sources have become necessary for our economy's continued growth. But, Malik, surely the colo—well, the Numai settlement's leaders recognize that we continue to offer them a great deal of support as well?"

"They certainly do recognize that, and are willing to

lord it over us when the time is right," Shalowon said. "Without adherence to the pact as written, the colony could simply abandon its trade with us. It would not surprise me if they secretly want to ally with the Federation on their own, without us."

Malik said, "I can assure you, Prefect, that is not the case."

"But you can see," Shalowon said, "the Federation is courting us because it has its eye on the colony. From a strategic point of view, Rhaax offers nothing. Without something to tie us together, we have no unique appeal to a group of worlds as vast and as diverse as the United Federation of Planets. But the colonists might enjoy individual membership in a group that lets them avoid their obligations to Rhaax while we wither away and die."

Randa felt a growing sense of alarm as Shalowon voiced precisely what she secretly feared. Rhaax might have lied about having a biogenic weapon to wield against the colony, but the colonists did not need to bluff about the potentially devastating weapon they themselves held, one born of dependence. All that was required was for the colonists to cease interplanetary trade with Rhaax. Should colony leaders ever wish to bend the wills of the Rhaaxan people, the merest threat of such action would carry the weight of a dozen attack fleets.

"Can't the colonists see how Federation membership is best for us both, Malik?" She was unable to keep the sound of a plea from her voice. "Don't they understand that benefits are afforded to us both?"

Her aide paused before answering. "I am getting the idea, Prefect, that Shalowon's opinions of the Numai settlers' motivations are starting to color yours. Do you believe they are plotting against Rhaax?"

I wish I knew.

Her failure to say anything after a moment seemed to be answer enough for Malik. Nodding in resigned acceptance, he rose from the table and bowed his head. "At this point, I have little to add to this conversation, so if you will excuse me, I will return to my duties."

As she watched Malik leave the chamber, Randa hoped she might not hear any gloating words from Shalowon. It would make what she had to say that much more difficult. She turned to her remaining advisor but could not meet his gaze. Thankfully, he held his tongue.

"Please notify the science ministry of this new development," she said softly. "It might be best if they reviewed their studies and pursued new courses with haste."

"Say no more, Prefect," Shalowon said, nearly springing to his feet. "I cannot help but think this is the best way to proceed."

Randa kept her eyes on the table and slowly nodded.

But at what cost?

CHAPTER 4

Absently sipping from his glass, Fabian Stevens tried to clear his head of the day's events while sitting in the fourth new eatery he had tried in a week.

His feet and lower back ached from hours of walking, scouring warehouses and industrial sites, scanning and rescanning areas that raised the concerns of security specialists, peering into storage containers of all types, and ultimately writing and submitting reports for everything that he saw and, more typically, did not see. He had lost track of the times this routine had been repeated. Now that he had finished this latest site inspection, he and his team would be transported to the next location fitting the profile for weapons manufacture or storage and begin the seemingly futile process all over again.

In the weapons department, as far as Stevens was concerned, Rhaax III was turning out to be a dud.

He politely held off his meal order for a third time from a passing server, a heavyset Rhaaxan woman whom Stevens could tell was losing interest in him. He arched his spine against the unyielding wooden back of his seat, an uncomfortable bench in a cramped booth situated in what he hoped would be an inconspicuous area of the eatery.

Given the political climate of Rhaax III these days, he thought a low profile might be best for him and any fellow S.C.E. members, should they still join him for dinner as planned. A few weeks ago, Captain Gold had given permission for the crew to visit the planet during their off hours, and it had not taken long for Stevens to set his tastes on a small resort town in the planet's temperate zone, one with a respectable pub in walking distance to a quiet beach.

That was before the Rhaaxan Assembly decided to restrict the travels of Starfleet personnel to the limits of the capital city of Longon. The entire area was grimy and unappealing in Stevens's eyes, nothing if not the polar opposite of a resort town, and he found his amusement factor for all of Rhaax III dropping several notches since the dictum. Now, he was weighing the relative merits of his current surroundings with that of the mess hall back on the *da Vinci.*

At least this place has free snacks, he mused as he used a finger to flick a path around what appeared to be seasoned, toasted bits of purplish grain in a bowl. *I'm assuming this stuff is edible. Of course, I assumed that on Kharzh'ulla, and spent three days in sickbay for my trouble.*

A clatter of sound from the establishment's front door made Stevens look up to see a trio of Rhaaxans, burly laborers from the look of them and ones who obviously began their evening revelry much earlier than Stevens had, making their way through the dining area. They were laughing, one reeling a bit after a hearty backslapping from another, as they settled at a table near Stevens.

One of the trio, an older male judging by the harsh lines etching his orange face, made eye contact with Stevens and stiffened a bit. Stevens smiled and raised his water glass in reply, but the Rhaaxan loudly scooted his chair to face away from him. He leaned in to his fellow diners and said something in a low voice that elicited a derisive chuckle at the table.

The assembly's dictum meant Starfleet personnel faced much more frequent contact with the populace of Longon than they had in other locations. Stevens was quick to note that the residents of the capital city seemed more attuned to the political nuances of the *da Vinci*'s mission than the general public elsewhere on the planet. Not that the situation had led to anyone being in danger, but he felt that the general air of tension had been ratcheted up in the city. Stevens took another sip from his glass as his thoughts led him to one inexorable conclusion.

Duff would have hated this place.

Even with the unwelcome feelings he had been getting from the locals of late, Stevens did not waver in his support for the *da Vinci*'s mission on Rhaax III. In his time on the planet, he saw that the Rhaaxan society would reap many benefits from Federation membership. While being warp-capable for only a few years, the Rhaaxans' general enthusiasm for learning and for accepting offworld cultures was obvious to him, politics aside. He also understood the tactical advantages that a starbase or outpost of some sort in this system would afford the Federation given its proximity to the Romulan border. It seemed on the surface to be a mutually beneficial arrangement.

With that, it was obvious why Federation leaders wanted these people and their planet thoroughly checked out by Starfleet personnel. The idea that the Rhaaxan Assembly would threaten its own colony with compliance or destruction obviously went against the grain of Federation thinking, and the thought of colonists being strong-armed by leaders on another planet rankled Stevens. Growing up in the Rigel Colonies and assisting with his parents' shuttle service there, he had a great appreciation for the struggles of a burgeoning colony and the drive and goals of the people who lived there.

Okay, too much thinking and not enough eating, Stevens thought as he felt his stomach grumble. He toyed with the idea of trying the purple stuff before him, when a clear voice rose above the surrounding background noise.

"Mr. Stevens, you are in violation of a direct order," said a voice from right behind him. "No one is to be in a civilian area without a security escort."

He smiled in recognition as the speaker made no attempt to disguise her voice. "I don't pay much attention to orders like that, Commander, since my girlfriend runs secur . . ."

Stevens's voice trailed off as he looked up to see Sonya Gomez accompanied by her escort, Domenica Corsi. "Uh, hi," he said, fumbling a bit at the appearance of the very girlfriend he had just glibly mentioned. "I didn't expect to see you both down here."

Gomez laughed as she slid into the booth seat across from him, and he shot her a glare in return. She obviously enjoyed seeing him embarrass himself in front of Corsi, whom they both knew continued to be unsettled by mentions of her personal relationships while on duty. The *da Vinci*'s security chief was known among the crew for her strict, professional demeanor, something she had told Stevens many times would not change where he was concerned no matter what their personal connection might be.

"The commander asked me to accompany her for dinner," Corsi said, allowing a slight smile as she slid into the seat next to Stevens. "At least *she's* mindful of a standing security order."

"I guess my request for an escort got lost in the shuffle," Stevens replied. "Mind pulling double-duty for us?"

"It depends on what they've got to eat in this . . . place," Corsi said, running a fingertip along the tabletop and scoffing at the greasy streak it created. "What is it you see in these bars? The foo—"

"Oh good, more Starfleet," came a loud voice from the nearby group. "Guess we'd better behave, boys. We have guests tonight."

Making eye contact once again with the aged laborer, Stevens tried to smooth things a bit by laughing along with the man. "And here I was the one trying to behave," he said, but the man returned only a deadpan expression. Turning back to the table, Stevens said in a lower voice, "They've been drinking."

"That's obvious," Gomez said. "We ought to leave."

Shaking his head, Stevens replied, "This is the first time they've said anything all night, and if we get up and go, it'll look like we know we don't belong here. It'll be fine."

Gomez looked at Corsi, who shrugged in reply. "Okay, but at the first sign of trouble, we're out of here."

"Promise," Stevens said as he searched the dining area for their server. "So, how go the inspections?"

Gomez sighed and slumped a bit in her seat. "Nothing new, if that's what you mean." Both engineers knew better than to talk in public about the one key find they had made several weeks ago. In fact, Gomez had not wanted to talk much about that discovery at all, even in the relative privacy offered aboard ship. She claimed that Ambassador Marshall had ordered her not to discuss the subject, a directive that, so far as Stevens could tell, was not sitting well with her.

"Sometimes," Gomez continued, "I get the feeling they're trying to hide something from us, but damned if I know what."

Stevens shrugged. "There's some discomfort from my Rhaaxan escorts, kind of like they're just waiting for the other shoe to drop on their admission request. But I'm not getting a feeling of anything underhanded going on, if that's what you mean."

"I'm not sure what I mean, but they seem to be watching us pretty closely for people who claim they've got nothing up their sleeves." Rubbing the back of her neck, she added, "We can talk more about it later. I'm just glad to be sitting for a change."

"Fine by me," Stevens replied. "I haven't seen a menu yet, but I'm sure we're in for a taste treat to please the senses."

"Or assault them," Corsi said. "I think I smell some sort of petroleum by-product coming from the kitchen."

Stevens laughed. "That's gravy, my dear. I saw someone eating an open-faced sandwich smothered in the stuff. I don't know what it is, but I'm going to try it."

"Then maybe you could eat somewhere else," Corsi retorted.

"An excellent suggestion," announced a baritone voice. "Then I can take his seat." Stevens turned to see a smiling Mor glasch Tev standing alongside Carol Abramowitz.

It was not long ago that Stevens would have refused to yield his place at any table to Tev, the *da Vinci*'s recently added Tellarite second officer. His haughty and self-important demeanor rubbed Stevens wrong, especially since Tev now occupied the position once held by his deceased best friend, and Tev fit into the shoes of Kieran Duffy like a square stem bolt in a round socket. Still, Stevens knew he played an equal role in the two of them getting along as shipmates, so he had done his level best to set any raw feelings aside and be civil.

"Pom glittathay na," he said, gesturing to the seats opposite his.

Tev gave Stevens a look of genuine surprise. "That's as close to a proper intonation of my native tongue as I've heard from a human other than Bartholomew in quite a long time. And with a southern-continent accent, I might add. *Gradunk, merchubo.*"

"Uh, sure, I think." Stevens smiled. "It's been a while since I've practiced my Tellarite language skills."

"Especially in a bar," said Abramowitz, smirking as she slid into the seat next to Gomez. "Come to think of it, I remember the last time you—"

"Moving right along," Stevens blurted to cut her off. "May I ask, before the lieutenant commander here does, just where is your security escort?"

"Why, I brought her," said Tev with a nod toward Abramowitz. "But I hardly expect any trouble."

Stevens was about to point out that Abramowitz was a cultural specialist, not a security guard, but he froze as he watched Tev turn and approach the table with the vocal Rhaaxan laborers. "Pardon me, might I make use of this empty seat?"

The elder Rhaaxan turned from his conversation to look up at Tev. "Oh, be my guest, Starfleet," he said. "Take it and go home."

"I'll just take it over here, thank you," Tev said. "There's no need to cause a problem."

As Tev returned to the booth with his chair, the man called back, "We had no problems until you arrived here."

"We are here by invitation of your own assembly, sir," the Tellarite replied. "Perhaps you might do well to pay closer attention to the dealings of your leaders." He smiled to his companions as he slid his seat to the table. "So, what's for dinner?"

Stevens moved to put a lid on what he thought could brew into a conflict with the locals. "Tev, those three look like they've had a bit much to drink, so it might be a good idea to . . ."

"Please, Specialist," Tev said with a wave of his hand. "I don't want a problem either, but I'm hardly one to shy away from a civil conversation."

Stevens looked to Gomez with wide eyes. A civil conversation in a Tellarite's opinion typically included name-calling, slurs against one's appearance and heritage, and a good deal of shouting. "Uh, Commander?"

"He's right, Tev," she said. "Those guys—"

"Hey, Starfleet!"

Stevens winced. It looked as though the shouting would begin from the Rhaaxans' table, after all.

"Perhaps *you* might tell us what our leaders are doing?" the elder Rhaaxan asked. "Maybe you could also tell us how to run our colony and our businesses, as well?"

Tev turned toward the shouting man. "By Kera and Phinda, I might have quite a number of good ideas for dealing with your colony," he said, "starting with your letting it develop rather than making empty and cowardly threats."

The Rhaaxan bolted from his chair, which tipped and clattered to the floor. "I do not make threats that I cannot back up."

Tev rose as well, but in a calmer manner that Stevens hoped might not translate to the Rhaaxan as a challenge. "There's no need to show off for your friends when it is obvious you are in no physical condition to best me in a fight."

Knowing this was not the time for Tellarite candor, Stevens got up and put a hand on Tev's shoulder. "Look, why don't we all just agree to respect each other's positions and eat in peace."

But the idea did not slow the approach of the Rhaaxan worker, who staggered a bit as he stepped forward. "I have a better idea." He took a swing at the jaw of the stocky Tellarite, who easily dodged the drunken punch. The worker followed with a second swing, which found Tev's paunchy gut but was not enough even to make the stocky officer waver from his stance.

Tev stepped forward, drawing a breath and sucking his large belly inward before huffing and throwing out his chest and stomach. The impact knocked the Rhaaxan to the floor, but before he could scramble to his feet, the two other laborers were up and heading over to the brawl.

Corsi squirmed in her seat in an effort to reach her phaser while sitting in the cramped booth. Stevens saw that Gomez also caught sight of the weapon now coming up in her hand.

"No, Domenica!" she shouted as she slapped the combadge on her chest. "Gomez to *da Vinci.* Five for emergency beamout. Now!"

As Stevens felt the telltale sensations of the transporter's energy beam, he wondered what Captain Gold's reaction would be.

I can just hear it now, he thought. *"This is just what I was hoping to avoid down there, and I'm . . ."*

CHAPTER 5

"Very disappointed in all of you," Gold said, pacing the floor before the quintet of his crew assembled in the *da Vinci's* observation lounge.

The last thing the captain expected to be doing before bed was hearing a report on a planetside bar brawl and meting out punishment to his highest-ranking officers. It was not that word of an altercation on Rhaax III took him completely by surprise, but were he to have made a list of likely candidates for that first blowup, the names of the five persons before him would not have been at the top.

"Tev, I understand the need for self-defense," he said, sizing up his second officer, "but knocking down a Rhaaxan, and a drunk one at that, is unnecessary in the least."

Returning his gaze, the Tellarite said, "It seemed to be a civil conversation to me, sir. I will not make that mistake again."

"I'm sure that you won't." Turning to Corsi he said, "Gomez was right to bail you all out of that place before someone saw a Starfleet officer with a phaser draw down on some drunks. I'm sure there were alternatives, Corsi. Let's explore them next time."

As Corsi offered no answer, he continued, trying hard not to sound like a lecturing parent. "People, we need to be sensitive to the situation on Rhaax III. The assembly, as I see it, is having second thoughts about inviting us here, and we aren't leaving until we can straighten out a mess that we as the Federation had a hand in creating. Those folks on the planet, the ones we deal with as inspectors or chance upon as civilians, have all sorts of conceptions about our presence here. The accuracy of those conceptions is not something we should debate in public—not among ourselves, and especially not with the Rhaaxans. Am I clear?"

A round of affirmative answers came from the crewmen as the door to the briefing room slid open and Ambassador Marshall entered. Gold deliberately did not look in the man's direction, intent on continuing his talk with the crew. "Now, regarding future contact with the Rhaaxans, our best—"

"Captain, if I might interrupt," Marshall said, drawing a quiet sigh from Gold. "I think it would be best for us to discuss how we should handle contact with the Rhaaxans before giving new orders to the crew."

Us?

"Ambassador, I am very certain about how we ought to proceed," Gold said. "How I direct the crew won't affect your mission or your discussions with the Rhaaxans."

"Why, of course it will, Captain, if riots break out every time someone on the planet is spotted in a Starfleet uniform."

"What happened down there can hardly be described as a riot, Ambassador."

"Nevertheless, Captain," Marshall replied, "I just think you and your crew would be more effective on this mission by staying on task and being more sensitive to our hosts."

Drawing a breath to keep from snapping a retort at the ambassador, Gold instead turned to his officers. "We will continue this later. You are dismissed."

"Not Commander Gomez, please," Marshall said. "I have need of her right away."

Gold watched as the other four left, with Abramowitz flashing him a sympathetic look that helped take some of the edge off the slow burn he was feeling toward Marshall. Once the door slid closed behind her, he turned to the ambassador. "I had hoped that even you would show me some respect in front of my own crew."

Marshall stepped closer, and the move fired up a surge of defensiveness that the captain himself wished had not come so quickly. "For this mission, the crew is in essence as much mine as it is yours, Captain."

"Only the S.C.E. detail is under your authority," Gold said, reminding himself of that nuance as much as Marshall. "I still run this ship."

"Then please tend to it," Marshall said. "I need Commander Gomez to review these reports with me before my meeting with Prefect Randa."

"I wasn't done debriefing the commander."

"Yes, but my meeting is in less than an hour, so I must take precedence," Marshall said as he took a seat, Gold's own seat, at the briefing table. "I'm sure you understand. It might be easier if you allowed me to speak with the commander in private, please."

Gold squelched an urge to say anything more to Marshall once he saw the expression on Gomez's face. He could tell from her pained look that she hardly relished the idea of working with the ambassador but was bound by orders from Starfleet Command, and was equally certain she would come to him for guidance if she felt conflicted by her duties or responsibilities.

Realizing that his scuffles with Marshall were not making things easier on her or the rest of the crew, Gold decided at that moment to rein himself in. He felt sure that, should the situation deteriorate to the extreme, he could count on Gomez and the others to follow his lead and not be second-guessed by the ambassador.

He had intended to leave wordlessly, but Marshall spoke just as Gold stepped into the corridor. "One more thing, Captain: Please restrict the crew's off-duty activities to the ship, given the circumstances."

The captain closed his eyes for a moment to ensure his bearing remained in place, then turned back to the ambassador. "My crew is working hard on this assignment, Mr. Marshall, and I believe they merit a little down time when they can find it."

"Given the current climate in the capital city," Marshall replied, "it might be wise to remove the potential for repeats of tonight's incident. It would also help if you went down and apologized in person to that bar's proprietor. Pay for the broken glasses or whatever."

Not even bothering to respond to the request, Gold turned and left the room. As the door slid shut to block his view of the seemingly smug Marshall, he wished he could just as easily block the man from his ship, and his mind.

CHAPTER 6

As he walked the corridors of the massive Rhaaxan orbital platform with P8 Blue and Soloman, Tev made a conscious effort to keep from touching anything. Having brushed up against a bulkhead and pulling back a hand covered in grime, it was a mistake he was determined not to repeat. It seemed that everything, from the walls to the surfaces of control consoles to storage containers and tool lockers scattered throughout the station, was filthy. If he could have used anti-gravity boots to avoid making contact with the deck plating, he would have done that, too.

"If there is an afterlife and a place of damnation," he said, "then this could very well be its lobby." He grimaced as he tried once more to clean his still-soiled fingers on a small towel from his tool kit. Once again, his attempt failed.

Walking beside the *da Vinci*'s second officer, P8 Blue

said, "As an engineer, surely this is not the first time your hands have gotten dirty?"

Tev snorted derisively as he regarded her. "On rare occasions, of course, when no other alternatives presented themselves. Thankfully I have a structural systems specialist like yourself to help with such demands today. Who better to go traipsing through the innards of this overgrown boil on the buttocks of the universe?"

"That is just the lieutenant commander's way of saying he appreciates your skills, Pattie," said Soloman, using the affectionate nickname many members of the *da Vinci*'s crew employed for the Nasat. Indicating Tev with the wave of a hand, the Bynar added, "He expressed similar admiration for me just yesterday, when it became apparent that a thorough scan of the station's computer systems would require crawling through a service conduit to reach the primary computer core."

Tev said nothing, allowing his two companions their moment of levity. In the time since his posting to the *da Vinci*'s S.C.E. contingent, it had taken him a while to grow accustomed to the peculiarities of the team. Now that he had worked with the crew for several weeks, he had a better sense of their growing respect for him and his accomplishments, as he had for theirs.

Fabian Stevens in particular had taken quite a bit of time to warm to him, especially considering that Tev had replaced the man's best friend who had been killed during a previous mission. That was not to say that he and Stevens were close friends, but a mutual respect for one another's position and abilities had been formed. Despite this, Stevens still seemed to enjoy the verbal jousts in which the two of them engaged, though Tev knew the repartee was no longer as ill-humored as it had been in the beginning. It was indulged in by many of the team and often triggered by his own behavior, and though he would never publicly admit it, he rather enjoyed the banter.

Besides, when it came down to it, the *da Vinci*'s S.C.E. team was an impressive collection of talented specialists, and the missions they had undertaken over the past few weeks had engendered happiness in Tev for being a part of it. If maintaining the team's high standard of performance meant striking a balance between his forthright approach and the rest of the group's jocularity, then so be it.

That did not mean that they should be privy to his methods, however. *I do have a reputation to protect, after all,* he mused.

The humor also helped to make their current assignment bearable. Tramping through the mammoth freight transfer station, one of four positioned in high orbit above the surface of Rhaax III, had proven to be an even more strenuous task than Tev had predicted. Nearly three times the size of the smaller, modular-type R1 orbital stations used as starbases throughout Federation space for more than a century, the platform boasted three dozen cargo bays, each harboring its own docking port and ship maintenance services. There was also a central control room, engineering and computer sections, as well as barracks and support facilities for personnel assigned to the platform along with temporary berthing for the crews of visiting ships.

So far as Tev was concerned, this entire affair had amounted to one gigantic waste of time. In all the weeks they had spent scouring Rhaax III and its array of orbiting transfer stations, they had yet to identify anything even resembling a large-scale weapon, biogenic or otherwise.

What was that human expression? Chasing a wild goose? Tev had heard it used many times in the past by human engineers who believed they were working toward an unattainable goal, though he himself never had understood the analogy. While he was happy that the Rhaaxans seemed to have nothing hidden away that could cause the already troubled colonists even more strife, he almost wished they could discover something, anything, simply to provide a welcome break in their monotonous routine. In the time since he signed on, they had undertaken missions that were worthy of Tev's considerable talents—and that of the rest of the team, of course. But even the mission to Kharzh'ulla, difficult as it was for Tev personally, was preferable to this tedium.

He was at least thankful that the Rhaaxans working on the station seemed civil enough, particularly in light of the incident at the bar, as well as a few other skirmishes between *da Vinci* personnel and the locals in other locations. Captain Gold had seen fit to restrict the crew's shore leave activities to those areas and establishments where proprietors already had welcomed the Starfleet visitors, a move that seemed to satisfy many Rhaaxan dissenters. While there still had been the occasional verbal dispute, the violence appeared to be contained, for the moment at least, with the uneasy truce extending up to the transfer stations. The workers on all of the platforms were cooperating with the various inspection teams, and no negative incidents had been reported of which Tev was aware.

None of which meant that he was happy to be here.

"So," he said as they turned a corner in the corridor, "where do we stand on the inspection?"

Reviewing the tricorder she carried, Pattie replied,

"We are nearly finished, Commander. There are two more docking areas to examine as well as one computer subprocessing center."

Pattie's eight extremities made her the perfect candidate for moving about the variable gravity areas of the docking and cargo areas as well as the engineering sections, while Soloman's own diminutive stature was ideally suited to navigating the narrow crawlways connecting the complex's twelve computer subprocessing centers. That left Tev to take care of the command center, along with less glamorous areas of the station. He had not believed he would find an area of the orbital platform dirtier than some of the engineering sections, at least until he had seen the berthing spaces.

"Marvelous," Tev said as the Nasat completed her report. "With any luck, we can condemn this orbiting cesspool and get permission to maneuver it into the sun."

Soloman regarded him with confusion etching his pale features. "Unfortunately, the Rhaaxan Assembly is not likely to give us the authority to carry out such an action, Commander."

"Thank you for clarifying that," the Tellarite replied dryly, pleased that he and Soloman seemed immune to the sarcastic banter that was so characteristic of the *da Vinci* crew.

The deafening wail that pierced the air the next instant nearly made him jump out of his skin, the alarm echoing off the narrow walls of the passageway. The lighting panels set into the metal plates forming the corridor's ceiling changed from their normal white illumination to a warm, glowing orange.

"Alert," a lifeless, mechanical voice called out above the din, *"life support system fault, Beli Section. Dis-*

patch damage control team." The message continued to repeat.

"Where is that?" Tev shouted, trying to hear himself over the noise.

Checking her tricorder again, Pattie pointed down the corridor. "It is the next section, Commander."

"Let's go!" the Tellarite said, taking off at a trot down the hallway. "Perhaps there's something we can do to help."

With Tev leading the way, the three engineers turned another corner and scrambled through a large pressure hatch, entering what he recognized as one of the station's two main thoroughfares. Running symmetrically down both sides of the platform's long axis, the passageways accessed nearly the entire complex.

The first thing Tev saw was a group of five Rhaaxans, all dressed in the dark gray coverall typically worn by workers assigned to the station. They were moving frantically around a large, oval-shaped storage tank. Measuring more than twenty meters in diameter, he knew that this was one of thirty-six such reservoirs containing oxygen and other inert gases. Combined in the proper amounts by the platform environmental control systems, the gases served the Rhaaxans' life support requirements on the station.

"Shut down the flow, now!" Tev heard one of the workers shout as the three Starfleet officers approached the scene, and there was no mistaking the trail of gas jetting from the tank. A pale green vapor, it was escaping into the air and beginning to fill the corridor.

"What happened?" he asked as he approached one of the workers, a supervisor that he recognized from an earlier meeting named Tamaryst.

The Rhaaxan turned to him, the illumination from

the alert signals giving his orange skin an ashen pallor and accentuating the anger clouding his features. Tev saw that Tamaryst's expression appeared to be inflamed when the two made eye contact.

"What does it look like?" he replied. "One of my people accidentally punctured the storage tank with his torch." Looking away from the commander, Tamaryst pointed to one of his companions. "Get an emergency patch kit. We need to seal this thing before the whole tank bleeds out."

Stepping forward, Tev said, "We can help." Unslinging the tool kit from his shoulder, the Tellarite opened it and reached inside, extracting a laser welder. "I can seal that breach in no time."

"We can handle our own problems," Tamaryst responded, no longer even looking at Tev and instead watching the efforts of his four companions. "The best thing you can do is stay back and let us work."

Put off by the abrupt dismissal, Tev pressed on. "Now see here, there's no need to be rude or to panic. There are thirty-six of these storage tanks on the station. Surely the loss of one cannot be cause for such alarm, but if it is, then we can help get it sealed in a matter of moments."

"Commander," Pattie said from behind him. "I'm picking up some strange readings from that tank."

"Not now," Tev snapped. "Can't you see I'm trying to foster a little goodwill with our hosts?"

Moving closer, Pattie held her tricorder up for Tev to see. "Commander, the gas coming from that tank is not one of those used to sustain the station's life support system. It is an inert compound." Looking up to the Rhaaxan worker, she asked, "What is it supposed to be?"

"It is not your concern, Starfleet," the Rhaaxan supervisor replied, his expression darkening with each word, and Tev suddenly felt the hairs on the back of his neck stand up. Had they blundered into something more serious than a simple storage tank leak?

"Very well," he said, perhaps too quickly. "We will get out of your way. You're certainly more qualified to handle this than we are, after all. Let's leave these gentlemen to work," he said to the two specialists. As he took a step backward, however, he bumped into something. Much to his regret, it was not just another dirty bulkhead.

"I am afraid it is too late for that," the second Rhaaxan said from behind him. Tev started to reach for his phaser but the worker was faster, his hand darting out and snatching the weapon from its holster and leveling it at the Tellarite. "All of you stay where you are and keep your hands where we can see them."

His ire rising as the five Rhaaxans quickly relieved him and the rest of the away team of their phasers, combadges, and other equipment, Tev leveled a scathing glare at the leader of the group. "What is the meaning of this?"

"We cannot allow you to leave now," Tamaryst said. "You might report what you have seen, and we are not yet ready for anyone to know what we are doing here."

The twinge of alarm Tev had felt moments before had now formed a knot in his stomach. After all this time and despite the numerous inspections the *da Vinci* crew had carried out, had the Rhaaxans still succeeded in hiding some kind of weapon, right here under their noses?

"That gas can't be lethal," he said. "Specialist Blue scanned it and determined the chemicals in that tank to be harmless."

Tamaryst nodded. "By itself, that is correct. However, when mixed with another such 'harmless' chemical, the result will be a compound that we have named jurolon."

"A biological agent, I take it," Tev said.

"That is correct," Tamaryst said. "It is designed to break down the components of the planet's atmosphere. It will be quite deadly to anyone living there, but the effects are temporary and after a time the planet will heal itself and be available to us once again."

Shaking his head in disbelief, Tev said, "You would actually kill everyone in the colony? That is insane."

"Correct again," the Rhaaxan leader replied. "Such an action would be insane. It is my home, after all."

The horrific revelation made Tev's jaw drop open in shock. "You mean . . . are you saying that you're a colonist?" For that to be true, it would mean that insurgents from the colony would have taken control of the orbital platform, which normally operated under the auspices of Rhaax III.

"We have been planning this action for quite a long time, Commander," Tamaryst said, "ever since the government of our homeworld directed an ultimatum at us. We did not know if they were lying at the time, but we could not afford to take that chance."

"But they were bluffing," Tev countered. "There's no need for you to attack. You'll be killing millions of innocent people for no reason at all."

"Do not mistake our intentions," the Rhaaxan said. "We do not wish to harm anyone, but existing under the constant threat of our homeland is not living. We want our freedom, to decide for ourselves whether we will join your Federation."

Tev knew that when it came to diplomacy, particularly when it involved the internal machinations of a planet's own society, he was very much out of his depth. "Listen, telling all of this to me is a waste of time. Let's take your grievances to Ambassador Marshall on my ship. I'm sure he can—"

"The time for talk is over," Tamaryst snapped, cutting him off. "We require a decision, today, once and for all." Indicating his companions, he added, "It is our job to see that the impetus for that decision is provided."

Frowning, Tev considered his options. He might be able to incapacitate Tamaryst if he moved fast enough, but he would not get much farther before one of the other Rhaaxans gunned him and his team down with their own phasers. Still, he could not stand by idly as these rebels turned this space station into a giant weapon.

An instant later, he learned he was not the only one who felt that way.

From the corner of his eye Tev saw a blur of gray movement a heartbeat before Soloman slammed into the Rhaaxan closest to him. The diminutive Bynar continued moving, snatching the phaser from the worker's hand even as his opponent crashed backward into the nearby bulkhead.

"Look out!" someone shouted, and Tev ducked to his right as the Rhaaxan behind him opened fire. The howl of phaser energy erupted in the corridor, and Tev spun to face another of the attackers just in time for something to strike him in the face. Stars exploded before his eyes, the pain of the assault so intense that he dropped to his knees. He reached for his nose and forehead with both hands as a wave of dizziness swept over him.

Around him he heard the sounds of scuffling feet and bodies crashing into bulkheads and one another, all of it punctuated by occasional bursts of phaser fire.

Through blurred vision he saw Pattie skittering up one wall to latch onto an overhead pipe, kicking out with another of her legs as she fought to stay out of reach. Then another phaser strike echoed in the hallway and Tev saw Pattie hit by the beam, its orange energy washing over her. Her body went limp as she dropped unconscious to the deck.

At least, Tev hoped she was just unconscious. The phasers had been set on stun, but what if the Rhaaxan had accidentally altered the weapon's power setting?

"Get the other one!" someone cried, and Tev saw that farther down the corridor, Soloman was ducking behind some kind of maintenance locker and shooting at the Rhaaxans, one of which was firing back in response. The worker wielding the other captured phaser was maneuvering for a shot while his partner kept the Bynar pinned down.

"Soloman!" Tev shouted. "Run!" With that, he heaved himself to his feet and lunged forward, wrapping the Rhaaxan in a fierce bear hug and driving him to the deck with such force that the worker dropped his weapon. The Tellarite pushed himself to his knees, intending to swing at his opponent once more when his vision was abruptly filled with the business end of another phaser.

"Enough," Tamaryst said, his voice seething with rage. Gesturing for Tev to get to his feet, he looked to one of his companions. "Well?"

The other Rhaaxan shook his head. "The little one disappeared into one of the maintenance conduits."

"Then go after him," the leader said, biting off every word.

"You'll never catch him." Tev hoped his boast was correct. With his slighter build, Soloman would be much better suited to navigating the crawl spaces. "At least, not before he finds a way to contact our ship."

"Quiet," Tamaryst snapped, aiming his phaser at the Tellarite's head again. To the others he said, "Contact the rest of our group. Get everyone out searching for him, except for those involved in the next phase. We're starting the process now."

"Now?" one of the other workers repeated. "But we're not supposed to start mixing until we get clearance."

"If we wait, that little Starfleet rodent might be able to call for help. Then where will we be?"

Nodding, the subordinate turned and ran off, presumably to carry out his orders and leaving Tamaryst to turn and glare at Tev.

"Do you realize what you have done?" the Rhaaxan asked. "Thanks to you, we now have no choice but to proceed."

You're welcome, Tev thought, sighing in resignation.

CHAPTER 7

Ignoring the pain in his elbows and knees, to say nothing of the bare skin of his hands being rubbed raw by his frantic scrambling through the access conduit, Soloman kept moving. The Rhaaxans did not have any type of internal sensor technology, so their only means of pursuit was trying to keep up with him. His smaller size provided his only advantage in these narrow crawl spaces, allowing him to move with greater speed and agility than anyone who might be chasing after him.

Without his tricorder, he was forced to rely on his memory of the access conduits, which he and Pattie had traversed several times during their inspection of the orbital platform's computer systems. For a moment Soloman considered heading for the station's central computer core, but he quickly abandoned that idea. If his pursuers somehow managed to figure out where he was going, they could coordinate their search and surround him.

What he needed to do was find some way to contact the *da Vinci.* Lieutenant Commander Tev would want him to warn Captain Gold of what the away team had discovered here, and the Rhaaxan government needed to be apprised of the threat to them as well. With their plans revealed, the colonists might be compelled to act earlier than originally intended, which meant that for Soloman, time was of the essence.

Since he had been unable to retrieve one of the away team's confiscated combadges from their captors when he launched his escape attempt, the Bynar reasoned that his best option was to find one of the computer terminals situated throughout the station's maze of service conduits. Used by workers when performing maintenance on the platform's various onboard systems, the terminals allowed direct interface to the main computer and its vast library of diagnostic software. It was an efficient setup, Soloman conceded, considering the limits of Rhaaxan technology. Though it possessed none of the sophistication of the global computer network on his home planet, it was enough for his purposes here.

If he could get to one of the terminals, of course.

Ahead of him in the conduit, something rubbed against metal. Soloman froze, even holding his breath as he looked and listened. It was hard to discern any sounds over the steady background hum generated by the station's power systems, and after several moments the Bynar neither saw nor heard anything. He was ready to move again when the sound repeated itself. A four-way intersection lay perhaps ten meters ahead of him, and Soloman's ears told him that the source of the noise was around the corner to his right.

He was sure it was one of the workers sent to comb

the conduits for him, no doubt having heard his own hurried movements as he fled through the crawl space, but was that person alone? Soloman heard no indications of additional pursuers, though without his tricorder there was no way to be sure.

Not that it mattered, anyway. He could not afford to sit here, idle, and wait for this situation to play out. The longer he stayed in one place, the greater the chances of someone else finding him. That left only one option.

As quietly as he could, Soloman removed his right boot and held it in his left hand. Aiming his phaser down the conduit, he tossed the boot so that it landed on the deck plating just before the intersection.

He received just the reaction he wanted as a tall lanky figure lunged forward, loosing a fierce howl of anger as he fired his own weapon. A green ball of energy spat forth and slammed into the wall, scorching the bulkhead plating. His movement was too quick and disjointed, however, the action pulling the man off balance. He fell forward, reaching out with his free hand to keep from tumbling face-first into the deck.

It was a wasted effort, as he ended up doing just that as Soloman fired his phaser and the orange beam struck the man, stunning him into unconsciousness. Once the worker's body settled to the floor of the passageway, the Bynar remained in place for an additional several seconds, listening for any signs that the momentary skirmish had been heard.

Satisfied that he was alone in the conduit once more, Soloman took a moment to search the prone colonist but found nothing that might prove useful. Next, he checked the sign on the bulkhead at the intersection to get his bearings, smiling to himself as he read the markings. If his memory was accurate, he was not all that far from a junction point that would lead him to one of the maintenance computer terminals.

Then he felt it.

First it was a minor vibration in the deck plating beneath his feet. It grew in intensity with each passing second, moving into the bulkheads and pipes surrounding him. Now it was accompanied by a deep rumbling sound from the depths of the space station, overpowering even the power plants' omnipresent hum. What could be causing all of this? So far as Soloman knew, only one system aboard the orbital platform could cause this type of commotion.

The engines.

We are moving.

CHAPTER 8

Alarm klaxons wailed across the bridge of the *da Vinci,* echoing off the bulkheads and driving directly into Gold's skull.

"Captain!" Shabalala shouted from the tactical station. "Orbital Station 4 is moving out of position and beginning a descent toward the planet!"

"Kill the alarm and go to yellow alert." Gold rose from his command chair. "Shabalala, put the station on screen."

The image on the main viewer shifted and he recognized the stout, utilitarian lines of one of Rhaax III's four orbital cargo transfer platforms. It was his first time viewing one of the stations this closely. More than half the size of Spacedock, the Rhaaxan platform possessed none of the more artistic blending of form and function that characterized Earth's primary starship maintenance facility. Even from this distance, Gold could make out the numerous docking ports and cargo storage bay hatches adorning the station's outer hull.

"Hail them," he said, silently counting as contact with Orbital Station 4 was attempted and his anxiety level increasing with each second the link was not established. It only got worse when Shabalala shook his head.

"No response, sir."

"Tev and the away team are on that station," Gomez said. "Have you tried contacting them?"

Nodding, Shabalala replied, "None of the team is answering, Commander."

Sitting at one of the bridge's rear science stations, Stevens turned in his chair. "Captain, the station isn't just falling from its orbit. It's a controlled maneuver, descending toward the planet at a constant speed and moving under its own power."

"Where the hell is it going?" Gold asked. "It'll burn up if it enters the atmosphere." What was happening over there? Already on board as part of his assigned inspection duties, Tev would have called in the moment anything unexpected occurred. Was he hurt? What about the rest of the away team?

Oh no.

It was so simple, he realized. Even though the station likely would break up as it passed through the atmosphere, killing everyone aboard, the facility's size and mass would still be enough to cause widespread damage when it impacted on Rhaax III's surface. And if some lunatic was currently maneuvering the station so that it would fall on or near a populated area . . .

"How much time until they enter the atmosphere?" he asked.

Shabalala checked his console before replying. "At their present course and speed, about twelve minutes, sir."

"Something else, Captain," Stevens called out. "Sensors are detecting a massive chemical reaction underway inside some of the modules storing oxygen and other compounds for their life support systems."

"Is it a threat to the people on board?" Gold asked.

Stevens shook his head. "I can't say just yet, sir."

"Well, find out," the captain snapped.

Though Marshall had been standing silently at the back of the bridge to this point, Gold knew that he would not be able to hold his tongue much longer. The captain's suspicions were confirmed when the ambassador stepped forward.

"How many people are aboard the station?" he asked.

"Sensors show two hundred and five life signs," Shabalala reported.

"You have to do something, Captain," Marshall said, his face a mask of anguish.

"I *am* doing something, Ambassador," the captain replied. Despite being irritated at the diplomat's observation of the obvious, Gold chose to ignore it and channel that energy elsewhere. Turning back to the viewscreen, he ordered, "Wong, move us into transporter range."

"Captain," Shabalala called out, "I am receiving an incoming hail from the station."

"On-screen," Gold said.

The viewer changed images again, this time to show a Rhaaxan male, muscled and wearing dark gray worker's coveralls. His orange features were clouded in apparent anger.

"Federation ship," the Rhaaxan said, *"our quarrel is not with you, but rather the government of our home planet. Do not attempt to interfere with us in any way.*

You are directed to keep your vessel out of range of your weapons and matter transfer systems. We have your officers in custody here and though I do not wish to harm them, I will kill them if necessary."

"What do you want?" the captain asked.

"Our freedom, once and for all. Either that is granted today, or everyone on Rhaax will die."

The transmission ended, leaving the *da Vinci* bridge crew with the viewer's image of Orbital Station 4.

"Someone sure has issues with authority," Stevens said.

"Stow that," Gold snapped as he turned from the viewer. This was no time for the tactical specialist's unique flavor of jocularity. "Gomez, please tell me they're bluffing over there."

Gomez already was moving to Stevens's station on the upper bridge deck. "Working on it, sir." To Stevens she said, "Let me see the sensor data on that chemical reaction."

Letting his people tend to that, Gold used the delay to make his way across the bridge to where Marshall stood and tried not to take too much satisfaction in the diplomat's ashen expression.

"We've been looking for weapons the Rhaaxans might be developing," he said, "and all this time the colonists have been planning their own attack? How the hell did they manage that?"

Blinking rapidly as realization sank in, Marshall shook his head. "The colonists never even hinted at any such action, Captain, not once. This is completely out of the blue."

"Or just very well guarded," Gold countered. The idea that they might have been so completely deceived despite the work Gomez and her team had done, and after suffering through all of Ambassador Marshall's supercilious nonsense, galled him, but it was nothing compared to the sense of dread he felt at what the colonists might be capable of doing.

"Captain," he heard Gomez say. "I think we might have something." He moved to the science station, where Gomez was leaning over Stevens's shoulder and studying the information scrolling across the display monitors above the workstation.

"What is it?" Gold asked.

Stevens tapped a command string and the image on his station's center monitor shifted to show an array of chemical formulas and mathematical computations derived by the ship's scanners. "This is the new compound being created," he said as he froze one image and pointed to it. "I've got the computer chewing on it, but without a sample to analyze it's going to take time." Suddenly the tactical specialist snapped his fingers. "Computer, show me the design specs for the orbital stations. I want to see the environmental subsystems."

A moment later the request was answered and Stevens nodded. "Look," he said, indicating what Gold took to be design diagrams for a massive storage tank. "This is one of the areas where the chemical is being mixed. Now, see these valves positioned on the exterior of the tanks and connected to hatches on the station's outer hull? This is part of the system used to purge the storage tanks for maintenance. Ordinarily the contents of the tanks would be vented to space."

"That's it," Gold said. "The chemical must be something they can release into the atmosphere, and the station itself is the delivery vehicle." He nodded as he started to fit the pieces of the puzzle together. "With all the ship traffic coming in and out of those stations, it would be a simple matter to move that material into position over a long period of time. For all we know, they've been planning this for months, or longer."

From behind him, Shabalala said, "Captain, I'm picking up an incoming transmission from Rhaax V. It appears to be a recorded message intended for Prefect Randa and the rest of the assembly."

"This should be joyous news," Gold said, more to himself than anyone else. He found it interesting that the colony leaders would choose to send a recording rather than use the subspace communications equipment furnished to each planet's governing body by the Federation Diplomatic Corps. The intent had been for the leaders to interact with one another and with the Federation mediators in real time, despite the vast distances separating their two worlds and the delays experienced when using their conventional communications equipment. To Gold, the colonists' intentions were clear: they had something to say, and they did not want any interruptions.

"Put it on the viewer," he said.

A moment later the image of the orbital platform was replaced by that of a regal-looking Rhaaxan. He was dressed in robes similar to ones Gold had seen Prefect Randa and members of her assembly wearing, though his garment looked to be simpler in design and made from rougher-hewn material than the lavish clothing worn by his counterparts on Rhaax III. To the captain, the robes appeared to be an attempt at marrying Rhaaxan heritage with the unique identity the colony had tried to establish.

"People of Rhaax, this is Prefect Erokan, representing the Colonial Assembly and the people of Numai. For many months we have faced an impasse with the government of our homeworld, who have forgotten the basic

tenets of the original agreement that established the Numai colony. Rather than allow us to continue on as an independent entity until such time as the agreement calls for us to become a province of Rhaax, your government seeks to abandon that contract in favor of allying themselves with the United Federation of Planets. The Federation has made it known that it values our planet, perhaps more so than Rhaax and, by extension, all of you. Worried that they might somehow be left out of any arrangements made with the Federation, Prefect Randa and the Assembly have seen fit to threaten us with extinction."

"I see he's pulling his punches and taking the nice approach," Stevens muttered.

Though he glared at the tactical specialist, Gold said nothing. Instead, he wondered what Prefect Randa and her people might be doing at this moment. Without the ability to counter anything the colony leader might say, were they trying to prevent the message from reaching the Rhaaxan people?

"Despite repeated debates and discussions," Erokan continued, *"all our efforts to reach a compromise have failed. Therefore, we have decided that the time for discussion is over, and that we will no longer settle for simple compromise. The fate of both our worlds will be decided here, today, and in the presence of our Federation mediators. Either the colony of Numai will be granted its permanent freedom from Rhaaxan rule, or every living thing on your planet will perish."*

He paused, as if knowing that his words would be more effective if allowed to sink in for several seconds before saying anything else.

"Oh my God," Marshall said. "He'll incite a global panic down there."

"While Prefect Randa and her advisers may have been

bluffing when they threatened us, rest assured that the threat I bring today is quite real. As you receive this message, Orbital Station 4 is being maneuvered into position so that it can release a chemical compound we call jurolon, which will result in the total breakdown of all the life-giving elements of your planet's atmosphere. Simply put, all of you will suffocate."

Pausing again, Erokan stepped forward and opened his arms, and Gold was nearly infuriated as the colony leader actually smiled warmly.

"Of course, such tragedy can be avoided. It simply requires the Rhaaxan Assembly to guarantee us our freedom, now and forever. We await your response, Prefect Randa, but only until the sun sets on the capital city." Then the message abruptly ended, and the viewer returned to its image of the orbital platform.

Gold turned to Gomez and Stevens. "Find me a way to disable that damn thing, *now.*"

"Aye, sir," Gomez said.

Moving around the bridge toward the tactical station, the captain asked, "Shabalala, how long until sunset hits Longon?"

The lieutenant checked his sensor displays before replying, "Approximately two hours, Captain."

"Fine," Gold replied. "Hail the Rhaaxan Assembly. Get me Prefect Randa."

A moment later the image of the Rhaaxan leader filled the main viewscreen. There was no mistaking the harried expression clouding her pale orange features.

"Captain," she said, *"I trust you observed the message from Erokan on Rhaax V?"*

Gold nodded. "We did, Prefect. My people are examining the situation right now and looking for ways to deal with it."

"Ways to deal with it?" Randa replied, her expression one of shock. *"They threatened to destroy all life on my planet, Captain. What do you suggest we do in the face of that?"*

Holding his hand up, Gold said, "Please, Prefect. This is not the time to react emotionally. We haven't had time to examine all the options yet."

Stepping forward until her face nearly filled the viewscreen, Randa glowered at him. *"There can be only one response to such menace. That station must be destroyed, but we no longer possess the means to do so ourselves. I therefore implore you to take on that responsibility."*

Gold shook his head. "Out of the question. We have no way of knowing how many innocent people are aboard, not to mention I have an away team over there right now."

"Captain," he heard Ambassador Marshall say from behind him, "we may reach the point where choosing between a small number of people on that station and billions on the planet is our only option."

Ignoring the diplomat, Gold turned to the science station. "Gomez, Stevens. What have you got?"

"If we can get close enough," Stevens replied, "we might be able to target the exhaust ports for the purge system with phasers, but it'll require pinpoint precision."

"What about disabling the station itself?" the captain asked. "Targeting its engines or locking on with a tractor beam and pulling it away from the planet?"

Gomez stepped away from the science station. "It's too big for our tractor beam, sir, and even if we knocked out its engines, its momentum would still carry it into the atmosphere."

"And if we disable the exhaust ports," Stevens added, "they could still release the tanks manually, and there's no way to be sure they'd burn up during reentry without releasing their contents."

From the viewscreen, Randa said, *"Captain, if you do not try, the colonists are certain to unleash that poison upon us."*

"Prefect," Gold said, trying very hard to keep his emotions in check, "unless we have a solution with a reasonable chance of success, all we'll do is help them put their plan into motion sooner. Sunset doesn't fall on the capital city for two more hours. Let my people have that time to find another option."

Randa shook her head. *"If you are unable to act, then you leave me with no other alternative."* The prefect then turned to someone offscreen. *"Send the signal."*

"What are you doing, Prefect?" Gold asked.

Returning her attention to him, Randa replied, *"I have dispatched orders to one of my military vessels, which has been maintaining a concealed position on the far side of the moon orbiting Rhaax V. It carries twenty-four ballistic missiles, which have been armed with a biological weapon of our own devising."*

"You're lying," Gold countered. "All conventional weapons were accounted for weeks ago."

"Please, Captain, give my military advisers credit. They are long practiced in concealing information and matériel from the prying eyes of inspectors and accountants. Removing the missiles from the inventory databases was child's play, though arming them with the biogenic agent was a bit more difficult." Pausing, she smiled grimly. *"Actually, I have you and your crew to thank for that. If not for the revelation provided by Commander Gomez, we would never have been able to complete our weapons research, to say nothing of employing it with such speed."*

The Rhaaxans had been monitoring communications

between the *da Vinci* and the inspection teams. It was the only logical explanation for the prefect's comments. They had taken what Gomez and Stevens had found and run with it, developing some perverted weapon that would allow them to make good on the bluff that had started this entire mess in the first place.

David Gold did not like being used, by anyone, and it was only with a physical effort that he forced his features to remain fixed. "Prefect," he began, but got no farther before Randa interrupted him.

"I have also sent my own message to Prefect Erokan," she said. *"The rebels on the space station must immediately surrender themselves and allow the platform to be boarded, or else the missiles will be launched. If they follow through with their attack, the missiles will still be launched."*

"You can't be serious," Marshall said. "Prefect, surely you realize what you're proposing?"

"Indeed I do, Ambassador," Randa replied. *"I cannot stand by and allow my people to be threatened. Either we will all live through the day, or none of us will."*

Silence engulfed the bridge as the communication was severed, with only the background sounds of the various consoles and the omnipresent hum of the *da Vinci*'s engines to fill the void.

"Mutually assured destruction," Gold said after a few seconds, "otherwise known as an interplanetary game of chicken. I never thought I'd live long enough to see anyone engage in such insanity."

The question now was: Which side would flinch first?

CHAPTER 9

"That lying witch!"

Standing next to Pattie in one of the orbital platform's cargo bays along with nearly fifty Rhaaxan workers and covered by a squad of at least twenty armed colonists, Tev watched as Tamaryst nearly lost control of his temper. The muscular Rhaaxan's fists clenched so hard that they shook visibly, and the commander was sure he might lash out at one of his subordinates at any moment.

Tamaryst turned to glare at Tev with unfettered rage. "This is the result of your Federation's interference," he said, pointing to the viewscreen mounted to the bulkhead of the cargo bay, where, only seconds before Prefect Randa had issued her response to the colony leader's ultimatum. "All this time, they were looking for a way to crush us, and you provided them with the answer. None of this would be happening if you had simply left us alone."

Snorting in derision, Tev replied, "Are you saying we drove you to create whatever hellish brew you have stored in those tanks? Was it the Federation who put a weapon to your head and forced you to take up arms against your own people?"

"Commander," Pattie said, her voice low and her tone one of warning.

Tev ignored her, instead pointing to the now inactive viewscreen. "And we didn't give the Rhaaxans anything, either. If Randa and her people have a weapon to deploy against you, then it's one of their own devising. They couldn't have come this far this fast without having done a lot of the research for themselves."

"Research they would not have conducted if their minds had not been poisoned with thoughts of joining the Federation." Clearly angry now, Tamaryst stepped closer. "Perhaps there is sufficient blame to share among all of us, Starfleet, but to deny that your presence here has been a disruption to our way of life is arrogant hypocrisy at best and criminal negligence at worst."

Suddenly he turned his attention to the rest of the people being held in the cargo bay, and Tev watched in admiration as the Rhaaxan's features molded from angered and scowling to warm and inviting, almost as if he had tripped some sort of emotional switch.

"I want to thank all of you for your cooperation," Tamaryst said, holding his arms wide in a display of entreaty. "Rest assured that if you continue to behave as you have, you will not be harmed."

"Then what?" Tev heard a voice call out from behind him. "What about those of us trapped up here on the space stations?"

"Yes," another voice said, "once you've destroyed our

home, what's to prevent you from killing the rest of us?"

"Enough!" the Rhaaxan snapped, making a chopping gesture with his right hand as he continued to pace. To Tev, it seemed that Tamaryst was beginning to doubt the orders he presumably was following, but could he also be starting to question his conviction for carrying out this heinous act in the first place?

More to himself than anyone else, Tamaryst said, "It will do no good to order the Starfleet ship to destroy Randa's missiles. The captain will refuse, and I cannot keep threatening to use the jurolon in order to command obedience. Sooner or later, they will force us to act or retreat." He shook his head. "Why does Prefect Erokan not advise us?"

As Tamaryst stopped his pacing and gazed thoughtfully at the deck plating for several seconds, Tev could see the rebel leader struggling with his own emotions and thoughts as he fought to reach a decision. The longer the Rhaaxan stayed in one place and said nothing, the larger the knot of anxiety in Tev's stomach grew.

"If we surrender now," Tamaryst said after a few moments, "there will be nothing to stop Randa and the Assembly from ordering our destruction. Therefore, our only choice is to attack now, while we have the advantage."

"Don't be a fool!" Tev shouted, his voice laced with such fury that the Rhaaxan and even a few of the guards moved back a step. "Aren't you forgetting something? Prefect Randa has already dispatched weapons of her own to destroy Numai, and her orders are to launch those missiles if you don't surrender this station. If you attack, so will she, and everyone will lose everything. What's the point of that?"

Beginning to pace the open area in front of the prisoners, Tamaryst said, "It is better to die free than to live as slaves."

"How very dramatic of you," Tev replied, making no attempt to hide his disdain, "and that's fine if you're making the decision for yourself. However, you don't have the right to make that choice for billions of others. A good many people down on Rhaax support Numai's position in all of this. Are you planning to kill them, too? Does that chemical of yours distinguish between friend and foe?"

Seeing the momentary doubt on the Rhaaxan's face, Tev pressed forward. "Tell me something, Tamaryst. Let's say that everything works out today and you get to go home, with your freedom and whatever else you manage to coax out of the Rhaaxan people. What will you do then? Your supporters down on the planet won't appreciate being used as pawns by you and your leaders, and you'll have lost their backing for all time. From this point forward you'll have to rely on threats and fear to get anything from the Rhaaxans, because they'll never trust you enough to deal with you in good faith ever again."

For a fleeting moment, as Tamaryst said nothing, Tev thought he might be getting through to the rebel leader and imagined he saw the hesitation in the Rhaaxan's eyes.

Then, it was gone, replaced by a steely determination that made Tev's blood run cold.

"You are right," Tamaryst said. "Our relationship with the Rhaaxans has been damaged forever. There seems to be no compelling reason to continue it any longer."

The blunt statement was punctuated by the

Rhaaxan's pivoting on his heel and walking away, leaving Tev, Pattie, and the rest of the prisoners to stare after him, many of them looking on with jaws slackened in horror.

On the bridge of the *da Vinci,* David Gold was considering his options and not liking any of them.

"Captain, you can't just leave the Rhaaxans to face that monstrosity," Marshall said, pointing at the main viewer and the image of the orbital platform, which was still lumbering through space and descending toward the atmosphere of Rhaax III.

Sighing in mounting frustration, Gold nodded. "I'm aware of that, Ambassador." Looking to Shabalala, he asked, "How long until those missiles reach Rhaax V?"

"Six point three minutes, sir," the lieutenant replied.

"Can you locate the away team on the station?"

After a moment, the tactical officer said, "I've located one Tellarite and one Nasat life sign in a cargo bay with forty-six Rhaaxans. Neither Tev nor Pattie are wearing their combadges."

"No Bynar readings?" Gomez asked. "Where's Soloman?"

Shabalala paused as he checked his sensor readings. "I found him, but he's in what looks to be a service crawl space in another part of the station."

"It's a safe bet Tev and Pattie are being held hostage in that cargo bay with the rest of the station workers," Gold said. "Can you get a transporter lock on them?"

"Once we get in range, sir," Shabalala said. "Get me there and I can transport everyone out of that bay." He looked to Gomez and smiled. "And Soloman, too."

Stepping down to the command well from where he had been standing at the rear of the bridge, Marshall asked, "What are you doing, Captain?"

"I'm putting an end to this nonsense, Ambassador." Gold knew that, despite the risk of engaging warp drive while still within the boundaries of the solar system, the *da Vinci* could easily beat the missiles to the colony planet. The rule against such practices had been broken more times than Gold could count, and though disaster had resulted on a few occasions when the maneuver was attempted by others, he trusted his people to handle the navigational demands should he give the order.

The problem with such a rash action was that it left Rhaax III vulnerable to the threat still facing them. Unless he factored that into his plan, of course.

"Stevens," he said, "enter your targeting data to the computer. I want to do this in one pass." Then he moved forward until he stood directly behind the conn and ops positions and placed his hand on the shoulder of the young lieutenant at conn. "Wong, lay in an intercept course to the station and stand by for my command. Coordinate with Stevens based on his target selections. Once we hit those marks, I want to be at Rhaax V thirty seconds after that."

"Aye, sir," Wong acknowledged as he set to work.

As he waited for his people to finish their preparations, Gold felt Marshall standing just behind him. Folding his arms across his chest and without turning around, the captain prompted, "Yes, Ambassador?"

"Your plan would seem to hinge on disabling the space station's ability to disperse that chemical, Captain."

Gold nodded. "Yes."

"But you said yourself that if we proceeded without a guarantee of success," Marshall said, "it would only cause the Rhaaxans to jump the gun."

"What I said was that we'd need a reasonable chance of success," Gold corrected. He turned to face the ambassador. "Under the circumstances, this is probably as good a chance as we're going to get."

Shock washed over Marshall's face. "What if you're wrong?"

"It's the same result whether we fail or do nothing." Gold looked over to the science station. "Stevens?"

The tactical specialist turned from his console. "Ready to go, sir."

"Captain!" Shabalala called out. "Something's happening over on the station."

All eyes on the bridge turned to the viewer, and at first Gold noted nothing different than what they had been seeing for the past several minutes. Then he saw it.

The station was slowing down, and beginning to tilt on its axis.

"It hasn't entered the atmosphere yet, has it?" he asked.

"No, sir," Shabalala replied. "It was still descending when it started to slow down. The station's braking thrusters are firing and its lateral movement indicates a possible direction change."

"Maybe Tev or somebody on board incited a takeover," Gomez offered, "a counteraction to take back the station."

Behind her, Stevens said, "No. Sensors show Tev and the others still locked in the cargo bay."

What the hell was happening over there? Gold stared at the image of the orbital platform, now quite definitely moving in a direction away from the planet, apparently accelerating as it went. Had the rebels responsible for the hijacking gotten second thoughts?

"Incoming hail, Captain," Shabalala said. "It's the station."

Gold nodded for him to put the hail through and once more the connection with the renegade Rhaaxan was established. The captain had no chance to say anything before the rebel leader exploded.

"What have you done?" the Rhaaxan said, his face a mask of rage.

Shrugging, Gold replied, "Nothing. I've been sitting here like you asked me to do." He smiled warmly. "Is there a problem?"

"We have lost control of the station! My people are reporting that they are trapped, unable to open any hatches or move out of whatever section they are in now. We have been locked out of the main computer and the navigational systems and we are hurtling into space!"

"Can we confirm any of that?" Gold asked.

Studying his sensor displays, Shabalala nodded. "All interior hatches have been sealed. Main computer access has been routed away from all interface terminals, except one."

"You don't think . . ." Gomez began, and even without looking Gold could almost hear the grin wrapped around her words.

A moment later, the image of the Rhaaxan disappeared from the viewer, replaced by that of Soloman. To Gold, the Bynar appeared to be hunched over a computer terminal jutting from the side of a maintenance vent.

"Captain Gold," he said, *"I have taken control of all onboard systems and redirected the station away from*

the planet. Lieutenant Commander Tev reports that they have seized control of the cargo bay where they were confined, and that everyone is safe. Awaiting your orders, sir."

Cheers and applause erupted on the bridge before a bark from Gold quieted everyone down. "Outstanding work, Soloman. First, jettison that sludge from the environmental systems. Next, coordinate with Tev and security to round up the rebels and detain them until Rhaaxan authorities arrive."

"Aye, sir," the Bynar replied, nodding formally.

To Shabalala, Gold said, "Notify Corsi to mobilize her security teams for transport. Alert sickbay, too, in case there are any injuries among the prisoners. Then get me Prefect Randa."

The bridge crew set about their various tasks as Gold turned back to Marshall. "Looks like we caught a break, Ambassador."

"It seems that way," Marshall replied.

A moment later, the leader of the Rhaaxan Assembly once again graced the main viewer, and Gold noted that she did not appear happy.

"I have good news, Prefect," Gold said. "My people have neutralized the threat on the orbiting station. Even as we speak, my security teams are preparing to transport over and secure it until you can send your own people up."

"We are most grateful for your quick resolution, Captain. I cannot thank you enough." Her expression, though, remained unchanged.

"Actually, you can," Gold replied, not liking the sudden tingle at the back of his neck. He unleashed his most charming diplomatic smile, the one reserved for official Starfleet functions attended by high-ranking flag officers, members of the Federation Council, and other people he normally did his best to avoid. "You can recall the missiles launched against Numai."

"No," the prefect replied, her expression one of apology. *"I do not think so."*

CHAPTER 10

Gold was sure he was hearing things. "I beg your pardon?" he asked.

"I have no intention of recalling the missiles," Randa said. *"You may have solved the immediate problem, but we cannot tolerate terrorist actions against our planet. I have no choice but to do everything in my power to ensure that such threats are not repeated."*

Feeling his ire beginning to rise yet again, the captain stepped closer to the viewer. "Prefect, you know I can't allow that to happen." To Wong he asked, "Is that course to Rhaax V ready?"

"Plotted and laid in, sir," the lieutenant replied.

"How much time before the missiles enter the atmosphere?"

At tactical, Shabalala said, "Less than three minutes, sir."

"Even with your ship's speed, Captain," Randa said,

"you cannot destroy all the missiles. Some will still get through, and even if it is only a few, they will be sufficient to send a message to the colonists never to attempt such a foolhardy strategy ever again."

Turning from the viewer and moving to his chair, Gold said, "Get her off my screen. Wong, engage." Two minutes. Was that enough time to intercept and destroy all of the missiles? Logic said no, emotion said yes, and Gold felt the pull from both as they went to war against one another.

Even with the ship's inertial damping field, he still felt the subtle change in the omnipresent vibration of the *da Vinci*'s engines as the vessel leapt into warp. On the viewer, stars elongated and stretched beyond the boundaries of the screen as the ship hurtled through subspace on its abbreviated journey through the Rhaaxan solar system.

Please don't plow us into a planet, Gold pleaded silently, but need not have worried. As fast as the trip had begun, it was over, with the stars reverting to distant pinpoints and the image on the viewer now dominated by the lush blue and green world that was Rhaax V.

"I'm tracking twenty-four missiles, all on course for the planet, Captain," Shabalala reported.

"Plot an intercept course," Gold said to Wong. "Coordinate with Shabalala for automated targeting and fire control. We're only going to get one chance at this."

How much of whatever deadly biogenic agent created by the Rhaaxans did each missile contain? What kind of damage could each weapon inflict? By failing to intercept them all before they reached their target destinations, how many people was he leaving to die?

"Captain," Gomez said, stepping down into the command well and stopping alongside his chair, "you—"

"Commander Gomez," Marshall snapped, cutting her off.

When the diplomat said nothing else, Gold frowned and turned in his seat. *What the hell is this about?*

"I don't have time for this sort of nonsense, Ambassador," he said, irritation lacing every word. "We're beyond diplomatic solutions now, and you're interfering with my people in the performance of their duties." Looking to his first officer, he said, "What is it, Gomez?"

Before she could even open her mouth to reply, Marshall said, "Commander Gomez and her S.C.E. detachment are still under my authority, Captain, and subject to my orders."

Why that might possibly matter at this critical juncture was a mystery to Gold. He could feel the eyes of everyone on the bridge turning to watch the rapidly escalating confrontation.

"We'll discuss your authority when I'm finished here, Mr. Marshall," the captain said. He could not afford this kind of lapse, not now. Returning his attention to the task at hand, he asked, "Wong, where are we?"

"Course computed, sir," the ensign replied.

"Phasers ready?"

Shabalala nodded. "Yes, sir."

"Fire at will."

Gold watched multiple beams of orange energy streak away from the ship on the viewer as the computer locked on to the first targets and fired. There was only an instant for him to note tiny distant explosions as the phaser strikes found their marks before the ship altered its course for the next battery of fire, and the sequence repeated again.

"Seventeen missiles destroyed," Shabalala reported after the third volley of fire. "Moving to target the next group." He looked up from his console a moment later, his expression filled with dread. "Sensors are picking up the first missile entering the atmosphere, sir."

Damn it!

Gold slammed his fist on the arm of his command chair. One more pass and they would have had them all!

"The other six are following," the tactical officer said, shaking his head in defeat. "I'm picking up detonations within the atmosphere."

"Move us to standard orbit, Wong," Gold said, his voice subdued. "Shabalala, get me Starfleet Command. We're going to need planetary disaster teams to be sent here as soon as possible." He felt the bile rising in his throat as he spoke the words. How long would it take for the biogenic weapon carried by the missiles to begin its work of poisoning the planet's atmosphere, and how fast would that reaction spread? As he rose from his chair, a sudden weakness coursed through his body as he envisioned the thousands of colonists, all gasping for one final tortured breath.

"Captain," Stevens called out, drawing the captain's attention from the viewscreen. "I think you should see this."

Gold looked to the science station and saw the very confused expression on the younger man's face. "What is it?" he asked.

"I'm not detecting any chemical reaction in the atmosphere," Stevens replied.

His own brow creasing in confusion, Gold moved until he was leaning over the bridge railing that separated him from the upper deck. "Were the warheads on those missiles empty? Did they malfunction?"

Stevens shook his head. "Each missile released a chemical compound, sir, but according to my scans, it's inert."

"Are you sure?" Gold asked.

"Absolutely. The compound is breaking down as it disperses through the atmosphere. I'm picking up residual traces, but it's having no destructive effect that I can find."

Pausing a moment to offer a silent thanks to whichever deities or omnipotent superbeings had seen fit to smile on them, Gold breathed a sigh of relief. The Rhaaxans had obviously made some error when manufacturing the biological weapon, taking the research information Gomez had uncovered and failing to capitalize on it in whatever manner the commander had originally feared.

"Most gracious are the heavens," he mused, "and the small favors they offer."

"Sir, I'm sorry, but the heavens didn't have anything to do with it," Gomez said from behind him. Turning from the railing, Gold saw Marshall and Gomez standing side by side. The ambassador was giving Gomez a look of angered annoyance, while the commander had an expression of relief and, if he was not mistaken, guilt.

"What are you talking about?" the captain asked.

Pointing to the viewscreen, Gomez said, "The missiles were designed to fail."

The utter absurdity of the statement kept it from fully registering with Gold at first. "What do you mean?" he asked after several seconds.

"The data they found was bait," Gomez said, "which I planted on Ambassador Marshall's orders to see if the Rhaaxans would use the information to act against the colonists."

"You deliberately furnished them with the information to create a superweapon?" Gold asked, his voice nearly strangled by the astonishment he felt.

"No, sir," Gomez said quickly. "Like I said, it was intended to fail. The information they obtained from us was designed to create an inert chemical. Originally, yes, the compound their scientists devised was lethal, but that was in order to satisfy test conditions. The formulae devised for the agent were sufficiently complex that it was easy to mask the elements necessary to render the entire mixture harmless as soon as it came into contact with the atmosphere of Rhaax V."

"That's impossible," Stevens said as he rose from the science station. "You showed us all the—" He cut himself off.

Gold shook his head. "You set it up in such a manner that you even fooled your own people. You did it that way so you'd be the only one involved."

Gomez's response was simply to nod.

"That's right, Captain," Marshall said, "I ordered Commander Gomez to put this plan in motion. After the Rhaaxan's bluffed threat, we had to find out if they were willing to carry out a true aggressive action of this magnitude if given the opportunity." Shaking his head, the ambassador's expression was one of grim regret. "As we have just seen, they appear to be quite willing."

Though he understood how difficult it must have been for Gomez to be torn between her loyalty to him and her duty to obey Marshall's orders, Gold still felt the sting of betrayal from his first officer. On the other hand, she did speak up, finally. Based on the look of anger on Marshall's face, Gold had to wonder if the truth would ever have come out if she had kept quiet.

"You had the authority to give that order?" Gold could not imagine the Starfleet Diplomatic Corps or even the Federation Council advocating such an outrageous venture.

Marshall stiffened in response to the question. "The Federation wants these people as members, Captain, and I've been sent here to resolve the dispute between the Rhaaxans and their colonists. Once it became obvious that all conventional diplomatic measures were proving ineffective, more drastic action was called for. I've been given a great deal of latitude to accomplish my mission here, and I'm confident that once the facts of the matter are presented to the Federation, they will agree with the decisions I made."

Shaking his head in disgust, Gold said, "There'll be plenty of time to sort out this idiocy later." He turned his back on Marshall, unable to keep the disappointment from his face as he regarded Gomez for an extra few seconds. The captain took no satisfaction when she failed to meet his gaze, but then he pushed the issue away, tabling it until a more appropriate time.

"Shabalala, open a channel to both prefects," he ordered as he returned to his chair. A moment later, the image on the main viewer was split in the middle, with both Randa and Erokan looking out at him.

"Prefect Erokan, I'm sure you'll be pleased to know that the missiles launched against your planet were ineffective. The chemicals they carried proved to be harmless to your atmosphere."

"That is impossible!" Randa exclaimed, her voice nearly a shriek.

Gold shrugged. "Believe it, Prefect. Sorry to ruin your plans. Feel free to file a report with Starfleet Command at your earliest convenience."

"Thank you for your assistance, Captain," Erokan offered, but Gold waved it away.

"Don't thank me. I wasn't able to stop all of the missiles. You got lucky, that's all." To both prefects, he said,

"We have a problem here, one that I intend to resolve very quickly, after which I'm taking my ship the hell out of here. What you do after that is up to you, because I'm certainly not planning on giving a damn one way or another."

"Now see here," Randa said. *"We would not be in this situation were it not for Federation interference. You cannot walk away from the damage you have caused here."*

Rising from his chair, Gold began to advance on the viewer. "Pardon my faulty memory, but was it not you who petitioned us for Federation membership?" To Erokan he said, "As for Numai, you called on us to mediate your dispute with Rhaax, and you applied for Federation membership as a separate body, did you not?"

"That's true," Erokan said, *"but—"*

Gold cut him off. "I don't deny that we might have botched some things with regard to your situation, but let's not forget the simple truth upon which this entire sordid affair has been erected: We're only here because you wanted us here and because you couldn't settle your own disputes yourselves. Now that you've amply demonstrated that you're not mature enough to handle your responsibilities within a larger interstellar community, you want us to clean up your mess for you. What do you want us to do? Assuming we can even put a stop to this insanity you've created, what's to prevent you from trying again tomorrow? Why should we bother? *Why are you worth saving?"*

For what Gold believed might just be the first time since being elected to their current positions, the prefects were speechless.

"Good," he said. "I see I've given you a lot to think about. You do that and get back to me." With that, the captain made the motion of drawing his finger across his throat, and Shabalala immediately severed the connection.

No one said anything for several seconds, and Gold himself merely stared at the image of Rhaax V's surface slowly rolling past as the *da Vinci* continued its orbit. Finally he shook his head, the events of the past hour having nearly sickened him.

"Captain," Marshall said, "I remind you that I am still in charge of this mission. If any resolutions are to be offered, they will be offered by me."

Turning from the viewer, Gold leveled a withering stare at the diplomat. "Your mission is over, Ambassador. I just completed it for you. The only thing left is the cleanup, and for us to iron out a few nagging details." He indicated the door to his ready room. "I'd like to talk with you and Commander Gomez in private, please. *Now.*"

CHAPTER 11

David Gold had never considered himself a violent man. Of course, he had been involved in various forms of conflict throughout his career, from individual fights to space battles, most especially during the brutal two years of the Dominion War. He took pride in his ability and willingness to go to any length in order to find non-violent solutions to problems no matter their size or scope. Even on those unfortunate occasions where he had been forced to take life, he had resorted to such action only after every other option had been exhausted, and spent much time afterward reflecting on whether or not there had been another alternative he might have overlooked. He was comforted by the thought that subjecting himself and his decisions to such intense scrutiny played a key part in ensuring that he never wavered from his convictions.

It was precisely that level of restraint, nurtured and

refined over a lifetime, which prevented Gold from knocking Ambassador Gabriel Marshall through the bulkhead of his ready room.

"Mr. Marshall," he said, "with all due respect, have you lost your mind?"

The diplomat's jaw dropped open in response to the blunt query. He said nothing for several moments, for which Gold was actually thankful. When he finally did begin to recover, his trademark overbearing demeanor returned in force.

"I might ask you the same question, Captain," he replied. "You forget your place."

"Let's get something straight," Gold snapped. "Your authority on this ship ended the moment those two planets started shooting at each other. Your authority over me ended the moment you elected to keep information from me that resulted in members of my crew being placed in danger."

Marshall snorted. "If I'd informed you of my plans, would you have cooperated?"

"Absolutely not," the captain replied, "and you knew that, which is why you made an end run around me to Starfleet Command and shanghaied my people." He glanced at Gomez, who stood silent near the door, before continuing. "I know that your mission parameters placed the ship's S.C.E. team under your direct command, but I'm pretty damned certain that order wasn't intended to let you tamper with the relationship between Rhaax and her colony. Something tells me that somebody's eyebrows are going to rise more than a bit when they read the report I'm submitting about all of this."

Shaking his head, Marshall frowned. "Captain, given the current challenges facing the Federation, we are in need of new allies now more than ever. We must continue to expand if we are to remain healthy and vibrant. The Rhaaxans represent a valuable asset to us if they can be helped to overcome the obstacles they face. That is why we are here."

To Gold it sounded like so much public relations doublespeak. "I realize we've had our share of problems in the last few years, Ambassador," he said, working very hard to keep the distaste from his voice, "but it would seem helpful to remember that the Rhaaxans' state of affairs is one that the Federation must take responsibility for creating. While it might have been an honest error or a massive lapse in judgment, I don't think it justifies continuing to manipulate an entire civilization in order to create a solution that reflects our best interests. I'm pretty sure the Federation will believe that, too. After all, I'd hope we learned something after that mess with the Ba'ku."

During the Dominion War, that peaceful civilization had become the focal point of one of the most embarrassing incidents in Federation history, to Gold at least. High-ranking officials and Starfleet officers had conspired to drive the people from their world in order to harness for their own ends the life-prolonging effects of metaphasic radiation surrounding the Ba'ku planet.

After the crew of the *U.S.S. Enterprise* thwarted the plot, the details of the conspiracy were made public during a lengthy series of trials and courts-martial for those involved. Explanations and excuses were offered, citing the need to maintain the health and security of the Federation and the hardship in doing so during a climate of war and its aftermath. Promises were made and commitments pledged anew to the principles upon which the Federation had been founded, including the highest standard of all, the Prime Directive.

"I think that incident is still fresh enough in a lot of people's minds," Gold continued, "that it'll invite all sorts of unwanted and unpopular comparisons to what's happened here. I just don't see how your actions can possibly be justified or accepted."

Marshall replied, "My intention was to draw the Rhaaxans out and see if they would develop the biogenic agents if given the opportunity. As it happens, we also learned that the colonists were harboring their own weapon."

"And it was a stroke of luck that they didn't get to use that weapon," Gold countered. "If you thought they might do something like this and still went ahead with your plan, then you're even more dangerous than the people who built the damned things."

"It was a calculated risk," Marshall said, "but I was confident that Commander Gomez and her people would be able to stay on top of the situation. There may have been a few bumps, but ultimately that's what happened."

Shaking his head in disbelief, Gold stepped from behind his desk. "How many times does this sort of nonsense have to happen before we finally learn that taking sides in these types of disputes is disastrous for everyone involved? Have we forgotten the forty-year civil war on Mordan IV that was caused by a Starfleet captain? And what about Kirk on Neural or Talin? Those are required study at Starfleet Academy, and still perfect examples of what happens when you muck with a planet's culture. Isn't any of this on the Diplomatic Corps' reading list?"

Marshall drew himself up to his full height, his chest puffing out and his brow knit in irritation. "I've listened to as much abuse from you as I'm going to, Captain. Rest assured that your conduct will factor prominently in my report to your superiors." He said nothing else as he turned and exited the ready room, leaving Gold alone with his first officer.

"I have to say I'm disappointed, Gomez."

Nodding, Gomez replied. "I know, Captain, and I'm sorry. Marshall ordered me not to discuss the matter with anyone, including you. Even before I knew what he had in mind, I went to Captain Scott for help, but he'd been given similar orders about the mission. I knew what we were doing was crazy, but when the orders came from Starfleet I had no choice, sir. I can't tell you how hard this has been for me."

Gold sighed in frustration. He had never been tolerant of "just following orders" as an excuse, but Gomez had raised a valid point. If the orders given to her came from the highest levels of Starfleet Command to cooperate with the Diplomatic Corps, was she not supposed to infer that the orders were lawful and issued in such a manner that those obliged to follow them would not find themselves in a moral or ethical quandary?

He moved back behind his desk and dropped into his chair, indicating for Gomez to take one of the two seats before him. Sighing, he said, "When I first accepted command of the *da Vinci,* I thought I was comfortable with the notion that part of my crew could be accountable to someone else without going through me if the situation called for it." Salek, a Vulcan and the ship's previous S.C.E. team commander until his death during the Dominion War, had also served as Gold's first officer and aided him in adjusting to the ship's unorthodox rank and personnel structure.

"But after what's happened here," he added, "it's obvious that this is a policy vulnerable to abuse. You should never have been put in the position of having to keep secrets from me. There has to be some form of redress to ensure that officers caught up in these types of situations can't be forced to withhold important information, particularly from ship commanders." Leaning forward in his chair, he added, "Not to mention, I don't think I'm content with my and the rest of the crew's being a bunch of chauffeurs that people like Marshall can just drag into any mess they decide to create."

Gomez grimaced at that. "For what it's worth, Captain, I've never viewed you or the crew in that way. I think after this much time we've proven we work better together than separated, which is why I hated Marshall's putting me in that position. I just didn't know what to do, so I concentrated on making sure the Rhaaxans developed an ineffective biogen." She shook her head as disbelief and anger clouded her features. "And as for the colonists, we never saw that coming. We should have anticipated that they might do something themselves, but they'd never even hinted at anything like that. I can't believe how easily we were suckered." Looking up to meet Gold's gaze, she asked, "What do you think the Federation Council is going to say about this?"

"If they have any sense," Gold replied, "they'll deny the Rhaaxans' *and* Numai's application for membership, at least for the foreseeable future. Beyond that, the prefects were right. We did cause some of this, and we have a responsibility to fix it. I expect that Marshall or someone else will be here for quite a while, working with the Rhaaxans and the colonists to find some kind of permanent, peaceful solution."

"I wonder how the citizens of both planets will react when the actions of their governments are made public?" Gomez asked.

The captain shrugged. "They'll have plenty of explaining to do, I suspect. Maybe now they'll stop and see just where all this insanity has left them. I'd be very surprised if there weren't calls for resignations and elections to select new leaders." Nodding more to himself than anyone else, he added, "All things considered, that might not be such a bad thing."

No matter the outcome, Gold knew it was a dispute that would be a long time in resolving. Regardless, the captain was sure that this would be recorded as yet another dark chapter in the annals of Federation diplomatic history, but would it be the one to provide some bit of wisdom and perhaps prevent another such incident from happening in the future? Gold doubted it.

More important, to him at least, was his concern that what had happened here would have lasting effects on him and his relationship with his crew. This mission had highlighted not only the myriad problems that plagued the Rhaaxans' grand aspirations to become Federation members, but also exposed a glaring flaw in what many had believed to be an effective organizational design that supported the unique demands of S.C.E. detachments being ferried by Starfleet ships.

Looks like I'm going to have a long talk with Captain Scott one of these days.

It was an issue David Gold wanted addressed, quickly, before it caused more damage to the bond between a ship's captain and its crew.

FAILSAFE

David Mack

CHAPTER 1

The sky was a blackish purple bruise, filled with banks of swollen storm clouds that dragged heavy coils of rain across the barren plains. Crashing thunder echoed off the distant mountains and rolled away into gritty rumbles. The cold, bitter wind smelled of dirt, and for a moment it dispelled the thick stench of rotting flesh that rose from the hastily excavated pit in front of Venekan Army Trooper Genek Maleska.

Wind-whipped dust stung his face. He lowered his goggles and lifted his face mask, both of which became caked with a mix of brown dust and chalky lime powder from the pit. Maleska could barely see an arm's length in front of his face, but he heard the growl of the excavator's engine as it revved up. He listened to its heavy treads grind forward then stop. A moment later the ground shook as the gigantic industrial vehicle filled a quarter of the pit with fresh-dug black earth.

The falling load of dirt kicked up its own gust of wind and blew most of the lime off the overlapped rows of X'Mari corpses that lined the bottom of the pit, four layers deep.

Maleska coughed. He felt his chest tighten and knew he was moments away from a second taste of his breakfast. He planted the butt of his rifle on the ground as he dropped to his knees and pulled his face mask down and out of the way.

His vomiting didn't last long. The acidic bile burned in the back of his throat. He licked his teeth and spat twice to expel the sour taste from his mouth. Lifting his arm to sleeve the flecks of food and spittle from his mouth and chin, he stopped as he saw that his uniform was shrouded from head to toe in a thick coat of dust. He put his mask back on.

Another load of dirt made a trembling impact in the grave pit. Then the sky darkened as if a giant black curtain had been pulled across it. A loud clap of thunder was followed by a scattered fall of fat raindrops sweeping in from the plains. The sky broke in a sheeting, heavy downpour. The dust coating his uniform turned to mud and washed away in slow, dirty rivulets, revealing the gray-green patterns of his camouflage fatigues.

The excavator's work lights snapped on. The huge machine pushed another mound of soil into the pit. Other piles of dirt began to gradually melt away as muddy flash-floods. As another segment of the pit was filled in, he looked down at the rain-cleansed faces of the dead X'Maris. Their midnight-blue skin and coppery hair lay tangled together, their bodies intertwined like broken, tragic sculpture.

He removed his goggles, mask, and helmet and let the rain wash over him as he pulled his light-blue fingers through his silvery hair. He hoped that the war would end soon, so he could go home and be a civilian again.

A fiery streak sliced through the canopy of storm clouds and blazed across the sky, passing over his squad and racing toward the horizon. Work halted as the two dozen Venekan soldiers scrambled to the northeast edge of the ridge to watch the burning object make planetfall. It had almost reached the horizon when it hit the ground and was swallowed into the perfect darkness of the mist-swept landscape.

"Radio!" Maleska shouted. His radioman jogged over to him and handed him the digital two-way handset. Maleska pressed the secure-frequency switch. "Sync-Com, this is Five-Nine *Jazim*, over," he said. He stared into the darkness, in the direction of the fallen fireball, while he waited for Synchronized Command to respond. A few seconds later, a tinny, digitally processed voice squawked back over the radio.

"Five-Nine Jazim, *Sync-Com. Go ahead."*

"Sync-Com," he said, choosing his words carefully, "we've sighted an unidentified aerial object traveling north-northeast over our position. Estimate touchdown approximately eighty-five *tiliks* from our current location. Please advise, over." Raindrops pelted his helmet with a rapid-fire deluge for several long seconds while he awaited Sync-Com's answer.

"Five-Nine Jazim, *hold your present location for dust-off. Twenty-third Mech Lance'll lift you out of there as soon as the storm breaks. You'll help them recon the UAO crash site. Over."*

"Sync-Com, we confirm, holding for dust-off and recon. Five-Nine *Jazim* out." He stowed the digital radio handset in the radioman's backpack. The rest of the soldiers were still gathered at the edge of the ridge, staring into the rain while trading rumors, guesses, and wagers among themselves.

"Snap to!" he barked. The soldiers turned to face him and straightened to full attention. He prowled in front of the men, his bootsteps splashing in the broad puddles that were growing steadily larger and deeper. "As soon as this storm breaks, we're being lifted out," he said. "Norlin, get back on that excavator and fill this in before it turns into a lake. Everyone else, standard cleanup and perimeter watch. Move out!" The squad scrambled back into action.

Maleska watched the excavator push another wet heap of dirt into the last uncovered segment of the X'Mari mass grave. As the dark-blue faces of the dead vanished beneath a tide of mud, the young noncom feared that the object he'd just watched fall from the sky had been a Venekan military aircraft—one whose crew and ordnance were now in enemy hands.

He glanced at his watch and sighed. Sunrise was more than an hour away, and he could already tell this was going to be a very long day.

Ganag crept forward in the pouring rain, fearful of the strange and smoldering tube-shaped object that had just gouged a ragged wound across the Kelvanthan Plain and come to a stop here at the base of the Scorla Hills. The X'Mari teenager kept his rifle aimed squarely at the object as he moved closer to it.

His cautious footfalls were all but inaudible through the pattering white noise of the storm. From behind him, the beams of his two friends' handlights crisscrossed in tight formation as they lit his path, casting mirror-twin shadows of his gangly adolescent body in front of his feet.

He knelt beside the battered, black object and held his hand above its surface. No heat radiated from it. He touched its cool, slick wet surface and ran his hand along it, feeling its scuffs, cracks, and other points of damage. Resting his rifle against it, he leaned closer to study the emblem etched onto its flat top surface. He had never seen anything like it, not on any flag of the world.

"I don't think it's Venekan," he said over his shoulder.

"Whose is it, then?" Lerec said, his voice quavering. Ganag wondered whether Lerec was too young to be in the field. Most of the scouts had been at least fourteen years old before they picked up weapons. Lerec was only twelve. The boy had insisted that he was ready and had gone out of his way to prove he could shoot, run, and spot as well as the older scouts. Now, less than ten days later, the kid was losing his water during his first real field patrol.

Ganag traced the lines of the round-edged, triangular emblem with his dark-blue fingertip as he considered Lerec's question. "I don't know," he said a few seconds later. "I've never seen this crest in any of the books. And I've never heard of a missile that could navigate without fins."

"I wouldn't call what it did 'navigating,'" said Shikorn, who was fifteen, just one year younger than Ganag. "If you ask me, I'd say it fell." Shikorn had a point; the object's descent had been very erratic.

Ganag was about to ask Shikorn for the radio when he heard the sound of truck engines approaching from inside the Scorla Pass. Without a word, the three boys scrambled to cover behind a nearby cluster of scrub bushes. They pressed themselves against the ground and held their breath as four trucks emerged from the pass and drove directly toward the fallen object. The mud-spattered vehicles' headlight beams, dimmed by slashing rain, swept over the trio as the trucks passed by.

The vehicles came to a stop in a circle around the object. With the engines still running, the drivers and passengers got out. Even in the stormy darkness, Ganag was certain that all of them were X'Maris. Then the leader emerged from behind the far truck. Ganag recognized him as Hakona, a war chief of the X'Mari Resistance. Ganag tapped Shikorn, who nodded his confirmation. The two youths stood up and pulled Lerec to his feet along with them. Ganag called out to the group of adults.

"Friendlies," Ganag said. "Scout Team *Kalon.*"

The X'Mari adults aimed their rifles at the three boys. "Sector code word," one of the men said.

"Vashon-zelif," Ganag said. The adults lowered their weapons. Hakona walked toward the three scouts.

"Have you seen anyone else near here?" Hakona said.

Ganag shook his head. "No, sir. We only just got here ourselves, a few minutes after we saw it hit."

"Everybody in the *zilam* hemisphere saw it hit," Hakona said. "We need to get it to a safe location before the Venekans get here. Help us put it on the flatbed."

Hakona stomped on the accelerator pedal with such force that he almost expected the corroded floor of his vehicle to crumble under his feet. Every bump and divot in the road made the speeding flatbed truck rattle like a child's toy.

He glanced at the cracked mirror on his door. The other three vehicles of his convoy were close behind him, keeping pace and following his lead, down to every curve he fishtailed through at unsafe speeds. He couldn't yet see the gray light of predawn, but he felt it coming.

The downpour had ceased a few minutes earlier, making the roads a bit easier to see. He and the other drivers in his convoy had turned off their trucks' headlights and activated their night-vision goggles. He hated the monochromatic gray-green displays' hypnotic quality, and he struggled to remain focused on the twists and turns of the Scorla Pass.

He heard the first explosion come from behind his vehicle. The glare from the blast flared his light-intensifying goggles to blinding white. As he tore them away from his face, a second explosion transformed his vehicle's few remaining windows into stinging glass projectiles.

The heat of the blast shriveled his short, ragged hair and filled the cab with an acrid stench. By the time the third explosion rocked the narrow canyon of the Scorla Pass, he was aware of nothing except the dizzying sensation that the laws of gravity had been suspended.

The wind screamed through the open side doors of the jumpjet, its constant roar drowned out by the high-frequency screech of the jet aircraft's engines, which became even more deafening as the afterburners kicked in.

A seam of sky along the horizon began to show a hint of gray, a harbinger of the new day. Maleska crouched in front of the open side door, watching the ragged landscape of the Scorla Hills blur past beneath the wings.

Seated in the darkened main compartment of the broad-bodied jumpjet, their backs pressed against its gunmetal-gray walls, were his motley-looking soldiers. Most of them kept their rifles clutched between their knees, barrels up and safeties on. Norlin, a short-timer who everyone could tell was all but burned out after spending too long in country, slumped in his harness, mouth hanging open to give his snoring free rein. The young footman's rifle was laid like a bridge across his knees, the barrel pointing toward the rear of the troop compartment.

The jumpjet banked hard to the left, and Maleska tightened his grip on the rappelling harness over his head. A sharp hiss preceded the release of a volley of missiles from the jumpjet's wings. Their smoky exhaust trails snaked inside the troop compartment, and the soldiers awoke to the bitter stench of spent chemical propellants, which made Maleska cough. Over his own hacking gasps, he heard the dull reports of the missiles striking their targets on the ground below.

The troop compartment's ruby-hued lights clicked on, and the engines whined as the pilots fired the braking thrusters. The outer engines rotated into a takeoff-and-landing configuration, and the jumpjet began a quick, vertical descent.

The co-pilot's voice crackled inside Maleska's helmet headset. *"Snap to,"* he said. *"Insertion in twenty seconds."*

Maleska looked at his squad. "Snap to!" he said,

shouting over the engine noise. "Weapons hot. Two by two, standard cover. Search and secure. Yellik, left point. I've got right point."

The jumpjet touched down with a heavy, jarring bump.

"Move out!" Maleska said as he hopped out of the jumpjet through its right-side door, half of his twenty-four-man squad behind him, the other half following his second in command, Senior Footman Yellik, out its left side.

Maleska landed on his feet with practiced ease. His boots sank into the soft, muddy ground. He lowered himself into a crouched posture, weapon held level and aimed forward. Moving out of the way of the footmen who followed behind him, he dropped to one knee and scanned the perimeter through his rifle's targeting sight. There was no sign of movement on either side of the road ahead, or from the overturned burning vehicles that lay in the middle of the narrow, high-walled mountain pass. He looked back and saw all his footmen assembled behind him in proper cover formation. Glancing beneath the jumpjet, he could tell from the arrangement of feet on the other side that Yellik and his team were also ready.

He keyed his headset mic. "*Tikrun* Seven, Five-Nine *Jazim*. I've got boots on the ground, and I'm moving to secure the site, over."

"Five-Nine Jazim, Tikrun *Seven,"* the jumpjet co-pilot said, his voice rendered scratchy and mechanized by Maleska's headset receiver. *"Acknowledged. Standing by for dust-off.* Tikrun *Seven out."*

Maleska led his squad forward toward the fiery wreckage of the four trucks. The soldiers' steps made small squelching noises as they traversed the muddy road. Inside the shattered and bent vehicles, groups of four to six corpses lay in heaps, charred almost beyond recognition by the searing heat of the Venekan "sky cutters," small missile-delivered munitions that relied on scorching temperatures and thousands of deadly shrapnel-like projectiles to quickly neutralize enemy personnel.

Maleska marveled at the obviously overwhelming firepower that the jumpjet had unleashed against the small ground convoy. Beneath the mangled vehicles, the thin crust of pavement that had long ago been laid over this neglected road was now molten and glistening behind curtains of heat radiation.

The point squads reached the convoy's lead vehicle, a flatbed truck that had been flipped upside-down and rear-end-forward by the impact of the blasts that had erupted behind it. It was the only vehicle that did not appear to have been directly targeted by the aerial barrage. The road here was not melted but was spider-webbed with fresh fissures that emanated from the fiery debris behind it.

Yellik glanced inside the vehicle and aimed his weapon into the cab. The air was split by the angry buzz of his assault rifle. Maleska shielded his eyes from the incandescent muzzle-flash. Seconds later, Yellik eyed his handiwork and signaled all clear to Maleska, who keyed his mic.

"*Tikrun* Seven, Five-Nine *Jazim*. Site secured, over."

"Five-Nine Jazim, Tikrun *Seven. Acknowledged, site secure. Relaying to Sync-Com.* Tikrun *Seven out."*

Maleska kneeled beside the overturned vehicle and glanced beneath it. Secured to the flatbed was an oblong shape wrapped in a dark tarpaulin. He looked over his shoulder and snapped his fingers a few times in quick succession to get his squad's attention. "Norlin, Pillo. Crawl under and cut whatever that is free. Get it out here so I can see it."

With sour-tempered grumbling, the two enlisted men wriggled under the flatbed and began cutting the heavy cables that secured the object to the flatbed. Maleska stood off to one side and kept his expression neutral to mask his growing impatience.

Several minutes later, while the two men were still working, a trio of Venekan jumpjets landed down the road, behind *Tikrun* Seven. Three squads quickly debarked from the jumpjets and fanned out in either direction, far behind and far in front of the secured site. Following them up to Maleska and the wrecked flatbed was an officer whom Maleska recognized only by virtue of his rank and a few surprisingly accurate overheard descriptions: his division leader, Commander Zila.

Zila was a career officer whose face looked like it had been hewn from the mountains of Zankethi and tempered in the fires of combat. He had a reputation for never accepting defeat in battle, and he was rumored to be nurturing lofty political ambitions. Maleska didn't believe that a high-ranking officer like Zila would leave the safety of Sync-Com headquarters and set foot inside X'Mar unless there was something critically important going on—something that would require the commander's personal attention.

Zila strode up to Maleska and spoke through clenched, sepia-tinted teeth with a voice like a rasping saw.

"As soon as your men cut the truck's cargo free, I want them back on the jumper," Zila said. "But you stay here."

"Yes, sir," Maleska said with a nod. He turned as he

heard the sound of the truck's cargo falling free of its bonds and thudding to the ground beneath the truck. A few seconds later, Norlin and Pillo, now coated in mud and grease, pushed the cylindrical, shrouded object out from under the truck, rolling it ahead of them. As soon as it rolled free of the truck, it slipped away from them and began to roll toward the side of the road. Zila stopped it by planting his heel on it, like a conquering hero. Norlin and Pillo, still down on their bellies in front of him, stared up at him in awe.

"Get up," Maleska said, his voice sharp. "Yellik, take the squad back to the jumper, double time." Yellik snapped Maleska a quick salute, then barked orders at the rest of the squad as he herded them back into *Tikrun* Seven.

Zila watched them pile into the aircraft. As soon as the jumpjet door slid closed, he turned to Maleska. "Cut that cover off of it," he said. Maleska drew his utility knife and sliced the tarpaulin off the object.

The shredded fabric fell away to reveal an ordinary fuel drum—rusted, pockmarked with holes, and emptier than the promises of a politician. Beside him, Zila made a sound that was somewhere between a grunt and a growl.

As the sky overhead turned a bleak, hopeless shade of gray, Maleska's long day became just a little bit longer.

Ganag kneeled in the stern of the long, narrow skiff and slowly paddled it downstream. The skiff sat dangerously low in the water, which threatened to wash over the gunwales and swamp the small boat if Ganag tried to paddle too quickly. In the prow of the skiff, Lerec and

Shikorn lay back-to-back, sleeping fitfully beneath a thin, shared blanket of moth-eaten fabric.

The object from the sky was in the middle of the skiff, between Ganag and his friends. It was concealed beneath thick, gray sheets and sacks marked as grain but filled with feathers.

Ganag knew that Hakona and his officers were dead. He had seen the Venekan aircraft streak toward the Scorla Pass, and he'd heard the muffled explosions echoing off the hills. Just like that, every adult Ganag and his friends had known was gone.

Now it was up to them to carry this strange prize to safety—to the last bastion of the X'Mari Resistance.

Ganag stopped paddling for a moment and unfolded his map, which rustled in a frigid breeze that signaled the early onset of winter. This stream would carry him to the Ulom River within half a day. From there, he had only to let the current carry him and the skiff downriver. Once on the river proper, they would hide during the daytime and move only at night.

If we're lucky and careful, he thought, *we might reach the Resistance in four days.* He forced himself not to consider what would happen if the Venekans learned that it was to him and his friends that Hakona had entrusted the object.

The first reddish rays of dawn snuck over the horizon and slashed between the war-ravaged hills of northern X'Mar. Ganag tucked his map inside his shirt and resumed paddling with quiet resolve toward his destination.

CHAPTER 2

Commander Sonya Gomez leaned against the wash-basin in her quarters and sighed heavily. *Today is nothing,* she thought.

She had been silently observing the milestones of time's passage since "that day." The day that a routine salvage mission had become a gruesome tragedy. The day that more than half of the *da Vinci*'s crew had died in the line of duty. The day that Kieran Duffy, the man she'd loved, had gone to his death.

She didn't speak of her habit with the other survivors of the Galvan VI mission, and she hadn't discussed it during her Starfleet-mandated counseling sessions. She had simply noted the passing of the days and at regular intervals reminded herself.

Today marked no such milestone. Today was just another day like any other. Another day aboard the *da*

Vinci. Another day in Starfleet. Another day alone with her shattered heart.

Today is nothing.

She had been woken only minutes ago by a comm chirp in the middle of her sleep cycle.

"Bridge to Gomez," the voice had said, rousing her from a fitful slumber. After a moment of foggy-headedness, she had realized that the voice was that of Vance Hawkins, the ship's deputy chief of security.

"Gomez here," she had said, her voice halfway between a croak and a groan.

"Captain Gold needs you in the briefing room, Commander," Hawkins had said. *"He said it was urgent."*

"On my way, Chief," Gomez had said, then half-rolled out of bed and slouched into her bathroom.

She sighed again and let her weight rest on the washbasin. Looking up at her hollow-eyed reflection in the mirror, she wondered whether she had time to step into the sonic shower or perhaps just work some cleanser and conditioner into her dark, curly hair, which spilled in unkempt coils over her shoulders.

Chief Petty Officer Hawkins's voice echoed in her thoughts: *"He said it was urgent."*

She tied her hair back in a utilitarian ponytail, opened her closet, and grabbed a clean uniform. *No point getting all dolled up just to get my hands dirty.*

Fabian Stevens looked like something the *sehlat* dragged in. His hair was slightly disheveled. He could swear his eyes were filled with sand. His eyelids drooped and threatened to drag him back to sleep. His head lolled forward, and he caught a whiff of his replicated Colombian coffee.

He jerked awake, his eyes now stuck at wide-open. He took another much-needed sip of coffee and tried not to let himself become hypnotized by the sixty-cycles-per-second hum of the briefing room's overhead EPS conduits.

Captain David Gold sat at the head of the briefing room table, hands folded in front of him. Seated to Stevens's left was revoltingly wide-awake cultural specialist Carol Abramowitz, who casually scrolled through screen after screen of data on her padd.

Bleary-eyed, Stevens fixated on the steam rising from his coffee mug. Sitting opposite him was Hawkins, who leaned back in his chair and pensively stroked his dark, bearded chin.

Past the far end of the table from the captain was the main viewscreen, on which heavy-jowled and white-haired Captain Montgomery Scott, the officer who gave the Starfleet Corps of Engineers its marching orders, rolled his eyes impatiently.

"I apologize for the delay, Captain Scott," Gold said. Scott smiled and waved his hand, brushing aside the apology.

"No need, lad," Scott said. *"I remember what it's like living on ship's time. It's always midnight somewhere."*

Abramowitz put down her padd as the door slid open. Gomez entered and blushed as she saw the group was waiting for her. She took her seat at Gold's left. "Sorry to keep you wait—"

"It's all right," Gold said, cutting her off. "Captain Scott, the floor is yours."

Scott keyed some switches on his companel. The screen split to show two images: Scott on the left, and a schematic of a Starfleet Class VII Remote Culture Study Probe on the right. *"About a year ago, Starfleet lost contact with Probe Delta-7941 after it encountered an uncharted astrophysical hazard,"* he said. *"We thought it was destroyed. We were wrong."*

The image on the right side of the screen changed to a detailed schematic of one of the probe's internal systems. *"Four-point-six hours ago, Starfleet received a subspace signal from the probe indicating that it's crashed—and that its self-destruct failsafes have . . . well, failed."*

The image on the right side of the viewscreen changed again, to a solar-system diagram. *"The probe went off course and landed intact on this system's third planet,"* Scott said. *"Teneb is an M-class world, humanoid population, uneven levels of technological development between its many nation-states. A lot like Earth before the Third World War."*

"And no doubt protected by the Prime Directive," Gomez said.

Scott nodded, his expression grave. *"Aye, and that's where the wicket gets sticky. The Tenebians are a clever lot, but not as clever as they like to think. Depending on which one of their countries gets its hands on the probe's warp engine, they might reverse-engineer the thing . . . or they might blow themselves to kingdom come while tinkering with its antimatter pods."*

"There's an even worse scenario," Hawkins said. "They figure out how to control antimatter, and they turn it into a weapon that can destroy their planet. The probe could be used to start an apocalyptic arms race."

"Oy vey," Gold said.

Abramowitz looked confused. "Can't we remote-detonate it?" she said. Stevens swallowed a sip of coffee and shook his head.

"Nope," he said. "The remote detonator's part of the self-destruct failsafe—which failed." He took another sip of coffee.

"But can't we just beam it up?" Abramowitz said.

"Unfortunately, no," Scott said. *"The crash damaged its antimatter shielding. Trying to beam it up would cause an explosion larger than anything that world's ever seen. . . . And, there's another wrinkle to consider. . . ."*

"Of course there is," Gomez said, and smirked ironically. Scott continued without acknowledging her gentle sarcasm.

"The planet's dominant superpower has begun exploring space: orbital stations, lunar bases, deep-space telescopes. . . . Bringing a Starfleet vessel into orbit is a risk we can't take. You four need to land on the planet without the Tenebians detecting the da Vinci. *You'll go in undercover: no weapons, and with as little Starfleet technology as possible. We can't risk any more cultural contamination."*

Gomez furrowed her brow before tossing out another question to Scott. "Captain, may I ask why this operation isn't being handled by Starfleet Intelligence?"

"They asked us *to do it,"* Scott said. *"If the probe could be detonated without being fixed first, they'd handle it themselves. But they don't have anyone who can make these kinds of repairs in the field. . . . That's why I'm sending you lot."*

"Understood," Gomez said with a curt nod.

"All right, then," Scott said. *"I'm sending over everything in the database about Teneb and all the telemetry from the probe. . . . Are there any more questions?"* Everyone shook their heads to indicate that there weren't.

"Then Godspeed, and good luck. Scott out."

The viewscreen blinked to a bright blue field adorned

with the white double-laurel-and-stars of the Federation emblem.

Gold turned toward Gomez. "We'll reach the Teneb system in just over sixty-eight hours," he said. "I'll ask Conlon and Poynter to find you a hush-hush way to go planetside."

Gomez nodded. "Okay, good. Carol, I need you to go over all the cultural files on Teneb. Check the probe's crash coordinates and pay particular attention to the cultures and current situations in that region."

"Sure thing," Abramowitz said. "I'll let Bart know we'll need an alphanumeric primer for the planet's written languages."

"Good," Gomez said. She turned toward Hawkins. "Vance, check the database for information about the types of vehicles we might find down there. We might need to cover a lot of ground to find the probe, and I'd rather not do it all on foot."

"You got it," Hawkins said. Gomez turned her attention toward Stevens, who was trying to look attentive rather than jittery and wired on caffeine. He suspected, based on her bemused expression, that he was failing.

"Fabe," she said, "you look like I feel. Go get some rest, and I'll see you when alpha shift starts—" She checked the ship's chronometer on a display set into the tabletop, then let out a weary sigh. "—in about six hours."

The landscape blurred past. Wind whipped through cracks in the fragile glass windshield in front of Hawkins. He stomped on the clutch then slammed the gearshift lever forward. He felt the vehicle lurch as a jaw-clenching grinding of metal on metal screamed from the combustion engine. The pistons seized and smoke belched from beneath the car's dented red hood. The rapid deceleration made the two-passenger vehicle fishtail wildly, and Hawkins saw the gnarled trunk of a tree a split second before it crumpled the front end of the automobile into an accordion fold. The safety-harness strap that diagonally crossed his torso bit into his collarbone.

The simulation froze, its injury-and-mortality failsafe kicking in at the last possible moment. Hawkins's pulse raced and sweat soaked his brow and back. There was nothing simulated about the adrenaline rush that still had him shaking in his seat. He had never understood why some of his fellow security officers felt the need to court disaster in holographic simulations. He figured there was more than enough real danger in the galaxy without bringing it into a training program.

"Computer," he said, "load vehicle training program Hawkins Twenty-nine. Introduce random road-hazard variables and activate foul-weather subroutine." He was enjoying this training regimen. Tenebian motor vehicles and weapons were a good example of Hodgkins's Law of Parallel Planet Development: Many of their inventions closely paralleled those of early twenty-first-century Earth.

The environment re-formed itself around him. He now was seated on a squat, two-wheeled vehicle that was parked on a high-mountain road marked by steep grades and treacherous hairpin turns. Swiftly approaching from the horizon was a bank of storm clouds. *"Program ready,"* the computer said, its feminine voice unchanged since the day Hawkins had joined Starfleet.

He twisted the vehicle's handgrip throttle and was about to launch himself down the lonely, snaking road at the fastest speeds he could handle, when the door chime sounded.

"Hey, Vance," Stevens said over the comm. *"It's Fabe. Can I come in?"*

Hawkins reduced the cycle's throttle. "Sure," he said.

The hololab door appeared to Hawkins's right, taking shape on the rocky face of the cliff wall. The door opened and Stevens stepped inside the hololab next to Hawkins and his loudly purring machine. "Nice program," Stevens said, looking past Hawkins at the panoramic vista. "Teneb?"

"Yeah," Hawkins said. "Built it from database files. The vehicle specs are at least a few years old, but I don't think the basic operating principles will have changed much since then." Hawkins nodded toward the road. "Want to join me? Play a little follow-my-leader?"

"Nah," Stevens said. "Took me six weeks to master flying a Work Bug, and that was based on a system I'd already been trained on." He gestured toward Hawkins's motorcycle. "I wouldn't know where to start with one of these things."

"You don't know what you're missing," Hawkins said.

"No, but I know what *you're* missing," Stevens said. "The premission briefing. It started five minutes ago. They sent me down to get you. Apparently, someone with a security clearance turned off the hololab's main comm circuit."

Hawkins dismounted from the motorcycle. "Computer," he said. "End program." The road, the vista, and the cycle all vanished, revealing the compact space of the *da Vinci*'s hololab. Hawkins narrowed his eyes in mock irritation at Stevens. "Killjoy," he said. Stevens shrugged as he led him out of the hololab and into the corridor.

"That's the job," Stevens said. "You don't like it, quit."

"I can't quit," Hawkins said as he followed Stevens. "I'm enlisted."

"Yeah," Stevens said stoically. "Me, too."

Abramowitz switched the briefing room viewscreen image to one that displayed the national borders and prominent landmarks of an area within a one-thousand-kilometer radius around the crashed probe's last known coordinates.

The rest of the away team—as well as *da Vinci* second officer Lieutenant Commander Mor glasch Tev, chief of security Lieutenant Commander Domenica Corsi, chief engineer Lieutenant Nancy Conlon, chief medical officer Dr. Elizabeth Lense, and Captain Gold—listened as she detailed the findings of her hastily compiled research.

"This is our biggest problem," she said. "The entire region, which the indigenous people call X'Mar, is a war zone. The country of Veneka, Teneb's sole military and economic superpower, recently invaded X'Mar for its uranium resources."

She switched to the next screen of information. On one side were images of Venekan soldiers in uniform. On the other side were images of X'Mari civilians and Resistance fighters.

"The Venekans," she said, "are an ethnically diverse population, with a level of technology roughly equivalent to the best of early twenty-first-century Earth. The only Venekans we're likely to encounter during our mission will be soldiers. We have no hope of infiltrating their military, and we definitely won't be equipped to fight them, so we should avoid them."

She pointed at the various X'Mari images. All the X'Maris had skin tones of dark blue, and metallic hair colors ranging from coppery to dark bronze. "The X'Maris, on the other hand, are ethnically homogenous and highly xenophobic. Their army is composed primarily of irregular militias. Our best bet for moving through the region undetected is to pose as X'Mari civilians—and pray that we don't run into the Venekan Army."

Gomez nodded. "Thank you, Carol." Abramowitz sat down as Gomez looked to Tev, her second-in-command of the S.C.E. team. Even after having served with Tev for a matter of weeks, Abramowitz still found the Tellarite's omnipresent air of arrogant superiority off-putting. "Tev," Gomez said, "have you made any progress with tamper-proofing the away team's tricorders?"

Tev looked offended that Gomez would even entertain the possibility that he hadn't devised something unspeakably brilliant since breakfast. "Of course I have," he said. "I've outfitted them with a self-destruct circuit that you can trigger with a pre-set command phrase, on a timer, or by remote from another tricorder. Also, I designed an independent tactile sensor that recognizes whether the person touching the tricorder is human. If a non-human picks up one of your tricorders—*poof!* No more tricorder. I'd have brought one to the meeting except—" He held up his hands, and looked around the room. *"Poof,"* he said.

"Good, thank you," Gomez said. Abramowitz wondered if she was only imagining an expression of long-suffering on Gomez's face whenever the first officer spoke to Tev. Gomez turned her attention to Dr. Lense. "Doctor, how soon can you be ready to begin cosmetic surgery for the away team?"

"Give the word, Commander," Lense said. "Sickbay's ready when you are."

Abramowitz watched Gomez fluidly shift her gaze toward Chief Engineer Conlon. "And that brings us to you," Gomez said. "Nancy, are we *any* closer to formulating a plan for getting the away team onto and off of the planet?"

The petite chief engineer cocked her head at an odd angle and shrugged. "Maybe," she said. She sounded unconvincing.

"Maybe?" Gomez said, obviously wanting more details.

"Chief Poynter and I are still running some tests," Conlon said. "If we can iron out the bugs, we'll have an answer for you by tomorrow at 0800."

"I think you mean today, at 1900," Gomez said.

Conlon hesitated, tapped her fingers on the table as she parsed the order implicit in Gomez's remark, then nodded. "Right, that's what I said," Conlon quipped. "Today at 1900. No problem."

"All right," Gomez said. "Assuming we iron out the insertion and extraction plans by then, the away team will report to sickbay at 2100 to begin cosmetic modification. Does anyone have anything else?" A quick look around the room yielded no questions. Gomez stood up from the table. "Meeting adjourned."

Abramowitz picked up her padd, saved her notes from the briefing, and pocketed the handheld device as she followed the others out of the room. She had long dreamed of a chance to study a new alien culture incognito and *in situ.* But walking unguarded into a combat zone had not been what she'd had in mind.

"Dom, wait up!" Stevens said, calling out to Corsi. She was several paces ahead of him in the corridor, which was empty except for the two of them. It was rare to be able to steal a moment's privacy aboard a ship as small as the *da Vinci,* and Stevens figured he'd best take advantage of it while it lasted.

She stopped and half-turned to face him. The perfection of the blonde security chief's tall, athletic body was outshone only by the delicate symmetry of her face in profile.

He quickened his step and came to a stop beside her.

"Hey, Fabe," she said. "What's up?" Her manner was warm and relaxed. It was a side of her that most *da Vinci* personnel didn't get to see often, if ever.

Stevens had tried not to develop expectations when it came to Corsi. It had been several months since they'd shared a one-night stand that she had made him promise to never mention again—in part because Starfleet frowned upon fraternization between officers and enlisted personnel, and because Corsi simply didn't like having her personal life on display.

But a few months ago, when Stevens's best friend Kieran Duffy was killed in the line of duty, it had been her shoulder that he'd cried on. At the time, he and Corsi had been on the verge of . . . what? Romance? It had been hard to tell. But after their visit to her family and their return to duty on the *da Vinci,* nothing had been the same between them. For one thing, they no longer needed to pretend that they weren't friends. For another, much of the awkwardness that had marked the beginning of their relationship had long since passed.

Which made the awkwardness of this moment stand out.

"I'm not sure how to ask this," he said.

"Just spit it out," she said reassuringly.

Stevens nodded. The moment stretched out a bit longer than he'd intended. She kept her attention fixed on him while he studied the scuffs on his shoes. He looked up. "Why aren't you going on the away mission?"

She shrugged. "It's Vance's turn."

"But it's such a high-risk mission that I just assumed you'd want to—"

"He can handle it," she said, the corners of her mouth turning upward in a half-smile. "He's actually better qualified than I am for this kind of thing."

She reached out and pressed the turbolift call button.

"If you say so," Stevens said.

"Besides, he'll need high-profile field experience if he ever wants to become a chief of security. People in our line of work don't get promoted for sitting around pushing buttons."

Stevens heard the hum of the turbolift stopping a moment before the outer doors opened. Corsi stepped inside the turbolift, then turned to face him again.

"Anyway," she said. "Good luck down there. Be careful."

"Thanks," he said. "I will." The turbolift doors closed.

He stood alone in the corridor, staring at the closed door.

For months after their one-night stand, he hadn't noticed that she had always seemed to be at his side during away missions, even when protocol would have placed her closer to someone of higher rank. Now, however, she seemed content to leave his defense to someone else.

As he walked back to his quarters, he realized that, though he would never admit it, he was bitterly disappointed and more than a little concerned that this time out she wouldn't be there to watch over him.

CHAPTER 3

"Testing," Haznedl said. The ops officer's feminine voice was soft, barely audible through the subaural transceiver implanted in Gomez's middle ear. The sensation of having a voice inside her head made Gomez feel like she was hallucinating.

"Susan, can you boost the gain on my transceiver?" Gomez said. A moment later, Haznedl's voice sounded again inside Gomez's head, this time as clear as if she was standing right next to her. *"Testing,"* Haznedl said again. *"Better?"*

"Much. Thanks." Gomez sat on the edge of a bed in sickbay, staring down at her indigo hands. She was already attired in the rough, earth-toned cloth garb of a X'Mari civilian. Her tricorder was safely tucked away in a deep pocket along the leg of her pants. Her new, coppery hair spilled across the front of the heavy, dark-brown serape that covered her torso. Her feet were shod in heavy leather shoes, and each leg was wrapped from ankle to midthigh with a long, wide, supple strip of dark leather tied tight at the top with thin strips of hemp cord. Despite having been replicated less than an hour ago, it all smelled like vintage clothing, musty and rich with history.

Across from her, sitting on two other beds, were Hawkins and Stevens. Both men had already been cosmetically altered with nearly identical shades of dark-blue skin and dark-bronze hair. Only the slight difference in their eye color—Stevens had been given metallic-gold irises, while Hawkins's were now metallic violet—enabled her to distinguish them from one another. Both were dressed similarly to Gomez, except that the leather wrappings on their legs stopped below the knee. That was a gender-specific detail that Abramowitz had insisted on when she submitted the replicator patterns for the away team's disguises.

Stevens checked the settings on his tricorder. Hawkins tucked his tricorder under his serape and began stretching and testing the range of motion afforded him by the X'Mari clothing.

The door to the surgical suite opened and Abramowitz stepped out. The cultural specialist had been the last to undergo the procedure because she had been busy overseeing the others' transformations into authentic-looking X'Maris. Her skin was now midnight blue, and her new head of rust-hued, copper-flecked hair was tied in a long, large-knotted braid that hung straight down her back almost to her waist.

Abramowitz walked over to Gomez. "I have to fix your hair, Commander," she said. "Turn around for me?" Gomez turned and sat quietly as Abramowitz rapidly braided her hair. Within a few minutes she was finished. Abramowitz stepped in front of Gomez and looked over the first officer's disguise. "Perfect," she said. "And if I may say so, blue is definitely your color."

Gomez rolled her eyes and stood up. "Let's go."

The away team stood in the transporter room and stared at Conlon and transporter chief Laura Poynter. None of the away team personnel showed any sign of being willing to step onto the transporter pad. Conlon was quickly growing annoyed.

"You've got to be kidding," Gomez said.

"I'm not saying it's perfect," Conlon said. "But if the ship can't go into orbit to beam you down, then this—"

"Is suicide," Hawkins said.

"I won't lie to you, it could be a rough ride," Poynter said. "But we've got plenty of documentation on previous, safe uses of this technology, and we've tested the living daylights out of it."

"If I'd known you were planning on using a jury-rigged subspace transporter, I'd have aborted the mission," Gomez said.

Conlon rolled her eyes. "Do you think we'd let you step on the pad if we thought it wasn't safe? The transporter will work fine. My only concern is getting accurate beam-down coordinates from this distance." Conlon was actually more concerned about interference from Teneb's primary star, because Captain Gold had parked the *da Vinci* above the star's north pole to conceal the ship from Teneb's legions of satellites and radio telescopes. But given the level of agitation the away team was already exhibiting, Conlon thought it best not to tell them about that particular variable in the equation.

"Let's say you can get us down more or less in one piece," Stevens said. "How are you supposed to lock on to our signals to beam us up from this far away?"

"We can't," Conlon said. She continued before the team's groans of dismay got out of hand. "You can use a tricorder or the probe's transceiver to send a signal that'll let us know you're ready to come out. When we get it, we'll warp in, do a high-impulse flyby of the planet, and grab you with a near-warp transport before the Tenebians get too good a look at us. We can go from signal to beam-out in thirty seconds. In theory."

"If you can get us *out* with a near-warp flyby," Hawkins said, "why can't you beam us *in* the same way?"

"Captain's orders," Conlon said. "He doesn't want the Tenebians getting more than one look at us. *That* means you only get one shot at this. You all go in together, you all come out together. If you choose to abort, that's it—mission over."

Stevens rolled his eyes. Abramowitz brusquely lifted her hands in a gesture of capitulation. Hawkins shrugged.

Gomez stared at Conlon. "*Captain's* orders?"

"Uh, yeah," Conlon said. "Is there a problem, Commander?"

Sighing, Gomez said, "No, no problem. He's the captain, after all."

Conlon had felt odd being the bearer of Gold's orders to Gomez. She guessed that this was the captain's way of tweaking Gomez for what happened at Rhaax.

Gomez stepped onto the transporter pad. The rest of the team followed her and took their positions beneath the phase-transition coils. Conlon nodded to Poynter, who took her post at the transporter controls. Gomez frowned at Conlon.

"And away we go," Gomez said with flat sarcasm.

Conlon moved behind the control panel next to Poynter. "Conlon to bridge. We're ready, Captain."

"Stand by," Gold said over the comm. A few seconds later, he continued. *"Shabalala says the beam-in point is clear. You're good to go."*

"Acknowledged." Conlon nodded to Poynter. "Energize."

Poynter keyed in the transport sequence. The room filled with the deep hum of the energizer coils charging to maximum power, followed by the almost musical rush of white noise that accompanied the dematerialization sequence. As the away team's glowing silhouettes vanished from the transporter pad, Conlon prayed for their soft landing and safe return.

Abramowitz felt the irresistible tug of gravity as she began to materialize. She had warned the others that Teneb's gravity was just slightly higher than what they were accustomed to aboard the *da Vinci,* and to pace themselves accordingly.

The transporter's annular confinement beam released its hold on her. She had just enough time to blink at her majestic view of the moonlit Scorla Hills before she realized that she was falling.

The rest of the away team plummeted beside her. They had materialized in mid-air, more than five meters above a river. For a moment, she almost dared to hope the river would break their fall. The coursing water rushed up to meet her.

The away team splashed into the river. Abramowitz had barely registered the stinging cold of the water before her feet struck a slippery mass of rock that had been concealed just beneath the river's frothing surface.

Her left ankle shattered on impact. She shrieked in agony as her legs buckled. Her left femur broke as it slammed against the submerged boulder, and she fell on her side. Her left arm struck the jagged crest of the rock. She felt the bone break beneath her bicep, as she slipped swiftly beneath the frigid water.

She cried out in pain, tried to shout for help. She gasped for air and instead pulled water into her lungs.

Back to the surface, she commanded herself as she looked upward at the water-distorted crescent of Teneb's moon. *Use your good arm. Air! Swim!* Her body refused to obey. She felt leaden. She reached out toward the light as she sank. Her outstretched right hand seemed to be several meters away.

Then it was in the grasp of another hand.

She was back above the surface, gasping for air, with no recollection how she'd gotten there, being pulled to shore. She was so cold, almost numb, and she started shivering uncontrollably. She couldn't feel her feet. Her teeth chattered violently despite her attempts to stay still.

Hawkins carried her out of the water and gently laid her on her back a few meters from shore. Gomez and Stevens were right behind him. Gomez already had her tricorder out and was scanning Abramowitz.

"It's bad," she said, as much to the two men as to the injured cultural specialist. "Left ankle shattered, multiple breaks in the left femur, fibula, and tibia. Left knee joint dislocated. Multiple serious fractures in her pelvis. Broken humerus." Gomez put away the tricorder and took out a disguised emergency medical kit that Dr. Lense had put together.

"You two go find some kindling and firewood," she said to Stevens and Hawkins. "We have to warm her up before she goes into shock. Once she's stable, we'll move out."

Hawkins stopped Stevens with a gesture and pointed at Abramowitz as he spoke to Gomez. "'Move out'? She needs to get to sickbay."

Gomez opened her medkit and took out two transparent adhesive patches. She gently affixed them to the underside of Abramowitz's upper right arm, and they seemed to vanish as they absorbed into the faux-blue skin.

"We can't get her back to the *da Vinci* without aborting the mission," Gomez said. "Her injuries are serious, but they're not life-threatening. Once we stabilize her, we'll set her up with some camouflage and supplies. If we need any cultural advice, we can reach her on the subaural transceivers."

Hawkins looked like he was considering further protest, but a silent, withering glare from Gomez convinced him otherwise. "Yes, sir," he said. He turned and followed Stevens away from the river, up a slope toward some trees.

The dermal patches released their painkillers into Abramowitz's bloodstream. The pain in her leg abated. Gomez opened a watertight compartment in her backpack and took out a rolled-up blanket. She gently placed it under Abramowitz's head. "You'll be okay, Carol," Gomez said. "I promise."

"I'm going into shock," she said through a shaking jaw.

Gomez spread another heavy blanket over her and tucked it under her. "No, I'm gonna fix that right now," Gomez said. "As soon as the guys come back, we'll build you a fire. You'll be okay here while we finish the mission."

Abramowitz felt almost disembodied by the sedative side effects of the painkillers. She blinked slowly. A weak smile trembled across her lips. "Well, hurry up, then," she said. "No offense, Commander, but I want to go home."

Commander Zila hunched over the regional road-and-municipality map, his pale-blue hands planted flat and wide apart on the table on either side of the large, laminated document. It had been more than three days since the UAO had fallen from the sky, and he was still no closer to finding it.

On the opposite side of the table stood Legioner Goff, Zila's divisional second-in-command. Neither officer had enjoyed a decent night's sleep in three days. As they cross-referenced field reports here in Zila's meticulously organized command office, it looked like tonight wouldn't be any different.

"Where the hell can it be?" Zila said, slapping the table with his palm. "It's got to be somewhere in the hills."

Goff shook his head. "Can't be. We've cordoned every road and stopped every vehicle within five hundred *tiliks* of the impact site. We emptied every X'Mari camp we could find. It isn't there."

Zila pushed himself away from the table and paced in front of it. He scratched his head and thought aloud. "Maybe the X'Maris buried it," he said.

"Yes, maybe," Goff said. Zila could tell the legioner was less than convinced. He forced himself to consider other scenarios, no matter how implausible they might seem.

"If the X'Maris don't have it, and we don't have it, is it possible that there are foreign agents in play?"

"Definitely," Goff said. "But they'd still have to move the object. Sync-Com radar indicated it was about the size of a class-six warhead. Not exactly the kind of thing you can hide in a backpack."

"So we've intercepted everything on the ground, and found nothing," Zila said. "And we know the no-fly zone hasn't been breached." He stopped in front of the table and loomed over the regional map once again. He pressed his pale-blue index finger onto an *X,* drawn in grease pencil onto the map's clear plastic cover to mark the object's impact point. He traced the route of the Scorla Pass away from the impact point and into the hills.

Then he retraced his finger's path across the map, back to a notation on the map that was so tiny it almost escaped notice. "Hand me a magnifying glass," he said. Goff grabbed one off the shelf behind him and handed it to Zila, who put it to his eye and leaned down to scrutinize the map close up. "That's a bridge," Zila muttered. "It's a *flezzing* bridge. What does it cross?" Goff opened the cabinet beneath the shelves and grabbed a topographical map of the region. He unfurled the map, which was printed on clear plastic, and laid it over the road map.

A hairline-thin blue line snaked through the Scorla Hills and passed beneath the road map's infinitesimal bridge icon.

"It's on the water," Zila said. He followed the blue line of the Scorla Ria across the topographical map toward progressively lower elevations until it intersected a much thicker blue line. "By now it'd be on the Ulom River."

"But we're watching the river," Goff said.

"For smugglers and terrorists," Zila said. "Not for one small watercraft just floating by. Whatever carried the object out of the hills had to be small enough to navigate a narrow, shallow stream for more than a hundred and twenty *tiliks.*"

"How many safe havens are there along that stretch of the river?" Goff said.

Zila scanned the names of the towns that lined the Ulom River downstream from its intersection with the Scorla Ria. "Tengma. Raozan. Kinzhol. Lersset. They've all been short-listed as X'Mari guerrilla bases."

"Assuming that the X'Maris are the ones who have the object," Goff said.

"They have it," Zila said. "Pull all the regiments out of the hills and secure those four towns, now."

"Yes, sir," Goff said. He snapped a crisp salute and held it until Zila returned the gesture. Then he turned on his heel and strode quickly out of the commander's office.

Zila picked up a red grease pencil and carefully drew an *X* through each of the four towns he'd just marked for death.

Gomez tied her pack shut and slung it over her shoulder. A few meters away, Stevens and Hawkins were already packed and waiting for her to lead them onward to the crash site. The sky overhead was peppered with stars; morning was still more than seven hours away, and the crisp, cold bite of winter was in the air.

Abramowitz was swaddled in thick blankets and propped up in a sitting position against a large rock formation next to the river. Within her reach on her left side was a neatly arranged assortment of water canisters and provisions, enough to last for up to two days. On her other side was a large pile of dry kindling and an ignition device, all arranged next to a stone-ringed concavity in which a small fire crackled.

Hidden beneath her serape was her tricorder and Gomez's medical kit, complete with another day's supply of painkiller patches. The whole comfy setup was concealed behind a makeshift screen of camouflage netting that Hawkins had tied together from spare hemp cord and local foliage.

Gomez crouched next to Abramowitz. "You feeling any better?"

"I'm okay," she said with a nod. "Pain's under control, and I should be fine here—assuming you guys don't drag your heels."

"I like you all drugged up," Gomez said with a smile. "Makes you talk like an officer."

Abramowitz chuckled and groggily shook her head. "Nah, just a mean cripple. Now go, you're wasting time."

Gomez gently squeezed Abramowitz's shoulder. "Okay. Hang tight, we'll be outta here in no time."

Gomez stood up and stepped around the camouflage screen. She walked over to Hawkins and Stevens, took out her tricorder, and checked the readout. They did likewise.

"I'm tracking the probe's energy signature," she said. "Bearing one-eight-six. Range, four hundred fifty-four-point-three kilometers and opening at a rate of roughly three kilometers per hour." Both men adjusted their own tricorders.

“Range and bearing confirmed,” Hawkins said.

“Roger that,” Stevens said. “That heading takes us right past the crash site, thirty-two-point-four kilometers from here. That’s about . . . what? Six hours’ walk?”

“More like seven,” Gomez said. “We’ll check it out on our way south. Let’s move out.” She adjusted the shoulder straps of her pack for a bit more comfort, then started walking forward into the night as a flurry of snowflakes fell like a white blanket across the uneven path ahead of her.

CHAPTER 4

Trooper Maleska led his squad down a dark, smoky stretch of Kinzhol's main street. Broad scorches marred most of the buildings along this avenue. Not one had even a single window intact, and their façades were pitted with shrapnel scars and long trails of large-caliber bullet holes. Several had been reduced to broken-concrete foundations studded with shorn-off steel beams twisted in every direction.

He tuned out the slow-rushing roar of Venekan jump-jets cruising high overhead. Moments later, a loud explosion a few blocks away sent a glowing fireball mushrooming into the sky, followed by a plume of inky black smoke that melted into the night. The blast shook a cloud of dust off the ramshackle skeleton of a building on his left. He paid it no mind.

Debris was strewn in a chaotic jumble across the street. Maleska and his soldiers moved slowly, crouched low to the ground, their short-barreled rifles held level against their shoulders. The men on the sides of the formation crab-walked sideways while watching the flanks for any sign of enemy movement. All Maleska saw were civilians: some staggering aimlessly in shock; some cowering from him and his troops; some trying to preserve any semblance of their ordinary lives in the aftermath of a barrage of pyrotechnic horrors.

A knot of twenty-odd X'Mari civilians drifted across the intersection ahead of the platoon. They were ragged and filthy, and they moved with a random, desperate curiosity as they sorted through the rubble and dirt, looking for who knew what. In the middle of the four-way intersection there was a crater where a bomb had exploded. As far as Maleska could see, the roads had been shredded, as if a fiery blade had shorn off the top layers of pavement. Twisted strips of the roads' aluminum undergirders were scattered everywhere, wedged into vehicles and corpses, or jutting out of buildings they'd impaled.

A door banged open to his right. He turned and aimed his rifle. A X'Mari man backed carefully out of the doorway, helping another man carry a sofa. Behind them emerged a woman carrying an enormous duffel bag on her back and two large cases, one in either hand. Following her was a trio of children, the youngest barely old enough to walk, all clutching one or two favorite toys as they abandoned their home.

As Maleska and his squad neared the end of their patrol route, he thought he saw a discarded bouquet of white flowers on top of the overturned, blasted-out, carbonized frame of a car. As he passed the smashed vehicle, he realized that the bouquet was actually a dead, white bird.

The soldiers moved cautiously through a hazy wall of gray, fuel-smelling smoke and turned the corner to the checkpoint at the end of their assigned sector. As they broke through the veil of smoke, Maleska saw the street was littered with broken musical instruments. Standing in the midst of the shattered items was a lone X'Mari man who stared, silent and forlorn, into the hollow, charred shell of what had once been a music shop.

Maleska looked back at his squad. Yellik, who had been bringing up the rear, signaled all-clear. Maleska beckoned his radioman forward and accepted the radio handset from him. He punched in his security code. "Sync-Com, Five-Nine *Jazim*. We've finished our patrol. Sector *masara* all-clear. Over."

"Five-Nine Jazim, *Sync-Com,"* came the staticky reply. *"All-clear confirmed. Proceed due south on Genmeck Road and secure the river port with extreme prejudice. Over."*

"Sync-Com, Five-Nine *Jazim*. Secure the river port, acknowledged. Five-Nine *Jazim* out." Maleska looked down Genmeck Road toward the river port a half-dozen *tiliks* away. There seemed to be nothing left intact between here and there.

He motioned his squad forward and began marching south toward the river. A light flurry of snow began to fall. He watched the flakes melt before they reached the smoldering, scorched ground, and wondered if any part of this country would survive the Venekan Army's dubious mission of liberation.

Ganag let his oar drag broadside in the water to the left of the skiff, turning the sliver-shaped watercraft neatly into the broad mouth of a corroded, half-submerged sewer drain. The stench of excrement and industrial waste assaulted his nostrils. He paddled the skiff slowly into the pipe. His paddle *thunked* against the sides of the pipe with a low, hollow metallic echo. The sound reverberated down the length of the pipe and back again, waking Lerec and Shikorn.

Shikorn swept his long, tangled bronze hair out of his eyes. "I dreamed I'd been buried in *karg,*" he said. He sniffed, looked around, and frowned. "I was right."

"We needed to take cover," Ganag said. "The sun'll be up any minute." He reached up and secured the anchor line to a protruding valve handle. Lerec failed to suppress a sick cough that sounded dangerously close to a retch. "Shut him up," Ganag said, realizing only after he'd spoken that Shikorn was already placing a clean, folded cloth over Lerec's nose and mouth, as a filter. Moments later, the young boy's coughing ceased as he breathed through his covered mouth.

"Where are we?" Shikorn said, his near-whisper amplified by the close quarters of the pipe. Ganag pulled his own, threadbare blanket from his seat and unfolded it.

"On the outskirts of Lersset," he said. "Maybe five *tiliks* from the edge of town."

Lerec seemed calmer, but he was shivering now. "Why can't we go and get some food?" he said.

Ganag wrapped his blanket around himself and huddled down into the stern of the boat. "Because you'll be seen, we'll get caught, and we'll be killed," Ganag said. He curled up for warmth and closed his eyes. "Now be quiet and go back to sleep. Save your strength."

"I can't sleep," Lerec said. "I'm too hungry."

"How hungry can you be?" Shikorn said as he

crawled back under his own blanket. "You ate just yesterday."

"No, the day before," Lerec said. "And it smells here."

Ganag sighed. He tried not to let his frustration with the boy prevent him from getting to sleep. He'd done most of the paddling since the bridge in the Scorla Pass, and his arms felt like knotty wood. He was hungry, too, but sleep was more precious to him than food right now.

"You'll eat tonight, after we reach the Resistance," Ganag said. "Now go back to sleep before we drown you." Ganag didn't enjoy making Lerec suffer, but right now it was necessary. *Hungry,* he reminded himself, *is better than dead.*

The pre-dawn sky was dark with clouds as Stevens, Gomez, and Hawkins crawled, side by side, up a snow-covered slope toward the crest of a hill. The gravity on Teneb was a bit more than Stevens was used to, and he felt as though he were dragging a large, dead weight behind him. He also could have sworn that the snow on this planet was colder than the brutal winters back home in the Rigel colonies, though that was probably only his imagination. As they inched over the top, they saw the brightly lit cluster of activity half a kilometer below.

A kilometer-long gouge in the soil, caused by the probe's impact, had been cordoned off with what looked to Stevens like a lot of hastily erected, prefabricated metal fencing topped with razor wire. Dozens of technicians in bright orange, full-body protective gear paced back and forth inside the trench, stopping occasionally to take samples or examine small bits of debris.

Parked on either side of the impact scar was a fleet of vehicles ranging from several kinds of large trucks to assorted types of four-person utility vehicles to armored assault craft. Scores of uniformed Venekan soldiers milled about. Several of them patrolled the site's perimeter.

Along the outer edges of the base camp, a large, fixed-wing aircraft with rotatable turbine engines split the air with a high-pitched roar as it made a slow, vertical landing. As its landing gear touched down onto the cross-marked landing area, its side hatches slid open, and another twenty-four Venekan soldiers bounded out and jogged in formation toward the camp's central, tentlike command pavilion.

Stevens looked up as another pair of the same type of aircraft shrieked overhead. Gomez leaned toward Hawkins. "How many, do you figure?"

Hawkins narrowed his eyes as he studied the Venekan troops. "About two hundred on the ground," he said. "Based on the number of landing platforms, I'd say there are three more of those aircraft in the area, counting the two that just flew over."

Stevens checked his tricorder readout. "The probe's stopped moving, four hundred eighty-two-point-seven kilometers from here, on bearing one-eight-four-point-two." He looked down at the Venekan troops. "Think their buddies have it?" he said.

Gomez shook her head. "No, look at these guys," she said. "If they had it, it'd be halfway around the world by now."

Hawkins nodded in agreement. "Definitely," he said. "They'd want it as far from here as possible. Same would go for any foreign powers trying to scoop it up.

The fact that it's as close as it is tells me the X'Maris have it."

"Only one way to be sure," Gomez said. "Let's keep moving."

Stevens followed Gomez as she turned to shimmy back down the hill. He stopped as he saw the barrel of a rifle pointed at his face from less than three meters away. "Halt!" an angry male voice said. "Hands in the air!"

Stevens waited until Gomez raised her hands over her head, then he did the same, followed by Hawkins.

Three Venekan soldiers, dressed in gray-and-white camouflage, kept their rifles aimed at Gomez, Stevens, and Hawkins while three more Venekan sentries, in the same winter gear, circled behind the trio.

Stevens's pack was torn from his back and flung onto the ground, its contents strewn across the snow. Beside him, Gomez's and Hawkins's packs were given the same treatment. He looked down the snowy hill and followed the soldiers' footprints.

All six soldiers had been concealed beneath the snow and soil, buried into the hillside itself. *They must have been in position even before it snowed,* Stevens realized. *We crawled right past them on the way up.*

He heard Hawkins fall to the ground, followed by Gomez. He tried to brace himself, but the soldier's boot slammed into the back of his knee and his leg buckled beneath him. He was pushed face-first into the snow-covered dirt and winced as the Venekan's boot pressed sharply on his neck. Another soldier searched through his pockets. They found his tricorder and pulled it out to examine it.

"Let me see those," the soldier in charge said.

A moment later, Stevens heard the whisper-soft *poof* of his tricorder self-destructing at the molecular level, right in the Venekan's hand. Two more *poofs* were all that announced the loss of Hawkins's and Gomez's tricorders.

The soldier in charge sounded very unhappy about having just inexplicably lost three very important pieces of evidence. "First squad, take 'em down to camp," he ordered. "Second squad, police up the rest of their gear and log it in with the quartermaster. I'll notify Sync-Com."

Stevens felt the boot lift from his neck. He was yanked back to his feet. The flurries of snow that had followed them south from the beam-in point grew heavier as he, Gomez, and Hawkins were pushed forward and down the far slope of the hill toward the floodlit base camp below.

CHAPTER 5

"Are you part of the X'Mari Resistance?" the Venekan military interrogator said. Stevens sat still and said nothing. After he, Gomez, and Hawkins had been escorted down to the camp next to the impact scar, he had immediately been separated from the others and brought to this tent for questioning.

The space inside the gray canvas tent was nothing if not Spartan. It stank of stale sweat. A naked tungsten-filament lightbulb dangled over his head, hanging from a frayed black electrical cord. It cast a weak orange glow in a tight circle around the dull-gray metal chair to which he was handcuffed in a sitting position. Other than that, the tent was empty.

The interrogator paced around Stevens, staring suspiciously at him. His steps crunched on the frozen-dirt floor. "Let's start with something easier," he said. "What's your name?"

"Hang on, Fabian," Abramowitz said over the transceiver, which made her voice sound intimately close. *"Don't say anything yet. I'm still cooking up a cover story for you."* Now that the Venekans had, albeit unwittingly, destroyed his, Gomez's, and Hawkins's tricorders, Abramowitz now held the away team's only true high-tech resource. Gomez had opened a four-way channel a few minutes ago, and now the entire away team was listening in on his interrogation.

"Just relax and play it cool," Hawkins said, joining the conversation. He sounded like he was whispering. *"Abramowitz, did you download any Venekan legal data? Does Stevens have any rights in there?"*

"I'm not sure," Abramowitz said. *"Hold on."*

The Venekan interrogator stopped in front of Stevens and leaned down until he was almost nose-to-nose with him. He stared into Stevens's eyes. "Why were you observing our camp?" he said, an edge of menace implicit in his tone.

"Don't answer him until we know what they know," Gomez said. Stevens wondered if having a party-line transceiver in one's head was anything like having multiple-personality disorder. *Probably not,* he concluded.

The interrogator's breath was hot and foul. It reminded Stevens of curry and cilantro, with a hint of sickly sweet cinnamon. Then he reconsidered—the odor might not be from the man's breath at all. *Could be his cologne,* Stevens realized. *No way to tell. Can't really ask. Oh, well.*

"Which of you is in command?" the interrogator said. "Where's your base?" Stevens realized that the only thing that was keeping him from falling asleep with utter boredom right now was the remote possibility that, at any moment, the interrogator might summon someone else to continue the questioning.

Someone equipped with painful implements of persuasion. Someone unburdened by the weight of a conscience.

Abramowitz piped up over the transceiver. *"Good news and bad news,"* she said. *"Good news is, the Venekan Army has strict laws against the use of physical or psychological coercion in the questioning of military prisoners. Bad news is, they have no problem detaining suspects indefinitely without charge, as long as it's in a war zone."*

"Where are your weapons?" the interrogator said. Stevens raised his eyebrows and shrugged. Only after he'd done it did he consider the possibility that the gesture might not mean the same thing to Tenebians as it did to humans. Fortunately for him, the interrogator seemed to grasp his meaning just fine.

"Okay," Abramowitz said, *"I've compiled the thirty most popular male given names and the hundred most common surnames for X'Mari men in your age group, and cross-referenced them with demographic data for this region. Here's your cover: Your name is Menno Yorlik, and you're a textile trader from Navoc. We're neighbors of yours, traveling toward—"*

"All right, we're done," the interrogator said. He walked away from Stevens and stepped outside through a flap in the front of the tent. "Come get this guy," he shouted to someone.

Figures, Stevens thought. *Just as I get an alibi . . .*

A pair of soldiers stepped past the interrogator and entered the tent, followed by another officer, an older man whose hair was turning platinum white at the temples.

"Did he tell you anything?" the older officer said. The soldiers unlocked Stevens's handcuffs.

The interrogator shook his head with disgust. "I'm not even sure he can talk," he said.

The soldiers lifted Stevens from the chair and dragged him out of the tent and across the compound, to another empty tent on the far side. They led him inside and ordered him to wrap his arms around the tent's center-support pole. He did as he was told, and they slapped the handcuffs back on him before marching back out. *It could always be worse,* Stevens consoled himself as he eyed his predicament. *At least I'm not stuck here with Tev.*

"The patrol leader tells me you were the one giving orders to the other two," the interrogator said, his putrid breath warming the back of Gomez's ear. Gomez tested the strength of the handcuffs, which bit painfully into her wrists. The chair she sat on was lightweight, but its metal frame was strong—and not the least bit flexible.

"I know you're the one in charge of this scout team," the interrogator said. He shifted his weight and whispered in her other ear. "The penalties for you are going to be a lot worse than for your friends. Unless you want to cooperate?"

"Good-news-bad-news time again," Abramowitz said over the transceiver. *"Bad news first: He's not lying. If they convict you three as spies and decide that you're the one in charge, they can execute you on the spot."*

"What's the good news?" Stevens said, echoing Gomez's thoughts.

"I lied," Abramowitz said. *"There isn't any."*

"You X'Mari girls love to play soldier, don't you?" the

interrogator said, leaning uncomfortably close to Gomez's face. "Love to pretend you're one of the men?"

"No more than you do," Gomez said, breaking her defiant wall of silence.

The interrogator wrinkled his brow and glowered. "Droll," he said. "Does this mean you're prepared to start answering questions?"

"Only if you're ready to meet my conditions," Gomez said. The interrogator folded his arms and eyed her warily.

"Such as?"

"You need to go shave and wash your face," she said.

He chuckled. "Why?" he said, his condescension naked in its intent. "Do my rough looks scare you?"

"No," she said with a lethal smile. "I just don't want you to scratch me when you kneel down and kiss my cold, blue ass."

The interrogator sighed in disgust, turned, and stepped outside through the flap in the front of the tent. "You can take her back now," he shouted to the soldiers waiting outside.

Hawkins looked his interrogator in the eye, sizing him up from the moment he sat down and felt the handcuffs click shut around his wrists. The interrogator's face looked gaunt and his eyes drooped with exhaustion, as if he hadn't had a meal or a decent night's sleep in weeks. He wore the manner of a man trying to be intimidating, but his body language was that of a man who would much rather leave this job to someone—*anyone*—else.

The interrogator rubbed his eyes and sighed. "I don't suppose you'll cooperate, either?"

"Why wouldn't I?" Hawkins said casually. "We're on the same side." The interrogator blinked and actually did a double take.

"We're what?"

Hawkins looked around, as if he were genuinely shocked by the man's response. "What? You mean they didn't tell you?"

"Huh? Who didn't—? Tell me what?"

"I'm a Venekan agent," Hawkins said. "I'm undercover."

"Come again?" The interrogator was starting to sound upset.

"I'm infiltrating the X'Mari Resistance."

"What?" The interrogator sounded incredulous. "All three of you?" Hawkins rolled his eyes and shook his head.

"No, just me," he said. "I'm only using *them* to enhance my credibility. They're part of my cover."

The interrogator's eyes narrowed with suspicion.

"What agency are you with?"

Hawkins snorted derisively, as if the officer had just made the stupidest request in the world. "I can't tell you that."

"Why not?" the interrogator said.

Hawkins shrugged. "You obviously don't have the clearance for that information."

"The hell I don't!" The interrogator pointed furiously at the rank insignia on his collar. "See these stars?"

Hawkins tuned out the rest of the away team's laughter, which came in bursts over his subaural transceiver.

"If you had clearance," he said, "you'd have been briefed already. But you obviously don't know who I am, so you can't have been cleared. Sorry, nothing personal."

The interrogator inhaled sharply, then held his

breath, apparently concentrating on calming himself. He exhaled.

"I suppose you think you can trick me into letting you go."

"And blow my cover? Are you *crazy?* It took forever to win the X'Maris' trust. Pull me out now and the whole op's a wash. No, no way. Not unless you have specific orders for me to abort—which you don't, because you didn't even know I was here."

The interrogator covered his face with his hands and breathed in and out in a slow, measured rhythm. He massaged his temples with his thumbs. He stopped and looked wearily at Hawkins, who stared back at the man like he owned him.

"Do you have *any* evidence," the interrogator said, "anything at all, that proves you're telling me the truth?"

Hawkins arched one eyebrow and smirked at him.

"Do you have any that proves I'm *not*?"

The interrogator stared at Hawkins for a very long moment before letting out a sigh of defeat. He plodded to the tent's flap, pushed it aside, and walked outside as he issued one final order to the soldiers standing guard outside the tent.

"I'm done," he said. "Put 'em on a jumper and get 'em outta here."

A steady fall of snow had shrouded the ground surrounding the Venekan camp during the two short hours that Gomez, Hawkins, and Stevens had been held for questioning. The snowfall was heavier now, but, Gomez noted, not heavy enough to keep Venekan aircraft from flying. She, Hawkins, and Stevens—with their hands cuffed behind their backs—were escorted at gunpoint toward a waiting aircraft, or "jumper," as the Venekan soldiers called them.

The gray-and-white camouflaged vehicle's jet-turbine engines gave off a loud and steady whine, and wavering ripples of heat distortion rose from the thrusters' exhaust ports. Its two-person flight crew sat side by side in the cockpit, which was separated from the troop compartment by what Gomez concluded was a very durable-looking metal door.

Gomez was the first to climb the wide metal ladder and step through the jet's right-side hatch, just behind the wing, into its main compartment. Hawkins followed close behind her, with Stevens and their three-person armed escort boarding last.

"You three sit there," one of the soldiers said, pointing at a long, flat bench that ran the length of the compartment's right side. The trio sat down. Two of the soldiers kept their rifles aimed at them while the third shackled the trio together at the ankles. As soon as he backed away and sat down, the other two soldiers did likewise.

"Commander, I'm monitoring the signal traffic from the aircraft you just boarded," Abramowitz said over the subaural transceiver. Though she'd addressed Gomez, Gomez could tell from Hawkins's and Stevens's subtle reactions that Abramowitz was using an open channel to keep everyone on the team equally informed.

She could barely hear her over the engine noise inside the jumpjet. *"Your pilot just received orders to take the three of you to a place called 'Samara.' I checked the—"*

The engines shrieked then roared, and the jumpjet

wobbled slightly into a vertical liftoff. The hellish din drowned out Abramowitz's voice for several seconds. Outside the still-open side hatches, Gomez saw the horizon recede as the craft gained altitude. A pair of amber-hued lights next to the side doors activated. The doors slid shut and locked closed, then the amber lights turned pale blue. Once the doors closed, Gomez was once again able to hear Abramowitz.

"—appears that Samara refers to the Mount Samara prisoner-of-war camp, located roughly one hundred twenty-point-seven kilometers northeast of your current position," Abramowitz said.

Gomez felt her weight shift in response to the sudden acceleration as the jet's afterburners kicked in. *"I'll try to access schematics for the camp and maps of its surrounding terrain before you—"* Abramowitz stopped abruptly. Gomez glanced sidelong at Stevens and Hawkins, who wore similar expressions of concern. Seconds passed before Abramowitz transmitted again. *"Um, Commander,"* she said, sounding worried, *"I have company."*

Abramowitz quickly deactivated her tricorder and concealed it in a pocket beneath her serape. The sound of approaching footsteps drew closer, muffled only slightly by the freshly fallen snow. *Whoever it is probably saw the smoke from my fire,* she realized, and she chastised herself for not staying more aware of her situation. She'd been staring at her tricorder display for the past two hours and had lost all sense of time and place.

As the footsteps grew louder, Abramowitz steeled herself for a much-dreaded confrontation with a Venekan soldier. But the face that peeked around the camouflage drop was young, female, and dark blue. The girl's clothes were of distinctively northern X'Mari origin. Abramowitz surmised that the girl couldn't have been much older than twelve or thirteen. The teenager stared at her with wide, doleful violet eyes.

"I'm Lica," the girl said. Abramowitz hesitated, unsure what to say. The girl continued to stare unthreateningly at her.

"I'm Kinara," Abramowitz said, slipping into the cover identity she'd prepared for herself while convalescing here.

"We saw the smoke from your fire," Lica said. "Are you all right?" Abramowitz concealed her immediate wave of concern: *We?*

"No," Abramowitz said. "My leg is broken. I—" Before she could continue, Lica waved someone else over to join her. Abramowitz heard more footsteps, slower and heavier than Lica's. *Sounds like more than one person,* she thought. Two adult women joined Lica. Both were gaunt and bore haunted expressions; one looked to be in her forties, the other in her sixties or older. Lica pointed at Abramowitz.

"She's hurt," Lica said. "Her leg is broken."

The younger adult woman knelt next to Abramowitz and rested a comforting hand on her shoulder. "I'm Nedia," she said, then gestured toward the older X'Mari woman, who was garbed in robes that Abramowitz could tell had religious significance. "This is Mother Aleké. What's your name?"

"Kinara," she said.

"I'm going to check your wounds, Kinara. Is that all right?" Abramowitz nodded, afraid to refuse lest it raise suspicion. Nedia looked over the makeshift splints that Gomez and Hawkins had made for Abramowitz's left arm and leg. The woman's hands smelled strongly of antiseptic iodine.

"Who set these?" Nedia said.

"My friends," Abramowitz said.

"They left you behind?" Nedia said, alarmed.

"They were captured," Abramowitz said.

"By the Venekans," Nedia said. Abramowitz nodded.

Nedia turned her head toward Mother Aleké. "Her injuries are severe, and her friends have been taken by the enemy. We can't leave her here." Mother Aleké nodded gravely.

"Get a stretcher and some more help," Nedia said to Lica. The girl sprinted away, back the way she'd come. Nedia began to gather Abramowitz's supplies for her, while talking over her shoulder in a low, angry voice to Mother Aleké.

"How can the Venekans be such savages?" she said. "How can they treat women and children like this?"

"Because they seek to extinguish in us what they have lost of themselves," the elderly woman said. "They are empty."

"Yet *they* rule the world," Nedia said, her bitterness threatening to spill over into rage.

"To rule is to govern and care for one's people," Mother Aleké said. "The Venekans rule nothing. They merely hold people hostage."

Lica returned, accompanied by four more X'Mari women ranging in age from late teens to mid-fifties. One of them carried a crude stretcher. Nedia and another woman gently lifted Abramowitz and slid the stretcher beneath her. "Everyone," she said, "this is Kinara." The women surrounded Abramowitz and lifted her stretcher. "Don't be afraid, Kinara," Nedia said. "We'll take care of you. It's going to be all right."

The cluster of women carried Abramowitz and followed Mother Aleké up a knoll and away from Abramowitz's redoubt. Heavy, wet flakes of ash-gray snow fell from a dreary sky and smothered the surrounding hills. As the group crested the rise and began descending the other side, Abramowitz saw the narrow road that snaked through the Scorla Hills, reaching from the plains in the south toward the higher ground in the north.

Stretched out on that road, for more than a kilometer in each direction, was a column of tattered-looking X'Mari refugees, almost all of them women and young children. Many of them were wounded and wrapped in crude bandages freshly stained with their sapphire-tinted blood. Those women who weren't holding wailing infants bore the burden of carrying what few possessions they'd salvaged from their former lives. Most were poorly clothed, considering the quickly dropping temperatures.

The women carried Abramowitz on her stretcher into the middle of the refugee column, which resumed its grim and wordless march away from civilization, into exile.

CHAPTER 6

The flight to the POW camp was brief. Hawkins estimated the trip had taken only about twenty minutes from liftoff to landing. He, Stevens, and Gomez were ushered off the aircraft. They stood at the base of a small mountain, in the mouth of a gigantic off-round nook in its side.

The nook's sheer, rocky walls were almost completely vertical, rising several hundred feet toward the crescent-shaped lip of a snow-covered slope. Hawkins could barely see the top of the cliff wall through the falling snow.

The trio was met by a platoon of armed soldiers, who led them past several Venekan troop vehicles and through the camp's outer gate, into a wide-open parade-and-assembly area that was more than forty centimeters deep with fresh-fallen snow.

On his left, Hawkins counted three barracks, each

large enough to house fifty personnel comfortably. Tucked into the far left corner, against the front fence, was a structure that he guessed was probably the latrine. On the opposite side of the assembly area was a long building whose roof was festooned with chimneys and steam vents. *Probably the mess hall,* he decided.

Directly ahead of the trio was an enormous, ten-meter-tall concrete bunker that stretched nearly two hundred meters across, spanning the entire width of the nook. Rising from the bunker's center was a fortified command tower fifteen meters tall. At either end of the bunker was a guard tower equipped with a searchlight and manned by a sniper.

Set into the bunker on either side of the central tower, halfway between it and the guard towers at the far ends, were a pair of three-meter-tall gates. Each opened into a ten-meter-long, three-meter-wide corridor. On either side of both corridors were gatehouses complete with "murder holes"—narrow openings in the walls just large enough to point gun barrels through, in order to mow down people inside the corridors without the risk of the victims fighting back.

Gomez was ushered toward the right-side gate, while Stevens and Hawkins were herded toward the one on the left. The two men passed a platoon of soldiers marching in formation. Based on the size of the camp and the number of buildings and vehicles, Hawkins estimated that there was, at most, a single company of soldiers garrisoned here—no more than a hundred and fifty personnel, including officers and support staff.

The left gate opened. He and Stevens stepped forward into the dark, narrow corridor. As soon as they were past the outer gate, it closed behind them, and the gate at the far end of the corridor opened in front of them. Hawkins felt the eyes of the Venekan soldiers watching them from behind the murder holes as he and Stevens walked forward.

They stepped out of the corridor, into the men's prison yard. The inner gate clanked closed behind them. In contrast to the orderliness of the soldiers' camp on the other side of the concrete bunker, the prisoners' side was a shantytown of torn and rotting canvas and rusted sheet-metal lean-tos. More than two hundred X'Mari men and adolescent boys drifted like aimless shades or sprawled idly inside their pathetic shelters.

Like the soldiers' camp, the men's prison yard was circled by a seven-meter-tall chain-link fence topped with razor wire. In several places there were narrow gaps between the fence and the cliffs beyond, but Hawkins looked back and saw that the gaps had been sealed on either side of the concrete bunker. Along the right side of the prison yard, parallel to the center fences, was a slope-roofed latrine building, thirty-plus meters long.

To his right, beyond the center fence, was the women's camp. It was a near-perfect mirror image of the men's camp, down to the shoddy latrine building opposite their own. The two yards were separated not by a single fence but by two parallel fences, less than a meter apart, whose razor-wire toppings tangled together. There were nearly as many women imprisoned here as there were men. Standing in front of the women's inside gate was Commander Gomez, who looked back at Hawkins.

He heard her speak softly to him via the subaural transceiver. *"Gotta give the Venekans credit,"* she said. *"They sure do build a good concentration camp."*

"Yeah," he said. "Get past the fence and there's nowhere to go. Go through the gate and you get shot."

Stevens craned his neck backward and gazed up through the falling flakes of snow at the towering cliffs of rock that surrounded the prison yards. Then he looked at the concrete bunker, the guard towers, and the central command tower.

"It does have one flaw," Stevens said. Hawkins fixed him with a look that urged him to explain. Stevens grinned.

"It shows a fundamental lack of respect for nature."

Abramowitz peeked through one eye to see if any of the refugees were watching her. She had pretended to fall asleep a few hours ago to discourage them from talking to her, which would only increase the likelihood that she would be caught in a lie. She knew the X'Mari were xenophobes; if they realized she wasn't one of them, they would very likely brand her a spy and kill her.

The column had stopped moving several minutes ago, and the women who had been carrying her had put down her stretcher and stepped away. Realizing she had been given a fleeting moment of privacy, Abramowitz activated her transceiver and covered her mouth with her hand as she spoke.

"Abramowitz to away team, do you read me?" she said in a near-whisper. She looked around nervously while she waited for a reply.

Gomez's voice filled her ears. *"Gomez here. Are you okay, Carol? We've been trying to reach you for four hours."*

"I know," Abramowitz said. "I couldn't say anything

because I'm not alone. I got picked up by a X'Mari refugee column."

"Picked up? Where are you?"

"We're on a road heading into the high country. I don't know exactly where, but I'd say we're heading north."

"Carol, we need some tricorder magic," Stevens said, jumping into the conversation. *"Can you help us out?"*

"Not right now," she said. "Still too many eyes around. Maybe tonight, after they make camp and go to sleep."

"It's okay, we can wait," Hawkins said. *"They're about to serve lunch here and I'm starved."* Abramowitz's eyes widened with alarm. She hoped she'd heard Hawkins wrong.

"Tell me you haven't eaten anything," she said.

"Why?" Stevens said. *"What's—"*

"Didn't any of you *read* my mission briefing? *We can't eat the food* on this planet. Everything organic on Teneb contains a cyanic compound called thanacil. One mouthful and you'll be dead before you hit the ground."

Gomez stared in horror at the shallow tin of gruel in her hands. Abramowitz's warning had come just as she had reached the front of the chow line and been given her thrice-daily ration.

Lucky for me they made me wait near the back of the line, she thought. *Being low girl on the totem pole finally pays off.*

On the other side of the fence, Stevens and Hawkins were just now having ladlefuls of the saffron-colored goop swatted into their own dented tin bowls. Gomez stared at them, then at the plate of poison in her hands.

From behind her came a grumbled litany of protests and complaints. “What’s the problem?” one woman shouted. “Why isn’t she moving?” said another. A filthy ladle was waved in her face. “What’re you waiting for? Move it!” said the prisoner serving the food, shooing Gomez away.

Gomez turned and handed her tin to the woman behind her.

“I don’t want it,” Gomez said. “You take it. Enjoy.”

A soldier standing guard in front of Gomez grabbed the edge of her serape as she started to walk away from the chow line. “What do you think you’re doing?” he said.

“Not eating. Let me go.”

He snatched back Gomez’s tin from the woman behind her and thrust it back into Gomez’s hands. “Move along.”

Gomez held her ground and stared back at him. All activity and grousing on both chow lines ceased. Everyone watched the confrontation between Gomez and the soldier. “I don’t want your food,” she said, enunciating clearly and with growing defiance. “It tastes like death,” she said. She turned her bowl upside-down and emptied its sticky, yellow contents on the soldier’s well-polished black boots.

On the other side of the fence, Hawkins and Stevens followed Gomez’s lead, and dumped their own bowls of gruel on the ground. The soldier facing Gomez lifted his arm to backhand her—and paused as the yard resounded with the splatter of hundreds of bowls of gruel being emptied onto the frozen ground. Every X’Mari man and woman in the camp had dumped their food and now glared at the soldiers. The air tingled with hatred.

Gomez tensed and waited for the Venekans to respond.

The soldier in front of her lowered his hand and stepped back toward the serving table in front of the chow line. "You want to starve?" he said. He grabbed the pot of gruel and dumped its contents on the ground. "Fine. Starve." He motioned to the soldiers who had been monitoring the chow service. They followed him back through the gate to the soldiers' side of the bunker.

On the other side of the fence, in the men's prison yard, more soldiers did the same thing, spilling out the remaining food then retreating to safety on the other side of the gate.

Gomez wondered if she had led the X'Maris astray—most of them looked like they couldn't afford to miss too many more meals. As she pondered the morality of triggering an almost certainly futile hunger strike, a X'Mari woman who looked to be about Gomez's age stepped up to her and clasped her arm.

"Thank you," she said as her eyes brimmed with tears. "We'd forgotten how to fight . . . how to *resist*. Thank you for reminding us." She released Gomez's arm and shuffled away, weak and tired, but no longer beaten.

Gomez felt a wave of sympathy for the woman, for all the prisoners in the camp—but then she reminded herself that she wasn't here to take sides. She didn't know the history of the X'Maris or the Venekans, or what the issues of their conflict were. She was here for only one reason: to destroy a Starfleet probe before any of this planet's denizens—whether they be Venekans, X'Maris, or anyone else—turned it into a weapon.

"Thanks for the heads-up, Carol," she said as she looked across at Hawkins and Stevens. "Let us know the moment you can use the tricorder. We need to break out of here as soon as possible." *Before we starve,* she thought as her stomach growled.

The refugee column had covered several kilometers between midday and nightfall, and everyone was worn out. The task of carrying Abramowitz's stretcher had been shared by many dozens of women. A few would carry her for a while until they became fatigued, then others took their place. No one had asked for help or complained; the shifts had seemed to happen all on their own.

The snowfall had petered out a few hours ago, and a break in the cloud cover along the horizon had allowed a few golden rays of sunset to slant through the jagged peaks surrounding the refugees before darkness fell.

Now the group was quiet; a few women and old men remained alert, tending small fires or watching the road ahead and behind for any sign of unwelcome attention. Abramowitz's benefactors had set her up with a bedroll and made space for her inside their crowded tent. Now she was huddled among them, shivering despite the body heat that emanated from either side of her.

She pulled her heavy blanket up over her head to hide herself. Fishing her tricorder from its hiding place, she activated it and adjusted its display, reducing its brightness to avoid casting a telltale glow beneath her covers. She set it for silent operation, then interfaced it with her transceiver. *Thank heavens for fully integrated technology,* she thought as she accessed the tricorder's voice-synthesis function. She would let the tricorder generate an audio signal to speak for her, and use her transceiver to transmit it to the rest of the away team. No one in the tent with her would hear anything, because Abramowitz herself wouldn't have to speak.

Abramowitz to away team, she transmitted. She heard the tricorder-synthesized voice in her transceiver. It sounded human, but strangely lacking in affect. **Do you copy?**

"Gomez here. Did you go and catch a cold?" Abramowitz could tell that Gomez was kidding—the commander knew what a computer voice sounded like just as well as she did.

I have to let the tricorder do the talking. What do you need?

"Can you tap into the camp's P.A. system?" Stevens asked. *"If we can use it to transmit a properly focused ultrasonic signal at the right frequency, we might be able to trigger a controlled snowfall from the ridge above the soldiers' barracks and make ourselves a bridge out of here."*

I'll see what I can do, but it'll take time.

"Let us know when you're ready," Hawkins said. *"We'll be standing by to walk you through the details."*

Abramowitz began the slow, tedious process of scanning for weather-radar satellites that would help her gauge the snow density on the ridge, and looking for a "back door" into the POW camp's communications software.

Why couldn't they have been captured by a X'Mari chieftain? she groused to herself. *A few platitudes, a few gestures of respect, and I could've had them out in time for lunch. But, no, they have to go and get themselves locked up in a Venekan POW camp.* She sighed heavily as she tapped into Teneb's satellite-information network and began seeking out weather-radar systems.

Stevens and Hawkins sat next to the fence that separated the men's and women's camps. The crisscrossing searchlight beams that swept like clockwork over the prison yards passed over their heads. Directly on the other side of the fence, Gomez leaned sideways against the chain-link and stared at the sky.

In the hour or so that they had been waiting to hear back from Abramowitz, the weather had cleared considerably. The night sky was an unpolluted black field salted with stars. The air had grown colder and drier. Stevens watched his exhaled breath become gray ghosts that vanished into the darkness.

He turned and looked at Gomez, then he glanced skyward, following the direction of her gaze. A brilliant, cross-shaped constellation dominated that patch of the sky.

Gomez whispered through the fence to him. "Which one are you looking at?"

He answered without looking away from the stars. "The same one you are."

"Second from the bottom of the cross, right?" Hawkins said.

"Yeah," Stevens said, somber and reflective.

They sat together in silence for a few minutes. Stevens knew, just as he was sure Gomez and Hawkins did, that the star they were looking at was Galvan, and that none of them wanted to say its name. Hawkins finally broke the silence. "Y'know, sometimes . . . lately . . . I can almost go an entire day without thinking about it."

"I envy you," Stevens said. He knew that Hawkins's loss at Galvan VI had been just as painful as his or Gomez's. Hawkins had lost most of his colleagues on the security staff, including his best friend, Stephen Drew, during that fateful mission.

Another silence enveloped them. Then the mechanically neutral synthetic voice from Abramowitz's tricorder spoke to them through their transceivers. *"Abramowitz to away team, priority one."*

Gomez put her hand to her ear, though it wasn't really necessary. "Gomez here. Go ahead."

"I have good news and bad news."

Stevens, Hawkins, and Gomez swapped dismayed reactions.

"The camp's public-address hardware is a closed system," Abramowitz transmitted. *"I wasn't able to access it."*

"What's the good news?" Gomez said.

"I'm using an alternative method to trigger your snowfall."

Stevens suppressed a stab of panic. "*What* method?"

"I found a derelict Tenebian satellite that was scheduled for atmospheric reentry and changed its descent profile."

The trio's looks of dismay turned to terror.

"You're crashing a satellite into the mountain?" Hawkins said. "Isn't that a little . . ." His voice pitched with disbelief. ". . . *imprecise?!*"

"We'll know in about thirty-five seconds. I suggest you take cover."

Stevens was about to say something about the importance of leaving engineering to engineers when a fiery streak slashed low across the sky overhead. *Oh, no,* he thought, then he sprinted to catch up to Hawkins, who was already running between the tents, shouting to wake up the other male prisoners. Gomez ran through the women's yard, shouting for the women to retreat to the far side of their camp.

A crimson flash on the mountainside above the camp lit up the night sky. One second later, a cataclysmic boom shattered the night. X'Maris and Venekans alike awoke in terror. A surreal, deathly silence washed over the camp.

Then the rumbling began. Low, almost inaudible at first, then it grew louder. Stronger. Closer. The ground trembled. A gentle rush of air gave birth to a blustering wind.

The camp's alert klaxon wailed. X'Mari prisoners scrambled out of their fragile shelters. Half-naked Venekan soldiers fell over one another as they fled their barracks.

The mountain roared, drowning out the siren. The avalanche exploded over the top of the cliff and plummeted in a roiling white cloud toward the camp. It seemed to fall in slow-motion, but as soon as it hit the ground it spread across the camp with terrifying speed, sweeping up tents, sheets of metal, and everything else in its path.

From beyond the concrete barrier, Stevens heard the soldiers' barracks snap like dry twigs crushed underfoot. "Get behind the latrine!" Hawkins shouted to the X'Mari men, who already were running in that direction, away from the oncoming wall of churning snow, dirt, and ice.

The crowd broke like a wave against the latrine building, flowed around its sides, and reassembled behind it.

Stevens and Hawkins were trapped in the middle of the group.

"Push it over!" Hawkins yelled. With strength born of panic, the prisoners heaved against the back of the free-standing structure and tipped it forward, pointing its angled roof toward the raging gray-white crush that was about to hit it. "Get inside!" he hollered. The men leaped inside the overturned but otherwise intact building, piling on top of one another.

The avalanche struck the sideways-facing latrine roof and shoved the building forward ahead of the snowfront. It crashed liked a battering ram through the first chain-link fence, then the other. Snow and ice from the avalanche surged through gaps in the walls and shattered ventilation grates.

Stevens's lower body became cocooned in snow and earth from the building's open side, which was scooping up the ground like a plow blade. He scrambled away from the incoming snow, climbed beside the other men, and pressed himself against the splintering roof.

Then the avalanche slowed. The building's slide halted halfway across the women's prison yard. The wood-frame building creaked and moaned ominously. "Out!" Hawkins bellowed. "Now!" The X'Mari men fell over one another as they rushed to exit the buckling shell of the latrine building.

Hawkins and Stevens helped up a few older men and young boys who had fallen and pushed them out ahead of them, then leaped to safety themselves as the weight of settling snow and ice crushed the latrine building into pulp and toothpicks.

Stevens lifted his head and looked around. The camp was pitch-dark. "Avalanche must've knocked out the power," he said to Hawkins, who brushed himself off then offered Stevens a hand and helped him to his feet. Stevens looked back at the massive, steep slope of snow that had buried more than half of the camp and one of the two guard towers.

He ducked reflexively as a crack like a gunshot echoed off the cliffs. Then he heard the sound of snapping wooden planks and turned to see the central command tower topple, break apart on the concrete wall, and collapse into the women's prison yard. When he turned back toward Hawkins, Gomez was there.

"Are you two all right?" she said.

"Couldn't be righter," Hawkins said.

"Define 'all right,'" Stevens said.

"Let's go," Gomez said.

Stevens and Hawkins followed her up the icy slope. As they hurried over the buried concrete wall, the X'Mari prisoners swarmed past them and rushed ahead and down the other side to confront the Venekan soldiers, most of whom had narrowly escaped the avalanche by leaving their weapons—and most of their uniforms—in their barracks. Only a pair of soldiers, who had been on duty in the far guard tower, were still armed and in uniform. A handful of others, from the buried guard tower and collapsed central tower, were likely alive but trapped inside the concrete bunker and unable to join the fray.

Gomez led Stevens and Hawkins around the melee that was brewing just a few dozen meters away. The sharp reports of gunfire split the night and continued for nearly a minute as the trio sprinted away, dodging through the shadows and walking out over the camp's buried outer fence. Then the gunfire stopped, and from inside the camp Stevens heard the fearsome sound of the angry X'Mari mob attacking the unarmed and massively outnumbered Venekan soldiers. He, Hawkins, and Gomez clambered inside a Venekan Army truck, which was the only one of the camp's five vehicles that hadn't been buried by the avalanche.

Hawkins slid into the driver's seat and pressed the ignition switch. The engine stuttered then turned over with a robust growl. He shifted the vehicle into gear. "Next stop, the probe," he said as he pressed on the accelerator and steered the truck down the road and away from the camp.

"Carol, we're out of the camp and we have a vehicle," Gomez said. "Which way do we go?"

"Follow the main road for about seventy-seven kilometers until you cross a bridge over a river," the tricorder's synthetic voice instructed. *"After the bridge, the road forks. Go to the right. Stay on that road for four hundred forty-six kilometers, then follow another major road that branches off on the right. From there it's about one hundred sixty-four kilometers to the probe."*

Stevens calculated the total distance in his head and divided it by what he gauged to be this vehicle's maximum safe speed on icy winter roads. By his best estimate, it would take more than nine hours for them to reach the probe.

Hawkins upshifted and accelerated. "We'll be there in about five and a half hours, Commander," the security officer said. Stevens checked to make certain his safety harness was secured.

"Carol," Gomez said, in an overly tactful tone that Stevens had heard her use only when she was utterly livid, "in the future, please confer with me or another senior officer before you devise a plan and put it into action. That bit with the satellite was one of the most irresponsible, most dangerous stunts I've ever seen a Starfleet crewmember pull on an away mission. You could've killed us, not to mention hundreds of Tenebians."

An awkward, uncomfortable silence lingered inside the cramped cab of the truck, which hurtled through the night, all alone on a lonely stretch of winding road.

Then Gomez's mouth twisted into a crooked smile and she shrugged. "On the other hand," she said, "it worked, it had style, and we're all still here. So what the hell—nice work. Gomez out."

CHAPTER 7

Commander Zila stormed into his office. It was the middle of the night, and he'd just been woken by a damned footman who'd told him there was urgent news. Standing in the middle of the office was Legioner Goff, around whom five lancer-grade officers scurried, collecting incoming reports from the secure digital comfeeds. "This had better be important," Zila said, his voice rough and loud.

"The Samara POW camp was destroyed three hours ago," Goff said. He held out a printed report. Zila snatched it from his hand and scanned the damage reports and casualty lists.

"An avalanche?" Zila said. "You woke me for a *flezzing* avalanche?"

Goff took the rebuke in stride. "Turn to page two," he said.

Zila turned the page. The trajectory change of a satellite was the first thing he noticed. Then he saw its impact point. "Its navigational systems were hacked moments before it made premature reentry," Goff said.

"How many intelligence agencies in the world have that kind of capability?" Zila said.

"Three, maybe four." Goff handed another printed sheet to Zila, who accepted it politely this time. "I checked the camp's nightly report for new arrivals. Two X'Mari men and one woman, arrested at the impact site, northeast of Raozan."

"Arrested at the impact site," Zila said. "And eighteen hours later a satellite gets knocked out of the sky and lands above the camp they're being held in. Whoever they are, they're professionals, and well-connected."

"Very well-connected," Goff said. "An interrogator's report says that one of the prisoners claimed to be a Venekan agent working undercover, but he wouldn't say for which agency."

"I'll bet he's working for Councilor Urwon," Zila said, shaking with fury at the mere mention of his archnemesis in the Venekan civilian government. *That bastard's been undermining me ever since I was commissioned,* Zila raged. *He probably thinks he can beat me to the biggest discovery in history, cheat me out of another promotion.* "Where are the spies now?"

"On the move," Goff said. "The rescue team activated the signal beacons on the camp's vehicles to help with the recovery effort. One of them is on the Eruc Highway, heading south at nearly a hundred and twenty *tiliks* per hour."

"Exact position?" Zila said. Goff pointed to a red circle with a dot in its center, drawn in grease pencil on the transparent map overlay. "It's already past the Tengma turnoff," Goff said. "They're heading for Lersset."

"Get every jumper you can find," Zila said. "I want them loaded and in the air to Lersset now."

"Already done, sir," Goff said. "We'll be moving into the city from three directions by daybreak."

"Get my jumper ready," Zila said. "We're going down there."

"Fueled, armed, flight plan filed," Goff said. He snapped his fingers, and one of the lancers stepped up, holding Zila's foul-weather jacket open for him. Zila put the jacket on.

"Well done," Zila said with a nod. "Let's move out."

Hawkins parked the truck in a narrow, trash-strewn alley and turned off the engine. The town of Lersset was smaller than he'd expected, perhaps no more than a hundred thousand people. Its tallest buildings were four stories tall; most were shorter. It looked old, neglected, weather-beaten. He saw signs of skirmishes past—scorches, blast-pitting, broken foundations—but the town was not particularly war torn. Its dominant colors were shades of gray and brown.

The trio had made good time, finishing the trip from Samara in just under six hours, due in no small measure to the fact that Hawkins had kept the accelerator pinned to the floor for almost the entire journey. The real-life vehicle had handled less reliably than had its holographic simulation, but Hawkins chalked that up to poor vehicle maintenance.

Of course, the truck's tendency to fishtail wildly on fast turns was no doubt a key factor in why both Gomez and Stevens now looked nauseous as they staggered out of the truck, boots sloshing and crunching in the ice-crusted mud. Gomez leaned against the truck, and Stevens bent over and rested his hands on his knees while he steadied his nerves with long, deep breaths.

The sky overhead slowly changed hue, from black to royal purple. Sunrise was drawing near, and Hawkins was eager not to lose momentum when they were so close. "Commander, we should move while we still have cover of darkness," he said.

Gomez nodded and straightened her posture. "Right. Ready, Fabian?"

The engineer stood up, drew a deep breath, exhaled, and nodded once. "Yeah, I'm set," he said.

"Carol, you read me?" Gomez said. "Which way from here?"

"Out of the alley, right thirty meters. Then left, up the main avenue, forty meters."

Gomez led the way, and Hawkins and Stevens fell into step right behind her. Hawkins scanned every window and rooftop for sentries, snipers, or simply unwelcome observers. The city was quiet, not yet roused by the coming dawn. Gomez darted across the street, her mud-splashing footsteps answered by sharp echoes. She paused at the corner before the left turn.

"Vance, take point," she said. Hawkins slipped past her and moved down the street on its sidewalk, which was lined with dilapidated parked cars. He crouched low, keeping himself mostly concealed behind the row of vehicles until he'd covered roughly the forty meters Abramowitz had directed.

"Checkpoint," Hawkins said. "Where now?"

"Narrow gap between the buildings on your right. Slip through there to an alley behind the building on the left."

Hawkins scouted the street in both directions, then ducked across it to the gap. It was barely wide enough for them to move through sideways, single-file, backs to the wall.

Hawkins went in first, followed by Gomez, then Stevens. He inched ahead, scraping against the wet, rough-stone wall. They emerged in a wide alley that ran behind two rows of buildings situated on parallel streets.

"We're in the alley," Hawkins said.

"Go to the alley on your right, five buildings ahead."

Hawkins led Gomez and Stevens into the intersecting alley, which was cluttered with debris and overflowing garbage bins. It reeked of rotting food and stale urine.

Overhead, the sky was now a deep sapphire blue and getting brighter by the minute. "Checkpoint," Hawkins said.

"In the building across the street, second from the corner. Elevation ten-point-two meters above ground level."

Hawkins eyed the target building. It was narrow, three stories tall, and nondescript except for the garage door at street level, which was uncommon among the buildings he'd seen on the surrounding streets. The elevation Abramowitz had cited would place the probe on the building's top floor, where the window shades were pulled closed.

Silhouettes played across the drawn shades, overlapping one another and preventing Hawkins from making an accurate guess as to how many people were inside. The one thing he could tell from the occupants' silhouettes was that they were armed, whereas he—and the rest of the away team—were not.

The building's front door opened. Three teenage X'Mari boys stepped out the door and walked down the front steps to the street. They carried heavy backpacks and wore loose, flowing dark serapes that Hawkins could tell were being used to conceal long-barreled weapons. They moved quickly, without talking, and continued around the corner and out of sight.

The Starfleet trio huddled together in the alley.

"What's the plan, Commander?" Hawkins said.

"We sneak inside," Gomez said. "Cause a distraction. Keep the guards busy while Fabian fixes the probe. Start the timer, signal the *da Vinci* for beam-out, go home, and get some sleep."

Stevens and Hawkins stared at Gomez through narrowed eyes. "No disrespect, sir," Hawkins said, "but that's a bit vague."

"I'm open to suggestions," she said.

"Maybe Carol can drop another satellite on them," Stevens said. Hawkins struggled to suppress a chortle.

"It's still an open channel, Stevens. Watch it."

"Seriously," Gomez said. "Does anyone have any ideas on—"

"Cover!" Stevens said, pulling Hawkins and Gomez behind one of the putrid-smelling trash bins. From the street, ear-splitting explosions chewed up the pavement and turned parked cars into hurricanes of shrapnel. The rumbling blasts melded with the engine-roar of a pair of Venekan jumpjets screaming past, low over the rooftops.

The town quaked under the simultaneous impacts of hundreds of air-to-surface missiles, which shredded vehicles, collapsed buildings, and turned streets into jumbles of broken stone. Hawkins shielded his head with his arms and strained to think of a way to reach the probe before a Venekan missile destabilized its antimatter containment and vaporized most of this continent.

Trooper Maleska gripped the piping that ran from the front of the armored attack vehicle to its rear. He and eleven soldiers from his squad—all outfitted with body armor and anti-gas masks—squatted on top of the AAV. Each man hung on with one hand and balanced his rifle across his knees with the other as the AAV rolled down Lersset's eastern boulevard toward the center of town. Coils of smoke twisted through golden, horizontal shafts of dawn light as jumpers streaked overhead and unleashed their ordnance on suspected key enemy strongholds.

Perched on top of another AAV directly behind them was the rest of his squad, led by Senior Footman Yellik. Following them was a column of eighteen more AAVs ferrying nine more squads into town. Ahead of the column, panicked X'Mari civilians ran across the streets and in and out of decaying buildings.

The streets were lined with burning vehicles, incinerated only minutes earlier during the initial aerial assault. The squad's orders were simple: Neutralize all non-allied vehicles.

The column reached a major four-way intersection. The AAVs carrying Maleska and his squad turned left. Behind them, two more AAVs turned right at the intersection, while the remaining sixteen AAVs rumbled straight, toward the center of town.

Without warning, a spatter of gunfire ricocheted next to Maleska, off the top of his AAV's gun turret. "Down and cover!" he said. He jumped from the moving vehicle to the muddy, slush-filled street. The rest of his squad followed him. The splashing of their boots into the mud was swallowed by the growl of the AAVs' wide, armored treads pushing forward. He scanned the rooftops and windows, looking for the shooters.

He saw too many to count. Rows of windows on either side of his squad bristled with the barrels of various small firearms. The street echoed with the cracks of semiautomatic gunfire. Two of his soldiers were hit and fell dead next to him. He sprayed a long burst across a row of windows.

"Rockets!" he shouted. To his left, Norlin hefted a compact, shoulder-mounted launcher and fired a small rocket through a top-floor window in the building on the squad's left. The explosion sent jets of fire out six adjacent windows and caused the top floor to collapse in a fiery jumble onto the one below. On the opposite side of the street, Pillo and Yellik fired two more rockets and gutted another building. Clouds of smoke and dust rolled into the street, choking out the daylight.

Maleska keyed his helmet mic. "*Velkor* One, Five-Nine *Jazim!* Suppressing fire, forward left and right! Over!"

"Five-Nine Jazim, Velkor *One. Acknowledged."*

"Fall back!" Maleska said, stepping backward as he peppered the buildings ahead with short bursts of gunfire, even though he couldn't see through the smoke what he was shooting at. The lead AAV rotated its gun turret slightly to the left, while the second swiveled its massive gun barrel a few degrees to the right. They fired in unison, the booms low and deafening. Ahead of the AAVs, five buildings on each side of the street filled with flames, then imploded. For a moment the harassing fire from above stopped, then resumed from behind the squad.

Norlin and Pillo leveled their rocket-launchers toward the rear-flank buildings. Before Maleska could order them to hold fire, a pair of rockets were in the air, one racing toward each building's center point. The bright orange flashes turned the buildings into huge brick boxes filled with fiery clouds.

He watched greasy black smoke belch from the buildings into the street and was ashamed that he felt glad he wouldn't have to risk clearing the buildings room-by-room, as the law required. "*Velkor* One, Five-Nine *Jazim*. All secure." He looked around and counted his casualties. "Notify Sync-Com, we have three dead, four wounded for immediate medivac. The rest of us are up and solid. Over."

"Five-Nine Jazim, Velkor *One. Acknowledged, signaling Sync-Com for medivac. Holding for your go. Over."*

"Mount up!" he said, directing his men back onto the AAVs. There were actually nine wounded among his squad, but five of them were still walking and able to hold their rifles; he'd only counted the four who were still down and bleeding. His men piled on top of the AAVs, found their handholds, and hefted their rifles a bit less cavalierly than before. He climbed aboard, spared one last look back at the soldiers he was leaving behind in the muddy, dust-choked street, and keyed his mic.

"*Velkor* One, Five-Nine *Jazim*. All boots are up. Good to go. Five-Nine *Jazim* out." With a low growl of their engines, the AAVs rolled forward through the walls of smoke, forging ahead into the town to look for more enemy vehicles to destroy.

He loaded a fresh magazine into his rifle and tried to

convince himself that there most likely hadn't been any innocent noncombatants in the fourteen buildings that he and his squad had just incinerated.

As he scanned the road ahead, he couldn't decide what stank worse: the burnt bodies along the roadside, or the lies he was now telling himself so that his government wouldn't have to.

Ganag peeked out of the alley, then ducked back into the shadows and motioned Lerec and Shikorn to stay down.

"What's happening?" Lerec whined.

"Shh!" Ganag hissed, waving a threatening backhand at the boy. Shikorn placed his hand over Lerec's mouth before the boy complained again. In the street beyond the alley, a Venekan armored attack vehicle rolled slowly past, its heavy treads grinding up the brittle and heavily weathered pavement. Marching on either side of the AAV were several Venekan infantrymen, all wearing torso armor and anti-gas masks.

Ganag knew that the X'Mari Resistance had never used poison gas; he could only assume that the Venekans had equipped their soldiers to protect them from their own weapons.

I should've known better than to hang around, Ganag chastised himself. *Should've left as soon as we'd delivered the object.* After the sun had set last night, Ganag had left Lerec and Shikorn in the skiff to guard the object, and he had snuck into Lersset and made contact with Jonen, the Resistance leader whom Hakona had told him to seek out. It had been nearly midnight by the time he'd led Jonen and his commanders to the object, and a few hours more before they'd smuggled it back to the group's base of operations on the other side of town.

The commanders had rewarded the boys with fistfuls of cash and backpacks full of food, medicine, and ammunition, as well as new reconnaissance orders. *Should've left then, while it was still dark,* he thought. But they hadn't left; they had stayed to bask in the praise that the commanders had heaped upon them. It had felt good to be recognized for a change. To be needed.

Now we're just trapped, he fumed, as he watched three more AAVs roll past flanked by dozens more soldiers. *They must have the whole town surrounded. And it's probably because of us.*

The street buzzed with the angry roar of assault rifles. A massive explosion rocked the ground under his feet and knocked him down. In the street, a fireball laced with huge slabs of metal debris hurled a dozen Venekan soldiers backward through the air and dropped them like so many limp rag dolls on the muddy ground. A torrent of burning fuel rained down and turned the street into a lake of fire. The blazing liquid pushed into the alley, toward Ganag and his friends.

"Run!" he said as he sprinted past Lerec and Shikorn. He retreated from the fuel fire that was spreading rapidly into the alley. "Go right! We're heading for the river!" Neither of the younger boys questioned his order. They simply turned right and kept running, following a half-stride behind him.

The river would be dangerously cold. Trying to float submerged back to their skiff would be a risky proposition; there was a good chance they'd all end up with hypothermia, or catch who-knew-what kind of illness. *Sick is better than dead,* he told himself, *and it's our only way out of here.*

Fighting to remember every pathway and abandoned building between the alley and the river, he sprinted ahead to the next shortcut and prayed they reached the water before Lersset went up in flames.

The entire town was alive with the chatter of weapons fire and the irregular percussion of large explosions. Gomez could barely hear Abramowitz's whispering voice over the transceiver.

"Abramowitz to away team!"

"Gomez here."

"The refugees are getting ready to move out, I have to hide the tricorder. Have you reached the probe?"

"Not yet," said Gomez, who was growing both impatient and frustrated. She leaned out from behind the trash bin to see if the fire at the end of the alley had dwindled enough to allow passage to the street. A wash of searing heat stung her face. She ducked back behind cover. "We're kind of stuck."

Going back was no longer an option: A pair of missiles had collapsed a building in the intersecting alley behind them, blocking their only avenue of retreat.

"Well, you need to get un*stuck,"* Abramowitz said. *"The probe's moving. Street level, coming right at you."*

Gomez, Stevens, and Hawkins scrambled out from behind the trash bin and squinted to see through the flames and the wavy wall of heat radiation. From an alley beside the target building a truck emerged and pulled into the street, where it awkwardly navigated an obstacle course of burning debris. Inside the front cab of the truck were two Tenebian men with sky blue skin and metallic-gold hair. "Those aren't X'Maris," Stevens said.

"And they aren't wearing Venekan uniforms," Gomez said.

"Game on," Hawkins said. He ducked his head under his serape and ran toward the wall of fire. Diving through it, he rolled out the other side, singed and smoldering, but all in one piece.

Gomez and Stevens glanced at one another, then turtled into their own serapes. They sprinted forward, leaped through the flames, and hit the ground running.

CHAPTER 8

Gomez's running footsteps slammed against the cracked pavement and sent painful tremors through her shins. She had almost become accustomed to Teneb's gravity, but now, as she tried to sprint, she really felt it pulling her into the ground.

Hawkins was in front of her, and Stevens was right beside her. The truck carrying the crashed Starfleet probe rounded the corner and began climbing a gradual incline. Hawkins veered away from the chase, toward the building the away team had been staking out. "Hawkins!" Gomez said. "Where are you—"

"Playing a hunch!" Hawkins shouted over his shoulder. "Stay on the truck, I'll catch up!"

Gomez pushed ahead after the truck. In regular gravity, an unburdened run up such an incline would be no problem for her. But she watched the truck gain speed up the slope even as she felt the muscles in her legs begin to burn and ache. Several dozen meters ahead, the truck neared an intersection.

Stevens kept pace beside her. She sensed that he was holding back. "Don't worry about me," she said, gasping for breath. "Go." He hesitated for a moment, then steadily gained speed—not enough to overtake the truck, but enough to leave Gomez behind.

Stevens was running on fumes. He hadn't eaten in a day and a half, and he'd been pushing himself much harder than normal.

His throat burned with every ragged gulp of biting-cold morning air. Gusts of breath exploded from his mouth in clouds of mist that quickly evaporated.

Push through the pain, he told himself. *Pain is my friend.* He tried to force himself into a "runner's high," but he knew it was still far away, on the other side of a mountain of agony he wasn't prepared to scale.

The truck turned right at the intersection and disappeared around the corner.

He forced his legs to pump faster, fight harder against Teneb's merciless gravity. His grunts of pain became growls, then gasping cries. His body desperately wanted to stop. His leg muscles felt like knotted cable. Sharp knifing pains stabbed between his ribs with every frantic pull of frigid air.

He refused to slow down. He flailed through the right turn in a stumbling run. The truck was far ahead, fortuitously slowed by another maze of exploded car husks in the road.

A few more steps, he begged himself. *Just a few more steps.*

"Fabian!" Gomez shouted from behind him. "Take my hand!"

He looked back and saw a large cargo van hurtling up the road toward him. Hawkins was in the driver's seat, securely strapped in. Gomez stood in the open passenger-side door, her hand extended toward the exhausted Stevens.

He forced himself to keep running, alongside the van. He held up his hand and left it there until Gomez seized it and pulled him up, through the open door into the vehicle. He crouched between the two seats. Gomez got in behind him and slammed the door. "Thanks for the lift," he said between gasps.

"Jump in back and tell me what's there," Hawkins said.

Stevens turned and opened a narrow door that led into the van's cargo area. He squeezed through into the windowless space, which was dark except for the narrow shaft of daylight slashing in through the open door behind him.

He reached toward an overhead light fixture in the middle of the cargo area. The van swerved suddenly, and he tripped over a heavy object on the floor. He righted himself as Gomez joined him. He reached up and turned on the light.

The back of the van held an arsenal. Its sides were lined with assault rifles and submachine guns. Boxes of grenades and ammunition covered the floor. "Vance?" he said. "If you want weapons, today is Christmas."

"I figured that much," Hawkins said. "What've we got?"

Stevens looked around, more than a little spooked by the primitive, savage weaponry. "Projectile weapons galore, a ton of ammo, and a lot of grenades."

"Are the grenades smooth on the outside, or bumpy?"

"Like Cardassian neck ridges," Gomez said.

"Okay, those are high-explosives. Careful with those. Anything else?"

Stevens opened a long, narrow box. An odd weapon was nestled inside, packed securely in custom-cut blocks of foam. "I have an empty metal tube with a targeting sight," he said. He opened the large square box next to it. "And a box of . . . I have a rocket launcher."

"Good to know," Hawkins said. A staccato rattle of gunfire was followed by the sound of cracking glass. The van swerved wildly, tossing Stevens and Gomez back and forth against the walls of guns. "Load me up a small semi-auto," Hawkins said, "and grab two for yourselves. Bring extra rounds."

"I don't know how to load one of these things," Stevens protested.

"Neither do I," Gomez added.

"Didn't you guys read my mission briefing?" Hawkins said.

"Did you read *mine?"* Stevens retorted.

Another buzz of gunfire was followed by ricochets off the van's front hood. "No," Hawkins said grudgingly.

"Tell me what to do," Stevens said.

"See the open slot in front of the grip?"

Stevens picked up a submachine gun. It was much heavier than the phasers he was used to. "Yeah," he said, looking at the bottom of the weapon. The van lurched side to side again, but he was starting to get used to the chaotic rocking motion, and he swayed with it.

"Look for a clip full of bullets that fits into it and slap it in." Stevens and Gomez rooted through the boxes at their feet. Gomez found the matching magazines, jammed one into her weapon, and handed one to Stevens. He loaded his weapon while Gomez armed another for Hawkins. Stevens picked up the box of loaded magazines and moved back toward the van's cab.

"Stay down," Hawkins said. "We're taking fire."

Stevens crouched and shuffled back into the cab, pushing the box of ammo ahead of him. Gomez inched in behind him and handed a weapon to Hawkins, who ducked low behind the steering wheel and peeked occasionally to see where he was going.

The windshield was spiderwebbed with cracks radiating from a constellation of bullet holes. The engine roared as Hawkins stomped on the accelerator.

The passenger-side windshield exploded over Stevens's head. A storm of glass shards rained down on him and Gomez as bullets dented into the rear wall of the cab.

"Shoot back!" Hawkins said.

Gomez and Stevens lifted their weapons over the dashboard and aimed them out the shattered windshield in a vaguely forward direction. They opened fire. The weapons were incredibly loud. Stevens found his gun impossible to control—it jerked and jumped in his hand like it had a mind of its own.

By the time he and Gomez released the triggers, they were sprawled atop each other on the floor. Smoking bullet holes cut a path across the van's roof. The van's cab smelled of sulfur.

Hawkins was pressed down against his door and glowering at them. "Whose side are you on?" he shouted. "Use *both* hands. Short, controlled bursts. And watch your ammo."

Another sweep of enemy gunfire turned the rest of

the van's windshield opaque with damage. Hawkins punched the windshield with the flat of his palm and knocked it out of its frame. It slid across the bullet-scarred hood and fell into the street. Icy winds whipped dust into the cab and stung their faces.

Stevens and Gomez sat up and steadied their weapons on the van's dashboard as Hawkins swerved around more burning wreckage in the street. Stevens felt the flames licking at his face as they sped through a curtain of fire with a *whoosh.*

He opened his eyes and saw the escaping truck thirty meters ahead. The back of the truck was open. Two Tenebian men crouched inside, both brandishing large assault rifles.

The muzzles of the Tenebians' weapons flashed. Bullets zinged past Stevens's head. He held his breath and steadied his aim as he stared into the cold wind, then pulled the trigger.

Beside him, Gomez opened fire, her face a mask of grim determination, the frigid gusts watering her eyes with tears.

The weapons chattered in their hands.

They filled the back of the truck with a spray of bullets. The two Tenebians hit the deck as ricochets rebounded and tore out through the canvas-covered, wooden-plank sides of the truck, which Stevens guessed probably had been "borrowed" from a livestock or poultry purveyor.

His and Gomez's weapons clicked empty. He tried to pull the empty magazine out of the weapon, but it refused to come free.

"Press the release on the right side of the rear grip," Hawkins said as he aimed his own weapon one-handed out the front windshield. He spun the steering wheel through a tight right turn and peppered the truck ahead with more harassing fire.

Stevens fumbled with his weapon's release catch, then felt the magazine slide easily and fall from the weapon to the floor. He picked up a fresh magazine and slapped it in.

Beside him, Gomez locked and loaded. She nodded to him.

They sprung back into position, facing into the wind, weapons planted on the dash.

Looking back at them from the truck, now only twenty meters ahead and racing toward a Y-shaped merge with another road, were the two Tenebians—both of them aiming rocket launchers.

Stevens saw the look on Hawkins's face, and he knew: *We're so screwed.*

A moment before the Tenebians fired their rockets, their truck barreled into the Y-merge—at the same moment that a speeding passenger car raced into the merge from the other fork of the Y and accidentally broadsided them. The car caromed off the truck and spun into a dusty collision with a brick wall.

The Tenebians' shoulder-fired rockets careened off-target. One screamed into a deserted building to the left of the van. The other plowed into the street directly ahead of it.

Hawkins slammed on the brakes. The van skidded to a halt just shy of the explosion in the road, which kicked up a smoky storm of glowing-hot broken asphalt that pattered down onto the van. Past the smoldering crater, the rocketed building collapsed into a broken-stone mountain that blocked the street.

"Can we go over it?" Gomez said.

"Not in this thing," Hawkins said.

The security guard poked his head out his window, looked around quickly, then spun the van through a reverse whip-turn. He shifted gears and stepped on the accelerator. The van sped forward. He hooked a quick left turn, then made another left down an alley so narrow that a shower of sparks fountained from either side of the van as he accelerated.

"Chief," Gomez said, "where are you going?"

"I don't know," Hawkins said. "I'm making this up as I go."

Commander Zila monitored his army's drive into Lersset from a bank of monitors installed in his personal jumpjet. Sitting opposite him, facing his own bank of monitors, was Legioner Goff, whose attention had become much more narrowly focused during the past few seconds.

"What is it?" Zila said.

Goff held up a hand to signal that he needed a few more moments to concentrate. He looked up at Zila. "Reports of a van chasing a truck in southern Lersset, near the riverside. A recon unit says the two vehicles have exchanged gunfire."

"On my monitor," Zila said. Goff transferred the command-and-control screen to Zila's computer. The time-stamped reports scrolled quickly up the side of the screen while blurred, grainy images snapped by an aerial reconnaissance drone showed moment-by-moment details of the chase.

"That's it, that's our target," Zila said. "Order all forces to intercept and capture. No heavy munitions—I want those vehicles and their cargo intact."

"And the passengers?"

"Expendable."

Hawkins kept the accelerator pinned to the floor and barreled up streets, down alleys, and through the occasional vulnerable-looking fence. Stevens rode shotgun, his safety harness now securely fastened.

Hawkins glimpsed the morning sun as intermittent, yellow-orange flashes in the narrow seams between the decaying buildings he raced past.

Leaning forward, he glanced upward, then swung the van wide through a right-hand turn, followed by a quick left turn. Stevens held on to the dash with white-knuckle intensity.

"What're you following?" Stevens said. "Their scent?"

"No," Hawkins said, pointing skyward. "The planes." Several blocks away on either side of the van, flying low over the rooftops, were two Venekan jumpjets. They were approaching from different directions, but seemed to be converging on a point several blocks ahead of the van.

"Nice work," Stevens said.

"Well, Starfleet didn't hire me for my looks."

"Obviously," Stevens quipped.

"Don't make me come up there," Gomez said.

The buildings melted past in a blur as Hawkins pushed the van to its top speed. As the van rounded a long gradual bend in the road that ran along the river, behind the docks on the west side of town, the truck came into view.

Two jumpjets converged several dozen meters behind the truck. One aircraft assumed an attack position; the other dropped back over the river, to cover the leader's wing.

A ground-to-air rocket soared up from the back of the truck and sliced like a blazing scalpel through the leader's right wing. As the aircraft pitched nosefirst in a death-spiral toward the ground, a fiery chunk of debris expelled from its wing was sucked into the follower's left turbine intake. The second jet's left-wing engine exploded, taking half the aircraft with it in a massive, aviation-fuel conflagration.

Wreckage from the lead jumpjet struck the road and rolled like a Catherine wheel juggernaut over a row of decrepit dock warehouses. The second jet disintegrated in midair, scattering its debris in ephemeral, coal-black coils of drifting smoke as it splashed down in the river on the other side of the road.

Hawkins kept his eyes on the truck and his foot on the gas.

He pondered the tactical dilemma that was only seconds away from requiring an answer: *How the hell are we supposed to stop them when they have rockets?*

The question became moot as a sustained spray of large-caliber machine-gun fire, from an unseen source on the truck's left, shredded the wood-beam-and-canvas covering of its cargo area—and mowed down the two gunmen in the back of the truck.

From a gap in the several-kilometers-long row of dock warehouses, a flatbed truck swerved toward the smaller truck. Mounted on a pivot secured to the flatbed was the heavy machine gun whose handiwork Hawkins had just witnessed.

The flatbed's machine-gunner and another Tenebian man leapt into the now-open back of the truck that carried the probe. Both men drew small pistols from under their coats and fired several shots through the truck's rear window.

The attackers swiftly opened the truck's doors, pulled out the two men inside, climbed in, and commandeered the moving vehicle with hardly any loss of forward momentum.

Hawkins veered slightly to avoid running over the two dead Tenebians who'd just been thrown into the street.

"That flatbed doesn't have Venekan markings, either," he said, stating the baldly obvious.

Stevens shook his head in shock and disbelief. "How many countries on this planet are trying to steal this thing?"

"All of them," Gomez said without irony.

Maleska sat next to Yellik on top of the AAV as it rolled toward the turn for West River Road. From adjacent streets he heard the low rumble of two more columns of AAVs converging toward the south end of Lersset.

"What's going on?" Yellik said, shouting to be heard over the noise.

Maleska shook his head. "No idea," he said, his voice hoarse from yelling over the thick screech of low-flying jumpjets, which seemed to be leading the way. He had never seen this level of frenzy in either of his previous tours of duty in X'Mar.

Yellik leaned closer to him. He thought the man looked worried. "You don't think it's nuclear, do you?" Yellik said.

"I don't know," Maleska lied. "You know how it is. We're just the boots on the ground. Nobody tells us anything."

He looked back down the road and saw the column of AAVs growing longer with each block it traveled. He counted his men and was satisfied to see them all still accounted for. He sighed. *At least we don't have to hump into the zone on foot.*

Gomez leaned forward from the van's cargo area and assessed the situation. Hawkins was keeping the van a safe distance behind the truck and the flatbed, whose passenger now staffed its gun, leaving just the driver in the flatbed's cab.

The two large vehicles veered away from the river and sped into a vast industrial plaza that contained several mountains of construction-grade gravel. The flatbed was still on the truck's left, and the two were nearly parallel.

"I don't think they see us," Hawkins said. "I'd say it's now or never."

"Okay, what's your plan?" Gomez said.

"I was hoping you had one."

Gomez eyed the twisting, obstacle-littered terrain ahead. Then she saw six Venekan jumpjets, still several kilometers away but closing steadily. And she knew that the enormous, advancing cloud of dust rising from the city beneath the jets had to be the product of an army on the move.

"Can you get in front of them without getting us shot?" she said, nodding at the trucks.

Hawkins cocked his head to the side. "Maybe."

He swerved left onto a path that ran parallel to the road that the truck and flatbed were traveling on. The path and the road were separated by mound after mound of gravel.

Pushing the van to its limits, Hawkins quickly caught up to the two trucks. The wind cut like a meat ax at Gomez's face.

As the van raced past a wide gap between two conical gravel mountains, the driver of the flatbed turned his head and saw them. Behind him, his machine-gunner opened fire.

Large-caliber bullets chopped a wide swath across a slope of gravel in front of the van. Bits of rock bounced in through the vehicle's empty windshield frame.

The flatbed accelerated ahead of the truck as another dark gray gravel mountain filled Gomez's field of vision.

She pointed to the next gap linking the path and the road. "Cut across up there, and don't slow down!"

She moved back into the cargo area. Grabbing the bolted-down weapons rack along the wall to her left for leverage, she kicked open the van's rear double doors.

Reaching down, she opened a box of grenades. She took one grenade out of the box and armed it. The van lurched into a sharp right turn. As Stevens fired out his window at the flatbed, Gomez jammed the live grenade back in the box.

The van cut a hard turn across the industrial yard's main road. Gomez heaved the box out the van's rear door. Then she hit the deck and grabbed the first thing that didn't budge.

Behind the van, the flatbed raced into the intersection. A chattering burst of machine-gun fire tore through the van, unleashing a storm of metal fragments. Hawkins and Stevens yowled in pain. Gomez felt a sharp impact in the back of her left thigh, followed by an agonizing burning sensation.

A shrapnel-filled fireball erupted beneath the flatbed's

second axle, directly below the machine gun. The blast lifted the truck off the ground and dropped it in a burning, broken-backed heap. Gomez enjoyed a very brief moment of gloating until she heard the screech of brakes from behind the flatbed.

The truck carrying the probe was unable to slow down in time to avoid the crippled flatbed in front of it. Making a desperate left swerve up a gravel slope, the truck lost its traction and slid out of control. It clipped the back edge of the flatbed and rolled several times until it came to rest on its side, several meters from the flaming husk of the larger vehicle.

Hawkins stopped the van and shifted it into reverse. He backed up the van to the truck, which lay on its left side, helpless as an overturned turtle.

Gomez got up and stepped out the van's rear doors, her submachine gun still clutched in her hand. Every step with her left leg caused sharp jabs of pain to radiate from her wound.

She looked back as Stevens and Hawkins got out of the van. Stevens's door looked like it had been chewed up and spat out. Hawkins pressed down on a bloody wound along his lower right abdomen. Stevens limped beside him and clutched fiercely at the left side of his neck. "How bad are you guys hit?" she said.

"Flesh wound," Hawkins said.

"Grazed, but it stings like a sonofabitch," Stevens said. As Gomez got closer, she realized both men's faces and hands were covered in tiny nicks, scratches, and cuts that were only now beginning to bleed. She also saw that the right leg of Stevens's pants was shredded below the knee. He noticed her watching him limp. "Shrapnel," he said simply. "From the door."

They gathered in back of the overturned truck. The

probe was still securely fastened to the floor of the truck's rear section. Hawkins and Stevens loosened its restraints and lowered it quickly but carefully to the ground.

The low mechanical roar of approaching tanks, troops, and aircraft grew steadily louder, from both in front of and behind the trio. Except for the van, the two wrecked vehicles, and the gravel mounds, there was no significant cover in the industrial yard and no means of escape.

Hawkins stared into the distance, also tracking the Venekans' approach. "Make this quick, Fabian," Gomez said. "The Venekans'll be here any second."

Stevens ran his hand along the probe's casing until he found the probe's hidden access panel. "Stevens to Abramowitz," he said. "Carol, we need the tricorder to transmit the security code that opens the probe's maintenance panel." There was no reply. "Carol, do you read me?"

"I can't," Abramowitz whispered over the open channel. Even over the transceiver, Gomez could tell Abramowitz was speaking through a clenched jaw. *"They'll kill me."*

"Carol, if we don't get the panel open now, we're dead," Hawkins said. "Just get clear long enough to send the signal, and we'll beam outta here in two minutes."

"You don't understand," Abramowitz said, her voice rising with desperation. *"There's nowhere I can—"*

"Abramowitz," Gomez said. "Activate the tricorder and send the signal. *That's an order.*"

For several seconds there was no response. Then Gomez heard Abramowitz's muffled and dismayed answer: *"Yes, sir."*

The dust cloud followed the Venekan troops as they entered the industrial yard and fanned out around its perimeter.

Gomez heard the engines of large, heavy ground vehicles and the frantic clatter of boots growing closer.

A pair of Venekan aircraft cruised low overhead, stopped in midair over the river, hovered, then began doubling back.

Soft chirping noises accompanied the opening of the probe's maintenance panel. Stevens reached inside and deftly handled several delicate-looking gadgets. He reached deeper inside the probe and pulled out a tiny kit of Starfleet repair tools—which decades ago some genius engineer had, in a moment of rare foresight, thought to design into the probe itself for exactly this kind of emergency field repair.

"Good work, Carol," Gomez said. "Hang tight, we'll be outta here in a few minutes." Gomez watched Stevens work for a few seconds, then realized Abramowitz had not acknowledged the good news. "Carol, do you read me? Gomez to Abramowitz, do you copy?"

Silence reigned over the transceiver channel.

Abramowitz stared up into the crazed, maniacally gleaming eyes of teenaged Lica, elderly Mother Aleké, and the formerly gentle and caring Nedia. They and a dozen other women surrounded her.

Nedia had been the first to see the tricorder and alert the others. Now they all stared angrily at the high-tech device in Abramowitz's hand, as if it were the very embodiment of evil.

"What is this thing?" Mother Aleké said, her voice grave.

"It's hard to explain," Abramowitz said.

"It's a Venekan tracking beacon," one of the women said. "She's helping them follow us to the sanctuary."

"No," Abramowitz said, "I'm not, I swear. Please, I—"

"I can't believe I let you deceive me," Nedia said. "You said your friends were 'captured' by the Venekans?" Abramowitz nodded. "Was that before or after your friends built you that shelter? And collected the wood for your fire? Certainly, with your injuries, there's no way you did that work yourself."

"Yes," Abramowitz said, "my friends built my shelter. They were captured later."

"How could you know that?" Nedia said. "Unless they were captured close enough for you to have seen or heard it. But if the Venekans were that close to you, how could they have not seen the smoke from your fire? Smoke that we saw from more than two *tiliks* away?"

An even larger crowd was now gathered behind the circle of women surrounding Abramowitz. Nedia snatched the tricorder from Abramowitz's hand. "Or did they contact you with *this?*" In the moment between Nedia's grabbing the tricorder and her holding it up to the crowd, the device vanished—*poof.*

Nedia stared at the dissipating tendrils of vapor in her hand, then looked down at Abramowitz, her rancor now tinged with fear. The entire crowd had seen the tricorder vanish in Nedia's hand, spawning a wave of horror that rippled out into the troubled sea of refugees massed on the cold mountain road.

Mother Aleké pointed a gnarled, bony finger at Abramowitz.

"She is a spy," Mother Aleké proclaimed.

Mother Aleké drifted back into the crowd as dozens of X'Mari women kneeled down, picked up fist-sized rocks from the road, and carried them toward Abramowitz—who had done enough research on the xenophobic X'Mari culture to know there was nothing left she could say that would stop them from executing her.

CHAPTER 9

A voice distorted by electronic amplification resounded from across the industrial plaza. *"This is the Venekan Army,"* it squawked with ear-splitting volume. *"Lay down your weapons and surrender. This is your only warning."*

Gomez felt her stomach churning as humanoid figures—decked out in military body armor and carrying a variety of small arms—began to coalesce into distinct shapes, even though they were still obscured by the amber haze of the growing dust cloud.

"Talk to me, Fabian," she said.

"It's not good," he said. "I need a few minutes."

Hawkins shook his head. "Stevens, we don't have—"

"Look," Stevens snapped. "I'm not making this up. I'm telling you, I *need* a few minutes."

Gomez looked at Hawkins. "Help me unload the van."

He followed her back to the van. She hurried inside and handed two assault rifles out to him. "You can't be serious," he said.

"We don't have to win the battle," she said as she handed him a heavy box filled with loaded rifle magazines. "We just have to hold our position until Fabian arms the self-destruct trigger. But there's an entire army coming at us, so we need all the firepower we can get." She handed him another weighty box, loaded with short, round-nosed cylinders. "What are these?"

Hawkins glanced in the box. "Rifle-fired mini-grenades," he said. "Pump-action launcher. You can preload up to four." He turned and set down the box. Gomez took the rocket launcher from its box, handed it to him, and picked up the box of rockets next to it. She stepped out of the van and looked around.

"The wrecked flatbed'll give us some cover," she said, setting down the box of rockets. "I'll take the left. You take the front and the right."

She took off her serape, laid it on the ground, and piled rifle magazines and mini-grenades onto it. Hawkins slapped a magazine into his rifle and began loading mini-grenades into its secondary chamber beneath the main barrel. "Sir, you do realize these weapons have no stun settings," he said.

"Wound if you can," she said, jamming a magazine into her own rifle. "Kill if you have to."

She slung her rifle across her back. Grabbed the corners of her serape; pulled them together to make it a bundle. Jogged in a low crouch to the front edge of the van. Kneeled down. Opened the serape on the ground. Counted ten thirty-round magazines of rifle ammunition and ten mini-grenades. Loaded four mini-grenades into her weapon.

Gomez looked over her shoulder. Hawkins loaded a rocket into the launcher. Between them, kneeling behind the truck, Stevens worked furiously, his hands deep inside the probe.

She peeked around the corner of the van at the advancing clusters of soldiers. There were hundreds of them, advancing in groups of ten and twenty. Leading them in and providing them with cover were large armored vehicles equipped with sizable gun turrets.

Four of the six Venekan aircraft that had led the soldiers here hovered nearby, low over the gravel mountains, at angles ideal for avoiding the risk of cross fire. The remaining two aircraft stayed together and circled the industrial yard.

I can't believe I'm doing this, Gomez thought. *I came here to save these people, not kill them.* She closed her eyes and reminded herself of the destructive potential of the probe's antimatter fuel payload. *No choice,* she decided. *If we let these fools capture the probe, they'll blow up their planet trying to take it apart. Better for a few of them to die by our hands than for the whole species to die by its own.*

"This is your final warning," the distorted loudspeaker voice said with ear-splitting clarity. *"Put down your weapons and surrender, or we will open fire."*

Gomez looked again at Hawkins, who looked back at her, awaiting her order. She nodded to him, then aimed her rifle around the corner of the van at the Venekan soldiers, who had closed to within sixty meters of the vehicles.

She pulled the trigger. Her weapon roared like rattling thunder and kicked painfully into her shoulder. Two soldiers fell to the ground as their comrades ran for cover, firing back in Gomez's general direction.

The overturned truck stuttered with metallic echoes from scores of bullet impacts. From behind her came the *foomp* of Hawkins pump-firing a mini-grenade. As she heard it explode, the buzzing clatter of Hawkins's rifle joined her own.

Her weapon clicked empty. She gripped the pump-action slide underneath her rifle's barrel and fired a mini-grenade into the path between two large gravel slopes. The explosion kicked up an enormous cloud of smoke and dust. She ejected the empty magazine from her rifle and slapped in a fresh one.

Bullet holes poked randomly through the overturned truck, a few at first, then several more. A round zinged past Gomez, close enough for her to feel the wake it cut through the freezing morning air.

A phaser, she pined, *my kingdom for a phaser.*

Abramowitz lifted her right arm to shield her face as Nedia cast the first stone. Abramowitz cried out in pain as the rock slammed into her torso.

She turned away and felt the second and third stones strike almost simultaneously in her middle back. Another rock hit her in the back of the head, purpling her vision. Then she lost count of the blows as a flurry of rocks rained down on her.

One agonizing blunt impact overlapped another and another and another. Her shouts of pain became an unbroken string of sobs and whimpers. She struggled to crawl away from the mob, with her one good arm and leg. A jagged stone hit her left arm dead on the break. Flashes of pain coursed up her spine.

Her fingers clawed at the cold, rocky ground as she

pulled herself forward beneath the brutal onslaught. Her fingertips scraped across the thin layer of sand scattered atop the high mountain road. She heard the clamor of hate-filled voices and the shuffle of leather-shod feet following close behind her.

Another wave of stones crashed down on her back, her legs, her head. One banged off her temple. A warm, wet wash of blood sheeted across the right side of her face. Trickles of blood snaked out from beneath her copper-flecked, rust-hued faux hair to trace paths across her forehead.

She came to the edge of the road and looked over it, into the yawning gorge below. There was nowhere left to run to.

The mob surrounded her on three sides. The women cast their stones then left to find more—as another group of women, rocks in hand, stepped forward to take their places.

She put her arm back over her face and curled into as tight a ball as she could. Retreating into the uncomforting cocoon of her own shadow, she whimpered in terror and pain as the rocks continued to fall, without end and without mercy.

Ganag, Lerec, and Shikorn huddled together behind a stack of rusted metal barrels lying on their sides in a narrow gap between two abandoned riverfront warehouses. Just past the end of the gap was West River Road.

On the other side of the road was the Ulom River.

Rolling down the road was a Venekan Army unit comprising several armored vehicles and more than a hundred heavily armed troops. "Just a few more minutes," Ganag whispered to his friends. "As soon as they pass us, we'll get in the river and swim the rest of the way back to the skiff."

Shikorn nodded. Lerec stared in mute terror at the Venekan troops marching past. Ganag reached back and playfully mussed the young boy's dark-bronze hair. "Breathe," Ganag teased him. "Hold your breath *after* we're in the water."

Lerec smiled weakly but said nothing. The boys remained quiet and hidden, waiting patiently for the soldiers to pass.

Then the army column ground to a halt.

Shikorn leaned over to Ganag. "What's happ—" The first cracks of gunfire silenced Shikorn and sent the Venekan soldiers in the road scrambling off the tops of their armored vehicles and behind them for cover. Explosions filled the road with fire, smoke, and shrapnel. Furious, buzzing automatic gunfire came as much from the X'Mari Resistance fighters on the warehouse rooftops as from the soldiers in the street.

Ganag turned to his friends and pointed away from the road, back the way they'd come. "Back and right, to the gravel yard," he said. "It should be empty. We can cut through it to the river." He herded Lerec and Shikorn away from the fighting.

"You're sure?" Shikorn said. With a look, Ganag silently admitted that he wasn't. Shikorn frowned, but nodded and moved on ahead, keeping one hand on the shoulder of Lerec's coat to prevent the boy from lagging behind.

The three boys ran south toward the gravel yard as the pandemonium of battle echoed behind them.

* * *

Hawkins fired off two quick bursts toward the attackers to the front, then pivoted to pick off a soldier who was charging forward on the right flank to lob a grenade, which fell from the man's hand and detonated, taking down four more Tenebians.

He spun back toward the front and pumped out the last of his four pre-loaded grenades. It bounced off the turret of an armored vehicle that had stopped and turned perpendicular to the road to provide maximum cover for the troops advancing behind it. The grenade's explosive detonation almost drowned out Stevens's anguished scream.

Glancing sideways, Hawkins saw that Stevens had been hit in his upper chest, just to the side of his right shoulder. The impact had knocked him backward nearly two meters. His earth-toned serape showed the beginning of a spreading bloodstain. From the other side of the truck, Gomez glanced nervously at Stevens and Hawkins as she continued shooting.

"Stevens!" Hawkins yelled over the metallic peals of ricochets. He tensed to spring to the wounded man's side.

Stevens grimaced and held up his hand, signaling Hawkins to stop. "I'm all right," he said, his voice a roar of agony, his eyes tearing. He crawled back toward the probe, his right arm limp at his side. Reaching in with his left hand, he resumed working. The bloodstain spread swiftly across his serape.

Hawkins snapped off another burst toward the right flank, then another forward. His weapon clicked empty. He ejected the magazine and reached down to grab a fresh one, then realized he had just picked up his last clip.

He tuned out the terrible battering clamor of weapons blazing; the fear-colored din of soldiers barking orders over the cries of the wounded and dying; the acrid smell of gunpowder and the choking weight of oily smoke.

He switched his weapon to semi-automatic and picked his targets, popping off three shots forward, two more to the right, then turning forward again. The soldiers on the front and right flanks seemed to be holding back, unwilling to charge blindly as their fallen comrades had done. Instead, they stayed behind cover, each of them looking to make a lucky shot.

We're lucky they want the probe, Hawkins realized. *If not for that, those tanks would've just run us over.*

An armor-piercing round blasted through the overturned truck and shot through Hawkins's right leg, knocking him on his back. Three soldiers on the front flank saw him fall, and charged forward. Hawkins lifted his head just enough to aim his rifle over his knee and fired three more rounds, dropping all three men in quick succession.

He heard the turbine shriek of a jumpjet, which appeared from behind an enormous gravel mountain like a dark mechanical raptor. It had a perfect angle from which to sweep him, Gomez, and Stevens with cannon fire without hitting the probe.

He dropped his rifle and grabbed the rocket launcher. In a single motion he raised it to his shoulder and fired.

The projectile soared away with a sibilant *whoosh,* trailing a streak of white exhaust as it raced in less than a second to its target. It struck the jumpjet almost dead-center in its fuselage. The aircraft spat fire from beneath every hull plate. It wobbled and spun for a moment, then pitched toward the ground and tumbled chaotically, finally making impact on the slope of another mound of gravel on Hawkins's rear flank.

The blast felt like an earthquake. The gravel mound was transformed into a storm of speeding rock, suspended in a pyroclastic cloud that billowed over the rear third of the industrial yard. Dust and dirt blanketed the away team.

Hawkins's ears were still ringing from the explosion as he loaded another rocket into the launcher.

Stevens slumped against the probe and declared as loudly as he could, "It's armed." Gomez looked back at him.

"Good work, Fabian," she said. "Set it for thirty-five seconds, then signal the—" The bullet exploded through her chest half a heartbeat before Hawkins heard the crack of the sniper rifle that had fired it. Two more shots ripped through Gomez's torso as she fell toward Stevens. With his good hand, he plucked her rifle from her hand and tossed it to Hawkins, who caught it, braced it against his shoulder, and aimed it at the sniper on top of the gravel mound behind them on Gomez's side.

He fired as he saw the muzzle flash of the sniper's weapon.

The sniper jerked back and tumbled down the far side of the gravel mountain—just as his bullet slammed into Hawkins's lower left arm, just in front of the elbow. Flesh and muscle were shredded, the bone shattered. The shell exited Hawkins's forearm and lodged deep in his bicep. He collapsed onto his back, with one arm and one leg paralyzed.

"Stevens," he said through a mouth sticky with dust. "Set the timer. Send the signal." Stevens reached into the probe and keyed in a short string of commands.

Hawkins craned his neck back and gauged his upside-down perspective of the armored vehicle parked broadside not forty meters away. He fought to steady his one-handed aim with the rocket launcher.

A pleasant-sounding chirp from the probe confirmed Stevens's orders. *Just need thirty more seconds of delay,* Hawkins told himself. He fired the rocket.

The AAV flew apart in a devastating eruption of metal and fire. Its explosion effectively pushed the Venekans' front line back at least fifty meters, equaling the damage done to their right flank by the crash of the jet.

"Stevens . . ." The engineer limped over to him, his face stippled with Gomez's blood and shrapnel wounds from bullets that had penetrated the truck.

"Get Gomez's submachine gun," Hawkins said. "Hold the left flank."

Stevens gripped Hawkins's shoulder, then half-limped, half-hopped to Gomez and took the submachine gun that was still slung over her shoulder. He staggered over to Gomez's position and squeezed off a short burst toward distant voices in the dense gray-brown cloud. Hawkins reached down and loaded one more rocket into the launcher, just in case.

The weight of the barrage had driven Abramowitz toward the edge of the precipice until she was perched on its lip, one foot dangling over the abyss. She shivered uncontrollably; she wasn't sure whether it was because of the cold or her injuries.

Then the rocks stopped falling. Abramowitz hoped that she had passed out and been beamed up to the *da Vinci.* She opened her tear-filled eyes. She was still on the mountain road.

A girlish scream of rage echoed off the cliff walls. Abramowitz heard a few running footsteps coming toward her, then she felt a brutal kick between her shoulder blades that knocked her over the edge.

Her right hand flailed out, every instinct telling her to survive, to hang on until the last possible second.

She looked up and saw Lica standing over her. Her young violet eyes, scarred by war and its endless horrors, were filled with rage.

"I asked them to rescue you," Lica said, her voice quaking with fury. "They let you in because of me! It's my fault we have a spy!" Abramowitz said nothing. She clung by four fingertips to the sandy lip of stone.

"I have to cleanse myself," Lica said. She lifted her foot.

"No!" Abramowitz screamed. Lica stomped on Abramowitz's fingers. A pain like searing fire spiked through her hand. Sobbing with agony and desperation, she held on. The girl lifted her foot again. "Lica, don't!" The girl's foot smashed down on Abramowitz's slender fingertips and pulverized them.

The world washed past Abramowitz, like a child's watercolor painting left in the rain, as she fell through the mist toward the barren canyon floor several hundred feet below.

Commander Zila swallowed mouthful after mouthful of curses as he observed the battle from the air and snapped orders to Lancer Vecha, the weak-kneed and mind-bogglingly incompetent field officer leading the attack on the ground.

"I *know* you just lost an AAV!" Zila shouted. "Send

Eight-Two *Olik* around the right flank and have One-Three *Masara* lay down smokers to cover Eight-Two's charge."

"Commander," Vecha said, his voice swallowed by static, *"with all due respect, their position is too strong for a direct—"*

"There's only *three* of them, you idiot! And one's *dead!* Charge! Do it now, before I come down there and rip off your *renods!*" Zila punched the channel closed and looked across the compartment at Goff. "Now we're gonna see some results!"

A flash of light brighter than the morning sun enveloped the gravel yard. The blast tossed the jumpjet into a flat spin. As the aircraft's electrics went dead, Zila felt it begin a sickening spiral toward the ground.

"Move out! Double quick time!" Maleska barked marching cadences at his squad as they sprinted away from the X'Mari ambush toward the firefight in the gravel yards three *tiliks* up the road. He'd heard two resounding explosions even from this distance.

The X'Maris must have an entire regiment holding the gravel yard, he speculated. The combat zone loomed into view beyond the row of dock warehouses along the road. *What if it's another ambush? Should we wait for more orders?*

A synthetic bleating from the radioman's pack signaled a transmission from Sync-Com. "Hold up!" Maleska ordered. His squad halted and immediately crouched low and assumed perimeter-watch formation. The radioman kneeled in front of Maleska, who grabbed the digital receiver, turned toward the river to reduce the noise from the combat zone, and pressed the transmit key.

"Sync-Com, Five-Nine *Jazim*. Go ahead."

"Five-Nine Jazim, *reinforcements are needed at map grid* Xondi *Six-One,"* the Sync-Com coordinator squawked. *"What's your column's status? Over."*

"Sync-Com, Five-Nine *Jazim*. We lost our AAVs and more than half our company in an ambush on West River Road. Remainder of company is humping into the zone on foot. Over."

"What's your grid reference?"

"We're near the end of West River Road, roughly three *tiliks* from *Xondi* Six-One, and moving into—"

A nova-bright flash of light from the gravel yard coincided with a sizzle-hiss of static over the line. Half a second later came the cataclysmic thundercrack of a massive explosion.

"Down!" Maleska vaulted over the railing that ran along the road and dived over the river's edge into the water.

He hoped that his men would be quick enough to follow him.

The river was so cold that it prickled his skin, like needles jabbing him with electric shocks. He gasped in pain, losing half the breath he'd gulped before hitting the water.

Looking up, he saw the blurry, morning-sky silhouettes of bodies diving into the river above him. Then he realized debris was falling in with them—and that none of them were swimming down to escape the blast or up to get air. They simply bobbed on the surface like flotsam and jetsam.

Within seconds, the rumbling stopped. A film of dust and filth settled like a skin over the surface of the river.

Maleska surfaced to a scene as dark as night. Gasping hungrily for air, he coughed as he swallowed a mouthful of filthy water and smoke. He spat it out and wheezed as he stroked awkwardly to the river's edge and pulled himself out.

He looked around at the flattened building, the landscape of scorched ruins and smoldering ground, the mushroom cloud. The gravel yard, the warehouses along its perimeter, and the ship-loading cranes that had dominated its waterfront were all destroyed, crushed as if by divine retribution.

Lying among the ruins, shrouded in the gray dust of this backward country Maleska had learned both to loathe and to pity, was his squad, reduced to an assortment of gruesome sculptures: an outstretched hand over here; a half-buried corpse lying facedown over there.

He plucked a rifle from the ankle-deep ash that covered the road. Slapped the dust off it and puffed a breath into the barrel. Took out the magazine and inspected it; it was clean. He put it back in. Fired one shot into the river, just to test it, then slung it over his shoulder.

Turning his back to the river, he walked east across the field of destruction. The ground was hot beneath his boots. He wandered without thought past slag heaps that once had been AAVs, past the mangled wing of a jumpjet.

After a time, he reached the far edge of the blast's major area of effect. Here the buildings still stood, though there wasn't a window intact anywhere. The city was quiet with death, its secrets whispered on a hot wind that concealed its phantoms in wandering dust clouds.

He paused as he heard muffled sobs. He looked up from his boots, which now were caked in dried mud. Kneeling on the sidewalk, dusty and bloody and broken like himself, was a teenaged X'Mari boy, slumped in the street along the industrial yard's perimeter. He held in his arms two other boys, both of whom were dead, riddled with bullet wounds.

Maleska looked at their faces, which were masked in dust. One was practically still a child, no more than thirteen, the same age as Maleska's youngest brother. The other was a teenager, gangly and rugged-looking, cut down just shy of growing into manhood.

The kneeling boy wept bitterly, choking on his tears, seemingly oblivious of Maleska's presence.

A silhouette staggered out of a wall of sunlit dust farther down the street behind the kneeling boy. As the backlit man drew closer, Maleska saw that it was Commander Zila. The officer was scorched, wounded, maniacal. He carried an assault rifle at his side as he pitched from one side to another, lurching like a drunkard down the street toward Maleska.

Zila stopped and stared with wide-eyed contempt at the kneeling, weeping X'Mari boy in the street. He stared at the boy for close to a minute. Maleska stood like a statue, watching Zila. Without a word, Zila lifted his rifle and pointed it at the boy in front of the alley.

Maleska didn't think about swinging his own rifle into his hands; he simply did it. He didn't think about aiming at Commander Zila and pulling the trigger once, twice, three times. He simply did it, without thought, without emotion, without regret. The boy went on weeping as the echoes of gunfire faded.

Maleska walked slowly up the street, dropping his rifle next to Zila's body as he passed by. The sound of the boy's crying receded behind him as he wandered out of the city, away from the devastation, toward the faint and distant hope that he had seen his last day of war.

Stevens materialized in the *da Vinci* sickbay. He felt lighter the moment the annular confinement beam released him into the familiar, lighter-than-Teneb gravity of the ship he called home, but he collapsed to the deck all the same.

The transporter beam had grabbed him, Hawkins, and Gomez less than two seconds before the probe self-destructed, and the near-warp aspect of their beam-up had left him more than a little disoriented. *Of course, that could also be because I've lost a lot of blood,* he realized.

Hawkins and Gomez materialized on the deck beside him in roughly the same poses they had been in on the ground. On the other side of Gomez was Abramowitz, who was battered, bloody, and unconscious.

Even before the away team had fully materialized, Dr. Lense, Nurse Wetzel, and Medical Technician Falcão snapped into action, visually assessing each team member's status.

They surrounded Gomez. Lense called out a string of medical orders that was so fast and thick with jargon that Stevens couldn't follow it. The only orders he caught for certain were Lense activating the EMH and instructing it to perform emergency surgery on Abramowitz, and Wetzel activating a backup copy of the EMH to perform triage on himself and Hawkins.

Lense, Wetzel, and Falcão lifted Gomez's limp, bloody body onto a surgical bed and activated the sterile force field. The first EMH, meanwhile, moved Abramowitz to the *da Vinci*'s other surgical bed, activated its sterile field, and began his own surgical procedure.

The second EMH consulted a medical tricorder as he knelt between Stevens and Hawkins.

"Both of you have multiple shrapnel wounds, ranging from minuscule to serious," he said, reading from the display. "Multiple grazing wounds, cuts, and bruises."

"Yeah," Stevens said. "We know that."

The EMH scanned Hawkins. "You have severe damage in your—"

"Doc," Hawkins said, his temper rising. "I know where it hurts. Spare me the list and help me." The EMH drew back a bit, as if he were offended, then he turned and picked up a hypospray from a nearby equipment cart. He put the nozzle of the hypospray to Hawkins's throat and injected a sizable dose of medicine. Stevens saw the tension melt from Hawkins's body.

The EMH placed the hypospray against Stevens's jugular and administered another healthy dose of painkiller meds. It worked beautifully; Stevens felt no pain, no weight, not even the coldness of the deck beneath him. The duplicate EMH remained between the two men, working quickly to stanch the bleeding from their worst wounds, but Stevens couldn't feel a thing.

He lolled his head toward Hawkins, who, like him, was barely conscious. "Hey, Hawk," he mumbled, his own voice sounding oddly deep and dreamlike.

"Yeah . . . ?" Hawkins sounded like he was a lightyear away.

"All we wanted to do was help those people . . . and all they wanted to do was kill us."

Hawkins chuckled cynically. "That's the job, Fabe," he said with a grin. "You don't like it, quit."

Stevens grinned as his vision clouded over. "Can't," he said, letting go of an exhausted sigh. "I'm enlisted."

Hawkins wore an ironic looking grin. "Yeah. . . . Me, too," he said as Stevens followed him into medicated unconsciousness.

CHAPTER 10

Gomez's world turned red in an instant. An impact like a sledgehammer against her chest knocked her against the bottom of the overturned truck with such force that she bounced off it. Her legs wobbled beneath her.

A battering-ram of force slammed into her back. She watched a spray of her own blood jet out of her torso and stipple Stevens's horrified face with wet freckles. The mechanical din of battle washed away in a low roar, like the sound she'd heard as a girl while floating underwater off the coast of Vieques. The ground tilted up toward her.

Color washed away, leaving the world painted in shades of watery gray as she stood over herself, counting the bullet holes in her own back. Her body was facedown in the dirt, next to a pool of blood from Stevens's wounded shoulder. A shell casing tumbled into the blood, touching off a tiny ripple. *This isn't real,* she told herself. *A hallucination. A delusion.*

"Not bad as delusions go," her love said.

Gomez spun around and looked at Kieran Duffy, who stood, arms folded, wearing that damned knowing grin, his sandy hair tousled rakishly. Unlike the rest of the bleach-rinsed world, he was painted in colors brighter than life itself.

"But you're dead," she said.

"Then I guess we're even." He nodded toward her body. "So. You call this a plan?"

"It was so crazy, I thought it just might work."

He shrugged. "I've seen worse."

"So," she said, taking a cautious step toward him. "What happens to me now?"

He lifted his arms in an exaggerated gesture of ignorance. "I'm an engineer, not a fortune-teller."

Gomez turned back toward her inanimate body. The world around her was growing fainter by the moment, dissolving into smoky white phantoms.

"Regrets?" Duffy said.

"No," she said.

"But sorry it's over?"

"Yeah. . . . I guess I am."

"Shame you didn't see this coming," he said.

"I did," she said. "I expected it."

"Then why'd you lead the mission? Didn't have to be you."

"Yes, it did," she said. "This entire planet was at risk, and I was in command. It was—" She stopped, the words like a hang-fire in her throat. She turned back toward Duffy, who once again stood with his arms folded in front of him, his face masked by that enigmatic smile.

She tried not to say it, but couldn't hold the words inside. "It was my duty," she said. He nodded sympathetically.

"Yeah," he said, "I know what you mean."

The world around Gomez passed away into white oblivion. All that remained for her now was Kieran Duffy. She hadn't been aware of movement, but he was so much closer now, close enough that she could almost reach out and touch him . . . almost.

The ocean of pain she'd swallowed to fill the empty spaces inside her threatened to surge up and drown her. "I've missed you so much," she said, her voice trembling with sorrow.

"That's good," he said gently. "I should be missed."

"It's been so hard," she said. "So lonely. Nothing's the same, it's like I don't remember anymore."

"Remember what?" he said with a voice colored in love.

"How to live," she said. She didn't remember being touched, but his hands gently cupped her face. She became aware of a chilling cold all around her, and the only warmth she felt was from his hands. He smiled, but she didn't know what that meant.

"Don't be silly, Sonnie," he whispered. "Of course you remember. You just haven't wanted to. Not enough, anyway."

She closed her eyes and placed her hands over his and felt their warmth against her palms.

"Open your eyes, Sonnie," he said, his voice quiet, his breath warm as sunlight and soft as silk on her cheek.

She opened her eyes and looked into his. She saw her reflection in the dark pupils of his eyes, which looked blacker and deeper than space, like the abyss of time itself.

"Know what today is?" he said.

She trembled in his hands. "Today is nothing," she said.

"No," he scolded. "I taught you better than that. . . . Today is *everything*. . . . Open your eyes."

A flash blinded her as a flood of torment raged through her body, like liquid fire filled with needles. She felt suffocated, as if she were drowning. She reached out to Kieran, but he was far away and fading, painted in the unnatural shades of an X-ray image, coming apart like smoke in a gale.

"Open your eyes!" the voice boomed, filling her with soul-shaking irrational terror.

She was back in the gravel yard, pitching forward toward the ground. A third bullet ripped through her torso. Her body felt like lead. She sank like an anchor into Teneb's gravity.

Another blinding flash, another surge of excruciating pain.

Today is nothing.

She was back in the shuttlebay of the *da Vinci,* watching Stevens pilot Work Bug Two back into the ship with Duffy's lifeless body clutched in its cargo claw.

Searing light burned her eyes like she was staring into the sun. A crushing weight pressed in on her from every direction.

She was floating in the water, warm and safe at home.

"Open your eyes!"

The light flared then subsided as she pulled a ragged, painful breath into her fluid-choked lungs. She exhaled with a string of hacking coughs that filled her torso with hideous jolts of pain.

She was lying on a surgical bed in the *da Vinci* sickbay. She looked up into the faces of Lense, Wetzel, and Falcão.

Lense clasped Gomez's bloody right hand in both of her own and smiled. "Welcome back, Commander." She turned to Wetzel. "Keep her stable while I scrub in for surgery." Wetzel nodded and Lense stepped away.

As Wetzel adjusted the surgical bed's numerous devices and functions, she looked at Gomez. "Relax, Commander," she said. "You're home. We've got you."

Gomez watched Wetzel and Falcão work. Lense returned, clad in a surgical gown. *I'm gonna make it,* Gomez promised herself.

Lense stepped up to the surgical bed. "You were clinically dead for almost two minutes," she said. "Scans don't show any sign of neural damage, but I don't always trust scans. So, before I put you under for surgery, answer one question: What's today?"

Gomez smiled weakly at Lense. "Today is everything."

Lense considered that, then smiled. "Good answer." She nodded to Wetzel. Gomez felt the delta-wave generator fill her mind with soothing impulses to embrace a dreamless sleep. She put up no resistance and let herself drift away, confident she would awaken whole.

Abramowitz stepped out of the turbolift and reveled in the simple act of walking. The EMH had done a textbook-perfect job of mending her shattered bones. But as glad as she was to be back on her feet, she was even more relieved to be looking like her old self again.

Putting her back together hadn't been easy, however. The EMH had described her internal injuries as "shocking," and Lense had wholeheartedly agreed with his diagnosis. Consequently, Abramowitz had been forced to stay in postsurgical recovery for almost a day after Stevens and Hawkins had been discharged to bed rest in their quarters.

It could be worse, she reminded herself. *Gomez is still there.* Abramowitz had learned from the EMH that the first officer had been beamed up dead and with such grievous wounds that only Lense's stubborn refusal to quit could be credited with her revival. After surviving a seven-hour surgery, Gomez was expected to remain in sickbay for at least a few more days.

Abramowitz strolled down the corridor toward the mess hall, looking forward to a nice bowl of raisin oatmeal. And a Denver omelette. And some pancakes. *A day and a half of fasting on Teneb, and I come home to a day of injected liquid nutrients à la sickbay,* she groused silently. *Bring on the apple pie.*

She turned the corner and paused at the peals of laughter ringing out from the mess hall. Stevens's hearty guffaws came through loud and clear, rising joyfully above the chorus of chortles. He reined in his laughter as he continued.

"So this lunatic, he tells him that they're 'on the same side,' that he's a *secret agent!*" More chuckling and snorting filled the room. Abramowitz peeked around the corner. Stevens and Hawkins sat across from each other at the far end of the middle table, holding court before an amused audience that included Corsi, Haznedl, Poynter, Conlon, Konya, Vinx, and half of engineering. The table in front of Hawkins and Stevens was covered with plates of food and a variety of odd beverages.

"He's leaving out the best part," Hawkins interjected. "Here I am, trying to keep my game face on, and *this* knucklehead's *laughing*—over an *open transceiver channel!*"

"It wasn't just me!" Stevens protested with a laugh.

"I know, it was *all* of you!" Hawkins said, his face

bright with amusement. "I'm fighting not to crack a smile in front of this guy, but I've got the twit triplets giggling in my brain!"

A small, frightened voice inside Abramowitz's head suggested she clandestinely slip away to her quarters and come back to eat later. She told the voice to shut up and stepped around the corner into the mess hall. "Room for one more?"

Stevens, who was about to launch into the next part of the story, switched gears. "Hey! Look who's up and around!" The group broke into applause and whistles and overlapping exclamations of "Good to see you!" and "Welcome back!"

She moved to take a seat at the close end of the table, near the door. "No you don't," Hawkins said cheerfully, crooking a come-hither finger. "Up here, with us, in the seats of honor."

Haznedl and Poynter stepped apart to let Abramowitz pass by. She stepped around Hawkins, who ushered her to sit at the head of the table, between himself and Stevens. "What're we eating?" she said as she sat down.

"It's habañero happy hour!" Stevens exclaimed.

"Burritos, fajitas, *hasperat*—if it'll light your tongue on fire, it's on the menu," Hawkins said.

"And for those of us still not cleared for active duty," Stevens said as he placed a large frosty beverage in front of her, "real-tequila margaritas, courtesy of a transporter chief who shall not be named." Poynter feigned innocence as she looked at the ceiling and whistled.

Abramowitz picked up her drink and took a sip. It was sweet and tart and cold and fiery all at the same time. She wasn't sure whether she liked the ring of large-grain salt around the edge of the glass, though it took the edge off the drink's more sour notes. Stevens lifted his glass in a toast, and the rest of the room followed his lead and lifted their glasses.

"To Carol," he said, "who stopped the rest of us from eating bowls full of poison—"

"Technically," Abramowitz said, "alcohol is also a poison."

"Quiet, I'm toasting you. Stopped us from eating bowls of poison so she could drop a satellite on our heads instead."

Amid the laughter, Corsi grabbed Stevens's sleeve and tugged on his earlobe. He made an exaggerated yowl as she pulled him toward her. "You were going to eat a bowl of poison?"

"It was an accident," he said, grinning as he squirmed loose and played to the crowd. "We were in this POW camp. . . ."

Abramowitz tuned out the rest of Stevens's rehash of the mission. She pretended to pay attention, in between washing down the insanely searing-hot *hasperat* and burritos with mouthfuls of her lip-puckering margarita. A few times every minute, she caught herself stealing sidelong glances at Hawkins.

His close-cropped hair flattered the crown of his perfectly rounded dark head, and the corners of his mouth curled winsomely behind his neatly groomed goatee.

A woman would have to be blind not to see what a handsome man he is, she thought. The echo of that notion lingered until another, more cautious voice intervened. *What am I doing?*

She couldn't stop looking at him. A few times he happened to glance back, laughing at some detail of Stevens's story, and she pretended to laugh along. She desperately wanted to reach out and put her hand over his. To touch his arm. To . . .

Stop it, you're irrational, she chastised herself. *You're feeling drawn to him because he pulled you out of the water. You were injured, you were delusional, in shock. Just some silly imprinting psychology, just a Florence Nightingale effect, just . . . it's just . . .*

She swallowed another generous gulp of her margarita. The alcohol infused her body with a warm glow that, unlike the effect of synthehol, was entirely impossible to ignore.

Just stop rationalizing, she commanded herself. *No more thinking. Feel. What do I* feel?

Turning her head, she looked unabashedly straight at him. She let go of her thoughts and forced her eternally chattering mind into a moment of silence.

She felt intrigued. She remembered talking with him during one of the premission briefings, and feeling respected. She saw the keen mind behind his eyes, the candor of his smile, the relaxed confidence that radiated from him . . . and she felt deeply, powerfully, undeniably attracted.

He noticed her unbroken stare. For a moment he looked taken aback, then he smiled at her. "What?" he said in a sub rosa tone. "Something in my teeth?"

She shook her head and answered in a voice for his ears only. "That vehicle-training holo-program you made?"

"What about it?"

"Would you show it to me?"

"Sure," he said. "When would—"

"How 'bout now?" she said, cutting him off. He peered inquisitively into her unblinking gaze.

The first tremor of a sly grin tugged at the corners of

her lips. She knew that Hawkins was good at "reading" people, and she wasn't exactly concealing her intentions in this rare unguarded moment.

He didn't answer right away, and Abramowitz's mind became a panicked whirlwind of all the awkward, innocently devastating things that she feared were about to issue from his mouth.

Then he spoke. "Love to."

He stood up and waited for her to join him. She blinked, realized it was really happening, and stood up.

"Where are you guys going?" Stevens said. "I'm just getting to the—"

"I'm gonna teach Carol how to drive," Hawkins said. "Don't forget to tell them about the . . . uh . . ."

"Flying monkeys?" Stevens said, clearly baiting him.

"Right," Hawkins said with a snap of his fingers. "The flying monkeys."

Abramowitz followed Hawkins out of the mess hall to the turbolift. "It's a great program," he said, his mind clearly not on the small talk he was spinning. "Very versatile. Plenty of environments to choose from. I think you'll really enjoy it."

"I'm sure I will," she said as the turbolift door opened. They stepped inside and stood unusually close together in the middle of the car.

Abramowitz felt like someone else—or maybe she finally felt like herself—as she lowered her head and flashed him a grin from beneath her slightly drooping black bangs.

The doors had barely begun to swish closed as she reached up, with three decades of suppressed passion suddenly unleashed, and pulled him into a hungry kiss.

He didn't pull away.

She didn't think about letting go.

BITTER MEDICINE

Dave Galanter

CHAPTER 1

"I'm reading the Starfleet warning buoy now, sir." Susan Haznedl tabbed at the ops console, then turned back to the bridge's center seat. "And also another warning hail, very weak."

Captain David Gold motioned to the speaker overhead. "Let's hear the other."

Haznedl nodded and worked her console again. "Running it through the translator, sir. There's not much of it, so it might take a few moments."

"I didn't see in the report that there was an original warning," Commander Sonya Gomez said, stepping down to the side of the captain's chair from the upper bridge.

"The *Lexington* sent the Starfleet buoy from two parsecs out," Haznedl replied. "The signal I'm getting is very weak. I doubt they picked it up."

"*Lexington* didn't have time to stop," Gold told Gomez,

"but two Allurian ships running salvage in this area are missing with all hands, and reported a hazard before contact with them was lost. It was enough for Starfleet to leave the buoy and dispatch us."

Twisting from ops, Haznedl gestured with a roll of her head toward the speaker above. "I have the translation now, sir."

"We issue this extreme warning to avoid our vessel at all costs. There is no hope, there is no cure. Beware."

Cryptic, Gold thought. "Is that all?"

Shrugging slightly, Haznedl's hands ran quickly over her controls. "There's probably a datastream, too. And there might be more audio, sir, but there's almost no power behind the signal."

Gold pursed his lips and continued to wonder just how much danger for his ship and crew was aboard that alien ship. Starfleet hadn't heard the "no hope, no cure" message they just had. "What did our sensor scan find?"

"A few ion trails, Allurian in signature," Haznedl said. "I'm not sure how far we can track it, but they both head in the same direction: three-one-two, mark one-eight."

"Launch a sensor probe," Gold told Lieutenant Anthony Shabalala at tactical. "Three-twelve, mark eighteen."

"Aye, sir."

Pulling in a long breath, Gold stared for a moment at the alien ship on the forward viewscreen. It wasn't particularly artistic in design. It looked more . . . efficient, for lack of a better word. "If there's some hazard aboard that ship that spread to two other ships . . ." he said more to Gomez than anyone.

"I'll brief Dr. Lense," Gomez said, turning immediately toward the turbolift.

"Level-one safety procedures on this one," the captain called after her.

"A shuttle for decon?"

"Only thing I know that spreads death from ship to ship is something contagious or something toxic. The away team can beam to and from the shuttle, but full medical tests are to be completed *there* before anyone comes back *here.*"

"Yes, sir."

Dr. Elizabeth Lense had come quickly to the bridge when Commander Gomez told her of the possible away mission. It had been a while since she'd been off ship, and she had to admit to looking forward to an opportunity to get out of sickbay, if only for a few hours.

"I'm not sure we even need an expedition," Captain Gold told her, putting into doubt that she might get the chance. "Closer sensor scans suggest this ship is derelict for a few hundred years at least. Probe telemetry shows the drift pattern."

"I thought the probes were tracking the Allurian ion trails," Gomez said.

The captain rose from his chair and walked to Haznedl's ops station. "They are," he said, pointing to the graphic display of the probe data. "It would seem the Allurians were headed in the direction the derelict came from."

"*Something* caused those ships to be lost with all hands," Lense said. "I'd like to investigate it, Captain."

"I understand," Gold said, resting one hand on the back of Haznedl's chair and motioning to the ship on the viewer with his other. "I'm considering it. What about life signs on the derelict?" he asked Haznedl. "*Lexington* said none."

"Indeterminate. There's too much radiation to get a good reading."

"Their engines," Gomez offered. "Half the ship is irradiated. It'll definitely need structural repair, if we don't declare it a hazard and destroy it."

"All right, then that's the mission." Gold pivoted and returned to the command chair. "To determine which, and then make it happen."

Lense nodded her understanding. "Commander Gomez said the message buoy talks about 'no cure.' If the Allurians contracted some disease, then took it away from here, we'll need to investigate—not destroy—the source of that contagion."

"That's a point and a half, Doctor," Gold said with a sigh and smiled. "Finish readying your team," he told Gomez as he lowered himself back into his seat. "And make it a small one, until we know what we're dealing with."

"I don't believe there'll be a need for security, Commander." Dr. Lense, having put her EVA suit on before entering the *da Vinci* shuttlebay because she didn't want to bother struggling with it in the close quarters of the shuttle, double-checked her medkit for everything she thought she'd need.

"Commander Gomez's orders, Doctor." Lieutenant Commander Domenica Corsi attached a holster to her EVA suit and made sure her hand phaser fit snugly inside it. "There might not be any people alive on that ship, but that doesn't mean there's no automated security." She picked up a larger phaser rifle from next to her left boot, checked its safety, and leaned it against one shoulder.

"Okay." Lense nodded, then turned to Gomez as she entered the hangar deck. Gomez held the top half of her EVA suit under one arm, and was only wearing the bottom half. "I'm sure I don't have to tell any of you how important it will be to make sure your EVA suits are kept completely intact," Lense said, "even if there's ample life support over there. We'll be using this shuttle to beam over, and if you have an occurrence where you believe your suit is compromised, you'll beam back to the shuttle. Any questions?"

Gomez smiled and held up the bulky helmet and EVA shirt. "I just didn't want to pilot out the shuttle in the suit. But yes, we understand. I'll find engineering on the ship, and check out the engine design. Starfleet wants full specs on it, and it's in obvious disrepair but I'll find out the extent. Domenica, make your way through the ship as best you can, and see if anyone is still poking around on board. Report every fifteen minutes."

Corsi nodded and the three boarded the Shuttlecraft *Kwolek*.

Lense never cared for beaming into any place with an EVA suit on. Somehow it seemed more claustrophobic, as if the suit beamed in first, and then she beamed into it. That was why she'd kept her eyes closed until she felt the transport process end. When she opened them, "obvious disrepair" seemed like an understatement.

There were pods along the wall before them, electronics falling from their sides, wires and insulation hanging out from panels here and there and . . . well, everywhere. There were also a lot of squiggles and symbols on the walls, but it didn't look so much like art as it looked like graffiti, or at least some kind of writing.

"This is their sickbay." She realized this as she looked from the writing to the consoles on which they had been scrawled, and the several beds against two of the gray walls.

"It scanned as being the safest from the radiation leaks." Gomez's voice came over the EVA's comm systems as the commander flipped open a tricorder. *"Which I guess a sickbay would be, usually. Ours is more shielded, too."*

Lense broke out her own tricorder—a medical one—and opened it a bit more awkwardly than Gomez had. Sonya was used to working in EVA suits from time to time. Lense had trained in them, had to use them sometimes, but generally didn't get as much practice as the rest of the S.C.E. crew.

"Atmosphere is nitrogen/oxygen mix, but I'm reading a high level of CO_2*, carbon monoxide, and other trace gases,"* Gomez said.

"Breathable, but we should stay in the suits."

"Agreed," Gomez said. *"Domenica, life signs are still indeterminate, so let's secure this deck first, then I'll spiral down to engineering and you go up toward what might be a bridge. Once it's secure, maybe we can get this engine under control."*

Corsi nodded, opened her own tricorder easily, and held her phaser rifle ready in the other hand.

"Elizabeth?" Gomez turned to Lense.

"I can set up shop here. If there is an infectious agent on this vessel, this is the place we'd find it anyway. It's probably also where the Allurians beamed in." She glanced down at her tricorder. "Oh!"

"An idea?"

"I can scan for Allurian DNA." The doctor jabbed at the tricorder for a few moments, reconfiguring the scanning filters. "Traces. They were here. Within the last ten days, I'd say."

"You okay to go it alone?" Gomez tossed a thumb over her shoulder. *"I thought I'd start by seeing if I can find a power relay on this deck and bring you more than lights. Maybe some of these consoles will have data we can access."*

"Sure."

Corsi soon found a door into what was presumably a corridor. Gomez quickly followed her, and Lense was then alone. With a deep breath, she stiffly walked toward a desk and put her case down on it.

There was something mildly spooky about being on an empty starship. An empty *alien* starship multiplied that by a factor of ten. Being confined to a space suit focused that foreboding feeling even more.

As she reached for the case at her feet, Lense thought she heard a sound. She cocked her head toward the doorway—fruitless since external sound was delivered via the same speaker system in her helmet that transmitted the voices of the other members of the away team.

"Domenica?" Lense took a step toward the door. "Sonya?"

She heard the noise again, a tinny sort of scraping sound, she thought, but from the opposite direction to the door, obviously, since she was looking that way and there was nothing there. Using an input pad on the lower sleeve of her suit, she increased the gain of the external microphone. She heard nothing unusual, and thought that perhaps her mind was merely playing the tricks it could when one was alone and in a somewhat spooky setting.

Opening her case, Lense pulled out a scanner that was a bit stronger than a normal medical tricorder, and set it to humming on the tabletop in front of her. Signs of an active virus in the air were beginning to show when she heard the scraping sound again. She wasn't imagining it.

"Lense to Gomez."

"Gomez here."

"Where are you, if I may ask, Commander?" Lense tried to keep the nerves from her voice.

"I don't have a map. I'm in a corridor heading into what's either their engineering deck, or some other place they have some large radiation leak happening."

"I just meant are you close by. I heard a noise."

"What kind of a noise?"

"Muffled. Like a shuffle or a scrape. Life signs *were* indeterminate."

"Do you want me to send Domenica back?"

"I . . . No. It could be a processor glitch in the suit's sensors."

After a brief pause, Gomez said, *"I'm sending Corsi."*

Lense shook her head and righted a chair that had been on its side on the deck. "Sonya, there's no need. I'm fine."

"Mysterious ship, Elizabeth. Let's play it safe."

"Fine. Lense out." Now she felt stupid. She was a professional. Why was she calling for help after hearing a shuffle? Then again, she didn't call for help. She called for information. And really, being cautious was probably the right way—

Shooof. There it was again. But the EVA suit's speakers were in back of the helmet and didn't really give her a sense of the sound's direction as the human ear would. "I'm not hearing things," she whispered to herself, and switched her tricorder from bio mode to area-scan mode. It wasn't as accurate as a tactical tricorder, but it would do.

She spun around. The tricorder told her there was a life form close by. Radiation was hampering the reading, but it was on this deck. It wasn't human, if the readings were right, so it wasn't Corsi. Then again, the readings may not have been right.

Lense searched the perimeter of the room, and it wasn't long before the proximity of the readings told her behind which panel to look. She considered calling for Corsi or contacting Gomez again. But whoever was with her was hiding . . . and if worse came to worst, she had her phaser.

She slid the panel away, but nothing lay beyond. At least that she could see. On the cuff of her EVA suit was a light, and Lense tentatively switched it on and pointed it forward into the alcove.

Two eyes reflected back, like a cat's eyes might, and instinctively she shrank away for a moment, pulling the light back. When she shined it back into the wall's recess, just a moment later, the eye reflections were gone.

The being attached to them was not. Eyes scrunched closed, shaking in what Lense hoped was fear rather than a prelude to some attack, the smallish humanoid seemed to be attempting to back itself as far into a crevice as it could.

"Lense to Gomez," the doctor spoke into her comm as she took in the small form's smooth head, slight limbs, and ridged brow. "We have a survivor."

"On my way. Domenica, meet me at the doctor's location, double time."

Other than shaking, despite Lense's now attempting to coax relaxation with soothing tones, the ship's lone inhabitant didn't move until Corsi and Gomez arrived, and then only with a rocking once it heard their voices.

Lense had moved her light beam from directly on the being to slightly above it, so now the . . . was it a child? It looked like a child. In any case, it was cloaked half in shadow.

"There could be others," Corsi offered, and Lense noticed the woman's tricorder was stowed and the phaser rifle was steadied in both hands.

"Check each deck. Let's be sure," Gomez said. *"I think the doctor and I have this handled."*

Corsi nodded and left again with an *"Aye, Commander."*

Her tricorder back from tactical to bio mode, Lense said, "I don't think she, or he, is an adult. Judging by the size of the controls and chairs."

"The universal translator isn't going to work if he doesn't talk," Gomez said.

"Hi there," Lense said into the dark alcove and reflective eyes. When she spoke, those eyes flashed for a moment, then closed shut again.

"I don't think that's working." Gomez went to the nearest computer console and pulled off an access panel to the electronics below. *"Let me see if I can get their computer to talk to us. From that, maybe we can get enough for the UT to allow him to understand us."*

As Gomez worked, doing whatever it was that engineers did while others waited, Lense couldn't help but wonder what terrified thoughts were behind the child's glowing eyes. If everyone else was dead, what had the poor thing seen? And now aliens had invaded her ship. Did she assume that Lense and Gomez had killed her parents?

Looking away for only a moment to see what Gomez was doing, Lense noticed that the small child took the opportunity to try to shrink even farther back into the recesses of the access way. There was nowhere for her to go. Sometimes such a situation could nearly paralyze Lense's decision-making process. Different cultures reacted differently than humans. Attempting a soothing tone could be "fighting words" for another race. What one culture would see as a submissive stance, another could see as an overture to attack.

"Got it," Gomez said finally, and Lense watched the child flinch. The computer panel came to life, and Gomez used a tricorder to access its functions. *"This might work."*

A computerized voice began to speak. *"Fotanet ba'alest. Dolah pocheeny sot ba touh begh. Sooft dabrah gren co'olat retnala'ag borft plumadal."*

The doctor frowned. "Nothing. Shouldn't we have enough with what we got off the warning broadcast?"

"It probably wasn't enough. You know some take longer than others. I'm not even sure the ship's translator data was beamed into the EVA suits' version before we left."

The child, Lense noticed, didn't particularly like whatever the computer was saying. But maybe she was just reading into the alien's expressions.

"Pocheeny kahlahct pathelet rathib t'binchekt. Aldasna contaminated sodithbrash throughout. Life dochmaba bar'ut systems cobnida maintained oht-langrah, so it is only pocheeny we fear."

Gomez smiled. *"Getting there."*

The computer continued. *"If we survive the next tests, it is my hope that we can determine why Dobrah is immune."*

"That's the end of the log."

It was enough. Lense was able to put it easily together. "Dobrah?" she asked the child. "Do you understand me?"

The alien child said nothing. She, or he, sat frightened, and shook in her fear.

"We won't hurt you," Lense said, attempting her most soothing voice. As an aside to Gomez she added in a whisper, "We might look less imposing if we weren't dressed in EVA suits."

"I'd imagine."

Lense put her tricorder down and showed her open hands, which skewed the light on her wrist at an odd angle and cast the child in even more shadow. "Dobrah, we're here to help you."

"G-go away." The slight voice was weak, but Lense sensed that wasn't physical weakness, just insecurity. "Go away go away go away go away go away go away go away go away go away—"

"Back up," Lense told Gomez. "Let's give him some room."

"Him?"

"Just a guess. I don't know why. Call it intuition."

"I'm a him," Dobrah said, still fearful but also sounding a bit insulted. "What are you things? Why are you here? Go away go away go away go away go away—"

"Don't be afraid," Lense said. "Are you alone?"

The boy didn't answer. He was rocking back and forth, arms holding his knees close to his body.

"We're humans," Lense told him, still stepping away, giving him space, but answering his question. "We're both—" She almost said females, but every culture looked at sex differently and who knew how his would see woman. "We're both from the Federation."

"I . . . I don't know a planet Federation. I have a ship. My ship. Go away. There are no planets. Go away go away go away—"

"What planet are you from?" Gomez asked, and Lense cast her an annoyed look. She didn't seem to know how to talk to a scared child.

"Go away!"

"Dobrah, we're here to help you, but we have to know where you're from."

"I'm from Earth! Now go away. Go away go away go away go away—"

Lense and Gomez exchanged a glance. It wouldn't have been the first time that the universal translator had done that. Many worlds' own name for their planet was something simple, like "home" or "earth." They'd have to see if there were star charts on the computer that would tell them where the boy's home planet was.

"Dobrah, are you alone on this ship?"

He looked up, stopped rocking, and looked at them, perplexed. "You're here."

Unable to suppress a chuckle, Lense said, "I meant usually alone."

"Yes. Others came. I hid."

"Why?"

"I don't know who they were. They went away. You should go away!" He was rocking again. Lense considered completely backing away for a while—just remaining in the room until he got more used to them.

But it didn't seem that necessary. The boy's intelligence was obvious, and the catch in his voice was more and more slight as time went on. He was becoming less scared and more curious. "Will you sit down?" Lense asked him as she backed up farther and motioned to one of the beds. She then pulled herself onto another of the beds a few feet away.

Dobrah inched slowly out of the alcove and close to the first bed, but didn't sit. "Why are you here? Are you real? Are you really real?"

"Of course we're real." Lense turned to Gomez. "If he's been here for some time he may be prone to hallucination. He might not know if we're real." Then she kneeled down to be more at the boy's level. "We're here to help you, Dobrah. This ship isn't safe—"

"This is my home," he interrupted. "This is *my* ship. You must leave! *Leave!* Go away!"

He answered so quickly that Lense almost allowed herself to become defensive about whether it was a proper home right now or not. "All right. How long has it been your home?" she asked finally.

Looking away for a long moment, it took Dobrah a while to answer. Something about him suddenly changed. As if he'd decided he wasn't imagining them and they were really there. "A long time, I think." He said it softly, and Lense wasn't sure if that was because he was sad, or just unable to know how long anymore.

"Alone?" Lense asked.

"Some of it." He was rocking again, not looking at them. "Everyone is gone. You must go! Leave me alone!"

"Did they d—" Gomez began, but Lense cut her off with a look.

With a light movement of one finger to the arm of her EVA suit, she turned off the external speaker so only Gomez would hear her over the comm. "We have to be delicate here. The computer record said he was immune to whatever killed everyone on this vessel. That could leave him with a star-mass of guilt."

"Sorry," Gomez said quietly.

Lense turned her speaker back on. "Do you know what happened to everyone?"

Sadly, his eyes still cast away, Dobrah's voice was slight. "Everyone?" he asked. "Everyone's gone . . . *Everyone.*"

CHAPTER 2

"Where's the boy now?" Captain Gold asked, his voice laced with a light thread of static, probably due to the radiation.

"With Dr. Lense. Commander Corsi is sure the ship is otherwise . . . uninhabited."

"Why did you hesitate?"

Gomez huffed out a breath. "I almost said abandoned, but that doesn't really fit, does it?"

"No. Not if they all died. Any bodies?"

"We found one," she said. "An Allurian. Looked like he was wearing a personal shield belt rather than an EVA-like suit. It failed, and the radiation probably got him."

"Probably?"

"The tools aren't here for a proper autopsy, the doctor tells me. It could also be some virus that we believe only the boy is immune to. She'd like some equipment beamed over to the shuttle, which we'll then bring over here. I'll need a few things as well. Engineering is locked down with a protective bulkhead. It looks like the Allurians tried to get in, but didn't have what to do it with. We do."

"Transmit a list. We'll get it to you." There was a pause, then Gold continued. *"If the Allurians left that ship with a disease . . ."*

"We'll try to find out, sir," Gomez assured him. "Anything from the probe telemetry?"

"We have a course to follow, as soon as you folks are finished over there."

"I don't know how long the autopsy will take. And we're unsure of what to do with the boy. This ship isn't very stable, and Dr. Lense can't give me a clear answer as to whether he carries the disease. She hasn't even isolated it yet. The tools to do that are on that manifest I'll send."

"Get to it, then. I want to know what we're dealing with."

"Aye aye, sir."

In the time it took for Corsi to completely search the rest of the ship, and for Gomez to find engineering and talk with the captain about their equipment needs, Lense had cleaned up the alien sickbay and learned where a lot of things were kept, or were supposed to be kept. It looked as if the Allurians had done some looting.

She'd also been talking with Dobrah a lot as she worked, and the boy had finally decided to sit on one of the beds and watch Lense with tremendous interest and intent. He was doing more and more of the talking, and he sounded more comfortable with her now. In fact, he sounded like he'd not talked to anyone in months and wanted to make up for it.

"What're you doing now?" he kept asking.

She indulged every question as cheerfully as possible. "Well, I'm using my tricorder—it's a computer and scanner—to read labels on all these containers and shelves. It looks like a lot is missing."

"Are you a healer?"

"Yes. A doctor." She took a box, read the label, and put it away again.

"A doctor or a healer?"

"There's no difference in my language, really. Well, there can be. But I guess I'm a doctor who is a healer."

"My mother was a healer," he said, and she couldn't tell what was in his voice when he said it.

"I— She was?"

Dobrah leaned forward on the bed and kicked his feet up. "You look like she looked when she was fixing things and making it all neat in here."

Lense wanted to ask what happened to her. But she knew. "Was that her voice we heard? On the computer?"

He rolled his head around in what seemed to be like a nod. "I used to listen to it sometimes, when things worked. Because she mentions my name. I don't want to forget what she sounds like. I do sometimes. Forget. I don't want to forget."

"No, of course not." She tried to imitate the head roll as he did it.

"Gomez to Lense."

"Lense here."

"Stand clear of the beam-down point, Elizabeth. Our equipment is on the shuttle. I'm going to have the computer beam it over."

"Okay."

"Energizing."

In the center of the room, several large containers sparkled into existence with a hum and flashes of light.

Dobrah stretched his neck to see it all. "That's a lot of stuff. What's it do?"

"Well, some of it I don't recognize, so that's for Commander Gomez." Lense smiled at him and walked toward the crates.

"And the other stuff?"

"It's medical equipment."

"Are you going to run tests on me?"

She turned back toward him, feeling her own brow knit. "Why would you ask that? Did . . . did your mother and other doctors run a lot of tests?"

"Yes." He seemed unconcerned about the tests, she thought, based on his nonchalant tone.

"Mine won't hurt," she told him.

"Promise?"

"Promise."

"What did you find, Doctor?" Sliced with more static than before, Captain Gold's voice sounded far away.

"The Allurian we found died from a plasma bolt, sir. Weapons fire. The energy signature matches what we have on file for Allurian weapons."

"One of his own people killed him?"

Lense nodded, despite the comm link being audio only. "After he'd already sustained cellular damage from this vessel's radiation."

"Maybe to put him out of his misery?"

"Why not treat him?" Gomez asked. Lense had almost

forgotten they'd been sharing the comm link to brief the captain.

"They were looting the sickbay," Lense said. "They may not have had the supplies."

"Allurians aren't known for stealing medical technology." Gomez's connection was local and sounded stronger, but still crackled with static here and there.

"I know. But my scans indicate there is a contagion here. Viral in nature, and Dobrah is only alive because he's immune."

"Would the Allurians' personal shields have protected them from it?" the captain asked.

"Commander Gomez checked the settings on the shield we found on our dead body. It was attuned to block the radiation on this ship, and nothing else. We found no external air tank."

"If that was still working, the Allurians would have recovered it," Gomez added.

"Unless it was airtight, they still would have been infected. There are virions of complex construction in the air, and they're aerobic. If they were here long enough, I might be able to tell if the Allurians contracted the disease. Lipids are present and are located in the virion envelope. The fatty acid composition of viral lipids and host cell membranes would perhaps be similar, meaning I could tell in what species of host any particular virion was replicated."

Captain Gold chuckled. *"I'm going to assume that means you can breathe in the little devils and you might be able to prove the Allurians did. What kind of virus is it?"*

"Level Four, I'm guessing, in whatever the—what did we find out their names are?"

"Dobrah's people?" Gold asked. *"Abramowitz is still*

going over what you could salvage from the one computer bank you were able to access, but their own word for their race is the Shmoam-ag."

"Well, the Shmoam-ag created themselves a nasty virus, near one hundred percent fatal."

"Definitely engineered?"

"I've probably only scratched the surface of the morphology, but determining that was the easy part. All the classic signs. Highly advanced, too, with both RNA and DNA coexisting in two separate sections. That's a virion with more than five-point-six percent nucleic acid combined, with the complete genome coming in almost sixty thousand nucleotides long. While what I've managed to decode is minimal, it's filled with information that's . . . well, it couldn't be considered natural."

"I see."

Lense wondered if she'd been too specific, but Gold had long since proven his ability to withstand barrages of technobabble, whether it was Gomez and her people's engineering jargon, Faulwell going on about a language, Abramowitz on a culture, or Lense herself with medicine.

"And one of the rooms off sickbay even has a quantity of the virus in several production stages. I'm not sure why. But it's a viral lab like any we might have—multiple airlocks are used to enter and exit, and one of the signs translates to what we'd call a warning about a 'no-sharps' area—to prevent the puncturing of the biohazard suits that are worn to enter the lab. We found those, too."

Probably taking all that in, the captain turned his attention to his first officer. *"Gomez, what about engineering?"*

"I still don't have access to the engine room. I do have

access to an auxiliary control area nearby. I've set up radiation shielding in that room, which is allowing me to bring those aux systems back online. With those, I might be able to use an automated system to bring the engines under control for a closer look."

"How much time would that take?"

"Six, maybe seven hours, if things go well," Gomez said.

"And what about you, Doctor? It's possible the Shmoam-ag didn't have a cure for themselves, but could there be one for other species?"

"It's a possibility, but too early to know."

There was silence for a while as Gold perhaps considered his command options. *"We need to catch up to the Allurians in case we have to stop them before they infect others. Gomez, use the shuttle's comm array to enhance our ability to communicate at a distance. Would either of you like us to beam over anyone to assist you?"*

"Captain, I think it's best if we limit anyone else's exposure for the time being," Lense warned.

"You three are safe, aren't you?"

"For the time being I'd assume so, but the more people here, the more we risk an accident exposing someone."

"Understood. We'll be under way within the hour. If you need any additional supplies or equipment before we leave, let us know. Gold out."

"You assume so?" Gomez asked over the comm, once the captain had left the channel. *"Anything I should know?"*

"No, but I don't know all we're dealing with. If we go back to the shuttle, I recommend we leave the EVA suits here. Beam right out of them, and back in when we return. Just to make sure nothing goes back with us that the transporter decontamination couldn't handle."

CHAPTER 3

"Where do you get your food?" Lense had thought to ask Dobrah this question several times in the nine hours they'd now known each other, but other questions—or sometimes just listening—had taken precedence.

"The canteens. There's a lot of food. I like most of it."

Lense nodded and continued hovering over the recently beamed-over equipment she'd set up on one of the sickbay's beds, but she was sure to make eye contact with the boy often. Gomez was focusing all her efforts on venting the radiation in the engineering compartment, and Corsi was helping her. The doctor was happy to have Dobrah's company, considering she was claustrophobically confined to her EVA suit. And the way he was talking to her, Dobrah was ecstatic to have the fellowship as well.

"What kinds of food don't you like?" Lense asked, and noticed she was a bit hungry herself.

"Oh, all the crumbly stuff. Tobah sticks and sanbell butter. Things like that."

A smile turning up the corners of her lips, Lense couldn't help but notice that the universal translator was especially good with duplicating the tone of Dobrah's age. His speech was more . . . informal. As time went on, and the translator "knew" him better, Lense supposed it sounded more like he would really sound to her if she knew his language.

"I don't like things with seeds," she told him. "Sesame seed rolls or poppy bread."

Dobrah wrinkled his nose in sympathetic distaste and slid down from his seat on the far bed. He slowly made his way closer to Lense as he looked over her array of scanners and computers with mild interest. "Are you going to cure me?" he asked after a few minutes of silence.

Pushing out a long breath, Lense took a step back from her work. "You're not sick."

"I'm the only one who isn't."

For the first time it occurred to Lense that the boy might know quite a lot about his situation. It was obvious by what little of the sickbay logs she'd been able to salvage—most were not on the one console they'd gotten to work—that extensive tests had attempted to figure out why he was immune.

"Do you know a lot about this disease?"

He paused for a moment, perhaps not unsure what to say but more to gather his thoughts. He moved his head from shoulder to shoulder in a motion Lense had discovered was rather like a shrug. "I know I can't get it, but I have it like everyone else."

"You're a carrier."

"Yes. I wasn't *really* that scared of you when I saw you. I was more scared you'd catch the Pocheeny."

"That's what it's called?"

"Yes."

"Why did you think we'd get . . . Pochieny?"

"Pocheeny."

"Why did you think we'd be infected if we were in these containment suits?"

"My mother used to wear one, too. She died of it. I killed her."

The words sliced into Lense and she took his shoulders in her arms and kneeled down. "No. Dobrah, it's not your fault."

"I can never leave this ship," he told her, rolling his head in a Shmoam-ag nod. "I kill people."

"Then we're just going to have to cure you," Lense told him, and as soon as the words left her lips she felt they were a mistake. And yet, she continued. "And then you won't have to worry about it anymore, okay?"

"I like you," he said, his thin lips flattening into an innocent smile. "You remind me of my mother." Quickly the smile turned into a terrible frown. "I—I don't want to kill you, too."

She pulled him close, embracing him, and he hugged his arms around her neck very, very strongly. She hadn't known him long, but she wanted to cure him now—to make sure he didn't live in fear of killing others, and more important . . . alone.

"He knows he's a carrier," Lense told Gomez and Corsi as they took a meal break back on the *Kwolek*. Lense took a bite from her turkey sandwich. It was the first she'd eaten in over twelve hours, and she needed the energy. She was also glad to be out of the EVA suit, and even though it had given her complete mobility, she felt the need to stretch as if she finally had room to do so.

"You told him, or he already knew?"

"He knew." Lense chuckled as she gulped a little juice. "He said he was hiding from us to protect us."

"Do you believe that?"

"I think he was hiding to protect himself and us both, actually. But it's sweet that he wants to be protective. He's such a boy."

"You sound like you really know him," Corsi said. "We've only been here a day."

"We've talked nonstop. It's actually been a bit hard to concentrate on my work sometimes, but I have found out more about this virus."

Gomez gulped some Earl Grey tea from a mug. "Anything we need to report to the captain?"

"Not yet. I think I'd have trouble explaining it to someone who isn't a biologist at this point. It's all data, not a conclusion." Lense looked under the bread. She'd forgotten mustard. Oh well. "How about you?"

"We've vented enough radiation to enter main engineering. If we don't determine where the radiation is coming from soon, it will build up again—with us inside. I wish we had some detailed schematics, but the computer core is too close to engineering and there's nothing stored locally on any console we've found. You wouldn't have been able to bring up anything in sickbay if there weren't personal files stored there and not yet dumped to the central core."

"That explains why there's only a few days' worth of files," Lense said more to herself than the others. "Once

I'm done mapping the entire viral genome, I'll probably need that core data from Dobrah's mother's research if I'm going to cure him."

Gomez looked up from her bowl of noodles. "Cure him?"

"There must be a cure. No one engineers something this complex without there being a cure coded in somewhere."

Since Corsi didn't usually involve herself in the scientific discussions, Lense was surprised to hear her pipe in: "You've never known a designed virus to not have a cure?"

"Of course. Bastards like T'sart who worked for the Romulan Empire, or the Cardassian Crell Moset . . ."

"Then how do you know—"

"I'm going to cure him. I'm going to find a way." She said it again, and the words clattered to the deck like a dropped dinner plate.

"Okay," Gomez said slowly, but Lense had turned away and couldn't see her expression.

"I need to get back."

Beaming directly into an EVA suit seemed as if it would be tricky, though Lense knew it was not. Still, she felt uneasy until the process was finished and she was able to step away from the beam-down point. Dobrah appeared from nowhere to greet her.

"You are back!"

"Yes," she smiled through her transparent visor. "We had dinner. Did you eat?"

"Not yet."

"Well, why don't you go get something and bring it

back? Keep me company while I work?" She patted her gloved hand on the top of his smooth head.

"Sure!" He ran off and was back quickly, before Lense really had time to set up her next experiment. She decided to talk while he ate, and so she only monitored the continuing viral genome-mapping the computer was performing.

Dobrah talked and talked, and when Corsi and Gomez beamed back down he said hello to them cheerfully and then continued. Lense worked on, listening happily if not completely.

At some point into the night, Dobrah fell asleep and Lense was able to work uninterrupted. She didn't know if this was normally the room in which he made his bed, but it likely was. Their sickbay was relatively shielded from the radiation pouring from the ship's engines, and the boy was perhaps smart enough to—

No. That wasn't why. This was where his mother had worked. No wonder it was here he'd spent most of his time.

His mother . . . where was she? Why were there no bodies of the crew, of his family?

Perhaps they *were* somewhere.

Grabbing a tricorder and setting it to scan for Shmoam-ag DNA, Lense followed a path out into the corridor after telling the device to ignore Dobrah's life sign.

As she walked, vectoring this way and that as the halls would allow, she homed in on the DNA signatures without life, and wondered if she was fooling herself into thinking she could cure Dobrah. She didn't think so, but she instinctively knew it had been a mistake to promise it. In mentioning it to Gomez and Corsi, she'd been hoping their reaction would be mild and unconcerned, in an attempt to make herself feel better about having said it. Their reaction was anything but. She tried to think positively, however. The Sherman's Planet plague had seemed impossible at the start as well. There was a confidence in her now that hadn't been there since before the war. Confidence alone didn't bring results . . . but it helped.

"I'm not so sure I can do this," Corsi said in complaint.

Gomez didn't have time to argue the point. *"You're all I have, Domenica. This is far more complicated than I thought. This engine design is—"*

Corsi smiled. "Totally alien?"

Laughing briefly, Gomez asked, *"Did you just make a joke?"*

"It's been known to happen." Corsi attempted to hold in place the tubing Gomez needed as the engineer laser-soldered it into place. "What exactly are we doing, anyway?"

"You're holding a conduit in place against a valve so I can seal it. Then we're going to attempt to reroute plasma to an area where their cooling units still work."

"And you know how all this works just from the schematic on the back of the panel we pried off?"

"Partly." Gomez grunted as she struggled to get her hand where it needed to be in the cramped space.

"Only partly?"

"The other part is guessing."

Corsi felt her brow wrinkle. "Uh . . . I don't like the sound of guessing."

"Give me some credit, here," Gomez said as she fired

the hand laser and melted the rim of the conduit onto the valve. *"It's* educated *guessing."*

"Am I going to blow up?" Corsi asked, feeling some of the laser's heat find its way up to her hand.

"Not on your own," Gomez said dryly.

"That's not funny at all." Pressing her lips into a thin line, Corsi took her hand away from the now attached conduit when Gomez motioned for her to.

"Relax. The danger here is that we'll have worse radiation leaks." She got up as Corsi did, and they both slid the access panel back into place. *"Okay, I'm done with this one."*

"This one?" Corsi asked. "How many more are there?"

"Nineteen."

"You know why I like my job better than yours?" Corsi asked as she picked up the tool kit to her left as Gomez did the same to the one at her right.

"Why?"

"Because if we do blow up, at least I won't know it's about to happen."

CHAPTER 4

"Wong, hold us out here at twenty thousand kilometers. Match the Allurian vessel's drift rate." Captain Gold studied the ship on the main viewscreen. It was a ramshackle design, he thought, more for function than form. And even function wasn't that great. The Allurians were often scavengers, and their ships could look like mishmoshed, makeshift afterthoughts.

"Aye, sir. Matching."

"Shabalala?" Gold turned toward tactical.

"Scanning, sir," Shabalala reported. "Minimal power output. Reactors are online but engines are at null thrust."

"Their drift vector suggests inertia from last plotted course," Wong said.

Shabalala nodded his agreement. "There are no weapons charged, and their shields are down. Deflector is on—probably automatic."

"Haznedl? Any response to our hails?" Gold stepped down from his command chair and rubbed his left palm against his side to stifle an itch.

"None, sir."

"Life signs?"

"None, sir."

A knot was beginning to form on Gold's neck. They were not finding any helpful information so far, and it made him uneasy. "There were two Allurian ships. Scan the area. See if we can find the second one." He made his way back to the center seat. "And let's put out a warning buoy on this one. Just in case."

"This ship needs more than one person can do." Frustrated, Gomez tossed her hyperspanner back into the tool kit and twisted her neck back and forth, without a decent way to massage it within the EVA suit.

"What am I, an overstuffed chair?" Corsi asked.

"You're a help, Domenica, but you're not an engineer. We've been at this for four and a half days now, and moved maybe an inch in shoring up these weaknesses." Gomez pulled herself toward the tool kit and reached for the spanner again, deciding to give it another try. "We really need Pattie on this one. This ship is a structural nightmare. It's an ion engine system, very complex, and at least three hundred years old. It doesn't look like it's had maintenance in half that time."

"Are you saying it's a lost cause?"

Gomez sighed. "I don't know. It is if I'm the only one working on it. Maybe if I had the full team . . ."

"For now all you have is me."

Gomez smiled. "Is this a pep talk?"

"Yes."

"Well, *we* might just keep this engine from exploding." Gomez pulled in a deep breath. "Back to work?"

Gesturing to the panel in which they'd been toiling, Corsi said, *"Lead the way."*

He was sleeping so soundly, looking so peaceful, Lense didn't want to have to wake him. She wondered how often his sleep was this serene. He'd slept in the sickbay as she worked every night for the last three nights. When they first found Dobrah, he had all the signs of an emotionally disturbed, lonely, abandoned child—rocking himself, repeating to them that they must leave him alone. His turnaround was almost instant. That suggested to Lense that the boy was still very disturbed, but in a period of relief due to his first companionship in . . . how long?

She hadn't yet been able to figure that out, but had a better idea once she'd toured the ship looking for Shmoam-ag DNA. But that had only given her a guess. A more in-depth look into his biological makeup would pin it down, and that was why she needed to wake him. She'd lost track, however, of how long he'd been asleep. She leaned down, almost but not quite caressing his smooth forehead, from his thick brow back across his scalp. She'd promised him a cure. What if she had to settle for his relocation to some Starfleet Medical isolation ward? He'd have company at least, but . . . what kind of a life would that be?

"Dobrah," she called softly, "wake up."

The boy stirred lightly, groaning a bit, thick with sleep.

"Dobrah?" She shook him just a bit, pushing into his arm with her protected hand.

His unfocusing eyes looked up glassily, reflecting in the light. "Mama?"

Innocent and sweet, the word cut right through her heart.

"No, honey. It's Elizabeth."

"E-liz," he said groggily. "You're still real."

She nodded. "I need to run a test on you. Can you lie straight for me and not move?"

"I can do that." He straightened, lay back, and seemed to go right back to sleep.

"Good," she told him, and patted his stomach. "Sit tight."

Retreating to one of her large scanners, Lense pointed the main sensor at the boy and began her intensive scan. The results poured in, flooding her screen. After several minutes the scan was done. She ran it again. And then again. Dobrah slept, and she ran it a last time. The results did not change.

Dobrah wasn't just a carrier. He was a virus factory. And he had been that for a very long time. But there was something else that worried Lense, and the next scan would have to be on herself.

Repositioning the scanner to the next bed over, Lense laid herself down and gave the computer a command to begin the scan remotely.

The scanner would have trouble getting through the EVA suit, but for her purposes that was just fine.

After what seemed like too long a time, the computer bleeped that it had finished, and Lense swooped toward the display screen.

She ignored the data on her own body after a cursory glance confirmed she was not infected, and focused on information about her EVA suit. She then went back to the finished genome map of the virus, and all the reports on different lipid profiles from selected virions. It was all as she suspected, and horribly so. She compared it with the data on Dobrah's clothes . . . and knew she needed to contact Captain Gold.

"Lense to Gomez."

"Gomez here. Go ahead."

"Can you spare Corsi up here for a while?"

"Problem, Doctor?"

"No. Well, possib—" She wasn't even sure where to begin about the problems this could cause, for them and especially for Dobrah. "No. I just need to— Why don't you and I talk to the captain while Domenica stays with Dobrah?"

There was a long pause, and Lense imagined Gomez was exchanging a worried glance with Corsi.

"On our way. Gomez out."

Lense pushed out a breath, and the slightest amount of condensation formed in front of her mouth on the EVA suit's visor window. It was a long wait, at least for her, until her crewmates arrived in sickbay.

First through the door, Gomez immediately asked, *"What's wrong?"*

Waving off the concern with both hands, Lense assured her nothing desperate had happened. "It's not a crisis," she admitted. "But it is . . . there's something about this virus that is different than most. And we need to let the captain know." She looked at Corsi and motioned to Dobrah. "In case he wakes up, will you stay here with him? Let him know we'll be back?"

Corsi nodded as Gomez ordered the computer to beam them out of their EVA suits and back to the shuttle.

As soon as she'd materialized from the transporter beam, Lense grabbed the nearest tricorder and began scanning for the Pocheeny virus.

"What?" Gomez asked as Lense ran the tricorder's scanner over both of them. "What's wrong?"

Closing the tricorder with a snap, Lense let out a sigh of relief. "Nothing. Thank God."

"Okay, Elizabeth, why don't you tell me what this is all about?"

"It will save time if I tell you and the captain at the same time."

Gomez nodded, and they took seats in the front cabin to open a channel to the *da Vinci.*

CHAPTER 5

"*Oy vay iz mir.*" Captain Gold shook his head somberly and sank into the *da Vinci*'s command chair. He turned to ops again. "Are you sure, Haznedl?"

"No life signs on the planet, sir." The ensign sounded crestfallen.

"Shabalala?"

"Confirmed, sir. Signs of major cities, but no power output."

"I read the technology, Captain," Haznedl said. "Just no activity. The second Allurian ship *is* on the planet. Crashed. By the spread of the debris field I'd say their orbit decayed."

"When?" Gold asked.

Haznedl shook her head. "A week ago, perhaps?" She stabbed at her console and peered at the scanning data. "There are satellites around the planet, sir. Some for communication, some possibly for defense."

This was interesting, Gold thought. "Any working?"

"A few of them."

"See if we can pull data from any computers aboard them. Get Soloman on it ASAP. We're not risking an away team."

Haznedl twisted toward the command chair. "Captain, Commander Gomez is hailing us."

"Put her on."

On the forward viewscreen, the image of the planet washed away, replaced by Gomez and Lense looking back at the *da Vinci* bridge crew.

"Captain," Lense began, but Gold cut her off.

"We found the Shmoam-ag homeworld, Doctor. Followed the second Allurian vessel's ion trail all the way here. We've not scanned for it yet, but I'd bet my socks that your virus has been here."

"No life?" Lense asked.

"None."

"I'm not surprised."

The captain's jaw tightened and he felt his nostrils flare. So much death . . . it unnerved him. "Explain."

"I've found two very disturbing things. One about this virus, and another about Dobrah," Lense said. *"I was looking at virion lipid profiles to determine if any of the Allurians who'd been on board had showed signs of infection. For this to happen, the virus would have had to become contagious via the Allurians. Viral lipids with this Pocheeny virus are present and located in the envelope of the virions. We can know what race was spreading the virus by looking at the fatty acid composition of the viral lipids, because they are similar to host cell membranes. Generally, these fatty acids are of host origin, derived from plasma membranes."*

The captain shifted in his chair. "Where is this going, Doctor? You're about to give me a cough."

"I'm sorry for the viral biology lesson, Captain, but this is important. Lipid profiles on the virions I studied did suggest Allurians were infected—"

"We know that. We've found their two ships: one derelict, the other now a crater on the Shmoam-ag homeworld."

"There shouldn't have been time for the spread of as many virions with Allurian lipids as I found."

"Maybe the Allurians were aboard longer than we thought."

"Dobrah says otherwise and has no reason to lie," Lense explained. *"He said they were there twice. The second ship was probably looking for a cure for the crew of the first. But this time the virus knew how to hurt them, and when the Allurian we found began showing symptoms quickly, I think his comrades killed him and left him behind. But he could have been remembering wrong, so I checked it out anyway. I thought to compare the rate at which Dobrah's body creates the virus. I found fatty acids that came from Allurian hosts."*

"I don't understand. Are you saying that Dobrah is related—no, you're not saying that." Gold leaned forward and looked into Lense's eyes with intent. "What *are* you saying?"

"I'm saying that Dobrah isn't just a carrier of this virus, he's a living colony. Or rather, because he is immune to the disease itself, it uses him as . . . a home base, for lack of a better phrase."

Staggered by the thought, Gold noticed Gomez was looking at Lense with the same expression he must be wearing: disbelief. "Is that . . . I've never heard of such a virus."

"There isn't one. Not a natural one. It's why the genetic code for this virus is so large. The virus is in-

structed to infect one being and then return to its home colony."

"To what end?"

"Virions with Allurian fatty acids that didn't make it back to Dobrah's body have one genome profile," Lense said, speaking quickly and moving her hands a bit. *"Virions that did make it back to his body have a slightly different genome profile—a larger one. I believe this virus is programmed to learn the genetic code of those it infects, and return that information, if it can, back to its host. The goal? So that it can infect others of that species better, and faster, by adding the newly infected's genetic weaknesses to the virus's very genome."*

Gold bit his lower lip, thought for a moment, then said, "You said there were two disturbing things you've learned. Please tell me that this was the more disturbing of the two."

"I wish I could." The doctor hesitated, then seemed to try to push through with what she wanted to say. *"Dobrah . . . his clothes . . ."*

"Spit it out, Lense."

"His clothes have the virus throughout. Bonded to, in an inert state, every fiber. Waiting for someone to infect. I tested my EVA suit as well. The same inert virions are working their way through the material, on a molecular level. Friction against the air is enough to agitate them through."

Gold stood and took a step toward the viewscreen. "My God—you're not infected—"

"No. No, we're not. But another week in the same EVA suits . . . we would be."

"Where's Corsi?"

"With Dobrah," Gomez answered the captain.

"Why?"

"He . . . he's sleeping," Lense explained. *"I didn't want him to wake up and wonder where I'd gone."*

"I see. Gomez, what's the engineering situation?"

Gomez frowned. *"That ship is being held together with hope and flopsweat, sir."*

"Can you get it stable enough until we return?"

"Yes, sir. Corsi and I stopped most of the radiation leakage, and shielded the rest."

"Long term?"

"I'd need my full team for at least a week."

"Return to the Shmoam-ag vessel. I'd like to have a word in private with Dr. Lense." Gold pushed himself from the command chair. "Transfer to my office," he told Haznedl, and marched off the bridge.

Seconds ticked by like centuries, and Gold reappeared on the shuttle's comm screen just as Gomez was beaming out. Lense wasn't completely sure what the captain wanted to speak privately with her about, but she was *pretty* sure and she wasn't looking forward to it.

"Captain?"

"Two nights ago, a progress report from Commander Gomez voiced her concern that you'd made a promise you don't know that you can keep. And I wasn't going to let it concern me until you just told us what you'd learned about this damned virus."

"Captain, I—"

"You were irresponsible, Doctor!" the captain barked, eyes wide with anger. *"That boy might actually think you can cure him. He's a child, an orphan, who's been alone on that ship for—for God knows how long!"*

"Probably a hundred and seventy or a hundred and eighty years."

Caught off guard, Gold paused in his dressing down of the doctor. *"Do you want to explain that, Lense?"*

"I suspected it when I saw where he got his food. Children don't clean up after themselves well, especially without adults around. There were empty food containers, not for months or years, but for decades. I'm almost surprised there was enough food to last, but this is a large ship and held a lot of people. I also wondered where all the dead bodies were—of his parents, and the crew." She looked up, saw the captain was listening intently and the anger had left his expression, at least a little, and so she continued. "Dead bodies on a space ship without life support last forever. Dead bodies that decay on a space ship with modern filtration systems are mostly filtered and scrubbed by the ship's systems, given enough time, until only bones are left. I took a walk one night, late, looking for remnants of Shmoam-ag DNA. Throughout the ship, mostly in what seem to be crew quarters, there are bones. A lot of very old bones. This ship has been not just his home, but a drifting graveyard."

Gold nodded his understanding, but his voice still held an indignant edge. *"It's admittedly a tragedy. But if anything, it makes it that much worse if you've given this boy false hope."*

"With the resources of Starfleet—"

"Do you expect me to take him aboard, even in isolation? Do you expect Starfleet to build a base out here dedicated to curing him? How long before doing that leaked out to people who might want just such a disease to use on their enemies and would do anything to use that boy as a weapon? You tell me, Doctor, what would happen if that boy found his way to an inhabited world?"

Unsure of what she expected from the captain, Lense didn't really know how to answer his questions either. "We can't just leave him alone here," she finally told him.

"I don't know what we can and can't do yet, but one thing's for damned sure—we can't take him with us. Unless you can tell me he's cured. Can you cure him?"

She knew it wasn't more than a question to make a point. He knew she couldn't, not in the time she'd thought she could before. Now, perhaps not ever. "I don't know. With time—"

"How much time did you say before you caught the disease? A week?"

"With a new EVA suit, and the right precautions, sir . . ."

"And you want me to just leave you on that ship with him? Alone? For how long?"

"As long as it takes."

"Listen to yourself, Doctor." He let out a breath, then spoke in a quieter tone. *"Back on Sherman's Planet, when we had our little chats, I joked that I was your substitute counselor. If I really had that position, I'd be wondering if you're bipolar right about now. If you're not sure you can do your job, you're thinking you can cure in a few weeks a disease you've only known the specifics of for a matter of hours? Is that fair to that boy?"*

"I . . . No. It's not."

Gold leaned across his desk and seemed to be peering into the shuttle cabin. *"What are you going to tell this boy when we have to leave him, without a cure, and maybe now without hope?"*

"I don't know." She shook her head and cast her eyes away from the captain. "I don't even know."

*   *   *

"Where did you go?" Dobrah asked.

Lense patted the boy on the shoulder and then the top of his head. "Did you wake up?"

"Domenica was here," he said with his rolling head nod.

"Sonya and I had to talk to our captain," Lense told him as explanation, and she realized she'd never lied to the boy. Except when she told him she'd cure him.

"Sonya came back."

"I know. I stayed to talk a little longer."

"Are you healthy?" It might have been an odd question for him to ask, but Lense knew that in the context of his life, where he'd seen everyone around him die, it wasn't.

She nodded, trying to make her tone sound not so sad. "I'm fine. I need to work as hard as I can right now. I have about four more days before my ship returns, and I'll need your help. Can you help me?"

Dobrah smiled, and his eyes seemed to reflect more light when he did so. "Sure. I used to help my mother."

Pulling her own lips into what she hoped wasn't a sad smile, Lense gave him a quick hug. "Well, you'll help me, too, just as good."

They worked, long into the next day. Dobrah left for food twice, at Lense's insistence, but she decided to labor nonstop. She wasn't exactly sure what she was looking for, but had hoped there was some sequence in the virus's genome that would turn it off. It wouldn't cure anyone who had the disease, if any such individual were still alive, but it might turn the virus inert and ineffective, and allow the boy to live a normal life.

At a certain point Lense remembered asking Gomez if it would be possible to get the sickbay computer running. If she could use its calculation and simulation power, going through the genome would be faster.

Gomez replied something about barely keeping the ship together and being there as soon as she could, but hours later she'd not shown up.

"Shouldn't you sleep?" Dobrah asked at some point.

Lense thought it had been perhaps forty hours since she'd last done so and while she was extremely tired, she knew time was limited. Before leaving the shuttle, she'd made sure to take some vitamin and energy supplements, however, and she believed those would last her. "I'm fine," she told him, and continued to hover over the computer console in front of her. "But you should sleep if you're tired—"

He'd moved without her realizing and was now next to her, pulling her arm toward one of the beds. "Get sleep," he demanded, looking up with bright wide eyes that reflected the glow of the lights above. "Stay healthy." He was pleading. "Don't get sick."

Allowing him to tug her away from the computer, and she *was* so tired that she might not have been able to stand her ground if she'd tried, Lense moved toward the closest bed. "Okay, okay," she assured him as she slid up onto the bed. "I'll rest here a little while, don't worry." She knew she wouldn't be able to sleep, lying on such a bed, in an EVA suit. There was just no way to get comfortable in one, but she lay on her side and closed her eyes just for him.

She was asleep in seconds.

"Elizabeth?" Gomez shook Lense's EVA suit lightly.

Stirring to wakefulness, and a bit startled by Corsi and Gomez standing there, Lense sleepily asked, "How long did I sleep?"

"I don't know," Corsi said dryly. *"When did you fall asleep?"*

Pulling herself up to a sitting position, Lense checked the chronometer on her suit sleeve. "Four hours," she mumbled. "Where's Dobrah?"

"We just got here," Gomez said, helping the doctor to her feet. *"I think you should go back to the shuttle for some real rest. I don't see how you can sleep in that thing."*

"I can't go back now. I've slept enough." She scrambled toward the bed on which Dobrah usually slept. "Maybe he went for food—"

"Domenica's going to take a break. I'm going to get power to the diagnostic computers in here, like you asked. You're going to go back to the shuttle and rest."

"No, I—"

Determined, Gomez's lips were pursed and her mind obviously set. *"That wasn't a request, Elizabeth."*

"Sonya . . ."

"This is how it is: Domenica will join you, Dobrah probably went for food, it will take a few hours to get this working." Gomez motioned to the console of Shmoamag computers against one wall. *"That's an order, Doctor."*

"All right. Two hours." Lense finally relented.

"We'll wake you in three."

"If I wake up in two—"

Gomez pointed to the beam-down point. *"Go!"*

Corsi pulled Lense lightly to the place where they always left their EVA suits, and ordered the shuttle computer to energize the transporter. With a sparkle and a flash, only the suits remained.

CHAPTER 6

Before she fully awoke, Lense was aware of the world around her: the feel of the thin blanket against her cheek, the dimmed light from above, the mildly uncomfortable bunk beneath her, and the sound of Corsi lightly snoring across the cabin from her. She made a sleepy mental note to mention it to Corsi again, and that she could cure it. Of course, Corsi would deny that she snored, just like she did every other time Lense had brought it up since they were first assigned to be cabinmates on the *da Vinci* shortly after the end of the Dominion War.

Cure. With her mind wrapped around that word, Lense was suddenly completely awake. "Computer, time," she croaked through a dry throat.

"Current sector adjusted time is sixteen forty-three hours and twelve seconds."

Feeling like she'd been asleep for a month, Lense then asked the date.

"Stardate 53801.9."

Lense grunted an acknowledgment as she squeezed on her boots, took a quick drink of water, and readied herself for beaming back to the Shmoam-ag ship.

"It's not three hours," Corsi said as Lense ran her fingers quickly through her curly black hair.

"I thought you were sleeping."

"I sleep very lightly."

"You snore," Lense said. "I can fix that."

Corsi rolled her eyes the way she always did. "I do not snore."

"I heard you snoring."

"Must be a clogged thruster that's keeping us from drifting."

"Must be. Well, I can fix it if you want."

Sitting straight up, Corsi repeated herself. "I do *not* snore."

"Sure."

"You're trying to annoy me so I won't stop you from beaming back early," Corsi said, slipping her boots on.

"You can't."

The security officer shook her head. "What is it with you?"

"I don't know what you mean."

"You're killing yourself working nonstop."

"It's the only way to find a cure. I've done it before—on Sherman's Planet, remember? I can do it again."

"That wasn't as bad a disease as this one. What if there isn't a cure?"

For too long a moment, Lense said nothing. She felt she might cry and tried to subdue the feeling. "There has to be a cure," she whispered.

"Why?" Corsi asked softly, in a tone Lense hadn't

often heard from her. It was sympathetic. "Because you want there to be one? That's not very scientific."

"No," she said, more to herself than to Corsi. "It's not."

Lense materialized into the EVA suit, which took a little extra time than a normal beamdown because the computer checked to make sure the suit was upright, hadn't been compromised, and so on. It didn't give her extra time to think, because of the nature of transporting, and yet stuck in her mind was Corsi's accusation that she'd not been very scientific of late. And on a personal level, it was true. She'd allowed herself to get involved with her patient, and he wasn't even supposed to be a patient. Her mission was to find out what had happened to the Allurians, not to cure a disease in a week that had destroyed two ships and an entire planet.

She was a doctor, however, and her urge to cure this poor boy had been too strong, and in ignoring her better judgment and promising what she couldn't deliver, she'd perhaps broken the cardinal rule of medicine: do no harm.

Did she believe, when she told Dobrah that she would cure him, that she actually could? After all, she was Elizabeth Lense, valedictorian of her class in Starfleet Medical, beating out the legendary genetically enhanced Julian Bashir, and savior of Sherman's Planet.

Was it confidence? Or worse, overconfidence? Or was it just shallow compassion, as when a doctor must sometimes hold dying patients' hands and assure them everything will be fine.

Really, it didn't matter what was in her head. She'd done it, and Corsi and the captain and her own conscience were all right that she'd made a very big mistake.

Once she took a step, having fully materialized, Dobrah turned away from where he was watching Gomez and ran to her.

"You are healthy?" he asked.

"Yes," she replied, kneeling down to him as best she could. "I'm healthy. I got some rest. Where did you go? To eat?"

"No, I sometimes walk the ship. I visit . . ." His voice trailed off.

"Where, Dobrah?"

"I visit my mother."

"I understand." His mother had died, probably in whatever room she'd kept quarters. It made sense that Dobrah sometimes visited her and had long ago gotten used to the idea that the bones left were nothing to be afraid of. "Why don't you go eat? I've got some work to do, okay?"

"Can I bring it back here and eat with you?" the boy asked.

It was interesting that after so many years alone, Dobrah had quickly slipped back into needing and seeking the authority of an adult. Of a parent figure. "Sure."

Once he'd moved off in a way that could probably be described as a scamper, Gomez looked after him, then turned toward Lense. *"He adores you."*

"I've spent more time with him than anyone has in over a hundred and fifty years. He'd adore you, too, if you'd done the same."

"Maybe. But he doesn't stop talking about you."

Lense wasn't surprised, but hearing it wasn't making the truth of the circumstances any easier. "Are you done?"

"I've been done. It's just off to preserve power. I can bring it back online when you're ready."

"You've linked in the universal translator?"

"Of course," Gomez said.

"Let's go, then."

With a few stabs at a control console, Gomez lit up a series of monitors above them. Alien symbols were replaced by familiar letters and words as Gomez input a translator algorithm. *"You're online."*

Nervous tension tightened Lense's shoulders. She hoped against odds that whatever data had sat dormant for decades on the computer banks before her would lead to an answer, for her . . . or Dobrah. In the moments it took to learn the logical system of the computer interface, Lense had managed to talk part of herself into the idea that all the Shmoam-ag had been missing was some little piece of medical knowledge. Some small shred that she possessed but Dobrah's people had missed. Something that would fall into place and allow her to find a cure.

Dobrah had returned with his dinner and fallen asleep by the time she found answers to all her questions. Placing an isolinear storage chip into an access port of her tricorder, Lense collected the log entries of Dobrah's mother and father—the two lead scientists who'd studied the Pocheeny and tried to cure it.

Tears welled in her eyes, and one rolled down her left cheek, but the EVA suit kept her from wiping it away. Lense now understood whom the Shmoam-ag were trying to save . . . and it had not been Dobrah.

"Is this data correct?" Captain Gold asked. "Are we sure?"

"Soloman said it's probably a spy satellite, sir," Carol

Abramowitz said as she snugged a strand of hair behind her ear. With her other hand she gestured to the screen to her left and leaned back into the science station chair so the captain had a better view. "The databanks were shielded and there's little degradation. It collected media and government broadcasts from all the various Shmoam-ag nations. And when the governments were gone, and the media broadcasts stopped, it continued to collect visual and scanner data."

"So they created this virus themselves?"

"One of the nations did," Abramowitz said somberly. "But it spread quickly, possibly before it could even be used as a weapon. The translation isn't clear on that, and it will take further investigation."

"Only the children were left?" Gold shook his head with disbelief.

"All carriers. I assume by design. Dr. Lense will be able to confirm, I'm sure."

Lense was a sore subject with the captain, and his neck knotted with the mention of her name. He wasn't sure what to do with her yet—the second time in a year he'd been in that position with her. At least this time, she'd broken no regulations, but she'd acted irresponsibly and it didn't sit well with him.

"And after the adults were gone?"

"That's when the broadcasts end, but sensor data that was collected suggests widespread violence, probably other disease, too. What if our children were left to run a highly technical society? How would they survive?"

Gold shook his head. "They wouldn't."

CHAPTER 7

When Lense got the call that the *da Vinci* had returned to the area, she'd actually been finished with her final report and calculations for over two hours. With the computer restored, Dobrah was showing her a game he used to play with his father, and sometimes his mother, but he was very clear that mothers didn't often play it. Lense had slipped into being a mother figure to him, and she knew that, but wished he wouldn't keep making it so clear.

Nonetheless, watching him have fun was contagious and lightened her heart, even if she knew their time together was now limited and soon she'd have to leave him.

When Gomez hailed her to let her know they were ready to beam back to the ship, Lense promised she'd be back after a while, and she and Dobrah would have to have a long talk.

"About what?"

"The future," she said quietly.

He rolled his head in his nodlike way and said he understood as he continued to play his game.

Lense beamed out, once again leaving her empty EVA suit behind with Dobrah.

When back on the shuttle, she did several scans that confirmed there were no stray virions that had contaminated any of them, or the shuttle itself, and it was safe to return to the *da Vinci* hangar bay. When they would need to beam back to the Shmoam-ag ship, they could do so from the main transporter room.

After an additional decon and a quick change of clothes, Lense was meeting with Gold and Gomez in the captain's ready room. Those ice-blue eyes of his bore down on her.

She didn't even know where to begin. How could she explain getting so lost in this one particular patient? And how could she keep herself from slipping back into the emotional pit that she'd felt herself falling into?

"Doctor? Gomez says you've learned a lot. So have we. I don't suppose you've found a cure for your young friend."

"No, sir. He'll cure himself." She handed him the padd with her full report and findings. "Dobrah's mother understood, and logged in her journal, that the Pocheeny virus uses children as incubators and homes for viral colonies."

"We found the same—evidence that the adults on the boy's homeworld all died, leaving the children to fend for themselves. They were either unable to, or the virus killed them when they reached adulthood."

"It wouldn't have killed them. Upon reaching puberty, the virus would have died off. It rewrites the child's

DNA to allow it to survive, and then rewrites its own to die upon production of certain enzymes and glandular secretions. It's a very sophisticated virus, meant to destroy an entire world of people, but leave their children so that anyone prepubescent could be saved, educated, and taught not to hate their enemy."

"An enemy that would have killed their parents?" Gold asked.

"Secreted onto an enemy planet, how would anyone have known what happened until it was too late? And what would children understand except that all the adults are dead, and these new adults have arrived to help?" The doctor shook her head at not just the waste, but the perverse morality. "The problem was, the virus was incomplete before it got out of containment. Dobrah's parents never knew exactly which of their planet's governments meant to use it on any of a number of enemies, but they saw where the genome was supposed to be coded to not infect any animal with Shmoam-ag DNA, but could have been coded only to affect one person with a very specific DNA. They perfected the latter, and not the former."

The captain nodded and sank a bit into his office chair. "Why were they on the ship?"

"The crew and scientists lived on the ship—they were the equivalent of our Starfleet, from the way it looks, and I got the impression that other ships in their fleet had been infected already." Lense gestured out the captain's office window and toward the Shmoam-ag ship visible nearby. "This vessel was their last hope—no infection. Dobrah was the only child aboard, and . . . it's not really mentioned, but I got the impression that his parents infected him once they knew he would survive eventually. They isolated him in their sickbay and only came into contact with him in suits like ours. They didn't understand that eventually the virus would work its way in anyway."

Gold rose, looked out the port window, and still turned away from Gomez and Lense, asked, "How long before he reaches puberty?"

"From the medical texts in the database, the Shmoam-ag have an average lifespan of over two thousand years. Dobrah is a little over two hundred years old, I believe. He'll no longer be a carrier of the virus at perhaps three hundred years old, maybe three hundred fifty."

"And then?"

"Soon after the viral colony dies, the virions that surround him won't have anyplace to return, and it will die out. By now, the Shmoam-ag homeworld, if no one is still alive there, is probably safe."

"Gomez?" Gold turned and looked at his first officer. "Can that ship last another hundred and fifty years?"

She nodded confidently. "With my full team, and another week or so of work, it can. So long as regular maintenance is done."

He gazed at Lense. "They'll be safe?"

"So long as EVA suits are changed out every week, and always left on that ship."

"See to it," Gold told Gomez. "Dismissed."

Both began to leave, but the captain motioned Lense back to her seat. "Not so fast, Lense. You don't get off that easy."

Of course not, Lense thought glumly. *Nor should I.* "Aye, sir."

"I've cooled down some since we last talked."

Lense had nothing to say to that, so she merely nodded.

"My concern was that you thought you could cure this disease, and blithely told him so. Maybe you were just trying to comfort him. But if you put the idea in his head that he can leave that ship now . . ."

"I didn't. At least, I hope I didn't. But we've not talked about it."

"Gomez tells me that he looks up to you. If you're thinking of staying, you'd have to resign your commission. And eventually you'd run out of EVA suits on your own."

"I know that, sir. I wasn't planning on resigning. I wish I *could* stay. It might be possible to find a cure, still. Certainly Dobrah's mother thought so."

Suddenly Gold's tone of voice shifted from annoyance to something softer. Maybe it was pity. "First you beat yourself up because you couldn't heal and cure everything. Then you thought—after a run of admitted successes—that you maybe could. Now you realize you can't again."

"You're playing counselor again."

"In a way. It takes a certain amount of ego to do what you and I both do—make life or death decisions. It's not a sin to believe in yourself."

Lense cast her gaze downward. "And what if I convince someone else to believe in me as well, and I'm wrong?"

"It's not a sin to be wrong, either." The captain knocked on the table and she looked back up at him. "It's not."

"Begging the captain's pardon, that's not how it feels."

"Well, part of that may have been the talking-to I gave you. Part of it is that the bottom fell out of your dream."

"This job . . . this ship . . ." She shrugged, unsure how

she could express her disappointment—both in herself and in life in general. "We overcome so much, and always come out on top. On Sherman's Planet, they were talking about building a statue to me. I guess I figured I'd always find the answer."

"You did find the answer, Doctor, it just wasn't what you wanted. Life's like that sometimes."

"I didn't want to lose this one." She felt another one of those tears coming, but only a bit, and it probably just moistened her eye rather than rolled down her cheek.

"You didn't. He'll be cured, someday."

"Years after we're dead," she said somberly.

"You lose patients sometimes. It happens. This one will outlive you. Certainly there's some comfort in that."

"He'll be all alone."

Gesturing toward his door, Lense rose as Gold continued to reassure her. "Well, I think we can manage to stop back from time to time, when we're passing by this way. And I have no doubt you won't be giving up your search for a cure, right?"

"Yes, sir."

"And . . . I have an idea about what we can do regarding the boy's loneliness."

She stopped, turned and looked at her captain. "Sir?"

"Let's go have a talk with some of our illustrious corps of engineers."

Dobrah's mother smiled down at her son, dropped to one knee, and embraced him so tightly that the boy made a happy grunt. She took his head in her hands and put it under her chin in what Dobrah had told Soloman she'd often done.

Lense couldn't help but take the Bynar's arm and give it a squeeze through their EVA suits. "I can't believe you did this all in a week."

"The holo-emitters are only in this room. It should be . . . sufficient for now."

"It's fantastic." Lense felt her face tighten with a wide grin.

Dobrah pulled the hologram of his mother toward the two Starfleeters. "Mother, this is E-liz. She's a doctor like you. And this is Soloman. He looks a little like Uncle Lintemuth, doesn't he?"

Switching the external speakers off, Lense asked Soloman privately, "He does understand this is a hologram, yes?"

"He does," Soloman replied discreetly, then put his externals back on. *"Pleased to meet you. I have heard much about you."*

Dobrah pulled his mother back to the computer console where they'd been playing, and Soloman turned completely to Lense. *"He's just pretending. He said he enjoys how interactive it is."*

"To get such a good representation of her, I guess there was a lot of data in her computer?"

Soloman nodded. *"Yes. Personal logs, physical profiles because of her work. For the father, too."*

"He played a game with his father already," Lense said, and had to try not to beam so much—the smile was beginning to hurt her cheeks. "I got to 'meet' him, too. Right now I think he's pretending his father is fixing the engine."

"It's good to see we've made him so happy."

"What if it breaks down?"

Soloman seemed unconcerned. *"We will be notified of any ship's problems via subspace alert. And there will be frequent visits by other science or engineering vessels."*

"I told him he'll eventually be cured," Lense said, continuing to watch Dobrah interact with the hologram. "That someday, when he's older, he'll be able to leave this place. When he's closer to being an adult."

"How did he react?"

"It's hard to tell. I think, being so long-lived, he might even sense time differently. Our visit here for the last three weeks might be a blink of an eye in his lifetime."

"If I may . . . I think some of us have made an emotional impact." Soloman could sometimes be cryptic, and so Lense didn't ask him how he knew that or what he meant. She just assumed Dobrah had said nice things about his Doctor "E-liz."

"He's very happy with the holograms of his parents," she said.

"We asked him exactly what holograms he'd like, and how they should act," Soloman told her. *"I am not surprised he is happy."*

"It makes me happy as well."

"Do you want to say good-bye to him?" Soloman asked.

She thought a moment about getting a second good-bye, but it might be too emotional for him. Or for her. "We said our good-byes once. I think I'd just like to beam out watching him this happy, with family."

"Very well." Soloman led the way the few steps to the transport point.

"Lense to *da Vinci.* Two to beam out." She kept focused on Dobrah for a last moment, wished him a silent good-bye, and then closed her eyes. "Energize."

Once the transporter effect had faded, all that remained were two EVA suits.

Dobrah looked back to them and frowned for a quick moment before smiling and running to the computer console he'd been taught how to operate by one of the nice Starfleet people.

He pushed the panel as he'd been shown, and confidently spoke to the computer. "Run program 'E-liz.'"

To one side of the image of his mother appeared a hologram of Dr. Elizabeth Lense.

Taking her hand, and his mother's hand, Dobrah pulled them both toward his computer game on the opposite wall. "You play, too," he told the Lense hologram. "Until you come back from being away."

SARGASSO SECTOR

Paul Kupperberg

CHAPTER 1

"Odds are it's right where you left it, David."

David Gold could hear the familiar mix of amusement and exasperation in his wife Rachel's voice as though she were in his cabin with him. How many times had she said those same words to him in the course of their marriage? How many misplaced socks, coffee mugs, padds, and combadges had elicited that very statement? Not, to David Gold's mind, that they were particularly helpful words, even if she did locate, finally, the missing object. If he could *remember* where he had left it, he wouldn't need to ask her. "It's right where you left it" ranked up there with "it's always in the last place you look" on the scale of Useless to Nonsense. But his forgetfulness seemed to amuse his wife, bring out the protective mother-hen in her during his all too infrequent stretches of time home.

For Rachel's part, it had taken her a long time to understand how her husband, a solid and steady Starfleet officer, could possibly have attained such a level of domestic absentmindedness. Aboard the *U.S.S. da Vinci,* he was responsible for the safety and well-being of forty crew and the operation of a ship often tasked with missions of literally world-saving proportions. It was a job that required focus and concentration, the ability to keep a million ever-changing details in mind at once, to make split-second decisions based on often incomplete data, to see not just the trees for the forest, but every last leaf on every tree while simultaneously maintaining a detailed overview of the status of the entire forest.

Why then, could he not remember where he left his socks?

Gold smiled at the memory of Rachel sharing with him her theory on that very subject several years back, during one of their rare anniversary celebrations together. "I finally figured it out," she had said. "It's *because* you don't have the luxury of forgetting on the *da Vinci* that you need to be able to just relax, to *not* have to remember every little thing when you're home."

"And," he said, taking her hand across the table, "because I know if I do forget, I always have you there to remember for me."

"And I always will," Rachel said. She had remained true to her word.

Which was all well and good, Gold thought while down on his hands and knees to search the floor around his bunk. And for that reason alone, he wished he was indeed back home, because then all he would have to do was shout out, "Rachel, have you seen my wedding ring?" and she would shout back, "Odds are it's right where you left it, David," and then, with her lovely face alight with the aforementioned amusement/exasperation mixture, she would march into the room and walk straight, without a sign of hesitation, to the missing item.

Gold sat back on his heels and puffed out a breath. If asked to testify in a court of law, he would have had no choice but to swear that his ring was nowhere to be found in that room. As captain, he was assigned the largest cabin on the ship, which wasn't saying much on a vessel the size of the *da Vinci.* Its small size—not to mention a lifetime of discipline as a Starfleet officer—forced him to keep his cabin squared away. A place for everything and everything in its place, and before he had gone to sleep last night, the place for his wedding ring had been on the shelf where he left all his personal items every night. What were the chances he had defied the habit of a lifetime and put the ring somewhere else?

The captain glanced at the time and knew he should be getting to the bridge. With the ship gearing up for a new and protracted—albeit fascinating—mission, it would be bad form for the captain to schlep onto the bridge, late for alpha shift. The continuation of his search would have to wait until later, even as the fact of its disappearance would gnaw at the back of his mind for the rest of the day, driving him crazy.

Straightening his uniform tunic, Captain David Gold stepped through the sighing door of his cabin and into the corridor. Thanks to the futile search he was a few minutes behind in his morning routine, which usually included walking to the bridge with his first officer, Sonya Gomez. He just assumed the commander would have gone ahead, anxious, as he knew the ship's senior engineer was, to sink her teeth into their new assignment. But, to Gold's surprise, Gomez was herself just coming down the corridor, her forehead creased with frown lines as she juggled a steaming cup of tea and two padds in her hands.

"Good morning, Gomez," Gold said.

Gomez stopped dead in her tracks, as though taken by surprise at the sound of his voice. "Captain," she said, and blinked at him. "I thought I missed you this morning."

"I thought the same of you," Gold said. He nodded at the jumble in her hands. "Problems?"

"Nothing *but* this morning," she said. "First thing off the bat, my padd experienced some sort of fatal error and crashed. It wiped *everything*."

Gold shook his head. "Oh my," he said with considerable sympathy, knowing that engineers kept half their lives and all their thoughts and ideas on their padds. The captain and commander continued on their way to the bridge.

"I didn't think it was that big a deal at first since I back up my padd onto the mainframe every night. But when I tried to download the files to a new padd, the computer said they had been corrupted . . . not to mention my backup padd also went on the fritz." Gomez shook her head. "I've done a considerable amount of preliminary work on this clean-up job and I *need* those notes. I just hope Soloman can talk some sense into the computer and help retrieve my files."

"I don't remember the last time I heard of a padd failing like that," Gold said.

"I know. And I had two in a row go south on me. What are the odds?"

"It's shaping up to be one of those mornings for me as well," Gold agreed. "I hate to think of it as an omen of things to come."

Gomez chuckled. "Why, Captain. I never knew you were superstitious."

"Oh, I've been known to dabble in superstition," he said. "Although I'm willing to concede that both our current situations are most likely random acts of capricious nature."

"In other words, bad luck."

"Exactly."

Gold and Gomez exchanged smiles, then stepped onto the crowded bridge of the *U.S.S. da Vinci.* The captain noted a larger than usual complement of bridge, engineering, and S.C.E. crew present this morning. They were gathered in clusters around different monitoring stations, huddled over padds and tricorders, or simply watching the breathtaking scene spread before them on the ship's viewscreen. The captain smiled, sharing as he did their excitement for the work that lay ahead. But his was not to stand and gawk in awe—much as he would have loved to join the justifiably flabbergasted observers. His was to keep his attention focused on the big picture so this diverse and brilliant crew could work their respective miracles.

"Good morning. A status report, please," Gold said by way of announcing his presence.

Tactical Officer Lieutenant Anthony Shabalala seemed to be the only member of the crew to take note of Gold's presence, snapping to attention and saying, "Holding steady, Captain, at half a parsec from the edge of the debris field. We've been scanning since our arrival three hours ago and, as expected, have so far found no life signs within range."

Gold noted that Gomez had joined a cluster of her fellow S.C.E. crewmates around one of the science stations and was already deep in their animated discussion.

Right, Gold thought, holding up his hand to cut off

Shabalala's recitation. *Time to give these leaf counters a bit of a look at my forest.*

"Ladies and gentlemen," the captain said at a volume that cut through the ambient murmur of some two dozen voices. "Observation lounge. Thirty seconds, if you please."

That, Gold noted with satisfaction, got their attention.

CHAPTER 2

Sonya Gomez was not the least bit surprised to see that everyone arrived at the morning briefing on time. It was a measure of the job that lay before them that this team of scientists and engineers, men and women, humanoid and otherwise, who had traveled the universe witnessing and accomplishing some pretty amazing things, were as excited as they were to get started. Who could blame them, considering what lay spread before the *da Vinci* across half a light-year of space?

Even as everyone settled in seats around the conference table, all eyes were glued to the monitor on the wall, glowing with the same image that had captivated the crew members on the bridge. Gomez could certainly understand their fascination and, in fact, shared their excitement. It was impossible not to as she looked upon the breathtaking expanse of hardware that blocked the *da Vinci*'s way through space.

For as far as the eye could see and their sensors could scan, there was nothing but ships, hovering motionlessly in an endless band that looked as though it stretched to eternity. Starships. Interplanetary craft. Shuttles. Ships of comprehensible design and purpose. Ships whose purpose would likely take years to determine. Ships of every size and shape imaginable, of materials known and mysterious. Ships powered by solid fuels and solar sails and nuclear engines and warp drives and black hole technology and ships beyond the imaginings of any of the *da Vinci*'s knowledgeable crew of engineers and scientists. Ancient ships carrying markings that identified them as belonging to races known to have disappeared tens or hundreds of thousands of years before humanity took to the stars. Others branded in languages lost to time and distance. Ships, some of which, preliminary scans showed, were millions—if not more—years old.

Literally millions of ships . . . and not clue one as to how they might have gotten here or why this little sector of space had become the repository for millions of years worth of derelicts and wrecks. A cosmic junkyard whose very existence made the engineer in Sonya Gomez shiver with delighted anticipation of the secrets examination of them would yield.

Gomez reluctantly tore her eyes from the nearest screen at the sound of Captain Gold clearing his throat. The rest of the crew did the same, but she noticed it was only seconds before they began to cast surreptitious glances back at the silent vista.

Gold, she thought with a private smile, had also taken note of the crew's less than undivided attention. "I think it's safe to assume," the captain said from his seat at the head of the table, "that all hands are aware that the *da Vinci* has reached its destination." He gestured in the direction of the screen, tacit approval for his mesmerized crew to resume looking for themselves. "As you also know, this sector has only recently been opened to travel by Federation vessels. Short of the mapping expedition that first discovered this Sargasso Sea of space, the *da Vinci* is the first ship through."

"The realm was previously in the Breen's purview," Lieutenant Commander Mor glasch Tev added. "Once they scurried out of sight when the war ended, many of their claims, including this region, suddenly disappeared."

P8 Blue, the ship's Nasat structural systems specialist, made a clicking sound that Gomez had long ago learned indicated curiosity. "I beg your pardon, Captain," she said. "That term you used, Sargasso Sea? I'm not familiar with it."

Gomez saw Carol Abramowitz, the ship's cultural specialist, open her mouth to offer an explanation, but Tev spoke up first. As usual, she noted wryly to herself. But she had long since reconciled herself to the Tellarite's propensity for arrogance that went beyond even the societal norms of his rather blunt-minded species. His was a people who spoke the truth as it was on their minds, to whom such human social niceties as tact and courtesy were just fancy ways of lying, and Tev was way up on the obnoxious scale even by Tellarites' high standards.

"It is a Terran term," Tev said. "A reference to an area of Earth's North Atlantic Ocean, also known as the 'Bermuda Triangle,' a fabled sea of lost ships. *Legends,"* and here he bit down on the word as if to let one and all know what he thought of unsubstantiated tales of undocumented phenomena, "abound of ships entering this area and disappearing, some to reappear months or even years later, derelict, their crews gone, often with half-eaten meals still on their mess tables. Aircraft are also said to go missing in the so-called 'triangle.' It's interesting that you mention it, Captain, considering our current location."

"Yes indeed, Tev," said Gold. "I considered its relevancy when I chose it as a metaphor."

"Yes, sir, but I understood you to utilize the term in reference to the aggregation of derelict vessels, which is one *myth* about the Sargasso Sea," Tev said. "Whereas I refer to a scientific *explanation* for both the sea and the phenomenon we now face."

Gomez fought back the instinct to jump in and reprimand her subordinate for the tone he was taking with their superior officer. She knew Gold wasn't offended by Tev's arrogance. All the captain saw was a good officer who was damn good at his job, if a bit unorthodox in his approach to military courtesy.

"The Sargasso is a sea within a sea, if you will. It's a two-million-square-mile ellipse of becalmed sea, named after the sargassum, a species of seaweed that covers and is native to the area, several hundred miles off the east coast of the North American continent. The area is surrounded by the Florida, Gulf Stream, Canary, North Equatorial, Antilles, and Caribbean currents, some of the strongest ocean currents on Earth. They all meet and enclose this sea, separating it from the rest of the Atlantic Ocean and creating a stagnant sea. The Sargasso rotates slightly, changing position with the surrounding currents as a result of seasonal changes, but it is otherwise a calm area.

"Therefore, anything drifting into the surrounding currents will make its way, eventually, to the Sargasso

Sea. Once caught there in the essentially still water, it is unlikely to ever drift out. Hence, one assumes, its reputation as an area from which sea craft might disappear, although I fail to understand how the sea currents would account for the disappearance of aircraft as—"

"*Yes,* Tev. That's all very fascinating," Gold said in an attempt to get his officer back on track.

"Of course, sir," Tev said smoothly. "My point is, our own Sargasso Sector came into being in essentially the same fashion as the one on Earth. That is, by surrounding 'currents'—in this case, of course, celestial forces—which have isolated this area and created a becalmed 'sea' out of which these trapped or abandoned ships cannot drift."

Tactical Systems Specialist Fabian Stevens whistled between his teeth. "This band of junk extends about half a light-year on the east-west axis and almost twelve AUs on the north-south. I won't even try to calculate how much area that covers. What kind of celestial forces are we talking about here?"

Tev shrugged. "It's a fairly unusual confluence of events," he said. "Ringing the Sargasso Sector are, in no particular order, one perfect binary black hole system, one system of unusually high magnetic activity, and no less than two quasars captured in some sort of complex mutual orbit, the result of which is a stasis zone, enclosed by the pull of the different gravitational and magnetic fields. This is a particularly ancient system, so such anomalies are to be expected."

"To have *four* such anomalies arranged close enough to create this dead space," said Gomez, "but in such perfect balance so they don't interfere with one another. . . ." She looked over at Soloman, the Bynar computer specialist. Able to interface directly with computers, she knew she could always trust him with rapid calculations. "What are the odds, Soloman?"

Soloman smiled. "Depending on how you choose to view it, either some several trillion to one against . . . or fifty-fifty."

Tev shook the precisely groomed dark brown fringe around his neck. "That's preposterous," he snapped.

"Odds," said Soloman, "really, are nothing more than a numeric representation of the probability of a certain event either happening or not happening. In a game of poker, you might need one specific card to fill your hand, say the ace of diamonds. You draw one card. The event you are calculating is whether or not the card you draw will be the ace of diamonds. Therefore, you either draw the ace of diamonds or you *don't* draw the ace of diamonds. Fifty-fifty."

Tev was scowling. "You're playing with semantics. What if you need two cards, or three? Or if the variables are far more complex, on the cosmic scale of four balanced anomalous systems?"

"Depending, of course, on how complex a model you wish to construct, you can always introduce a wider set of variables, treating each bit of the equation as a separate piece and come up with a more comprehensive number. But at the lowest common denominator," the Bynar said, "the equation will always reduce down to yes or no. Opened or closed. Binary. Can this happen? Yes, it can. No, it can't. Fifty-fifty."

Gomez tried to cover a smirk as Tev crunched Soloman's numbers for himself. Everyone but the literal-minded Tellarite realized the Bynar was having a little fun at his expense. Still, while the captain might tolerate the tangents their discussions often wandered off on, it was time to get back to the business at hand.

"We'll have plenty of time to study that," Gomez said, taking back, at a nod from Gold, control of the discussion. "In fact, Tev, you'll take the point on that. Pattie," she said to P8 Blue, "you'll lead up charting, cataloguing, and structural survey of the derelict ships. Bart and Carol, you two will catalogue what you can of language and culture as we go along. Likewise, Soloman, you'll recover as much of their computer systems as time allows for later analysis. Dr. Lense will handle the examination of any biological remains we may find."

Gomez nodded at Chief Engineer Nancy Conlon. "Your crew standing by for some heavy-duty demolition, consultation, and reverse engineering duties, Lieutenant?"

"We're ready," Conlon said, rubbing her hands together in anticipation. "I hear there are some pretty amazing propulsion systems waiting for us to get our spanners on."

"Then," said Gold, "it sounds like we all know what we need to do." He tapped a tabletop switch and called to the bridge. "Wong, proceed to point alpha at half impulse. Shabalala," the captain added, "warm up the proton-torpedo tubes. Demolition begins in precisely twelve hours. Let's get to work, people."

CHAPTER 3

Pattie hauled herself into the shuttlecraft's copilot seat next to Soloman and, as it conformed itself to her insectoid body, buckled herself in.

"I have completed the checklist on the external sensor arrays," she said. "Primary and backup systems are running, all datastreams feeding to the *da Vinci*'s mainframe."

"I'm ready here," Soloman said, tapping his combadge. "Shuttlecraft *Shirley* to Ensign McAvennie, we're set for bay doors to open."

"Roger, Shirley," came the reply from the shuttle control officer. *"Doors opening. Have a safe trip."*

Pattie clicked and buzzed with excitement as Soloman piloted the shuttle through the forcefield that held the vacuum of space at bay. "Some of these ships," she said, "are remarkable. One would need a lifetime to adequately investigate even a few of them."

"And we have," Soloman said with a glance at the

time on the console, "less than ten hours to make a sweep of the first half dozen before the *da Vinci* begins to destroy them."

The *Shirley* drifted from the bay and Soloman lit the thrusters. The *da Vinci* had settled into a stationary position less than a thousand kilometers from the edge of the debris field, a thin layer of wreckage and dismembered parts from countless vessels that swarmed around the conglomeration of derelict ships like the sargassum that covered the surface of the sector's earthly namesake.

Pattie clicked in regret. "Yes, it's a pity. Some will need to be destroyed to clear the way through the sector, but we'll try to move those we safely can. Either way, we can't risk doing anything to these ships until we've run an analysis on each and every one we propose to tamper with in order to determine the safety of such a move. At any rate, we've known from the start that our mission was to be as much about demolition as hard science."

"I understand," Soloman said, setting course for the closest of the derelict ships, a massive dark structure of many facets, an ill-defined smudge that blocked the stars. "A convoy of colonization ships are on course to pass right through the Sargasso Sector and the very conditions that hold these ships block any easy alternate route, preventing the convoy from altering course to go around the obstruction. But that doesn't mean I have to like the situation. These ships are an invaluable scientific and cultural find. To destroy so many without proper study merely to clear the way for navigation . . . well, it just feels wrong."

"I'm sure you won't find any onboard or in Starfleet who disagree with you," Pattie said. "But this colony's been in the planning stages for a year and a half. Those cargo ships are good for barely warp four for six or seven hours at a stretch. If they tried going around the Sargasso Sector, it would add nearly a year to the voyage, time their resources and changing conditions in their destination system don't give them. Like it or not, they will be passing through this system in less than one month and there better be a clear path for them to take."

The Bynar nodded and said, "Yes. We destroy them reluctantly." He looked at Pattie with sad eyes. "That doesn't make them any less gone."

"No," Pattie agreed and the two crewmates traveled several hundred klicks in silence. Finally, in an effort to lighten the mood, the Nasat said, "By the way, I enjoyed your joke on Tev. Last I saw him, his fringe was still ruffled trying to work out your theory on chance."

"Well," Soloman said modestly, "sometimes it's difficult to resist the temptation to put confusion in his path." Then the Bynar smiled. "Fabian told me I did a wonderful job of messing with his head."

"Absolutely. A clever simplification that makes just enough sense to be irrefutable. Sensor arrays are coming online now," Pattie said suddenly.

The view from the *Shirley*'s window was blocked by the looming blot of the black ship. Soloman deftly worked the controls. "Holding steady at optimum sensor range," he said. "Scanning for a computer core. Yes, it is a simplification, but once I said it, I started to wonder if it was in fact nonsense."

Pattie cast Soloman a skeptical look. "I have many more legs than Tev. It is far more difficult to make me stumble."

"No, I am serious. Take the example of a flat two-faced object, such as a Ferengi betting coin. Chance says that in any given set of tosses, the coin will come up heads or tails in statistically equal numbers. It's either/or, therefore fifty-fifty."

Pattie said, "But that's the case only in very simple systems. In the case of a poker game and the drawing of a specific card, there are not two choices involved, there are fifty-two, therefore increasing substantially the odds against drawing the necessary card."

"Ah, but the choice *isn't* between picking the hypothetical ace of diamonds against any *other* specific card in the deck. In any individual example of drawing a card, it comes down to yes, you *will* draw the ace, or no, you *won't* draw the ace."

Pattie waved four of her eight legs at Soloman and turned her attention to her sensors. "Now you're messing with *my* head," she said.

"Believe what you will," Soloman said, but the Nasat was fairly certain she saw the whisper of a smile on his lips as he said it.

Lieutenant Commander Mor glasch Tev stood at the tactical station on the *da Vinci*'s bridge, looking as sharp as a Starfleet recruiting poster. Fabian Stevens wouldn't swear to it, but from the way the Tellarite was briskly keying his way through the weapons system checklist and snapping out comments and commands to engineering, Tev just might have been having fun. The reason Stevens wouldn't swear this to be fact was that he didn't think he had ever seen Tev having fun before and therefore didn't know that he would recognize the phenomenon were he to actually witness it.

Nonetheless, ten hours before the demo was scheduled to commence the commander was on station, checking systems that both Stevens and Shabalala had, in fact, checked an hour earlier when coming on duty. And which would be checked again, later in the day, when Joanne Piotrowski came on duty for beta shift. If that wasn't a party, what was?

"Everything in order, Commander?" Stevens inquired.

"Seems to be," Tev muttered, distracted by information he was studying on one of the displays. "Has the targeting analysis been completed yet?"

"Yup. We've located an isolated pocket of derelicts that appear to be inert where we can start. No life, energy, or radiation signals from any of them," Stevens said. "Six of the ships were giving off anomalous readings, which is probably some sort of ambient energy signature, but we've sent Soloman and Pattie aboard the *Shirley* to take a closer look before we commit."

Tev nodded. He tapped the keypad, then nodded again at the targeting data scrolling across the screen.

"Odds are," Stevens said, "they'll check out just fine."

Tev's attention snapped from the console to Fabian. "What did you say, Mr. Stevens?"

Stevens said, "I said I'm sure the ships will check out fine."

Tev narrowed his eyes. "Mm, yes." Stevens allowed himself a quick grin as Tev turned his attention back to his work. *Gotcha,* the engineer thought, pleased with his little dig at the itch Soloman had planted in Tev's mind. *You definitely messed with his head, my Bynar friend. We'll make a practical joker of you yet.*

"Targeting is programmed into the firing system," Tev announced a few moments later. "I'll send them to the active buffer as soon as Soloman and Blue clear those last six ships."

"Do you want me to isolate this console to preserve your settings?" Stevens asked as the commander completed his task.

Tev pondered the suggestion for a moment. "Yes, why not?"

"Sure," said Stevens. "Doesn't pay to take chances, does it?"

Stevens could feel Tev's stare boring through his skull, heard the little rumble of a question caught deep in the Tellarite's throat, but pretended as though he was unaware of either and went about his business.

Gotcha again, Stevens grinned to himself.

The *Shirley* skimmed past the dull black metal of the first ship, its sensor arrays reaching and probing into the deepest recesses of the massive derelict.

"Nothing," said Pattie. "Not a blip from inside that thing. The outer hull is emitting low-level radiation, which would account for our preliminary anomalous readings, but everything else is flatline."

"Negative on the computer core as well," Soloman confirmed.

"Whatever powered this hulk was long ago depleted . . . not that I could locate a propulsion system, let alone any spent or residual materials. This one's a thorough puzzle. Unless we find another like it somewhere else, we'll never know what made her run."

Soloman piloted the shuttle toward their second target, some two thousand kilometers from the starboard side of the first. "Then let's move on. We're down to less than nine hours, with five more ships to scan."

A red light began flashing on the heads-up on the

window before Soloman. An urgent beeping tone accompanied it.

Pattie looked over, clicking questioningly.

Soloman frowned at the display. "According to the instruments, the *da Vinci*'s weapons systems have just targeted the *Shirley*," he said in a voice more confused than frightened. "We're about to be fired upon."

"*Captain*?" The urgency in Lieutenant Songmin Wong's voice made David Gold stop short and tap his combadge in the corridor where he was on his way to engineering.

"Yes, Wong?"

"Ship's computer has taken control of targeting and fire controls, sir," the conn officer quickly reported. *"Forward torpedo tubes are activated and locked on to the* Shirley."

Gold had begun running before Wong finished speaking. "Try manual shutdown. Override power to the weapons systems. How the hell did this happen?"

"Don't know, sir. According to the conn, everything's normal and weapons are offline."

Gold had sprinted into the lift, standing impatiently while it delivered him to the bridge. "They're obviously not. Keep trying the overrides. I'm on my way."

"*Shirley* to *da Vinci,* come in, *da Vinci,*" Pattie buzzed urgently into her communicator. "We're reading a weapons-lock on our position. Please advise."

Soloman said in disbelief, "It's no mistake. We've been targeted. I'm putting up maximum shields."

"For all the good they'll do against more than a few torpedo hits. This is madness," Pattie said. "The *da Vinci* isn't responding."

"There might be trouble onboard," he said. "Who knows what could have been lurking in one of these derelicts, waiting for a functioning vessel to come along?"

"What are the chances of that?" Pattie snapped as the urgent beeping turned to a continuous high-pitched whine. Both knew what that new alarm meant . . . that the *da Vinci* had fired.

"Perhaps better than we might think," murmured Soloman and began what he knew to be an entirely futile evasive maneuver.

"I have torpedo away," shouted Lieutenant Wong as Captain Gold raced onto the bridge.

Sonya Gomez was just moments behind him. "Captain . . . ?"

Gold held up his hand, his eyes glued to the viewscreen in horror. The *Shirley* was visible, looping tightly around to dive down behind the massive black ship. He expected to see, in the next second, the brilliant white flash of a torpedo tracking it, but the moments ticked by and it did not come.

"Captain," Anthony Shabalala said from tactical. "We didn't fire."

"Gold to Shuttlecraft *Shirley,*" the captain said. "You are in no danger, *Shirley!* We experienced a malfunction in the fire control that *simulated* targeting and locking, but it was only a simulation."

"I've taken the entire weapons system offline and isolated

them from the power grid," Shabalala announced. "All systems responding normally now, Captain."

"Shirley *to* da Vinci."

"Yes, Blue," Gold answered, in obvious relief. "Are you both all right?"

"Affirmative, sir," she responded. *"We were, needless to say, more than a little concerned there for a moment."*

"So were we," said Gold. "I would understand if you wanted to return to the ship until we've located the problem."

"That won't be necessary," Soloman's voice came over the communicator. *"We're unhurt and undamaged. The cause of the malfunction is, I assume, being eliminated even as we speak."*

"Then by all means," Gold said. "Proceed. Thank you. *Da Vinci* out." He turned to Gomez, who had moved to a science station and was reviewing the ship's internal log. Every action performed by ship's computer was automatically recorded on a separate memory unit encased in materials designed to survive the most catastrophic deep space accident. "How did this happen?" he asked her.

Gomez's eyebrow shot up in surprise. "According to the log, it didn't."

CHAPTER 4

Chief Engineer Nancy Conlon backed away from her latest handiwork in the *da Vinci*'s cramped engine room, carefully, as though afraid to take her eyes off the patchwork of connectors and relays lest it all fall apart.

"Okay," she breathed at last. The petite lieutenant turned to face the operations console, which was, at present, manned by her best junior engineer, Ensign Max Hammett. "Let her rip."

Hammett reached out to play the controls. "Alrighty then," he said. "Engaging impulse power." He tapped more keys. "While that warms up, we can patch the new intermediary modular into the grid." Conlon watched his fingers flash across the touch screen, her eyes flicking every few seconds to the new unit as though expecting to see smoke pour from it.

A green light flashed and Hammett turned to smile

at Conlon. "Online and checking out at optimum, Lieutenant. Nice little patch job there."

"Well, they're going to need more tractor beam for the job ahead than the *da Vinci*'s rated for," Conlon said. "Figured I should be able to reroute the power feed through the main impulse engines to amp her up to where we need it."

"You figured right."

"I'm clever that way." She grinned. "Okay. So, let's power down for now. We won't be able to field test this contraption until they've cleared the first targets for removal anyway."

Hammett gave her a thumbs-up and began to key in the shut down commands. After a few seconds he said, "This is weird."

"What is?"

"The panel's not responding. I can't take the new module offline."

Conlon squinted over at her suddenly troublesome creation. "Why not?"

"Good question. There's nothing wrong with the interface. Scans are still reading optimum." He paused and scratched at his chin before shrugging. "Must be a bug we missed."

Conlon laughed without humor. "Oh, well, it was too much to expect it to work the first time around. I'll pull the module and we'll run a new diagnostic, maybe get lucky."

Conlon and Hammett both found themselves lunging off balance as the *da Vinci* surged suddenly forward, as though yanked by a pull on an invisible rope. The chief engineer grabbed on to an overhead handhold and looked sharply over at the ensign, who had caught himself on the operations console. "What the hell was *that?*" she demanded. "Did the engines just kick in?"

Hammett looked over his readouts. "Negative. Engines are offline and locked down. That wasn't—" He gasped, his words breaking off in midsentence.

"What?" Conlon followed his astonished gaze to the console. "Who engaged the tractor beam?"

"Wasn't me," the ensign said, his voice tight as his fingers worked quickly over the controls. The tractor beam had targeted and locked on to one of the derelict ships at the edge of the Sargasso Sector, but without the *da Vinci*'s engines to provide a counterforce to hold the Starfleet vessel stationary, it acted instead to drag the ship toward the targeted vessel, like a fish reeling in the fisherman.

"Cut it off," Conlon instructed. "It's dragging us on a collision course with that wreck."

"Trying, Lieutenant. Damned thing's not responding."

Nancy Conlon swore under her breath and knew what she had to do. The souped-up tractor beam was functioning exactly as designed—except that no one had activated the thing and it was no longer responding to commands. But touching the module while it hummed with energy with a mind to disconnecting it was a short walk to suicide. She hefted a spanner and growled to Hammett, "Cover your eyes!"

And threw the tool at the module.

There was a brief flash of energy as the spanner knocked loose a series of interface adapters, severing the connection between the impulse engines and the tractor-beam generator. This was followed by a jolt and the stumbling backward of a couple of steps as the tractor beam released its hold on the distant wreck. The unit powered down.

"Engineering to bridge," Conlon said, still breathing hard.

"Something you want to tell us, Conlon?" Captain Gold's voice responded tightly.

"Eventually, sir. Soon as we figure out what just happened. Something went seriously wrong with the tractor-beam modification."

"Do we still have impulse power to correct the da Vinci*'s drift after our little unauthorized journey?"*

Conlon looked over at Hammett for an answer. "According to the diagnostics, everything's operating normally, sir."

Sonya Gomez's voice asked the next question. *"Nancy, was your glitch human or computer error?"*

Conlon shrugged. "I can't say for sure till I run a few tests," she said, "but I rigged that patch myself and I *don't* screw up that big."

"Not usually, no," came back Gomez's dry voice. *"Keep us posted."*

CHAPTER 5

"Can anyone explain this to me?" David Gold asked. "Has the entire crew suddenly turned incompetent, or does this ship have a serious problem?"

Sonya Gomez, to the right of the captain in the observation lounge, could only frown in frustration. "I seriously doubt the former," she said, "but can't find any evidence to support or deny the latter."

"How else do you explain it? Major failures in no less than three of our primary systems in only a couple of hours isn't standard operating procedure."

Soloman looked troubled, as though for a sick friend. But considering the Bynar's near-psychic connection to computers, his ability to communicate with them on an almost intimate level, perhaps humanoid and machine were close in ways his shipmates could never understand. "I have examined the ship's computer thoroughly, down to its source code," he said. "There's nothing wrong that I can detect, certainly nothing of a magnitude that might explain the lock and fire simulation of the weapons system, the communications blackout between the *Shirley* and the *da Vinci,* and the unauthorized activation of the tractor beam."

"And," Gomez added, "let's not forget the complete lack of a record of *any* of these events in the ship's internal log."

Stevens said, "That's what I keep coming back to. I mean, the log records everything from the rate of dilithium crystal decay to the different varieties of tea requested of the replicator by the crew, so what are the odds it's going to miss not one but *three* fairly substantial malfunctions?"

"On its own?" Soloman said. "I would venture to say the odds are so high as to be incalculable. But there is no sign of any outside influences on our systems. Whatever is happening is happening from within the *da Vinci.*"

Gold rubbed a weary hand across his forehead and looked around the table at the concerned faces of his crew. This was supposed to have been an easy one, a simple—if not delicate and vastly fascinating—job of clearing alien wreckage from a newly opened space lane. Each and every member of this crew was among the very best in their fields. Alone and as a group, they had encountered and solved more life and death problems than he cared to even think about, saving many lives—his own included—in the process on more than one occasion. But here they now sat, stymied by what appeared to be a computer glitch. He had to again ask the question that Gomez had glossed over at the opening of the meeting. "So can we rule out human error?"

Tev, uncharacteristically silent up until now, said,

"Absent any evidence to the contrary, I would tend to think we can, Captain."

"Thanks for the vote of confidence, Tev," Stevens said, surprised to hear the Tellarite take anyone's side but his own.

Tev looked at Stevens without expression. "It is no such thing, Specialist. I can merely conclude that since there has been a series of near calamitous events of which I was involved in but one, and knowing that all my actions were proper and by the book, that the others, too, must be the result of some other cause as well."

Stevens winked at Conlon. "Nice to know our backs are covered, isn't it?"

"All right," Gold said. "Our priority remains, as always, the successful completion of our mission. We've still got a tight schedule to maintain, which means everybody will be working twice as hard to do that *and* find and correct this problem. Whatever it is."

There were nods all around the table.

"Thank you, ladies and gentlemen," the captain said, rising. "And in the process, let's be careful, shall we?"

Carol Abramowitz was, she decided, as close to heaven as she had ever been . . . at least in terms of her professional life. The *da Vinci*'s cultural specialist kept coming back to the phrase "as happy as a kid in a candy store" to describe herself as she brought each new alien vessel's image up on her screen. Like the previous twenty or thirty ships—she had lost count—she had catalogued since beginning her shift on the second day in the Sargasso Sector, this one was unlike any she had ever encountered in any of her studies. Unlike any the *da Vinci*'s vast database of ships, comprised of records dating back to the dawn of human space flight, could match.

Her latest find lay four hundred meters long by three hundred meters wide . . . or, she thought with a smile, it could have been the other way around since the bizarre alien construction gave her human perspective no point of reference for top or bottom, fore or aft. To her eyes, it appeared to be made up of countless squares and rectangles of varying compositions, squished together into an angular whole that possessed a strange beauty all its own. Each boxy unit was marked with a different set of glyphs that might or might not have belonged to the same language.

"Fascinating," she breathed, unaware that she had spoken out loud.

"I'll say," said Language and Cryptography Specialist Bart Faulwell from his station near Carol. "By the time we're done here, the Federation's database of dead and lost languages is probably going to increase by tenfold."

"What I wouldn't give for a look at the culture of even a fraction of the civilizations that created these ships," Carol said.

"Soloman told me the older the ship, the less the chance of finding anything usable in their computer records. No matter how sophisticated their technology, a few million years is going to degrade just about any storage medium to uselessness, and, if it hasn't, it's not likely to be anything with which our technology can interface."

Carol laughed but her eyes remained fixed on her screen. "It's something, isn't it? Here we are, hundreds of light-years from our planet of origin aboard a ship capable of traveling from one end of the quadrant to the other, and the stuff we're finding here makes me feel like a chimp trying to understand the works of Shakespeare."

"That's a coincidence, your mentioning the Bard," he said. "I was just thinking of the line from *Hamlet,* 'There are more things in heaven and earth, Horatio, than are dreamt of in your philosophy.'"

"'O day and night, but this is wondrous strange!'"

Carol and Bart glanced up as Sonya Gomez walked into earshot, quoting the line that proceeded Bart's in Shakespeare's famous work. "And never more appropriate than under these circumstances," Sonya said.

"Hey, Sonya," Carol said. "How goes the engineering survey?"

Sonya's grin threatened to split her face. "Amazing. The range of ships we're cataloguing are, literally, mind-boggling. There are vessels out there from races that must have gone extinct before humanity was even an evolutionary glimmer on Earth. Subwarp solid fuel rockets, nuclear powered ships, impulse drives, black hole drives. . . ." Her grin did not fade even as she shook her head in wonder and confusion. ". . . including what may be at least a dozen variations on a transdimensional drive. There's stuff going on out there that none of us can even *guess* at.

"Of course, there's the rub," she said with a grin as she quoted *Hamlet* again. "Without knowing what ninety-five percent of those ships are, or were, we're faced with the possibility of disaster on a cosmic scale. All it takes is one energy source reacting adversely with another, or some previously unknown variety of particle or wave to be released and . . . *boom!* There goes the neighborhood, and maybe a solar system or two along with it."

Carol shuddered. "Ugh! I hadn't thought of that possibility. Good thing I'm too excited to sleep or that would keep me up at night."

"Rest assured," Sonya said, "we're playing it extra

safe. Anything we've moved we've been keeping in the same relative proximity to other vessels as it had been in the Sargasso. Anything we're not one hundred percent sure of, we're leaving where it is, and I've come up with what I think is a positively brilliant scheme to—"

Sonya Gomez's explanation was cut short by an urgent chirping tone from Bart's console. "Oh, for—" he blurted out, biting off an expletive before it could pass his lips. "I don't believe this!"

"Problem?" asked Carol.

"Looks like. Hold on a second." His face clouded with anger. "Computer, what's the problem with my file?"

Another chirp, and the soft, comforting feminine voice of the *da Vinci*'s computer replied, *"Please state the file name."*

"The one I've been working with for the last six hours," he said. "Sargasso, day two, linguistics."

"There is no file by that name," the computer replied.

His eyes wide with disbelief, Bart stared at the console. "This isn't possible," he said. "Check again for file 'Sargasso, day two, linguistics.'"

"There is no file by that name."

During Bart's exchange with the computer, Abramowitz quickly verified the safety of her own files, immediately dumping the contents onto her padd for backup and safekeeping.

"We've got serious computer issues, people," Sonya said in a tight voice. "Right when we need to be able to count on it most."

"Right now, I wouldn't trust it to count to ten," Bart said, slumping in his seat.

"Right now, I'm beginning to wonder if it even can," said Carol.

CHAPTER 6

Sonya Gomez was nervous.

In general, things had been going seriously wrong every which way she turned. What she wasn't forgetting she was losing and what she wasn't losing was breaking. And it wasn't just her, either. Everyone aboard the *da Vinci* was feeling it, all of them quivering bundles of nerves forced to juggle eggs.

She and her crew had suffered a few near-misses and project failures since starting the clearing of the Sargasso Sector. Tools and machines weren't working right. *People* weren't working right. A few crew members had taken to carrying good luck charms, although they all kept them out of her sight since she chewed out an ensign for rubbing a laminated three-leaf clover for luck. She felt bad, really, taking out her own frustrations on the unfortunate man, but they were supposed to be scientists and there was no room for voodoo in their line of work. She'd already disproved the so-called "curse of Sarindar" during her solo mission to the Nalori Republic, she wasn't about to succumb to this one.

So, yes, she was nervous, because here she was aboard the *da Vinci* and there—some two thousand meters away—was the object of the very delicate operation Sonya was about to attempt.

During any other mission, on any other day of her career, she would have been eager and, at most, cautious. Today she was just plain nervous. She had devised a fast and, more importantly, safe way to clear a substantial area of wreckage using a found resource that was proving far more abundant than initially suspected: Black holes.

A total of thirty-one ships within sensor range were powered by some sort of singularity-based technology, all, to Pattie's experienced eye, the handiwork of the same culture, if across an expanse of time. At some point in the past, a civilization near or adjacent to these parts developed black-hole technology similar to that used by the Romulans, and this was all that was left of them.

Each ship was equipped with from one to three chunky chambers holding its infinity-massed cargo in what appeared to be a sophisticated antigravity web. The study of how the engines managed to extract energy from this source would have to wait, but the singularities themselves, well, they were about to be pressed into service in an entirely different function.

"Engineering. Status?" Sonya said.

"Conlon here. Standing by on main tractor beam."

"Thank you. Transporter room, are you go?"

"Coordinates locked and standing by, Commander," said Transporter Chief Poynter.

This was a tricky maneuver under the best of conditions. They were playing with a black hole, packed in a containment device constructed by unknown beings at least seven hundred and fifty thousand years ago. So many things could go wrong.

And lately, Murphy's Law—that everything that could go wrong *would* go wrong—had become the law of the land. Not that the law wasn't part and parcel of the S.C.E.'s daily existence, but this was going to new extremes. If something went wrong with the extraction, the *da Vinci* and everyone on it would wind up with their mass stretched across infinity and devoured by the singularity. The only upside was that at this distance, given the limits of the tractor beam's effectiveness as a surgical instrument, it would all be over too fast for anyone to realize it was happening.

Which, she thought with bitter amusement, *is a hell of a pitiful upside.*

"Fabian?" she said to the crewperson temporarily taking Piotrowski's place at the bridge's tactical station.

Fabian Stevens, unusually serious, took a moment to crack his knuckles and shake out his right hand. "Ready," he said, taking hold of the joystick with which he was to direct a pencil-thin tractor beam.

"Very well, people," she said after one last deep breath, "let's begin. Transporter room, energize."

"Energizing."

The result of that order was played out on the ship's screen, on a strangely amorphous ship that seemed to undulate even though hanging motionless in space. Its pastel-streaked milky white surface looked more like cheap plastic than anything designed to survive the rigors of space. But here it was, by their dating techniques some three quarters of a million years after it had been built. Surviving.

Somewhere near the midpoint of the misshapen derelict, the transporter reached out and grabbed the molecules of a fifteen-foot-around section of hull. Unseen, it did the same thing to a series of bulkheads and decks, opening a tunnel for the tractor beam to follow to the containment unit. Transporting a singularity, even one as small as the nick of a pin contained in a null-gravitational state, was risky business at best, even if the vagaries of physics didn't make the amount of energy required to dismantle the singularity's near-infinite mass into transportable particles too great for the *da Vinci* to provide. So they were instead transporting the derelict piece by piece out of the way of the tractor beam.

"Doing good, Laura. How much more to go?"

"Four more decks, and the containment unit should be free-floating."

"That's your cue, Fabian. You up for this?"

"I'm fine, Commander." Stevens's smile was tired. "A streak of bad luck is just a self-perpetuating cycle. The first bad thing throws you off your stride, the second rattles you, by the third you're convinced you're jinxed, and everything after that is just you tripping yourself up worrying that you'll trip up. Personally, I don't buy into it."

"So we're all just neurotic?" Gomez asked.

Stevens grinned. "Each in our own way."

"Bridge, we're through the last deck. Sensors show the containment unit is free and clear."

"I copy that, Chief," Gomez said. "Fabian, ready on the tractor beam."

"Going in," Stevens said and triggered the beam with a tap of his fingers. His eyes were fixed on a three-dimensional image of the alien ship on his screen that served as a visual guide for the path of the tractor beam.

"Just like threading a needle," Gomez said softly.

"Contact," Stevens said. "Gonna start to ease it back out now."

"Scan of the containment unit looks good," Gomez said. "Go for the extraction."

There was silence over the next few moments as Stevens drew the squat alloy container from the bowels of the ancient ship, up past decks that had last seen movement most of the way to a million years ago. Soon, the unit would be in open space and in position for the next phase of the operation.

"What'd I tell you?" Stevens said. "No such thing as bad luck." The containment unit slid into view from inside the gutted derelict.

Gomez smiled and said, "I never for a second doubted you. But, just to be on the safe side . . ." She held up her hands, showing crossed fingers on both.

Stevens laughed. "If you want to know the truth, with my hands being occupied I had my toes crossed."

Tapping her combadge, Gomez contacted the engineer in the cargo bay. "Ensign Lankford?"

"Yes, Commander?"

"You may launch the drone at your discretion."

"Drone away, Commander. Through the cargo doors, locked on target and closing."

A small drone vehicle, about the size of a duffel bag, glided onto the viewscreen, on course for rendezvous with the containment unit.

"Two thousand six hundred meters and closing."

In just a few minutes the drone would ease up next to the containment unit and, on contact, would fire its main gas-propellant engine to push itself and the unit into the very heart of the field of wreckage.

"Two thousand three hundred."

At a predetermined distance from the *da Vinci,* the drone would detonate, shattering the containment unit and, of course, unleashing the black hole.

"One thousand nine hundred."

The singularity would begin to do what it did best, drawing everything within its event horizon toward and into its influence. Ships unmoved since forever would race toward the black hole, expanding into infinite mass before disappearing inside the thing's insatiable maw.

"One thousand two hundred."

It would sweep its immediate area clean and, not too long after it had sucked in everything it could reach, it would begin to feed on and collapse in on itself. Even a black hole so small as this one could exert its gravitational mastery over several hundred million square kilometers, a significant dent in this particular pile.

"Nine hundred klicks and closing."

There were risks, of course, but under controlled conditions, with the *da Vinci* moved to a safe distance to observe the event, they were—*If our luck holds,* she thought—acceptable. And this method, in addition to being fast, also offered some fairly attractive safety features of its own, most specifically in the case of the accidental release of any unknown but potentially hazardous contents of any of the ships.

"Three hundred klicks. Sensors are locked on target. Two hundred . . . one hundred . . ."

Everything from inert organisms to uncontrolled chain reactions would get caught up in the singularity.

"Two hundred meters."

Nothing unleashed could be more powerful than the gravitational pull of that tiny bundle of compacted matter. This would throw out not only the baby with the bathwater, but the bathtub and the whole bathroom as well.

"One hundred meters . . . ninety . . . eighty . . ."

If this worked, Gomez judged it would take a maximum of six strategically placed black-hole releases to open a lane wide enough for the approaching traffic through the Sargasso Sector. That would still leave several dozen lifetimes worth of intact derelict ships for future study.

" . . . Forty . . . thirty . . ."

At twenty-six meters, the drone's main thruster ignited and sent it slamming into the containment unit at several thousand KPH, relative. The struck object spun off at a tangent, while the drone, its trajectory altered by the impact, went streaking toward the not too distant rubble of another derelict.

"Dammit," Gomez growled. "We've got a misfire. Get us out of here, Robin. *Now!*"

The bridge crew sprang into motion, their voices rising with the sudden whine of the *da Vinci*'s surging engines.

"I have the drone impacting with the derelict in four minutes," Stevens shouted.

"We'll be at warp in *one,*" Ensign Robin Rusconi said from the conn.

"The containment unit," Gomez said heatedly as she scanned her console. "I've lost it in the clutter of the debris field."

"The unit would've been built to survive impact," Stevens said, but the look in his eyes was anything but confident.

"It's three-quarters of a million years old, Fabian," she reminded him. "Bet whoever built it didn't expect it to be in service that long. If it gets loose before we're out of range . . ."

He nodded, then pointed to his screen. "Got it! Plotting trajectory . . . it's good! The unit has clear sailing for a good hour, plenty of time to retrieve it."

"Warp one," Ensign Rusconi announced.

As the *da Vinci* pulled back from the Sargasso, Gomez and Stevens tracked the errant drone. By the time the little booster glanced off the side of the looming ship, they were well out of the danger zone. A misnomer, actually, as the result of the collision was almost nonexistent. The drone's mass was insufficient to do anything more than dent the larger ship's hull and cause it to begin to wobble slowly in its orbit.

Stevens looked over at Gomez and frowned. "Now, is what just happened bad luck or good luck?"

"Why do I think that luck had nothing to do with it?" Sonya said.

"'Cause," Stevens said, "we're scientists, not gamblers. We wouldn't have played this hand if the odds hadn't been in our favor."

"We need," Gomez said in agreement, "to find out just who the hell's been dealing us these crappy cards."

CHAPTER 7

The list of mishaps, accidents, and failures—both human and mechanical—was, Captain Gold noted sourly as he scanned the log, as prodigious as it was disturbing. As he had every right to be, Gold was extraordinarily proud of his crew and their record, but by the sixth day of operations in the Sargasso Sector, the crew of the *da Vinci* felt as though they had been chosen to serve as the butt of one long, elaborately cruel joke, the punch line to which was a nonstop series of disasters, major and minor.

Gold rubbed absentmindedly at the still-bare ring finger of his biosynthetic left hand. Like the fact of his still missing wedding band, this mission seemed to be jinxed by some bizarre corruption of all laws of probability. To encounter the occasional mechanical mishap or work accident was to be expected. To encounter nothing *but* was way off the charts of anything Gold had ever heard of happening on a Starfleet vessel.

Soloman had checked the computers six ways from Sunday and could discover no source of corruption or malfunction that might explain its behavior. Dr. Lense had examined every crew member for any and all physical or psychological causes of chronic klutziness, but likewise came up empty-handed. The captain had even had the ship's environmental systems checked for abnormalities, anything that might be influencing the crew or ship to act as they were, but there was nothing, not in the air, not on any level of the spectrum, *nothing* amiss.

It was, from all appearances, just a run of incredibly bad luck.

Still, in the aftermath of the black-hole incident the engineers had decided to suspend such potentially disastrous exercises until they sorted out the problems.

And Bart Faulwell hadn't been the last to experience some form of computer malfunction. The worst such incident occurred in the early morning hours of the fifth day as Rusconi executed a maneuver ordered by Tev to reposition the ship in preparation for a round of demolition. Though having entered the correct coordinates, as witnessed by the meticulous Tev and attested to by the operations log, the *da Vinci* had proceeded to spin, far in excess of programmed speed, into a near disastrous collision with one of the derelict ships before being brought back under control. The port nacelle had suffered serious damage, though no one, fortunately, had been hurt.

Another misfire had resulted in a grouping of thirteen derelicts that had not yet been scanned, examined, and cleared being demolished by torpedo. In this case, it turned out all right, but it could just as easily have gone the other way, ending in disaster.

But losses of data, environmental system failures, and strange malfunctions of the drives continued. Even the replicators had been acting up, churning out inexplicable creations in response to routine requests by members of the crew. Ensign Piotrowski had asked for a cup of coffee, regular, with three sugars. The replicator had supplied her with a three-tailed kkk'tukkiquith'quattkkk, a delicacy for whose molecular matrix it was not programmed.

Gold's own request for a snack of sliced vegetables had resulted in a platter of nugget-sized chunks of a thus-far unidentified isotope. Fortunately the sensors had instantly detected its powerful radioactive signature and alerted Gold before he had been exposed long enough for any harm to have been done.

But it wasn't just the physical dangers that seemed to be everywhere that were so draining. Worse was the constant petty annoyances, the lost tools, the misplaced personal effects, the wrong turns, the misremembering, the misjudgments. It was endless and endlessly distracting. How could the ship's conn officers execute orders knowing they could trust neither the computer nor their own judgment? How was the chief engineer supposed to do her job when she couldn't count on the tool she had put next to her on the floor just seconds before to be there when she reached for it again?

"Odds are it's right where you left it, David."

Gold chuckled and shook his head. He knew he was letting it get him down, but he had seldom in his career felt so frustrated. Yes, sometimes the situation did seem helpless, all options explored, exploited, and failed, but there was always something, no matter how desperate, to try, to *do*. But there wasn't anything to be done for a run of lousy luck. He had been in enough poker games in his life to know that it was all up to the cards, and if the right ones didn't come to you there wasn't thing one that you could do to change it. The problem was, while you could fold on a crummy poker hand, you didn't have the same option in life.

Certainly not when you were in command.

And so, even if David Gold couldn't provide them with the answers to this dilemma, he would at least give them his leadership. Which made it time to stop moping over his pitiful captain's log and get himself up to the bridge and *look* like he didn't feel as though the sky were falling all around him.

"Thank you, that'll be all," he said to the computer in his quarters.

"Unidentified user. Please state name and access level," said the computer.

Gold didn't bother responding, leaving his room with its missing rings and recalcitrant computers, wishing—without hope—for a reprieve from the misery.

Proving him an optimist, if not a realist, the answer to that wish was a loud, pain-wracked scream that pierced the air. Gold took off at a run toward its source, the turbolift at midship.

What now? he thought, expecting, from the sound of the scream, the worst and finding nothing less. Bart Faulwell was sprawled, writhing in agony, across the turbolift's threshold, clutching at his throat, his scream dulled to a moan by painful gasps for breath. Two security guards, Krotine and Lauoc, had already reached the red-faced language specialist and were alerting sickbay, but Gold couldn't see any obvious source for Bart's distress.

"He can't breathe," Lauoc said.

"What happened?" the captain demanded.

"Don't know, sir," Krotine stammered. "He just started gasping, then he went down, screaming."

Dr. Elizabeth Lense came running down the corridor and the helpful crewmates scrambled to make room for her. She passed her tricorder over Faulwell, frowning at the readout.

"How the *hell* . . . ?" the doctor muttered. She quickly shook off her surprise, then adjusted her hypo to deliver the proper medication. Administering the dose, she said, "Hold on, Bart. I've got you."

Faulwell's face had started to turn blue, his lungs unable to deliver oxygen to his starved blood despite his desperately heaving chest. Now, as the meds flowed through his system, his throat seemed to open and air flowed in. His dry, pained heaves quieted to gasps, then diminished to a wheeze as the color slowly drained back into his face.

Dr. Lense's tricorder scanned Bart again, and this time she looked up, smiling and satisfied with the reading.

"Anaphylactic shock," she said to Gold in answer to the obvious question. "Bart's had a severe allergic reaction to something. I've administered antihistamine and stimulants to open up his breathing passages. He should be fine."

"What's he allergic to?" Gold asked.

"According to his file? Nothing. Hence my confusion."

"This wasn't nothing, Doctor."

"Of course it wasn't," she said. She looked back at Bart, tapping him lightly on the cheeks. "Bart? Bart, can you hear me?"

Without opening his eyes, Faulwell said, "Yeah, yeah. Man, what hit me?"

"Did you eat or drink anything in the last half hour, Bart?" the doctor asked.

Bart nodded, his head still a bit wobbly. "Umm, yeah. Had an energy bar . . ." he said, then laughed weakly. "Didn't work."

"What kind? What was in it?"

Faulwell managed to open his eyes and, when he answered, his voice was noticeably stronger. "Peanut butter. My favorite. Why?"

"Peanuts," she said to the captain as though that explained everything. "To those allergic to them, the reaction can be quick and, without immediate medical attention, even fatal."

"Except I'm not allergic to peanuts," Bart corrected her and took in a long, shuddering breath as he raised himself up on his elbows. "I eat peanut butter practically every day. You could use my blood to create a *vaccine* for the stuff."

"Apparently not anymore," said Dr. Lense. "I'm sorry, Bart, but as of right now, I think you're officially off peanut butter."

"Aww," said Faulwell. He let his elbows slip out from under him and thudded back onto the floor.

"No need to be so dramatic, Faulwell," said the captain with a relieved smile.

Bart didn't answer.

"Bart?" said Dr. Lense, quickly activating the tricorder and taking a new reading.

But Bart Faulwell was dead.

CHAPTER 8

The captain's mouth had been dry for the past half hour. No matter how much water he drank, he couldn't seem to get enough moisture. Ever since Dr. Lense had been forced, after a nearly forty-five minute struggle, to accept reality and pronounce Bart Faulwell dead, David Gold had felt strangely drained of everything. One instant they had been talking, the next a man lay dead half inside a turbolift.

Nothing the finest care and technology could prevent.

It had gone beyond madness, Gold thought, getting himself a fresh glass of water from the replicator. He had lost crew before, lord knew. Salek and Okha during the war. 111 on the *Beast*. And twenty-three people in one, horrible incident at Galvan VI. But there, as senseless as so much death ever was, there had at least been a visible cause. A situation against which steps might have been taken, measures tried.

But what did they have now? Peanut butter. Bad luck? He looked at his senior staff, gathered with him in the observation lounge. Did he seriously intend to put forth the theory that this was all on account of simple bad luck? Finishing his water, the captain decided he had better let the others have their say before he dropped that particular *bubbemyseh* on the table.

"Faulwell's death," Gold said, "comes as a shock to everyone. It was as random, as unlikely an event as anyone could have foreseen."

"So senseless," said Sonya Gomez, fiercely.

Tev nodded. "What are the chances of an adult with no prior history of a problem developing so severe an allergic reaction to a much-consumed food?"

Soloman said, "Not likely at all. Yet far more so than a replicator producing a kkk'tukkiquith'quattkkk or an unknown isotope."

"Or anything else that's been going wrong. Think of it, what are the odds *everything* goes wrong *all* the time?" said Nancy Conlon. "This entire mission's been jinxed from the start."

"Jinxes do not exist," Tev said. "Bartholomew did not die from 'bad luck.' Luck is not intrinsically good or bad. It is just random chance. It is neither a cause nor an effect. It just is what it is."

"Besides," Soloman said, "it's not as though 'luck' or random chance possess physical qualities that can be quantified and manipulated."

"Bart is dead," Sonya Gomez said in a soft voice. "He was a dear man and a good friend and now he's dead because of something as ridiculous as snack food? I don't think so, people." She looked from face to face. "There's something wrong here. And it *is* bad luck, but something is helping it along. Maybe it's not anything we can measure, but you all feel it, don't you? I mean, we're *better* than this. All the accidents, the lost and broken tools, the equipment failures. We don't make these kinds of mistakes, and we sure as hell don't make them with the recent alarming rate of frequency. Something is influencing events. *Something* killed Bart."

Gold said, "What's left that we haven't already checked? And with chance against us, how do we propose to reverse our luck?"

"Really, Captain," said Tev. "You're not seriously suggesting that we proceed on the assumption of 'bad luck'?"

"If you have a better suggestion, Tev, I'd like to hear it," said Gold.

Tev opened his mouth to speak as the ready room door slid open.

Mor glasch Tev stepped into the room, saying, "My apologies for being late, Captain."

Mor glasch Tev, seated at the conference table, stared in disbelief at himself. "This isn't right," he said. "I am never late for meetings."

In the resultant uproar, the latecomer Tev appeared to slip, or otherwise disappear from the room, but no one could deny he had been present. If only for a moment.

"You, sharing the room with yourself is, without question, an impossibility," declared Soloman. "What better proof do we need that the very essence of probability is being tampered with?"

The Bynar and Tellarite looked at each other. Tev nodded in agreement.

"Wait . . . that's like saying because three plus three

doesn't equal eight, three plus three *must* equal eight," Gomez said.

"Not at all the same thing, Commander. When you've ruled out all that is possible," said the Tellarite, "the only remaining possible answer is the *impossible.*"

"To paraphrase Sherlock Holmes," Conlon said.

"Its attribution to a fictitious character does little to diminish its fundamental truth," said Tev.

Sonya paced the shuttle bay, deep in thought. She sometimes came down here, to the ship's largest open space, for room to move when faced with the seemingly insurmountable. That, and it was the place where Elizabeth pronounced Kieran Duffy dead. Coming here made her remember him, and helped her move on from the grief. Her near-death experience on Teneb had done a great deal to help in the latter regard, but she still liked coming here.

Every now and then, as she walked the length of the bay, back and forth, she found herself stepping over things that shouldn't be there. Chance had gone haywire, no doubt of that, she thought. Or been *made* to go haywire. Therefore, the odds of any event happening, no matter how unlikely under normal scientific law, had gone from one in numbers so large even the zeroes couldn't be counted to pretty much dead even. Like the cartoon cat chasing the cartoon mouse under her feet and out the cargo doors, through the force field and into the vacuum of space to implode into smears of paint. What were the odds of such a thing ever happening?

As mad as it sounded, Tev was right. It seemed the only possible answer.

And yet, what could affect so intangible a something as chance? She couldn't imagine some Yridan Bad-Luck Ray or Romulan Gotcha Beam being responsible. She couldn't imagine any technology capable of influencing probability.

And yet, as Bart Faulwell himself had pointed out the day the computer ate his files, *"There are more things in heaven and earth . . ."*

Such things as the universe of tech they were investigating, some of which, no matter how hard she might study it, she would never even begin to wrap her mind around. The theories on which they were conceived and the very logic behind the engineering eluded her, the end product too alien for this culture to ever understand. Some, she believed, operated on transdimensional power, although whether they actually traveled between dimensions or siphoned energy from other-dimensional sources she couldn't quite determine. Others seemed to rely on tachyon streams or the Uncertainty Principle or, in one case, little more than mineral water.

But probability?

Still, what was the Uncertainty Principle but chance? "The more precisely the position is determined, the less precisely the momentum is known in this instant, and vice versa," Heisenberg had said. One increased the odds of determining a particle's position by lowering those on knowing its momentum.

Which, too, came back to Soloman's earlier playful proposition that all odds could be boiled down to fifty-fifty. The Uncertainty Principle: you know either a particle's position or its momentum. Fifty-fifty. The same with Schrödinger's Cat: was the cat inside the box alive or dead? Fifty-fifty. Maybe here, for whatever reason, that had become, somehow, fundamental truth. There was as much chance of a ship outfitted with a drive that altered probability existing as there was for it *not* to exist.

Fifty-fifty.

She was putting her money on it being out there. And against, appropriately enough, all odds, it had somehow been activated and was screwing with chance.

What were the odds she would be soaked in a brief rain shower while standing in the cargo bay of a Starfleet ship with a controlled atmosphere? Infinitesimal, and yet, as her wet hair and uniform attested, no longer impossible.

"What did you call it?" asked Nancy Conlon.

"An Uncertainty Drive," said Gomez. "There was a similar, albeit fictitious drive, put forth in a twentieth-century novel by Douglas Adams. It worked, as I recall, by manipulating the laws of probability to move from place to place. But it was a humorous work, not meant to be taken seriously."

"Nobody's laughing," said Fabian Stevens.

"And you're saying you think that's what we're up against here?" asked Captain Gold.

Gomez shrugged and said, "I've eliminated the possible. Look, we're all agreed that chance is, by it's very nature, random but not capricious. What I mean is, there are rules. As Soloman said, flip a coin a set number of times and it will come out split evenly between heads and tails, every time. In a game of five-card poker, you stand roughly one chance in thirty-one thousand of holding a royal flush. Head a ship in a specific direction under an established mode of propulsion and it will travel at x-speed toward a fixed destination.

"But bypass physical propulsion, establish a set of odds for your vessel to simply *arrive* at a specified destination in a set amount of time, then manipulate the odds to make that arrival a sure bet, and you've got—"

"An Uncertainty Drive," said Soloman, a bit breathless at the very idea. "But it's mathematical insanity, Commander Gomez. The amount of processing power is unimaginable, and how would it go about affecting the odds?"

"It may seem insane," Gomez said, "but it's possible. I even have evidence." She touched a control on the table in front of her. The viewscreen on the far wall lit up with a half-sphere decorated with a moderately ornate panel.

"That looks familiar," Stevens said.

"It should—it was discovered on Deep Space 9 when you were stationed there."

Stevens snapped his fingers. "Right! That El-Aurian who opened the gambling joint on the Promenade!"

Gold looked at Gomez and Stevens. "You want to fill in for the rest of us, Gomez?"

"The El-Aurian Fabian's talking about got his hands on a device that altered probabilities."

Nodding, Stevens said, "It made all the neutrinos near the station spin the same way—and it made a pig's ear out of ol' Doc Bashir's racquetball game." He shook his head. "I lost a bundle betting on that game with the chief. . . ."

Abramowitz shook her head. "I don't get it. How can a machine make the impossible possible?"

"Impossibilities are merely things we've not yet learned to do," said Tev. "This very starship, its warp engines, were once thought impossible, as was creating artificial intelligence on par with biological sentience.

How many of us come from worlds that once believed the evolution of life on other planets was a statistical impossibility? As one who has himself experienced time travel, another historic 'impossibility,' I am inclined to accept that everything we today might *think* of as impossible just hasn't happened yet."

A chimpanzee in a conservatively cut and particularly dignified military uniform paused in their midst, checked something on the clipboard he was carrying, and continued on his way.

"That was different," said Stevens. He looked up and gave a helpless shrug. "Okay, so we buy the Uncertainty Drive. How do we go about finding it?"

"Already done," said Gomez. "I ran a broad spectrum scan, tuned to hunt for frequencies similar to the ones given off by that little doodad from DS9."

"And it worked?" asked Gold.

"What can I tell you?" Gomez smiled. "I got lucky."

CHAPTER 9

From the exterior it didn't look like much.

Not much larger than the *da Vinci*'s own length of one hundred and ninety meters, it was an elliptical tube of burnished silver alloy dotted with what appeared to be a random arrangement of portholes. It featured no openings for propulsion units or weapons pods, but then, Soloman thought, the Uncertainty Drive would alleviate the need for either. Simply increase the odds you will arrive at where you wish to be and, against all likelihood, there you will be. Or decrease the odds an assailant will be able to hit you, or increase them that an attacking vessel's propulsion or weapons system will self-destruct or malfunction, and you really have no need for defensive systems.

Ingenious and frightening.

"You're sure that's the ship?" the Bynar asked Sonya Gomez.

"No doubt about it," she said. "That's the one."

"Odds are," Tev added.

"Yes," Gomez agreed. "Odds are."

Captain Gold said, "We scanned this section of the debris field when we first arrived in the sector. How could we have missed it if . . . oh. Of course. Just bad luck."

"And it cost Bart his life," Gomez said. "If we'd only caught this ship in our initial scans, we might have known to stay clear of it and Bart wouldn't have had to die."

"The ship likely manipulates probability as much as a mode of protection as of propulsion," Tev pointed out. "No doubt it caused the odds *against* our sensors picking up its presence to fall to keep itself safe."

"Then why let us 'see' it now?" Gold said.

Soloman blinked as Captain Gold became momentarily, and against all odds, a six-foot marble Corinthian column. Sonya and Tev, their backs turned as they continued their scans, saw nothing.

"Soloman?" the captain said.

"Ah, yes. Well, perhaps it's determined that we're no longer a threat, that the odds have been reduced to such that nothing we do can possibly cause it harm."

"Even if that's true," Gold said, "why don't we simply quarantine this sector and just move a light-year or so down the line and create our pass through a section where there isn't an unlucky ship impeding our every move?"

Tev shook his head. "We can't just leave it as is, Captain. Now that we know what we're looking for it's plain to see that the area of ill-luck being generated by the Uncertainty Drive is an expanding field. We can't be certain—if indeed we can be certain of anything while under its influence—where, if ever, the expansion will cease."

"You mean this bad luck could engulf the entire sector?"

"With our luck, worse," Gomez said.

"Then what are our options?" the captain asked.

"Who's to say?" Soloman absently tapped on the tabletop. "With probability so mutable, we stand as much chance of defeating it with a conventional attack as we do by firing spitballs or by doing absolutely nothing. We don't even know why or how the Drive, as ancient as it appears to be, became operational after all this time."

Tev said, "I'm afraid I have to agree, Captain. When virtually anything is possible at any time, there's no way to predict anything with any degree of certainty."

Gold, Gomez, Soloman, and Tev all fell silent. A glowing blue and red Sarindarian butterfly flitted through the observation lounge, which, for just the blink of an eye, became a smoky, crowded cantina on Intar.

"Yes, I see," Gold said.

A four-hundred-year-old television program about a wacky red-headed housewife replaced the image of the Uncertainty Drive ship on the monitors.

"Gomez, have you been able to establish communications with the ship?" Gold asked suddenly.

"I've tried, but no luck."

Gold smiled without humor. "What are the odds if you tried again, you'd get through this time?"

She shrugged. "Fifty-fifty, I suppose," and activated the subspace comlink.

Soloman shook his head in disbelief and said, "You know, of course, I meant that in jest."

Tev gave him a long, hard look. "I suppose, then, the joke is on you."

"Captain!" Gomez called out, looking surprised.

"Greetings, U.S.S. da Vinci," said a soft, plain voice over the comm. *"This is the* Minstrel's Whisper, *flagship of the Khnndak Empire."*

Gold smiled. "We have contact!"

"I am Captain David Gold in command of the *U.S.S. da Vinci.* We are a scientific expedition representing a Federation of allied planets," Gold said, now seated in his chair on the bridge. "We come in peace, *Minstrel's Whisper."*

"Yours is a mission of destruction, da Vinci. *Your vessel will be held in an infinite-probability field until you can be taken into custody by the Empire."*

Gomez looked up helplessly. "It's misread our demolition efforts."

"Who can blame it?" said Soloman. "What concerns me is that it plans on holding us until its creators come to take us into custody."

"That ship's a million years old if it's a day," said Gomez. "The race that built it, let alone the entire Empire, has probably been extinct for millennia."

"It's a computer," Gold said. "Surely it must operate on a set logic system that we can speak to, reason with."

"Look what it's doing to us, Captain," the slender Bynar said. "I couldn't even begin to know how to reach it."

"Chance," said Tev. "It operates on the calculation and implementation of the laws of probability."

"Yes, along with the manipulation thereof," said Soloman. "Which makes it all the more difficult to approach when its ability to affect probability can *change,* from moment to moment, the very shape of reality."

Sonya Gomez threw her hands up in surrender.

"Then that's it? We'll never know how to communicate with the Drive because its very existence is forever changing how we perceive its communication? It's Schrödinger's Cat, all over again."

Tev nodded slowly, then said, suddenly, "Yes. Yes, it is."

Soloman peered at the Tellarite. "Something?"

"Yes," Tev said, a sudden surge of strength returning to his voice. Soloman realized that the S.C.E. second-in-command, like everyone else aboard the *da Vinci* since being caught up in the influence of the Uncertainty Drive, had been acting somewhat out of character. For Tev that meant a certain hesitancy in his voice and his usually unshakable confidence. The Bynar had been surprised that Tev had so readily accepted the fantastic explanation of an Uncertainty Drive, but now he realized he likely had been desperate for any outside explanation of their situation. Better they were under the sway of some scientific conundrum than that Mor glasch Tev had somehow become fallible.

"Schrödinger's Cat is a hypothetical expression of uncertainty," Tev continued. "A cat is placed in a box with a radioactive atom, a vial of acid, and a Geiger counter. Should the atom decay and the Geiger counter detect an alpha particle, the acid vial will be broken and the cat will die. But before the observer opens the box and observes the cat's fate—and, by extension, the state of the radioactive atom—they are in superpositions, that is the state of being both dead and alive, or decayed and undecayed, simultaneously. It takes the observer opening the box to 'observe' the cat and determine its fate and, again by extension, the fate of the radioactive particle."

"And . . . ?" prompted Gomez.

"And the one piece of the equation that remains unchanged," said Tev with no hint of smugness, unaware that for several seconds, he had, most improbably, became totally naked, "is the box."

Soloman blinked, averted his eyes and then smiled. "The box," he said, as though it was the most obvious thing in the world.

"What *about* the box?" asked Gold.

"The Drive is the box, Captain," said Soloman. "Whatever else happens *around* it, the box *remains* the box: a six-sided cube with very definite and precisely definable characteristics."

Now it was Gomez's turn to smile. "So the Drive isn't affected by the skewering of probability."

"I don't see how it could be," said Soloman. "It would need to operate within a sphere of unaltered probability, if only to serve as a baseline for reestablishing normalcy."

"So however bizarre it is *here,*" Gold said, "the Drive itself should be perfectly normal?"

"In theory, yes, it should be," said Soloman. "And that means there's a good chance I can reason with it."

And about as good a chance, he thought uneasily, *that the Drive had completely taken leave of its senses.*

Pattie and Soloman walked toward the shuttle *Shirley* sitting in wait on the docking bay.

"I'm sorry I can't go with you," Pattie said, rising up on her hind legs.

Soloman shook his head. "Two of us would double the chances of something going wrong."

"I understand," she said, clicking in concern. "I'm just worried, that's all."

"I doubt I'm in serious danger," Soloman said. "I'll

just be trying to establish a dialogue with the Drive." As he spoke, the *Shirley* impossibly became a passenger shuttle that disgorged a host of bipedal beings before closing its doors and sliding down a magnetic track to its next stop.

"Well," said Pattie. "Your ship could disappear out from under you, or you might become a species that finds your environment poisonous, or—"

"Or any number of equally remote 'what-ifs.' Haven't you noticed, Pattie, that for all the strange things that are happening, it is all of a mostly innocuous, if not disconcerting nature? I don't think the Drive wishes us harm, just to render us harmless."

"What happened to Bart was not innocuous," Pattie said sadly.

"No, of course it wasn't," he quickly agreed. "But his death was certainly, even among a crew of forty individuals undergoing an extraordinary run of bad luck, an anomaly. However, if you consider all the many trillions of beings that exist in the universe, all the possible interactions, encounters, and outcomes . . . well, really, how *unlikely* is it that, even under normal probability, just about anything *might* happen at any given time?"

The *Shirley* returned to its original spot, waiting for Soloman to board.

"In fact," said the Bynar, "you would no doubt find remarkable the case of elderly twentieth-century Earth twin brothers, both killed not two hours apart, hit by trucks while riding their bicycles on the same stretch of road."

"Yes, that sounds fairly remarkable," she agreed.

"Because they were brothers, dying so close together in so similar a manner?"

Pattie nodded. "Of course."

"Except the fact of their relationship, though of great interest, is irrelevant to the equation. You would likely have found the story less remarkable had I told it this way: Two elderly men in the same hometown died within two hours of each other, each riding a bicycle along a busy motorway in a snowstorm."

Pattie chittered. "Ah, I see what you mean."

"The truly strange things—the impossible appearances of beings, the improbable transmutations of objects—those are without a doubt caused by the Drive. But, ignoring that Bart regularly consumed peanut butter, and considering only that allergic reactions in humans can, in some cases, strike without a prior history, it might just be that his death was, truly, a freak accident. Perhaps having nothing to do with our proximity to the Drive and more to do with the random universe we are accustomed to dealing with."

"We'll never know, will we?" Pattie said. A rivet popped from the bulkhead overhead and dropped down on the Nasat's head with a dull thud against her exoskeleton. A second and third followed before she could scramble out of the way.

"Are you okay?" Soloman said.

"Concerned," she said. "There are no rivets used in the construction of this ship." Pattie's antennae quivered and she said, "Go, Soloman. Go talk to that crazy computer before what little luck there is keeping us alive runs out."

CHAPTER 10

Brightly colored party balloons adorned with the faces of cartoon characters flitted lazily past the *Shirley*'s forward window. Inside, a burly squat being in an antiquated and tattered space suit with a cracked visor seemed vaguely relieved when Soloman politely denied him permission to take the craft's copilot seat and wandered, by chance, out of reality.

Soloman was concentrating very hard on piloting the shuttle, trying not to be distracted by the increasing density of strangeness, such as when his heads-up display became a VR game featuring fairy princesses chasing after winged unicorns. The Drive had said they were being held in an "infinite-probability field," an area where there was every chance of anything happening. It no doubt had calculated such extreme odds as being necessary to prevent the *da Vinci* from doing anything it deemed a danger, but, as a winged creature of a species he could not identify wheeled overhead, screeching out its mating call, Soloman could only wonder how well the Drive was functioning. It was, after all, an ancient system, perhaps no longer able to properly calculate, control, or manipulate probability.

"This is the Shuttlecraft *Shirley,* of the *U.S.S. da Vinci,*" Soloman said into the communicator. "Requesting permission to dock with the *Minstrel's Whisper.*"

There had been a brief debate on the *da Vinci* over whether Soloman should have transported over to the other ship, but the Bynar had not been thrilled with the odds of having his molecular structure scrambled and successfully reassembled under current conditions. He would take his chances in the shuttle . . . a decision he thought he might soon regret.

The response came in the form, Soloman was fairly certain, of Romulan light opera. The translator chose to convert it into a haiku in a Ferengi dialect. "Please repeat, *Minstrel's Whisper.* Your transmission was . . . garbled."

The ship itself was faring little better than its attempts to communicate. As Soloman approached in the slow-moving shuttle, the *Whisper* randomly changed position every time he looked at or attempted to get an instrument lock on it. *The Uncertainty Principle,* he thought. *The observation of a particle changes how it acts.* What were the chances he would ever get to witness this subatomic phenomenon on a macro level?

About fifty-fifty, he supposed.

"Shuttlecraft Shirley. *Calculation of danger to* Minstrel's Whisper *under current probability level: sixteen to the twenty-third power. Permission to dock granted. Please follow indicators."*

The *Minstrel's Whisper* had apparently decided to once again occupy just a single place in the universe and stayed where it was as Soloman piloted the *Shirley* toward it. A line of blinking lights pulsed along the side of the silver craft, directing him toward the slowly opening maw of the cargo bay. And, in case he missed that, two unprotected dog-faced beings in greasy coveralls floated improbably in space on either side of the docking doors with brightly shining torches, pointing him to his destination.

Soloman found setting the *Shirley* down on a deck that couldn't quite decide its position or density the most nerve-wracking experience of the brief journey, but soon he was down and shutting down the shuttle's systems. Which, at the moment, apparently required the removal, from beside the thruster controls, of an old-fashioned key attached to a pair of large fuzzy, stuffed dice.

Soloman sighed. "Well," he said out loud, to himself, "at least the dice are appropriate."

The Bynar stepped from the shuttle onto a long red carpet that ran the length of the docking bay, flanked on either side by rows of formally attired footmen. Soloman tapped his combadge and said, "Soloman to *da Vinci.* I have arrived safely aboard the *Minstrel's Whisper.*"

"The number you are calling is no longer in service," replied a metallic, mechanical voice. *"Please check the number and dial again."*

Soloman frowned. "Hello?"

"We read you, Soloman," came Gomez's response.

"Good," he said. "I'd hate to feel like I was all alone in—"

Soloman's next step sent him plummeting down a hole that appeared, impossibly, in the metal deck-plate before him. He landed on his back in a twisting, slanted tube and proceeded to slide down this dizzying—and impossibly long—path, like a child caught on an amusement park ride.

"Soloman?"

Before he could catch his breath to answer, the slide leveled off and dumped him out into a plain, unmarked corridor lined with a series of short, round hatchways.

"Ow."

"Are you okay, Soloman?"

Rubbing his posterior, the Bynar rose to his feet. "Yes. I just rode a rather improbable alternative to a lift."

"I'm sure. Any sign of the Uncertainty Drive?"

One of the rounded hatches burped open and a giant green humanoid with a single eye where it's nose should have been started trying to squeeze through it. Soloman stared in surprise as the fingers on his left hand were briefly replaced by sensor probes. A line of game fowl from Naftali honked in chorus as they waddled past him down the corridor, disappearing around the bend.

"No doubt I'm close," Soloman said carefully. He looked around, brushing the web of an Arctyrrian narco-spider from his head. "Hello, *Minstrel's Whisper,*" he called.

"Please enter."

Soloman shrugged. "Enter where?"

"Probability of choosing correct portal: one hundred percent."

He thought he understood now. Whichever door he chose to enter would be the one that lead to the Drive. The Drive itself had altered the odds to make it a certainty.

Soloman approached a door at random and, when it

opened, he stooped to fit through it into the chamber housing the core of the Uncertainty Drive.

He could *feel* the world around him returning to normal. Creatures from other worlds and ancient times ceased scurrying and flapping around him. His limbs and digits no longer became something else, his uniform remained on his back, and things were no longer becoming other things for no reason other than probability allowed for it. Here, in the presence of the Uncertainty Drive, the odds ceased to conspire against sanity.

The Drive itself was hardly impressive. All that was visible in the low-ceilinged, ten-foot by ten-foot chamber—which, along with the evidence of the small portals, led Soloman to speculate that the creators of the *Minstrel's Whisper* had been a race short in stature, if not long on scientific know-how—was a floor to ceiling tubular chamber, transparent and filled with a bubbling gold liquid. It took him only a moment to realize that the bubbles traveling up and down the chamber did so in patterns.

"A protein solution containing organic memory matter?" Soloman asked.

"Analysis correct. I am Minstrel."

Soloman slowly circled the chamber. "I am Soloman."

"Yes. I calculated a ninety-nine point seven-two-three probability that you would be the one sent to interface with me."

The S.C.E. computer expert nodded, knowing he had to be careful until he had a sense of the Drive's operating parameters. "Where is your crew, Minstrel?"

"Insufficient data. I was briefly offline and rebooted to find the crew gone."

"Didn't you find that . . . odd?" Soloman asked.

"Improbable," the Drive corrected. "Minstrel's Whis-

per's *log contains incomplete data; analysis of probability incomplete."*

"Do you know how long you were offline, Minstrel?"

"Insufficient data."

"Do you know your current location?"

"Insufficient data."

Soloman found it interesting that an artificial intelligence of this obvious sophistication and complexity had made no attempt to fill in the gaps in its data. It could have easily requested the information from the *da Vinci*'s computers, or even taken simple star readings to determine the time and its location, yet it was strangely content to do nothing.

"I've come to assure you that the *da Vinci* has no hostile intentions toward you and ask to be released from your infinite-probability field," he said. "We wish only to remove obstacles blocking our space lanes."

"Probability of hostile action by da Vinci: *fifty point zero-zero-three percent.* Da Vinci *will remain in infinite-probability field until taken into custody by the Empire."*

On a mere three one-hundredths of a percentage point of chance, the Drive had determined the *da Vinci* to be a threat. Soloman wondered exactly what this intelligent computer that could not seem to figure out how to read a star chart to calculate its location or the passage of some million years of time was using to calibrate its determination of the odds.

"While we're waiting for the Empire to take me into custody," Soloman said, producing a deck of playing cards from his tunic, "might I interest you in a small game of chance?"

It was time he found out.

CHAPTER 11

Captain Gold waited.

Commanders of Starfleet vessels seldom had to endure the endless waits David Gold often found himself facing. True, he was the top man aboard the *da Vinci,* but aside from seeing to it that the ship got safely from point A to point B, much of his time was spent waiting for the various scientists and engineers under his command to finish their jobs before moving on to the next point on the map. Naturally, he took a great interest in what his people did and expected them to keep him fully apprised of their progress, but there really wasn't a whole lot for him to do while they built their gadgets and adjusted their gizmos. Absent an emergency, he was pretty much left to hang back and let his people do what they did best.

Which left him feeling, at times, very much like a third wheel. Sometimes that separation caused command issues, as happened at Rhaax a little while ago, but mostly it caused boredom. And sometimes, when an emergency did arise, the captain felt guilty that he might have brought it on by wishing for something to do to relieve the tedium.

If nothing else, the Uncertainty Drive was fast curing him of the desire for something to happen while he waited. At the moment, he would have given anything for some good old tedium in an environment that didn't make the impossible routine.

"Captain, look at this."

Gold looked. The viewscreen on the bridge showed a section of the Sargasso where the derelict ships were drifting into a new and very strangely recognizable pattern. "Is that . . . ?" he asked.

Gomez nodded. "Yes. Those ships are rearranging themselves into a diagram of a sodium chloride molecule. Common table salt."

"But . . . why?" Gold said with a shake of his head.

"Because the odds are that they can," Gomez said. "The readings in the field of altered probability appear to be intensifying."

A muffled explosion that caused the *da Vinci* to shudder and alarms to go off punctuated Gomez's words. It was quickly determined that a newly installed convection tube in the recently repaired port nacelle had, against all odds, burst.

"Those tubes don't just burst," Gold said angrily.

"They do when there are even odds that they might," Gomez said. "We've been experiencing more and more improbable failures over the last hour. Most of them were relatively minor, but what are the odds they can continue that way? The longer we're held here, the more likely the chance we'll experience a catastrophic failure, a structural abnormality, or even human error that could destroy this ship."

"We're just an accident waiting to happen," he said.

"Bet on it," Gomez agreed.

The lift doors opened and, as a kangaroo hopped onto the bridge, the *da Vinci*'s sensors chose that moment to crash.

Soloman settled himself on the floor beside the Uncertainty Drive and began shuffling the cards.

"Define 'game of chance'?" the Drive inquired.

"Diversions that are dependent on chance, such as the drawing of a specific card or the rolling of dice to achieve a specific number to determine victory or loss. Your civilization has no such games?" Soloman was surprised. Most civilizations across the universe had developed such games, and he would have guessed that a culture that developed this mode of travel would have such.

"The Khnndak attained mastery of probability millennia ago. Games of chance, under such conditions, would contain no element of risk."

"Yes, I suppose that's so," said Soloman. "Still, if you're interested, I could teach one such game to you."

"Explain."

Soloman dealt two hands of five-card poker, all faceup, to demonstrate to the Drive how the game was played. He quickly explained the fifty-two card deck, the different suits contained therein, the various odds of achieving the desired hands, and the methods of betting. A single simulated hand and the Drive indicated its understanding of the fundamentals.

The Bynar gathered the cards back up, shuffled, cut the deck, then dealt, turning the Drive's cards toward a visual sensor on the wall.

Soloman had drawn a pair of fours and three useless cards. In a real game, he would likely have folded his hand on such a pair, but there was more at stake here than winning a round of cards. "We each discard the cards that do not fit into our hands and draw an equal number of new cards in the hope of achieving a better hand." This he did, finding himself little better off than he had been with his original cards. He asked the Drive, "How many cards do you want?"

"I will maintain the initial selection."

"Really?" Soloman reached over and turned the Drive's cards, unprepared for the shock of seeing a perfect royal flush, just as he had dealt it.

"Remarkable," Soloman said. He gathered the cards, shuffled thoroughly, and dealt out another hand.

Even after drawing four new cards against an ace, he could not better the straight flush held by the Drive.

A third hand produced another royal flush for the Drive, followed by two full houses, a straight, two pairs (three times in a row), three of a kind, a third royal flush, and three more straights, all exactly the same. The best hand Soloman was able to achieve had been that initial pair of fours. After that, even the humblest pair of deuces had eluded him.

"Fifteen hands in which you've been dealt nothing less than three of a kind, including not just one but *three* royal flushes. In any individual hand the probability of a royal flush is some thirty-one thousand to one."

"Probability of drawing the five necessary cards: fifty percent for each individual card."

"But what of drawing *all five* necessary cards in every single hand? In fifteen consecutive hands," Soloman said, "the odds are mind-boggling. Where exactly does probability currently stand for us?"

"Probability is normal."

Soloman began dealing the newly reshuffled cards, one at a time, faceup on the floor. They came out of the deck in sequential order, by suits.

"This, Minstrel," he said, "is not normal."

A loud, high-pitched screech filtered up to the bridge from belowdecks of the *da Vinci*.

"What now?" Gold demanded.

Gomez signaled engineering and a stressed-sounding Nancy Conlon's voice said, without any preamble, *"You're* not *going to believe this one!"*

Gold closed his eyes and braced himself. "Try me."

"The warp drive . . . it's been replaced by steam engines, *Captain,"* she said. *"That noise was a pressure valve venting excess steam."*

Gold shook his head. *"Meshuggah,"* he said. "The whole universe has gone *meshuggah!"*

"Just our corner of it," said Gomez. "But the way the effects are spreading, the rest of the galaxy may not be far behind."

Soloman produced a small, coin-sized medallion from his pocket and held it up for Minstrel's visual sensor to inspect. The image of a starship was stamped on one side, the Starfleet insignia on the other.

"Maybe this will help," the Bynar said. "What would you calculate the probability of this disk, flipped through the air and allowed to land without interference one hundred times, falling with the side picturing the starship facing up?"

"Probability states the result to be fifty of one hundred such throws."

"That's correct," he said. "Each throw offers a fifty-fifty chance of landing on either side." Soloman flicked the medallion into the air with his thumb and watched it rotate head over tails before clinking to the deck.

"Heads, or starship side," Soloman announced. He picked up the medallion and prepared to toss it again. "There's still a fifty-fifty chance it will land on either side, but since the first toss came up heads, there is a greater likelihood—a three in four chance—that the next will come up tails."

Soloman flipped the medallion again, waiting for Minstrel to challenge his dubious statistical information, but the computer remained silent.

"Heads again." He retrieved the medallion. "Meaning there's now an even greater chance that the next flip *must* be tails."

But it wasn't. In fact, the medallion came up heads again and again. Sixty-two flips later and there was still nothing but the embossed starship's image facing the Bynar and the computer.

"Minstrel, what is the probability of so many consecutive flips being the same?"

"Probability: fifty percent."

"Excuse me?" Soloman said.

"Each toss of the coin offers an even chance of one side or the other coming up."

"Yes, on the basis of each individual toss," Soloman

agreed, "but when taken as a *set* of tosses, the odds increase exponentially."

Soloman tossed the coin for the sixty-third time and watched in surprise as it landed, this time, on its edge and stood there, perfectly balanced.

"And the odds of *this?*"

"Probability: fifty percent."

An answer which convinced Soloman, finally, that he was dealing with a mechanism that had lost all reason.

Aboard the *da Vinci,* Captain Gold and Sonya Gomez discovered that, improbably or not, the rest of the crew had gathered together in a three-foot by three-foot utility closet on the engineering deck. Which turned out well since the hull around the bridge deck had gone off somewhere, leaving the entire area exposed to the vacuum of space.

By the time the hull returned—minus all its electronics and decorated in a colorful but tasteful floral wallcovering—the starboard nacelle was showing fatal signs of metal fatigue and threatened to snap off at the slightest provocation.

Meanwhile, the CO_2 scrubbers responsible for recycling shipboard air had begun to spew lethal carbon monoxide rather than renewed and breathable air. A quick thinking, but improbable, Qwardian tree-slug with an engineering background shut down the environmental systems before the CO levels reached the danger point. Fortunately, a breeze blowing in from the mountains beyond the mess kept the *da Vinci* supplied with fresh air.

* * *

Gold, Gomez, and Tev watched the *Minstrel's Whisper* on the viewscreen in the captain's ready room. It was just one derelict ship out of millions, but one which random chance had vested with the power to destroy the *da Vinci.*

"Soloman is not answering any of our signals," the Tellarite said.

"Odds are," Gold said dryly, "his combadge isn't working."

"But Soloman is," Gomez said. "We've got to trust he's doing the best he can."

Tev growled deep in his throat. "So you're saying that the mind that conceived a statistical jest such as his 'fifty-fifty' theory is all that stands between this ship and its doom?"

"Well," said Gold, "when you put it *that* way . . ."

CHAPTER 12

Reason, Soloman thought, *should be left to the reasonable.*

But seeing as there was precious little reason to be had there in the Uncertainty Drive's den, he was best off taking another tact entirely.

When in Rome, he reminded himself before taking a deep breath and saying to the Drive, "Minstrel, do you know how long you were offline?"

"Query asked and answered. Insufficient data."

"I have the necessary data, gathered by the instruments aboard the *da Vinci.* You were offline for something in the vicinity of one million years."

"Probability: zero."

Soloman shook his head. "But you don't even know what happened to your crew. Have any of your attempts to contact your Empire met with success?"

The Drive made no response, but Soloman noted that

the flow of bubbles inside Minstrel's chamber had increased. He pressed on. "You set the probability that a coin could come down heads in sixty-three consecutive tosses at fifty percent," he said. "What chances would you give the *da Vinci,* arriving at any random point along a one-half light-year-long stretch of space, coming to rest within visual distance of any particular ship, in this case the *Minstrel's Whisper?"*

"Probability: fifty percent. The da Vinci *is either near the* Minstrel's Whisper *or it is not."*

Soloman realized that when he had initially encountered the Drive, it had been capable of offering odds—whether correctly calculated or not—other than fifty-fifty. The cards and the coin, meant to allow Soloman to establish the computer's concept of stable probability, seemed to have served only to confuse the device. That signaled to him a rapid deterioration of its processing abilities—and he doubted they would deteriorate in favor of the *da Vinci*'s survival.

"And the probability of your being dealt nothing but winning hands sixteen straight times?"

"Probability: fifty percent. Either one will be dealt the high hand or one will not."

"Then it stands to reason that there is a fifty percent chance that you were offline for one million years."

The logic was, of course, completely specious. It was as though he had said because it's possible to ride a bicycle without hands, it's also possible to take an unprotected stroll across the surface of a gas giant. One had nothing to do with the other, but Soloman was placing his faith in the fact that he stood a fifty-fifty chance of Minstrel accepting his argument.

"Logic error . . ."

The golden liquid began bubbling ferociously.

Soloman held his breath, suddenly convinced he had gone too far, too fast.

"*. . . Supposition irreconcilable with* Minstrel's Whisper's *two-thousand-year rating for organic memory matter.*"

"Minstrel," he said, exhaling and trying not to smile, "have you ever heard of Schrödinger's Cat?"

Torches lined the corridor of the *da Vinci,* filling the air with oily smoke. The crew, clad in monks' robes of coarse gray material, walked slowly along in double-file, chanting dirges in a language that none of them recognized.

Captain Gold felt as though his head were about to burst from the constant shifting of reality and the impossibility of everything that was happening to him and his crew. It was his responsibility to see that these forty beings under his charge came to no harm, but he was just so damned helpless in the face of this ancient and overwhelming alien technology. He would have felt humiliated had he for a second believed what they were going through was being done deliberately, but he knew better.

It was all just chance, science gone amok. What had he called it that first morning when he and Gomez had discussed their respective runs of bad luck? "Random acts of capricious nature." Only in this instance, technology was giving nature a helping hand.

Bart Faulwell had died because of it. His ship, this home to Gold and his crew, was, moment by moment, coming that much closer to destruction. Just before they all found themselves chanting in robes, the sensors had picked up an approaching and powerful electromagnetic pulse, apparently generated from the magnetic field that helped hold the Sargasso of derelicts in stasis. Of course, that was relatively minor compared to the kilometer-wide meteor hurtling on a collision course for the *da Vinci*.

Or, he noted with renewed alarm, the gradual disintegration of the *da Vinci*'s physical structure, as though the ship were made of spun sugar and had been dipped in a basin of water. The hull was melting away, inch by inch, exposing them all to the cold, unforgiving vacuum of space.

Gold tried to cry out, to warn his crew of the coming disaster, but all that came out of his mouth was the unintelligible dirge. Capricious nature couldn't even give him the comfort of prayer in this final moment.

But even had he been able to pray, the best he would have been able to summon would have been the kaddish.

CHAPTER 13

Captain David Gold opened his eyes and looked around the bridge of the *U.S.S. da Vinci.*

He sat, as was his custom, in the commander's chair in the center of the bridge. Wong, Shabalala, and Haznedl were at their respective stations, while Gomez and Tev were positioned at aft consoles, and other crew moved about in routines so blessedly familiar to the captain.

Gold knew, from the looks on the other faces around him, exactly what his expression must have been.

Shock.

A second ago, they had all been robed monks on a march to oblivion, singing a song to which no one knew the words.

A second ago, all hands had watched the slow, inexorable disintegration of their ship that promised to expose them to instant death in space.

A second ago . . .

And then, against all odds, their world had returned to normal.

"Soloman to da Vinci.*"*

Sonya Gomez jumped, startled by the voice coming over the comm. Her own came out in a surprised stutter. "Soloman? What, I mean, where are you?"

"Aboard the Minstrel's Whisper *and ready to come home."*

Tev leaned in and, trying to appear unruffled but failing miserably, said, "Has the situation been resolved?"

Gold was certain he heard Soloman chuckle. *"Indeed it has."*

Behind the captain, the lift hissed open and someone stepping from it said, "*What* situation?"

Gold sucked in a breath. Before he could turn to see if who he thought he had just heard was indeed who he believed it to be, one look at Gomez's face confirmed it.

"Bart!" she shouted and raced across the bridge, throwing her arms around his neck.

Bart Faulwell, hale and hearty as ever, staggered back under her affectionate assault. "Missed me *that* much between shifts?" he laughed.

Everyone on the bridge was staring at the language specialist in open disbelief. He looked from face to face, not sure what to make of their expressions and of the sniffling woman clinging to his neck.

"Uhm," he said, "have I missed something here?"

David Gold stepped toward the younger crewman and clasped his forearm in his hand. "No, Faulwell," he said in a voice momentarily choked with emotion. "We're the ones who have been missing something."

* * *

The command crew were there to meet Soloman in the shuttle bay. He stepped from the shuttle, casually flipping and catching the starship medallion, a satisfied smile on his face. He looked at them, Captain Gold, Sonya Gomez, Tev . . . and Bart Faulwell?

"Everything has, I take it, returned to normal?" Soloman stammered.

Faulwell smiled, "Surprise!"

Soloman looked to Gold, then Gomez. "But he was—"

"Dead," Bart said. "Done in by a peanut butter power bar, they tell me. Guess it was just too ridiculous a way to go for the powers that be to let it stick."

"This," Soloman said, "is *more* than I could have hoped for."

Gomez's laugh was loud with her relief. "Yes," she exclaimed. "Everything's back, one hundred percent. How did you do it?"

Soloman shrugged. "In truth, the Drive did it to itself. I merely helped point it in the statistically correct direction."

"Would you care to explain *how?*" Tev said impatiently.

"Of course," Soloman said. "As I suspected, the Drive, either because of age or," and here he smiled, "because of random chance, was basing its probability calculations on corrupted data. How else could the odds for the frequent impossibilities we were confronting have become so skewed in favor of their happening? Apparently, my attempts to ascertain its baseline for so-called stable probability through demonstrations of chance served only to confuse it. I think it was the coin toss that did it, but before I was done, Minstrel was operating on the assumption that all odds for all things were fifty-fifty."

"No!" exclaimed Tev in disbelief, glaring at his superior when Gomez failed to completely suppress a snort of laughter.

"Yes," the Bynar replied modestly. "I recorded the entire confrontation on my tricorder if you would care to check it. Anyway, it expressed doubt when I tried to explain that it had been dormant for a million years and had only just, by random chance, come back online. It was composed of organic components which were only supposed to function for two thousand years before deteriorating, a fact it could not reconcile with my claims of the vast passage of time.

"All those factors pointed to the solution to our dilemma. The Drive itself had established that it was functioning on the assumption that the odds of all things were even, so I told it the story of Schrödinger's Cat, reinforcing through the immutable laws of physics . . ."

"Some immutable laws, said the dead man," Faulwell chuckled.

"Immutable, then, under normal circumstances . . . the state under which the Drive believed itself to be functioning, by the way. I explained how the hypothetical cat is in a superposition of both life and death until an observer opens the box to determine the cat's fate. Alive or dead. Fifty-fifty.

"I explained that its great age was the cat and the vastly overdue life span of its materials was the radioactive particle."

"And you," said Sonya with sudden understanding, "were the observer!"

"That's as preposterous as your theory on probability," said Tev with unconcealed disdain.

"I couldn't agree more, but the Uncertainty Drive

didn't know any better. As far as it could perceive, I had opened the box to see whether the cat was alive or dead. And, as it was programmed to function under the Uncertainty Principle, it instantly understood that the mere fact of my observing it altered it. And since it was operating under the principle that something either was or was not—fifty-fifty, remember—it had only two states, or two probabilities, to choose from: function or nonfunction. Since it had been functioning, my observation could only offer it the alternative of nonfunction."

"You mean," asked Gold, "it just shut down?"

"On or off. Yes or no," Soloman said and directed his smile at Tev. "Fifty-fifty."

"Preposterous," the Tellarite grumbled and stalked out of the shuttle bay.

Bart Faulwell sat by himself in the forward observation deck, sipping a cup of coffee, staring out at the Sargasso Sector.

In the twenty-four hours since his . . . becoming not dead anymore (he felt silly using a word like resurrection, which was far too biblical for his tastes and, besides, didn't really describe his situation), he had hardly found a moment for himself. Everyone had wanted time with him to express their sorrow over his death and their happiness at his . . . well, not-death. And while he appreciated their sentiments—and how many people, really, ever got the chance to hear their own eulogy and learn how their death had affected those around them—he needed time on his own to digest the situation for himself.

Not that he remembered dying, of course. Or undying

either, for that matter. As far as he could tell, there had been no break in his life. It was as though he had taken a nap, nothing more.

But he hadn't been napping. He had been dead. Dr. Lense hadn't been mistaken. She had placed his body in a stasis chamber and his friends had mourned his sudden and senseless passing.

Except now he wasn't dead.

He had been there, of course, when twenty-three of his colleagues had died at Galvan VI. He had ridden the very same emotional roller coaster the *da Vinci*'s crew had experienced in the wake of his death, but now, suddenly, he *wasn't* dead and it was as though they had wasted all that sadness and emotion.

And how could they not resent him, on some level at any rate, for daring to cheat death when those twenty-three others could not? Duffy, Feliciano, Barnak, McAllan, and the others—they had stayed dead. Of course. That's what dead was, a final, irrevocable state. But Bart had, quite literally, beaten the odds and, while he was naturally happy to learn that reports of his death had been greatly exaggerated, he was also saddened that his happiness and good fortune was no doubt causing pain for others.

"Hey."

Bart heard Sonya Gomez's voice and, coming as it did on the tail of his particular train of thought, he winced. But he pretended not to and turned to her with a smile and waved her over to sit beside him.

"Sorry if I'm interrupting," Gomez said.

"You're not," he lied.

"I've just—" she said, then stopped herself. "I'm glad you're back, Bart."

He smiled. "Me too. It's freaky, though. Soloman figured that since the probability of my, you know, dying by peanut butter was so astronomical, when normal probability started to reassert itself, it just kind of spit me back out as too impossible to be dead. Or maybe it was that the odds of my staying dead were the same as my having died in the first place, but to tell you the truth, I couldn't understand half of what he was saying with all those numbers and equations."

"Me neither," she said. She reached over and took his hand. "You've been hiding in here, haven't you?"

He nodded and shrugged. "Sort of."

"Why?"

"Because," he said, staring into his cup, "I can't quite figure out whether or not it's fair. Not being dead, I mean."

"Now why in the world would you think that, Bart?"

He looked her in the eye, determined to get it off his chest, no matter how difficult it was. "Because of the others who died and didn't get a roll of the damned dice to bring them back. I mean, how the hell am I supposed to go blithely along with this fortuitous second chance of mine when I know every time you look at me you'll be thinking 'Why Bart and not Duffy?'"

Sonya looked down. He could see she was fighting hard to hold back tears. She and Duffy had found something miraculous together, something that had been ripped from her, never to be returned.

"You are such an idiot," she finally said.

Faulwell, taken aback, was forced to laugh. "Excuse me?"

"Yes, I loved Kieran and always will. Yes, I would give my left arm for five more minutes with him to tell him that. And, yes, I will miss him for as long as I live, but how shallow do you think I am, Bart?"

"I never said—"

"Listen, pal," she said with heat, "you've been given a gift. My God, we've *all* been given a gift. We've gotten back someone precious to us that we thought we had lost forever. It's a miracle, Uncertainty Drive or no Uncertainty Drive, and it just shows me that death doesn't have to be final, doesn't need to be the end. As long as we're alive, there's still a chance, still hope, no matter how infinitesimal."

Bart Faulwell could only sit and stare in wonder at his beautiful colleague. "I suddenly understand what Duffy saw in you, Commander."

"And don't you forget it, buster." Gomez released his hand and stood. "So, okay, I'll leave you alone now."

Faulwell stood with her. "Naw, I think I'm done here. Thanks."

Sonya Gomez smiled her most dazzling smile. "Don't mention it."

Two days later, Captain Gold logged off the computer after going over the day's reports. Since the finish of the *Minstrel's Whisper,* the opening of navigable lanes through the Sargasso Sector had proceeded without a hitch. The derelicts that could be safely moved were and those that were either of no interest for further study or deemed too dangerous to tamper with—including the now inert *Minstrel's Whisper*—were being disposed of under Gomez's black-hole demolition scheme.

Should their luck hold, the *da Vinci* would complete this mission well ahead of the appearance of the first colony ship.

Of course, their ordeal under the influence of the Uncertainty Drive hadn't been entirely without repercussions. There were several of the crew who would no doubt jump in worry that it was back every time they stubbed a toe or lost a possession. And Tev could be seen stewing whenever he was reminded by Soloman's presence of the Bynar's ridiculous probability theory that had been proposed initially to mock the Tellarite but which wound up saving the life of everyone on board.

And then, of course, there was Soloman's luck at cards. Ever since his return from his encounter with the Uncertainty Drive, he had displayed the most uncanny run of luck. Well, Gold thought, he deserved every winning hand for what he had done.

And speaking of hand, the captain was reminded again of his missing wedding ring. He had chalked its disappearance up to the Uncertainty Drive, but even after the Drive had shut itself down he still had not found it.

Perhaps this was simply a case of his actually having lost it. No improbability field or alien technology to explain it, just a very human case of carelessness.

But still, there was Rachel's voice . . . "Odds are it's right where you left it, David."

He went over to that shelf again, sure he wasn't going to find it because hadn't he been over this room, the shelf included, a dozen times and come up empty-handed? But he had to look, just to satisfy Rachel.

And, of course, as usual, she was right. The simple gold band was right there, where he had left it.

David Gold smiled and picked it up and placed it immediately on his finger. Chance was, however it came to you, a funny thing.

ABOUT THE AUTHORS

For more than eight years, **KEVIN DILMORE** was a contributing writer to *Star Trek Communicator,* penning news stories and personality profiles for the bimonthly publication of the Official *Star Trek* Fan Club. On the fiction side of things, his story "The Road to Edos" was published as part of the *Star Trek: New Frontier* anthology *No Limits*. With Dayton Ward, his work includes stories for the *Star Trek: Tales of the Dominion War* and *Star Trek: Constellations* anthologies, the *Star Trek: The Next Generation* novels *A Time to Sow* and *A Time to Harvest,* ten installments of the original eBook series *Star Trek: S.C.E.* and *Star Trek: Corps of Engineers,* the first installment of the *Star Trek: Mere Anarchy* miniseries, and the *Star Trek: Vanguard* novel *Summon the Thunder*. With Mike Sussman, Kevin and Dayton wrote *Age of the Empress,* a *Star Trek: Enterprise* novel published as part of *Star Trek: Mirror Universe* Volume 1:

Glass Empires. A graduate of the University of Kansas, Kevin lives in Prairie Village, Kansas, with his wife, Michelle, and their three daughters, and works as a senior writer for Hallmark Cards in Kansas City, Missouri.

DAVE GALANTER has authored various *Star Trek* projects, among these the *Voyager* book *Battle Lines,* the *Next Generation* duology *Maximum Warp,* the *S.C.E.* title *Ambush,* and the Original Series eBook *Mere Anarchy* Book 3: *Shadows of the Indignant.* He has also contributed short stories to the *Tales of the Dominion War* and *Star Trek: Constellations* anthologies. His not-so-secret Fortress of Solitude is in Michigan, from where he pretends to have a hand in managing the message board websites he co-owns: ComicBoards.com, a comic book discussion site, and TVShowBoards.com, a similar site dedicated to television and movies. He also edits and is the main contributor to his own blogsite, Snark-Bait.com, on which he babbles about philosophy and politics. Dave spends his non-day-job time with family and friends, or burying himself in other writing projects. He enjoys feedback on his writing, positive or negative, and would appreciate seeing any comments you have on his work. Feel free to email him at dave@comicboards.com.

Deciding there was more to life than retail and there were places that saw wintry precipitation, **ALLYN GIBSON** left EB Games after seven years and moved north this past autumn to Baltimore where snow is plentiful as are jobs that don't involve saying, "Would you like a memory card with that?" The new location has presented many new challenges—traffic, weekends without work, strange odors reminiscent of ground pepper sweeping in off the Chesapeake Bay. Curiously, these things make Allyn content. *Ring Around the Sky* was Allyn's first professional fiction sale, followed by "Performance Appraisal" in the *Star Trek: New Frontier* anthology *No Limits* and the critically acclaimed "Make-Believe" in the original *Star Trek* anthology *Constellations*. Beyond *Star Trek,* Allyn has published book reviews and pop culture commentary in magazines and newspapers, with upcoming fiction and non-fiction projects in various stages of development.

KEVIN KILLIANY has been the husband of Valerie Killiany for over a quarter of a century. The pair of them freely confess to being responsible for Alethea, Anson, and Daya. They are completely unrepentant and look forward to the next three quarters being just as much fun. In the course of the last forty or so years Kevin has been an actor; drill rig operator; unskilled laborer at a dozen grunt jobs in construction, landscaping, and demolition; photographer; special education teacher; short-order cook; warehouse manager; community college instructor; high risk intervention counselor; and paperboy. He is currently a community support services case manager, an associate pastor with the Soul Saving Station, and a writer. In addition to *Orphans,* Kevin's *Star Trek* fiction includes three short stories in the annual *Star Trek: Strange New*

Worlds anthology ("Personal Log" in Volume 4, "The Monkey Puzzle Box" in Volume 5, and "Indomitable" in Volume 7) and a second *Corps of Engineers* eBook, *Honor*. Kevin also writes Web content for game companies and has had over a dozen stories published by www.BattleCorps.com. His Whovian debut—"Men of the Earth"—appeared in the Big Finish *Doctor Who* anthology *Short Trips: Destination Prague*. In November 2006, Roc released Kevin's first novel, *Wolf Hunters*. Kevin lives with his family in Wilmington, North Carolina.

PAUL KUPPERBERG is the writer of hundreds of comic book stories, newspaper strips, books, and stories. A thirty-plus-year veteran of the comic book field—and former editor for DC Comics—he has written such characters as Superman, Superboy, Supergirl, Vigilante, Power Girl, Aquaman, Green Lantern, Doom Patrol, Captain America, Conan, Johnny Bravo, and Scooby Doo, and dozens of others, including fill-in issues of the *Star Trek* comic book. He is also the creator of the comic series *Arion Lord of Atlantis, Checkmate,* and *Takion,* has written online web animation, the syndicated *Superman* and *Tom & Jerry* newspaper strips, the feature "Trash" for England's *2000 A.D.* magazine, humor and parody for Marvel's *Crazy Magazine,* short stories for various fantasy and horror anthologies, more than a dozen young adult nonfiction books on subjects ranging from history and science to biography and pop culture, the Spider-Man novels *Crime Campaign* and *Murdermoon,* and the young adult novel *Wishbone: The Sirian Conspiracy* (with Michael Jan Friedman). Paul is Senior Editor of *Weekly World News* and lives in Connecticut with his wife Robin and son Max.

DAVID MACK is the author of numerous *Star Trek* novels, including the *USA Today* bestseller *A Time to Heal* and its companion volume, *A Time to Kill*. He developed the *Star Trek: Vanguard* series with editor Marco Palmieri and wrote its first volume, *Harbinger,* and its third, *Reap the Whirlwind*. Mack's other novels include *Wolverine: Road of Bones*; *Star Trek: Deep Space Nine: Warpath*; *Star Trek: S.C.E.: Wildfire*; and *The Sorrows of Empire* in the trade paperback *Star Trek: Mirror Universe* Volume 1: *Glass Empires*. Before writing books, Mack co-wrote with John J. Ordover the fourth-season *Star Trek: Deep Space Nine* episode "Starship Down" and the story treatment for the series' seventh-season episode "It's Only a Paper Moon." An avid fan of the Canadian progressive-rock trio Rush, Mack has been to all of the band's concert tours since 1982. Mack currently resides in New York City with his wife, Kara. Learn more about him and his work on his official website, www.infinitydog.com.

DAYTON WARD began his professional writing career with stories selected for each of Pocket Books' first three *Star Trek: Strange New Worlds* anthologies. In addition to the numerous credits he shares with friend and co-writer Kevin Dilmore, Dayton is the author of the *Star Trek* novel *In the Name of Honor* and the science fiction novels *The Last World War* and *The Genesis Protocol,* as well as short stories that have appeared in the Yard Dog Press anthology *Houston, We've Got Bubbas, Kansas City Voices* Magazine and the *Star Trek: New Frontier* anthology *No Limits*. Though he currently lives in Kansas City with wife Michi and daughter Addison, Dayton is a Florida native and still maintains a torrid long-distance romance with his beloved Tampa Bay Buccaneers. Visit him on the Web at www.daytonward.com.